LET IT REIGN

for my daughter,

    may you surround yourself with kind hearted people
who will help straighten your crown should it ever slip.

CATHRINE SWIFT

LET
IT
REIGN

Let it Reign Copyright © 2021 by Cathrine Swift.

All rights reserved. No part of this book may be used or reproduced in any manner whatsoever without written permission except in the case of brief quotations embodied in critical articles or reviews.
This book is a work of fiction. Names, characters, businesses, organizations, places, events and incidents either are the product of the author's imagination or are used fictitiously. Any resemblance to persons, living or dead, events, or locales is entirely coincidental.

For information contact :
Cathrine Swift
http://www.authorcathrineswift.com

Cover Design by Cover Dungeon Rabbit
Copy Editing by Bound by Words
Author Photo by Everlast Photography

ISBN
Hardcover : 978-1-7777158-1-6
Paperback : 978-1-7777158-0-9
E-Book: 978-1-7777158-2-3
Second Edition : June 2022

1.

August 31st, 1456

THERE WAS NO DENYING Queen Amelia had awoke on the wrong side of the throne.

Especially when her jaw still remained tight by early afternoon. The why of it was no secret either. In fact, *the why* had just waltzed into the throne room, causing displeasure to ripple up her spine. Alaric, her husband and unfortunately her king, stepped up onto the platform and carelessly collapsed into the matching high-backed chair next to her. Framed by ornate bronze and marigold velvet, he grinned wolfishly. Forever looking full of secrets and lies.

Her fist twitched as he crossed his left leg over his right knee, nearly brushing her gown with his boot.

She would rather ride naked and bareback on a horse through a blizzard than endure one more moment at his side.

Not that she had a choice. Wherever her happily ever after was, it was not with him.

"Good afternoon," he half-heartedly greeted in his familiar gruff drawl.

Her eyebrows rose, watching the leather clad knight to his right hand him a scroll. "Is it?"

Alaric's jaw tightened beneath the dark stubble, but otherwise he ignored her challenge, focusing instead on the list of names.

They had long ago stopped pretending their marriage was more than an abhorrent arrangement between her father and his.

The chilled air between them never wavered or warmed as the minutes ticked on. Not even as the sunshine beamed through the stained-glass windows and painted them in streaks of color. This kind of chill remained. It crept into the bones like an unrelenting icy wave that threatened to last forever. A wave that even wrapped in blankets and curled before a roaring fire, one would still shiver for hours.

Despite coveting the throne since her youth, Amelia disliked the entire supremacy model her husband seemed to thrive on. However, not as much as she loathed his twisted world views. His silky midnight locks, firm muscles, and captivating mahogany eyes continued to fail at charming her. After all, he had done nothing but prove himself to be a piercing thorn in her side. An irritating contract itching beneath her skin.

This past year as his wife had worn her down. He had scorned and refused every plea she made for reform until she became passive and mute. A fact she utterly hated herself for. So much that she had resigned to spending her days either in her tower, the kitchens, or the forest.

Yet, whenever duty called like it had today, she clung to the honor and *right* she still held to answer it. He could not keep her from listening to the villager's requests. Even if she was forced to sit next to him silently while he barked out ignorant rulings and dismissals.

But she had a feeling today would be different, at least if her poor mood had anything to say about it.

One by one, male villagers entered the throne room, each prepared to speak on behalf of their families or neighbors too unwell to travel the brief journey to the castle.

Desperate, simple requests tumbled from chapped and trembling lips, but their pleas were ignored. Alaric quickly dismissed them all, impatient to carry on with his day. As if this were all very boring.

He clearly did not give a damn, despite most requests involving the escalating taxes he had increased just last month. Which he had done—as he did everything—without consulting her.

Amelia's blood pounded in her ears with every Dathovielian turned away. Each desperate, unanswered plea made the pressure on her chest grow. As if someone were piling boulders atop her heart. Every word she craved to say clawed at her dry, useless tongue, desperate to escape and be heard.

This was too much. And entirely not enough all at the same time. *She* was not doing enough. Surely failing to defend her people made her just as bad as Alaric, if not worse.

A guard at the door announced their final guest for the afternoon, silencing her mind. This was her last chance. Blinking back frustrated tears, she forced herself to look up from her clenched fists and focus as the last villager entered.

His warm ivory skin suggested he had spent the summer working outdoors. Soft blonde hair—probably lightened in the same rays that had darkened his complexion—sat wildly atop his head. As if he had run his hands through it dozens of times while waiting. She had to blink again to finally hear what was being said.

"—are struggling to both feed our families and pay your collections on time."

Alaric sighed, his annoyance evident.

"You must understand the position your request puts me in. Let's say I grant your extension, despite having denied everyone else today. Would you take responsibility for the riots that would surely ensue?"

The man remained humble and brave, though his resolve was clearly beginning to waver.

"I beg you to reconsider, for my children. For my ill wife. We will not make it the month. I'd be willing to add interest."

For a moment Alaric seemed to consider the man's petition. In reality, Amelia knew he simply enjoyed their subjects seeking his mercy. He probably found this man's dreadful circumstances entertaining.

"As your king, it is my job to serve and guide you. The gentlest action is enforcing the payment date. Perhaps the consequence of an empty belly may remind you to manage your home better."

With a wave of his hand, Alaric summoned the leather clad knight on his right to escort the quivering villager away. But the man stepped out of reach, desperate hands locked in prayer as he turned towards Amelia.

"My Queen, please. Won't *you* help us?"

No one else today had addressed her directly, and it broke the final strands of submission. The other men had assumed she had no real power, and in a way, they had been correct. She had lost her will to fight, but she could find it again. And she would start right now.

Stomach churning, she stood, thanking the heavens for the layers of skirts concealing her trembling knees, and ignored her husband's narrowed gaze as she approached the man.

"What is your name?"

He bowed, hope flickering in his answer. "William, Your Highness."

She rested her palm on his calloused hands, regarding Alaric over her shoulder.

"How much does he owe you?"

The king shifted in his seat. "Thirty gold pieces."

Amelia's hazel eyes flashed violently. She spun in a swish of cobalt skirts and inky curls.

"No wonder he cannot pay!"

Alaric's gaze narrowed on her, but she refrained from cowering.

"You needn't concern yourself with these matters, wife. Taxes and collection are *my* responsibility."

"Yet my people and I face the consequences of your *responsibility*."

Teeth grinding, she turned to the decorated knight standing on her left. His skin, only slightly more brown than black shone, similar to the beloved timber trees surrounding the castle. Despite his five decades in service, he hardly showed any signs of it unless he was grinning warmly or his booming laugh was filling the room. At the moment he was still as a statue, though his dark, trustworthy eyes beamed proudly at her.

Placing his fist over his heart, he bowed, awaiting orders. "Yes, My Queen?"

"Constable Fredrick, would you please ensure William arrives home safely? The stables could certainly spare him a horse for the day. Also stop by the kitchens. I am certain Regina would happily prepare his family a basket of food. We have more than enough."

"And his debt?" demanded Alaric behind her.

She kept her eyes on the veteran knight as she addressed the king. "I will settle it myself."

Fredrick barely concealed his shock, glancing toward the throne. His prime duty existed to safeguard her life, which right now included protecting her from the king. After a moment, Alaric nodded consent, lips pursed into a thin line.

"I owe you a great debt, my gracious queen," William said, trailing out of the room behind the constable. "Thank you, thank you."

When the doors closed behind them, Alaric leapt to his feet, leering over her. The reddish fur collar of his black cloak and his scorching glare made him appear like a fox ready to pounce. Amelia did step back this time. Guards lined the walls on either side of them, but she had just sent away the only knight loyal to her, rather than the throne. Ignoring the tremor in her hands, she fixed the king with what she hoped was a strong gaze.

"What the hell are you doing? If you—"

"Save your threats." Amelia raised her hand, refusing to endure another of his testosterone-fueled rants. She dug thirty gold coins from a leather pouch hanging at her belt and released them into his greedy fingers. Alaric snatched the coins and dropped them into the silver collection box beside him. "If you starve the people to death, you will have no one left to tax. Remember that the next time someone needs to feed their family."

He sneered, gesturing for the knight on his right to come forward.

"Sebastian, please escort the queen to her chambers. She could benefit from a rest before our guests arrive this evening."

The dark-haired knight approached her, his kind, ginger eyes apologetic. An uncomfortable smile creased his sandy brown skin as he extended his arm to her. At least Seb had the decency to look sorry.

She strutted past him all the same, aching to slam the double doors in Alaric's face. Alas, the solid wood stood three feet taller than her. It would not have even budged.

Outside, she whirled around, capturing the knight in a fierce gaze.

"How can you stand at his side and say nothing? Do nothing?"

She had no right to speak to him this way, especially since today was the first she had stood up to Alaric so publicly. But she was furious. With Alaric, and with herself.

The knight bit his lip, his thick, black brows drawing together as he looked down, ashamed. Alaric had turned him submissive and silent too.

"Your Grace," he said finally. "He is king."

Amelia shook her head, disappointed. "I shall go to my rooms alone, Seb. Do *not* follow me."

Nodding respectfully, he moved to stand at ease, leaving her to stomp around the corner. In another life, they might have been friends, but she could never align with her husband's closest confidant.

~

Seb was forever grateful the queen addressed him with his birth given name, as opposed to the one Alaric assigned him as children.

As he returned to the bright throne room, he braced himself for what would surely be a king in a rotten mood. And sure enough, he found Alaric pacing and muttering before the thrones, his cloak whipping behind him.

The king's goblet sat empty and alone next to the collection box, a single drop of wine trailing down its side. The shards of glass crunching under Alaric's boots indicated he had shattered Amelia's matching goblet. Alaric dismissed the guards with a short bark, leaving Seb and himself alone in the grand room.

A simple and powerful sign that his next words were to remain private. Only it was Seb who spoke first, breaking the heavy silence.

"Are you alright, Ric?"

Alaric released a long sigh, throwing his hands in the air before perching himself on the arm of his throne chair, ankles crossed, and leather trousers wrinkling.

"I believed I'd squashed her argumentative nature... yet she remains difficult and rude. I expect the rare, minimal outburst, but her behavior today was far from minimal."

Seb hesitated, unsure if he should address Alaric as his boyhood friend, or as a king.

"Perhaps the time has come to consider being fully honest with Amelia, regarding your intentions for Dathoviel. She is an intelligent woman who surely senses the truths you hide from her."

Sliding back against the cushions, Alaric tossed his head and laughed. "An intelligent woman! Really? Have you ever met one?"

Seb rocked forward and back on his heels before snapping to attention and once more banishing the old, nervous habit. Luckily, Alaric hadn't noticed. Clasping his hands behind his back, he tried to stand tall.

"She is no commoner. Her education rivals most men we know."

Fingers steepled beneath his chin, Alaric shook his head, lost in thought.

"I cannot risk her informing Marcel. Her father may have been dim-witted enough to abdicate and hand over his crown, but I can't trust he'll stay complacent. If she will not yield to me... she may have to go."

Seb's eyes widened. "You would banish her from her own land?"

"A strong king does what he must, Sebastian. Ensuring proper freedom to rule my kingdom in peace may mean going to greater lengths."

"The people would never forgive you," Seb whispered.

Across the room, he glimpsed Fredrick pressed against the far shadowed wall. He must have left the villager behind in Regina's care temporarily so he could slip through the concealed entry and into the throne room. Fredrick himself had shown the secret tunnel to Seb back before Alaric's true colors were revealed and the castle was divided between the few loyal to Amelia, and the many terrified of the king.

Their eyes met far too briefly to communicate anything important as the veteran soldier disappeared behind the tapestry, but Seb kept his mouth shut, refusing to alert the king of what he'd seen.

"They will recover," Alaric boasted, his gaze focused out the window and oblivious to his surroundings. "Besides, Amelia would hardly be the first queen to lose her head."

~

Determined to continue acting out before she lost her newfound nerve, Amelia headed toward the north wing, briefly wondering if the phantom scent of her mother's vanilla perfume would greet her between the chapel and her father's suites as it sometimes did.

It was one of the many things she loved about the castle she called home. The tall, wide windows her great-grandfather, King Dathos had built into the stone were another. The few castles she had visited were dark and musty, but not hers. It had expansive, luminous halls, especially on days like today when the periwinkle curtains were secured back and the doors left open, allowing the sunshine and fresh air to pour in and splatter the corridors in gold.

The tension had nearly melted from her neck and shoulders as she rounded the corner, heading for her brothers' suites.

Navigating the corridors was easy given she had explored every nook and room the last twenty-eight years of her life. She bustled past the portrait hall and library, nodding to the four leather-clad guards stationed by the main entrance. The familiar clashing of weapons drifted in from the training grounds, beckoning her out.

How wonderful a ride down to the beach would be right now. She could taste the salty ocean air by just simply imagining how it would feel to dip her toes into the cool water. Perhaps she might submerge her entire body and wash away the anxiety pulsing through her veins. She would try and sneak out tonight before dinner, or better yet afterwards, and enjoy the full moon.

With a quick knock, Amelia peered into Brantley's room, smiling and shaking her head at his teenage clutter. Always in such a rush. He had clothes strewn about the floor and across his unmade bed, with books and mementos haphazardly stuffed onto his shelves and desk.

The young prince was seldom inside and today was no different. With autumn nearly upon them and winter never far behind, he was probably out in the forest, wondering where she was and absorbing every last minute of warmth. Closing the door once more, she selected a new destination and turned left. But with each door she passed on the way to her father's wing her steps began to stutter. Her confidence from earlier was already fading.

In an effort to keep from turning around, she began to count her breaths the way her mother had taught her. She was on her sixty-third inhale by the time she reached the end of the hall and was greeted by an ornately carved oak door.

Whichever servant had delivered the former king's tea this morning had failed to fully close it, so she took advantage of the thin opening and peered inside the study.

Now titled Lord—at his own request—Marcel lay sprawled with his feet up on the navy chaise. Was it sad that she had never seen him as happy as he looked now surrounded by books and half-empty bottles of amber alcohol?

Released from the weight of kingship, he was no longer required to be on his best behavior, yet the moment she knocked he began shuffling around in haste. Probably attempting to appear presentable. As if that were possible.

"En—enter!" he screeched.

Amelia stepped into the room, wishing as she often did, that he would open the windows instead of living in the dim. But she knew her mother's absence proved too significant in the light for him to cope with. The shadows endorsed his tight hold on denial.

"Good day, Father."

"What can I do for you, daughter?" he asked warily, tugging his linen tunic straight.

"We must discuss Alaric," she said, sitting across from him.

Marcel's shoulders slumped, head shaking in displeasure as he too sat. "You mustn't run to me every time your husband disappoints you. Marriage is hard work."

"It is not a marriage issue. He is on a path to destroy our kingdom."

Clearly exasperated, he sighed and smoothed back his thinning grey hair. She could hardly blame him, having grown just as tired of this discussion.

"Amelia, I know you believe I forced him on you—"

"Because that is precisely what you did."

"—but in his shoes, I doubt you'd make different decisions."

"I would! He is arrogant and dangerous; his new tax laws are *starving* our people. He might as well go to town and slay one man a day."

Marcel refused to listen. Despising politics had been only one reason he'd chosen to abdicate.

"Your emotions make you too sensitive. There is more to ruling a kingdom than you realize, Amelia. Alaric knows what he is doing. If you sense a disconnect, it's because he believes you hate him."

"I do hate him," she shot back.

"He is your king."

"He, is a bastard."

"Your duty is to your people, but you must also live as his queen. You know your responsibility lies in providing the crown with an heir."

Her stomach flipped aggressively at the mention of carrying Alaric's child. He had no right to be a father, and she no desire to be a mother.

"I am capable of running Dathoviel without him. While Brantley daydreamed out the window, I became an expert in our history, land, and laws. I know how to lead, and how to fight."

"It's not enough. I made my choice to enforce the law, Amelia. You must have a husband to rule."

"Would Brantley have needed a wife to rule?"

"Enough!" Marcel regressed to a tone from her youth. "You must stop this hysteria."

She did not give a damn about his tone.

"Are you aware Alaric canceled every annual festival? He decided this without consulting anyone. However, he has no problem using our staff and resources to organize balls and banquets at his whim!"

"Some would say full pockets are the sign of a righteous king."

She glared. "At the cost of the people's livelihood? Today I—"

Marcel lifted a silencing hand and it stung as if he had slapped her. "The crown rests upon his head, daughter."

"And *you* put it there. Alaric sits untouchable on the highest of horses, while our kingdom descends to hell."

Before he could respond, she stormed out, slamming his door. Sadly, it failed to provide the pleasure she had craved earlier in the throne room and did little to placate her fury. Letting her forehead drop against the cool stone wall she attempted to find her breath again, but failed.

She burned with desire for action and change, craving more than the limitations of her gender. How could they not see she held many of the answers that could help Dathoviel flourish again? But her words fell on deaf ears and the ease of submission and silence tugged at her resolve once more.

When she felt composed enough to walk, Amelia headed for her tower, craving a long, refreshing nap.

A gentle knocking roused the queen hours later.

"Come in," she called, sitting up and attempting the useless endeavor of smoothing her wrinkled gown.

Her handmaiden and most loyal friend, Olive, entered with a tray of tea and sandwiches.

"Regina prepared this to tempt you awake," she said, smirking. "You missed lunch, and dinner will be late due to the ball."

Amelia collapsed back against the pillows and pulled one over her face. As desired, it muffled her groan.

"Why must you remind me?"

Olive set the tray on the bedside table and perched on the edge of the bed. "It *was* organized for you, remember."

"Oh no," Amelia said, still muffled. "He organized it for himself to show off. The last thing I wish to do after this morning is celebrate marrying that bastard. Especially when my people are starving."

"I don't blame you. But, if you refuse to attend, I won't be permitted into the dinin' hall and there's roasted pig tonight. I'm uncertain how I shall ever forgive you if I miss it."

Amelia tossed the pillow aside with a huff, looking up at the handmaiden's teasing brown eyes. "Very well, but I attend for the food alone."

"Isn't that why we have balls? Besides watching Julian get all dressed up and *jester* around of course."

Grinning in sudden realization, Amelia threw her legs over the mattress, her slippers finding the carpeted floor with a thud.

"I should inform Regina to send all leftovers to the village."

Olive nodded, swinging her long blonde braid over her shoulder. "I'm relieved to see your fire has returned."

Amelia stood and quickly shed her wrinkled gown before slipping into her favorite saffron robe and padding barefoot over to the vanity where her crown rested on a pillow.

As Olive began braiding and pinning dark curls around her ears, she looked up and locked her friend's calm gaze in the mirror.

"Do you ever feel trapped here?"

Had anyone else asked this question, Olive would have been forced to lie, but they were always honest with one another.

"Yes, but I try to be grateful for the things I have. There are worse spots to be in for an unmarried woman my age."

Amelia nodded, supposing she was right. "When I go riding, I sometimes imagine never returning."

"Why do you?" Olive asked softly before her teeth clamped down on a dozen more pins.

Gripping the crown between her hands, Amelia caressed the peaked pearls and oval sapphires with the pad of her thumb.

"The deal my father made with King Viktor ensured Alaric would reign in Brantley's place, whether I married him or not. I could not let him rule my kingdom alone."

Olive's forehead wrinkled with concentration. "Life would be quite different if Brantley had accepted the throne," she said through the pins.

"I could not force him into taking it once he refused. To him kingship is like a prisoner's ball and chain."

"An unwillin' prince would make a better king than the current one," the handmaiden muttered and secured the final braid into place of the perfect nest she'd created for the crown to sit on.

"Once our mother died, no one else would protect him," Amelia said, her chest aching. "Certainly not my father. I married Alaric to protect Brantley from being forced into a life he did not want. *And* to protect our people."

"And you feel you've failed?"

Amelia shrugged, lifting the white pillow. "Despite this, I feel utterly powerless."

Olive gingerly lifted the crown from the velvet and set it in Amelia's hair, working to secure it.

"There's always the chance Alaric falls ill or is injured on one of those atrocious huntin' trips he's so fond of."

Amelia bit her bottom lip. "That would be too easy. Even then I'm sure the court would appoint someone else in his place."

She glanced toward the gown awaiting her on the body form in the corner. Her own personal ball and chain disguised as delicate daisies embroidered onto imported, pale blue silk. At least she had removed corsets from her wardrobe. She would burn every single one in the kingdom if she could.

Perhaps she still would.

The handmaiden removed the gown from the mannequin and held it open, eyebrows wiggling with excitement. She loved clothes.

After slipping on the matching heels, Amelia stepped into the skirt, already dreading its weight.

"Speakin' with your father prove useless as usual?"

Amelia held the bodice to her ribs while Olive laced the back. "He reminded me of my failure in producing an heir. Even *if* Alaric died, my father would surely continue to refuse my ruling Dathoviel solo. And if he will not approve, how will my people ever respect me without a king? Alaric is already bleeding them dry to finance his trips and celebrations. If that has not caused a riot, I'll need proof of something damning to inspire them."

Olive tied the yellow ribbon into a bow and tucked the tail strings away, then turned Amelia around to face her, gripping her shoulders. "You're not as powerless as you feel. They may just need reminding you genuinely care for them. To know they have another option."

A thoughtful silence drifted between them as Olive floated over to open the door. Supporting the weight of her crown, Amelia marched down the stairs, hope blooming in her once heavy chest. For the first time in months, her title slowly centered her. If her father and husband would not listen, she would uncover the power she needed elsewhere.

Perhaps, from *within*.

2

ALARIC TRUDGED INTO THE ballroom, surveying the tables with intense scrutiny. A fresh cloak hung from his broad shoulders, a similar crimson shade to the wine being poured by steady-handed servants. The flowing fabric settled around his leather-clad legs as he stopped to smooth a wrinkled creme table cloth.

His initial hope of seducing Amelia with memories of their wedding day and the care he'd given to her desires this evening had been purged following her episode this afternoon. However, he still wished to impress his guests and his standards remained high. Amelia may never love or trust him, but *they* would respect him.

At least, they would envy him.

Julian, the dark-haired, court jester, stood off in the corner, muttering to himself. Rehearsing and wringing his copper-skinned hands together. He really should have arranged to hear the japes and jabs included in tonight's performance in advance. Yes, all jesters were permitted to make fun of the king, but Julian in particular often took things too far. He certainly didn't bother hiding his dislike. It was mutual, and though Alaric desired to employ different entertainment, Amelia had made it clear he could not replace any staff without her consent.

So much for never respecting her wishes.

"We are nearly ready to welcome your guests, My Lord. Do you find *pleasure* in what you see?" Leah asked, appearing at his side.

Her complexion was slightly darker than the other servants born and raised in Dathoviel. Even in the winter. Typically, Alaric kept his distance from women unless they were pale, weak, and blonde, but from the moment he'd arrived in Dathoviel and saw Leah, he'd needed her to be his. And she'd been more than willing to be claimed.

Many other men were captivated by her and would gladly kneel at her feet for a night together, but he was the only one she seemed to love in return. And for that, he thanked the stars.

Stepping closer to her, his fingertips caressed up her spine, lightly tugging at the ends of her sweeping black hair, tipping her head back, exposing the tempting lines of her throat. As his hand slid lower and lower, her deep, hypnotic eyes further darkened, drinking him in. *Pulling* him in. Her lips parted slightly, her curves already molding to his chest as his arms snaked around her, out of his control.

A year later, he still didn't understand this power she had over him. How she could snap his resolve with merely a look. But he loved it. The freedom and the tension and the undeniable passion that always followed her teasing.

It was also nice not needing to conceal their relationship. The queen certainly hadn't seem bothered by it when he'd named Leah his official mistress. The court *had* complained, but it was good to be king. No one could truly tell you no.

"Your hard work will be rewarded," he promised, squeezing her waist.

"Perhaps after dessert?"

He leaned close; his breath hot against her throat. "Perhaps during."

Slowly, her teeth sunk into her lower lip before she peeled herself away, hips swaying. He had to grip the chair at his side to keep from following her to the kitchens.

~

Seb entered the ballroom a few minutes before the first guests were set to arrive. He'd retired his armor for the evening, instead choosing a taupe jacket with black toggles and simple trousers. His beloved cap with its ivory feather sat proudly atop his head. He felt as good as he looked, or rather he had, before realizing he'd dressed up for no one in particular. Perhaps he could have a drink and find enough courage to ask Olive to dance. *Doubtful.*

Resigned to spend the evening alone as usual, he approached the king.

"You've recreated your wedding reception," he said, eyeing the décor.

"Yes." Alaric sounded pleased, like he had been the one arranging flowers and configuring seating charts for the last two days. "I had hoped it would rekindle our romance. Given this afternoon however, my hopes are not high."

Seb clasped his hands behind his back, uncertain what romance he spoke of. Was his reference to Amelia's earlier outburst? Or when he'd threatened to behead her?

Whatever the king and queen shared now was not what poets like his late father wrote about. Nor what men went to war and died for. Alaric and Amelia *had* been on better terms when they first met, but they'd merely been two strangers making the best of their situation.

Seb recalled their picturesque wedding. A day, at the time, he'd greatly envied. The room overflowing with guests in colorful dress swaying to joyful music. The smell of delicious food, and the hum of excited chatter mixed with clinking goblets. Everyone had danced until the last candle melted away, and the final wine barrel drained. But the beauty of a single event could not equate to the bond needed for lifelong partnership. And a pretty party would hardly placate Amelia enough to give Alaric another chance. Or keep him from offing her when she didn't.

Seb searched foggy memories of his parents before their deaths, but failed as always. Even before they had left their desert land, and arrived in Petrovia, but he was too young then. They'd both been artists, passionate for one another and their crafts. Not that such passion had existed in his vocabulary as a child. He wasn't sure he fully understood it, even now.

~

Amelia noted the sentimental atmosphere of the ballroom and had promptly snarled at it. She held no desire to relive her wedding day. And Alaric had best not attempt to recreate their consummation either. He had a perfectly good tower of his own.

The roasted pig at least did not disappoint.

Amidst the chatter of dinner, Alaric stood, goblet in hand. Amelia forced down a mouthful of potato and looked up, his hand extending toward her. She forced a pretty smile and stood, months of practice helping her maintain a calm mask as he faced their guests.

"Many thanks for joining us tonight. We celebrate not only the anniversary of our union, but the joining of two powerful kingdoms, both rich with history and resources."

"Huzzah!" Marcel drunkenly slapped his table.

Alaric continued, jaw tight. "When my father told me the king of Dathoviel's daughter required a husband, I was overjoyed. To gain power alone is glorious, but to share the pleasure of ruling is... magnificent. Queen Amelia has watched me struggle to gain a firm footing as a leader. I hope in the years to come, her confidence and trust will grow, as I prove myself to you all."

Polite applause followed as Alaric passed a wooden box from Seb to Amelia. She lifted the lid and revealed a dazzling dagger nestled atop a protective bed of cream velvet.

In the candlelight the sapphire-encrusted hilt glittered, the long and elegantly arched silver blade flashing. Breathless, she felt the need to lift it from the box and hold it in her palm.

"I present Queen Amelia this dagger, along with a wish she will join me on a hunt one day soon. My mother always said that a man and wife who share interests, rise together. That a strong marriage makes a strong queen. And with her support, a wise king to lead a bountiful land." He lifted his goblet and the guests mirrored his action. "To Amelia, my wife, your queen. And all the days we shall share."

She had zero intention of ever joining one of his ghastly hunting trips, but she refrained from correcting him *or* returning the dagger. Despite it being from him, she embraced the strength the weapon brought her—the protection. With the dagger clutched to her chest, she drained her wine of every last drop.

Alaric's expression was focused as he studied her over the rim of his glass, like he was trying to figure her out. Perhaps wondering if she was worth all this trouble, or if she had bought his charade.

Once the final plate was cleared, servants came in to shift tables and create space for dancing. The tempo increased for a few songs, and Julian took a well-earned rest. Amelia had a bit more wine, showing off the dagger to Olive while Alaric chatted with his knights.

Then he was next to her, startling her with a hand at her elbow.

"My Queen, would you share this dance?"

Amelia genuinely considered his offer. He was an incredible waltz partner, if nothing else. A dance floor was the sole place his company proved bearable. Despite the fact she detested the way he financed these frequent balls, she'd always enjoyed a prime bash. Plus, the queen's first dance was always reserved for her husband. If she wished to dance with anyone else tonight, she had little choice.

He guided her to the floor and the guests dissolved to the edges, giving the couple space, but forever watching. Amelia willed herself to find comfort in the music as he drew her close. From the expressions of the women inspecting his every move, they clearly envied her.

Well, they were welcome to have him. The firm muscles beneath her hands and against her chest failed to excite her yet again.

"Do you recall when we met?" Alaric asked.

"I do."

The first night they had met, she accepted what fate had set before her. They danced and laughed, and she had shared her dreams for Dathoviel. Her desire to protect her brother from the title he evaded. She had laid all her cards on the table, not realizing he held his own close to his chest.

Her first and gravest mistake.

Excitement to become queen had blinded her to the dark hunger for power hidden within his eyes. There had been no mistaking it following their abrupt wedding ceremony and swift coronation, however.

Once the crown rested upon Alaric's head, the facade melted away. And by the time she understood Dathoviel was doomed under his control, he held the power.

Alaric's voice brought her back to the present moment. "I know we have contrasting opinions on how best to run the kingdom... but feel the harmonious way we float together around the dance floor? Try to understand, it is best to let me lead you through life in a similar manner."

She repressed the urge to stomp on his toes.

"I neither require your leadership, nor desire it."

He gripped her hand and lower back tightly. She winced and glared up at him. Their conversations were often blunt, holding little nuance and in a way, she was grateful for it.

"My parents had an arranged marriage as well, but over the years they worked to develop a resilient bond. My mother supported my father at every turn, and together they grew a vast empire. Meet me halfway, Amelia and I promise you'll grasp how well matched we are."

She laughed. "You are mad."

"We're both passionate people, and if we tried—"

"I do not approve of the way you treat my subjects, or rule my land. I despise how you collect and spend the wealth. I do not respect you as a king, a husband, or even a man. Therefore, I can never love you."

The song was ending and would provide an acceptable chance to escape. Alaric must have recognized this because he growled, clearly impatient, and tugged her closer.

"Give me more time to prove my process is worthy. The people will bow to us and worship the ground we walk on."

"I shall never rule in such a way. My people will not survive your brand of dominance. We are meant to lead and protect them. Not lord over them like gods."

Frustration flashed in his eyes when she attempted to retreat. He held tighter. For those watching, it probably looked seductive. To Amelia, his hand might as well have been locked around her throat.

"Release me," she spat.

"You will learn to respect me, *wife*."

His final word stung like a curse, branding her. It captured her voice and froze her blood.

Proving his control, he slowly freed her arm and waist—one finger at a time, his eyes cold and hard as they bore into her. Stepping apart, they clapped for the musicians in thanks, but he refused to release her gaze.

Dishes and forks clinked as dessert service commenced in the background. In costume, Julian strutted out, bells ringing with every step. It was time for his main performance. He bowed to the king and queen, a smile locked into his features. But she could see in his tawny and observant eyes that he understood their situation. And that he did not like it.

As the welcoming claps continued for him, Amelia darted from the dance floor. She dodged servants with colorful cakes and puddings, apologizing as she went. Avoiding eye contact with everyone, she snatched the box with her dagger inside and hastily escaped from the ballroom. She even ignored Olive's calls to wait.

Amelia did not care if her departure raised a few eyebrows. Alaric may be the king and her husband, but he could not stop her from leaving a room. She tore through corridors and up stairs, finally locking herself alone in her chambers. Her chest was heaving and she could feel her crown hanging crookedly despite the numerous pins Olive had used to secure it. The wooden box tumbled from her hands, splitting open with a thud. The dagger slid across the stone floor, finally stopping in a patch of fading light from the window.

Clutching the bedpost, she fought to steady her breaths.

With time, her heartbeat returned to its regular rhythm, and the ringing in her ears faded. Soon, the warmth and quiet of her tower enveloped her in a warm embrace. She removed her crown and set it on the bed, moving toward the sound of neighing outside her window. Hopeful to find her brother in the stables, she peeked her head out to look and spotted Brantley through the doors, saddling Gus; his Hanoverian gelding.

He had been absent from the party, but she had not bothered sending someone to retrieve him. No reason for them both to be stuck inside miserable.

Amelia headed for her wardrobe. One could only ride side-saddle so fast, and tonight she craved the speed. She reached into the back where a pair of her father's trousers and one of his shirts were concealed. Olive had tailored them so she could ride in comfort. She just needed to somehow remove this gown unassisted.

Smirking, Amelia reached for her dagger.

"Wait for me!"

Amelia burst into the stables, a triumphant smile glowing across her features as Brantley settled into his saddle.

The prince watched her rest against the door, winded and attempting to recover.

"What in God's name are you wearing?"

His words were accusing, but his eyes glinted, impressed by her gall. Shoving her sleeves up, she reached for a handful of water from the barrel. It wasn't the cleanest, but it was wet and not wine.

"Proper riding clothes."

"You better hope no one else sees the way you're dressed." He winked. "Especially Father."

"My fashion choices are the least of our kingdom's worries."

She waved off his warning, nuzzling Greta hello and feeding her a carrot from the crate by the door. As she passed by, she stroked Gus. The gelding munched toward her fingers. Chuckling, she returned to the box for a second carrot.

"Did you enjoy the party?"

"Not particularly." Amelia made quick, efficient work of saddling Greta. She leapt onto the horse's back, giving the chestnut mare a stroke. "Shall we ride?"

Greta gave an approving snort in response.

"I'll follow you." Brantley gestured to the open doors, his smirk a mirror image of his sisters.

Had they not been nearly a decade apart, they could have passed for twins.

"Let us see if you boys can keep up!"

They burst from the stables and dashed across the field surrounding the castle. Nightfall and familiar lush green land carried on for miles, occasionally peaked with rock and stone. Amelia felt the strength of Greta's movements beneath her as she held tight. She and Brantley had spent much of their youth in the stables. They had learned to ride and care for the horses early. An unusual task for a prince and princess, but a result of their mother, Diana, having interests in horse breeding.

She had always looked so majestic while riding. She had worn gowns *and* refused to sit side-saddle. Despite the scandal, no one had uttered a reprimand. They would not have dared. Not because she frightened them. She had simply commanded respect and adoration. Something Amelia desperately wanted for herself.

Over the years, Amelia and Greta's bond had developed into a fierce friendship. She had watched and assisted in the mare's birth as a child and had come to trust this animal with her life. More than any man or woman on earth. She could be herself in the saddle, a comfort she did not take for granted. Amelia had a hard time imagining riding another horse for the rest of her life. If she had a soul mate on this earth, she dared to believe it was Greta, and liked to think the horse felt the same about her.

As the four proceeded east, the wind whipped through the queen's loosening braids and Greta's similar dark mane. Their eyes fierce on the horizon, blind to the world around them. Heart-tugging in multiple directions, Amelia sighed.

How long would it take to reach? How easy would it be to continue straight through and never look back? Far past the fields, over the river, and deeper into the forests than she had ever explored. And beyond.

They had journeyed a reasonable distance from the castle when the horses slowed, requesting rest and water. Gallops turned to soft trots toward the south river as Greta and Gus fell in step beside each other. One rarely enjoyed riding without the other. Similar to their riders, they were brother and sister—though in their case; he was the eldest.

Amelia observed the stars pinging into the darkening sky while Brantley stared at his hands. It took her a moment to notice the sadness and guilt moving across his face.

"I owe you an apology," he said, his tone fallen.

"I honestly do not mind you missing the party."

"Not regarding that."

Amelia shook her head at him. He had said this all before, and there was no use in him saying it again. She understood. More so, she respected his decision.

"Brantley, you must stop doing this to yourself."

"How can I? If I'd agreed to take the throne, you wouldn't have been forced to marry Alaric, and our kingdom would be whole. This all happened because of my selfishness."

Amelia reached out, taking his hand. "I do not blame you for my marriage. We each have one life, and we must live it on our own terms. There is no shame in your craving for freedom and simple days."

"Yet, your unhappiness pains me."

He squeezed her fingers with his, finally meeting her eyes and she offered her best attempt at a comforting smile

"I am devising a plan to repair the damage Alaric has caused. The details are currently secret, but you shall be proud when I tell you."

"I'm always proud of you," he whispered.

September 1st, 1456

Refreshed the next morning, the queen rang for Olive to help dress her quickly so she could visit the chapel before breakfast. She could pray anywhere, but there she felt safest. No one could bother her while inside.

Including Alaric.

The chapel doors were tall, made of carved wood, and held two colorful pieces of stained glass. They stood open, the spicy scent of frankincense spilling into the hall. Each time Amelia passed through, it felt like stepping into her mother's arms.

Queen Diana had brought the panes with her when she had married Marcel, leaving behind a homeland much richer in resources than Dathoviel, and a fiancé she had not loved. It had created considerable gossip amongst the six northern kingdoms, but love had called her parents together and there was no denying their happiness was true. Until she had fallen ill.

Their romance had been Amelia's favorite bedtime tale. It became the standard she held her own future love story to. But adulthood reminded her daily that her reality would never be so romantic.

An elaborate gold cross stood front and center, awaiting her prayer. She approached it, mimicking its shape over her torso, and knelt, hands clasped in her lap.

"Heavenly Father, I come humbly before you today, wishing to know which of the paths I face is the right one to take. I could turn a blind eye on myself and the destiny I desire, and suffer in the silence of duty. Or I can rise up and give voice to those who are ignored. However, some of my actions will be dishonest. They will mock vows I have taken, and I may be forced to break a commandment or two. Yet, I believe you would not wish me to reject this calling. To ignore this rebellion against the fate I face. I know you created me for more than this."

She had not expected a light to shine from heaven or a literal voice to answer her, though she could imagine the response she hoped for. After all, prayers were often answered with knowledge already housed within.

You were created for more than this. Deliver your people, Amelia, for they cannot survive nor thrive in these conditions. You've been tested this past year, but now is the time to rise. To stand.

She pushed to her feet, eyes on the cross. Even if the words had not come from God, but from her own conscious, they were still as true. She would not turn her back on her people again.

"Whether my actions send me to the grace of your throne or the gates of damnation, I shall go knowing I did what I believed right."

The promise did not leave her lips lightly, and she prayed divine protection would follow her from the chapel.

Constable Fredrick was whispering with his most trusted knights when she entered the barracks, feeling quite out of place. When he saw her, he dismissed his men, his surprise clear. She overheard mention of increasing her protection detail before they returned to their rooms.

"Good morn', My Queen." Fredrick bowed to her. "How may I be of service?"

She fiddled with her belt, repressing the need to embrace him the way a daughter would, excited to share news with her father.

"Good morning, Constable. I trust all was well yesterday with the man I left in your care?"

He nodded, hands clasped in front of him. "Regina prepared enough food for his family and another, I imagine."

Something odd happened to his voice as he tripped over her beloved cook's name. Perhaps she could mention it next time she visited the kitchens. It would be hard to resist, considering how often she had caught Regina gazing out the window, her hands lingering in the sink for too long, whenever Fredrick ran drills with the new knights in the back field.

"I appreciate your words, considering the trouble that particular choice has me in with the king."

Fredrick wavered, perhaps wishing to tell her something? But untrustworthy ears could be anywhere.

"The remaining food from the ball is being prepared for the village, as requested."

"Wonderful." She smirked. "Please check in with Regina and see if she needs any help. You know those kitchen boys are so mesmerized by her they cannot help but to drop things. I would hate for all that food to go to waste."

He eyed her, like he knew what she was truly saying underneath the polite request. A wide grin split his dark lips open, showing nearly all his teeth before he cleared his throat and refocused on the conversation.

"I do believe what you're trying to do for your people is noble."

Amelia warmed at his words. "Your trust means more than I can express. You have always been a loyal man to Dathoviel and my family. I have come to ask if you would take a leap of faith and follow me on a mission."

"I would follow you anywhere, My Queen."

She lowered her voice, stepping close. "It would mean going against Alaric's wishes, and making moves behind his back."

He did not hesitate.

"I hold no love for the king. You have my unyielding loyalty."

"Thank you." Amelia clasped his hands in hers. "I wish to visit my people later today. I would like to deliver the food myself and see firsthand what is happening there, and I would appreciate your company."

Fredrick straightened his leather vest. "I'll begin preparations."

She watched him walk away with a sad smile. If only speaking with her father was that simple.

~

Alaric gazed up from the latest census scroll, his calculations lost when a squire burst into his study. What was his name again? Something with an H? Hector?

Desperate to be a knight, the young man was always eager to please, which came in handy, but it could also be bloody annoying. He would have to find a good use for the boy.

"Explain your intrusion!"

"Apologizes, My Lord," stuttered Henry? "I thought you ought to know. The queen has made travel arrangements into the village. I overheard the constable discussing it with his men moments ago."

No, Heath. It *must* be Heath.

"Very well. Thank you for your loyalty." Alaric dismissed him with a quick, hard glance.

When the door shut, Alaric sat silently, considering what to do. He could tell Amelia he knew of her plans. Or travel to the village himself and catch her in the act. Or even send spies with her to report back to him.

Or he could let her live out her fantasy, whatever it may be. Perhaps she would be too busy playing with the peasants like dolls, and stay out of his way. He had a trip of his own to prepare for, and the less time she spent in the castle, the better. He couldn't risk her foiling his plan. This was his chance to ensure his legacy.

Calmly, he stored the rolled parchment away in the hidden compartment within his desk drawer, ensuring it locked successfully.

Then he headed straight to his father-in-law's study.

Marcel must have been pouring himself a drink when Alaric knocked on his door because he was greeted with a tumbler of brandy and a look of surprise.

"I hope you don't mind me coming to you without warning, Lord. We must discuss your daughter."

The former king gestured for Alaric to sit across from him by the fire. His hair was obscenely out of place today, but his clothes at least looked freshly laundered.

"Regarding her disappearance last night?"

Disappearance. What a fascinating word choice for her nearly running down three servants before dashing from the room in tears. Of course, Marcel wouldn't actually admit anything was wrong with his daughter, but at least that meant he also wouldn't ask questions about the why behind her behavior.

What a dreadful excuse for a man.

"More than that." Alaric made a show of sighing and running his hands through his hair. "I regret to admit this because Amelia is a fine queen, but her wifely duties are lacking. She is once again undermining and avoiding me."

Marcel nodded knowingly.

"She has been a stubborn girl all her life. Too smart for her own good. If I'd known she would take those lessons to heart, I'd have forbidden her from entering the classroom."

"You mustn't blame yourself, sir." Alaric softened his tone, though it wasn't easy. "I strive to rule this kingdom and care for her, but she will not provide me an opportunity to prove myself. I'm at a loss."

"Her mother and I were lucky enough to marry for love," Marcel said, hardly focused on the conversation's main point. He looked dreamily out the window instead, spinning his wedding ring around his finger.

Alaric's own silver band burned on his left hand.

"Yes, Amelia told me of the love and passion you two shared the first night we met. How she wished for similar things."

"It is a wonder we did not have ten children," Marcel chuckled.

Alaric drained the glass, reminding himself that losing his temper with the old man would likely create more problems than solutions.

"Perhaps she requires more time? Patience? It's possible I've been too distracted trying to prove myself when I should have been getting to know her better."

"I'll speak with her again soon," Marcel promised, finally looking back. He eyed Alaric's empty glass, then his decanter, as if debating over sharing or saving his beloved alcohol. He decided not to. "Try not to worry yourself. Women come around sooner or later."

"Was her mother easy to handle?"

Marcel's eyes widened with sudden realization.

That's what he thought. Amelia had gotten her fire from someone, and it surely wasn't the man before him.

With a nod, Alaric set aside the empty tumbler, offered a handshake and departed from the dark, stale room. The man needed to open a damn window.

And bathe.

. 3 .

THE QUEEN'S CARRIAGE HALTED abruptly outside the main square and Amelia stepped out, squinting in the sunlight.

Olive followed with a wide, bright smile. Though her excitement over being free from the castle appeared to quickly dissipate into overwhelm. Behind them, Fredrick dismounted from his horse, giving the two accompanying guards a few short orders before moving to Amelia's side.

She surveyed every inch of every building as guilt consumed her. Why had she not come sooner?

The overall physical landscape had not changed, yet she struggled to recognize the village. During their early years, she and Brantley had often escaped from the castle to play with the other children. As they had grown older, the visits became less frequent, but she still remembered those days fondly. How many of the children she played with had young ones of their own? How many had Alaric inadvertently killed in the last year as he deprived her people of their most basic necessities?

The silence of the square was deafening as her memories faded away. There were no children running or laughing around the fountain. In fact, she could not spot a single soul. The once bright market carts were stripped to their bare bones, and a few were missing wheels. All life and color appeared to have been sucked from the neglected homes and wilted flowers. The banners and flags strung above shop doors, once boasting the bright gold and teal colors of their kingdom were now weathered and threadbare.

Shaken, Amelia turned to Fredrick for guidance, hoping her voice did not sound as terrified as she felt.

"Do you have any recommendations for gathering the people?"

His warm gaze swept the village. "The church and the tavern are the largest indoor spaces. We could also assemble here if you'd prefer fresh air."

"Indoors may be best," Olive said, eyeing the sky.

Amelia nodded, feeling the first raindrops on her temple. "The church has more seating than the tavern."

"I shall congregate anyone I find."

Fredrick took one officer with him to spread word to each house, leaving the other to watch over Amelia and Olive.

As they passed the dry, cracked fountain, the queen repressed tears, chomping down on her quivering bottom lip. Faces sporadically popped into view from the various homes, peeking at her. The men, women, and children she glimpsed appeared worn. Tired. *Terrified*. Olive kindly waved to a young boy in a nearby window, but he ducked down immediately and the faded cream curtain fell back into place.

"They must've hidden when they heard the carriage, fearin' Alaric's men comin' to collect more taxes."

Amelia cleared her throat. "This is not what I envisioned for my kingdom, Olive."

She could feel her heart in her ribs as she tried and failed to get a handle on her nerves, but they were nowhere to be found.

The handmaiden clasped her hand.

"You'll fix this. I believe in you."

Amelia's gaze settled farther down the road as a familiar man stepped out from a small cottage. Three small children bounded after him, gathering around his legs by the open gate. There was a bundle of knitted blankets in his left arm that must have been an infant.

A pale and ill-looking woman—his wife no doubt—followed next, leaning against his right shoulder for support upon reaching them. She had dark copper hair and thin lips, and surely, she would have been breathtaking had she not looked like a walking corpse.

Together, Amelia and Olive approached the peeling, white-washed fence.

"Hello, William," she said.

The small girl glanced up to her father. "Who are they, Papa?"

"Brianna, this is Queen Amelia, and her... *friend*?"

"Olive," she introduced herself gently.

Brianna, who looked about four years old, possessed her father's thick golden hair and the same jade eyes as her mother.

"The queen?" she breathed, mesmerized. "Papa says you saved him from the evil king. Have you come to save us too?"

Amelia knelt to the child's level, taking the two tiny outstretched hands in hers. "I came to try."

Brianna grinned and wrapped her arms around Amelia's neck, hugging tightly. "I knew it. You look like an angel."

"Brianna, we do not hug without asking permission first, remember?" the mother weakly scolded, trying to reach for her child. "Your Highness, I apologise."

Amelia continued holding the girl with a kind smile.

"It is quite alright, I promise."

William stepped forward to take his daughter's hand once she released Amelia. "Hannah and I can't thank you enough for the kindness and generosity you've shown us."

Amelia grinned. "I have come to hear from everyone in the village. Your concerns fall on broken ears when brought to my husband. I wish to change this. Will you join us at the church?"

William nodded. "We'd love to, but may I offer a suggestion?"

"I would welcome it."

"No one here is fond of your husband, and I'm sorry to say that your name is tarnished by association."

Precisely what she had been most afraid of. Her inaction the past year would be looked at just as harshly as the damage Alaric had caused.

"I understand."

"It may do you a service if William addresses those who gather first," Hannah suggested, her eyelids drooping. The poor woman looked like she may faint.

A second woman with lighter red locks appeared at the door and quickly approached the family.

"I think you best lay down," she murmured, wrapping her arm around Hannah's waist and guiding her back inside.

"I'll help you, Aunt Beatrice." The eldest son turned back to the cottage, gesturing for the younger boy to follow.

Brianna remained, seemingly rooted to the spot next to her father, her eyes never leaving Amelia.

William looked after his wife and sons, concern etched into his forehead. When he looked back to Amelia, the worry lines remained but were less prominent.

"With your permission, I wish to tell them what you did for our family. Act as witness that you have our best interests at heart."

Amelia's soul sighed in relief. "I would appreciate that, thank you."

~

The simple wooden church had been built fifty years ago. At the time, it had been the appropriate size to sit every villager, however the population had grown since. This forced a good majority to stand today, while the ill and elderly filled the pews.

Faces of various ages, colors, and creeds turned to him. Their chattering silenced. Now that they knew Alaric was not around their fear was gone, but contempt lived in its place. Amelia felt every cold, hard stare tearing into her from where she stood at the back of the stage. William gave Amelia a comforting smile before stepping up to the pulpit. He clapped his hands together, directing the villager's attention his way.

"Welcome! Thank you for interrupting your day to join us. If you've yet to hear, we have come together to entertain a message from Queen Amelia."

The crowd erupted into murmurs.

"What do we care to listen to her?" one woman from the pew shouted. "They never bother listening to us!"

William raised his hands. "I recognize your anger and I know your pockets and bellies are empty. But I assure you, your troubles are the king's doing and his alone."

"We cannot trust her," exclaimed another.

The room grumbled.

"I went before them both to ask for an extension over the taxes. The queen listened to me," William interjected. "She paid my debt to the king herself. When he threw me out, she offered me food for my family and a safe escort home. Food we shared with as many of you as we could. I implore you listen to her. She cannot help everyone today, but if she knows the problems, she can help little by little."

Amelia stepped forward, whispering her thanks as William moved aside, throwing her an encouraging nod. She had practiced what she hoped to say on the carriage ride over, but upon stepping forward, her mind went blank. She found Olive's comforting grin in the crowd and inhaled deeply, clasping her clammy hands together.

"I apologize it has taken me this long to come. I wish to hear any requests and concerns you have."

"Why should we believe you?" someone called out.

"Quite right!" barked a woman to the left.

"How do we know you haven't come under the king's wishes?"

Amelia prayed for calm, both within the space and her pounding heart. "I cannot undo the damage Alaric has done, but I can do this."

She gestured to Fredrick and the guards. Together the three men brought forward a large chest and opened it, revealing gold and silver coins. Weary excitement and longing drifted from the villagers.

"For us?" Brianna asked from below.

Amelia nodded.

"Anyone who shares their story with me today will be invited to fill their purses."

A line quickly formed down the center aisle.

The sun had set long before Amelia and her companions returned home, a result of the villagers insisting they join the feast she had provided. Everyone able contributed to the spread, filling in gaps the party leftovers failed to provide. Seeing their teamwork and gratitude eased the soreness in her feet and neck.

She had listened to story after heartbreaking story. Sickness, poverty, and hunger were repetitive themes throughout. Children who had to miss out on an education because they were needed at home. Adults who felt powerless to make change and provide for themselves and those they loved.

Comparing how the town felt when she arrived, to when they shared final farewells filled her with courage. The faces looked younger, hopeful even. And the air felt light, despite the darkness following sunset.

She *had* made a small difference.

Ready for sleep, she leaned over to extinguish her bedside candle, but a loud knock rattled her door. She froze. Alaric's powerful voice carried through the oak.

"G' evening, Your Majesty. May I enter?"

Her heart skipped a beat. She checked under her pillow for the dagger, fingertips finding the comforting metal. Night-time visits from the king normally meant one thing. But tonight, it could be anything.

Did he know about her visit to the village? Had he seen the chest of gold and silver missing from his vault?

"You may."

The knob turned and the door creaked open, his tall, broad frame filling the doorway. He had combed his hair and applied a woodsy scent, one of the few she could stand. He shut the door, eyeing the beauty tools on her vanity and the books on her shelves.

"We missed you at dinner this evening."

"I am teaching Olive to ride, and I suppose we lost track of time."

"Well, I hope you had a lovely... *adventure*."

"I enjoyed the fresh air." She sat up in bed, the dagger hidden beneath the quilt, watching him journey through her room. "What brings you to visit me?"

Alaric set aside the novel he had been examining and turned from the bookshelf to her. "It is time to try again, Amelia."

Relieved the conversation was not about the village, she hesitated to object, but the thought of his body on hers made her skin crawl. Even if he did smell like a forest.

"I am exhausted from the ride today."

He straightened his shoulders and inhaled, perhaps searching for patience. "We cannot keep avoiding this. The court grows tired of your excuses, and I of your father's berating. I'd hate to see what happens if we fail to present an heir."

It was not a threat. It was the truth, and she knew it as well as he. If they shared anything, it was the pressure to continue Dathoviel's dynasty. Neither of them had a choice in this. It was duty. Expectation. All part of the job description.

"Very well."

She tucked the dagger back beneath her pillow as he advanced toward her. He would never force himself on her; a sad comfort, really. A low expectation, but one she did not take for granted. Intimacy remained her choice and if she had truly refused, he would have walked out. Sharing a bed with her was hardly his favorite pastime either.

"I suppose I can't blame your lack of enthusiasm," he said, tugging his black tunic over his head and dropping it unceremoniously on her floor.

She avoided looking at his newly revealed skin and threw the blankets back, her night dress falling around her ankles as she stood. When his fingers went to the tie on his leather pants she looked up to his frowning face.

"I remind you I am still uncomfortable with kissing."

"Noted." He nodded diligently. "And I request your hands stay above my waist."

"When have my hands ever gone lower than your shoulders?"

She scoffed and he shrugged.

"Never, but it's only fair if we both have rules."

She could not fault him there.

"Ready?" she asked, her voice thick.

The vein in his neck pulsed. He nodded his consent and blew out the candle with one breath, hands finding her in the dark, molding her body against his to suit his needs. He was probably picturing Leah. She... well, she pictured someone who looked nothing like Alaric as she prayed no heir would be conceived tonight.

September 2nd, 1456

The dim dining hall the following morning saw only a father and son sharing an uneasy breakfast, awaiting the others to arrive and the sun to rise. Autumn truly had begun.

"Where is she?" Brantley mused aloud, scraping his bowl in hopes more oatmeal would miraculously appear.

Preferably with cinnamon this time.

Marcel looked up from his book, fork poised at his lips. "When a husband and wife are late to breakfast, you don't want to go interrupting them."

Brantley's face twisted with disgust. "The last thing Amelia would do is lose time in bed with *him*."

"Oh, son, not you as well." The lord's hands waved furiously, book and fork still firm in his grip. The flame of the candle he was using to read by flickered. "Our laws state Amelia cannot rule alone. I will no longer defend my actions to my children. What's done is done."

"It's a ridiculous law! One you should've changed when you had the power to do so."

"And *you*," Marcel said pointedly, jabbing the fork in Brantley's direction. "should have taken the throne, fulfilling your birthright when you had the chance."

Brantley's heart clenched with the familiar guilt. "Amelia is firstborn. She has interest and passion for this kingdom. What sense does it make to force an unwilling child to rule when you have someone qualified and willing, begging for a chance?"

"You were destined for greatness."

"Because I have a penis?"

Marcel's eyes widened before snapping into a glare. "This is the way we do things in our family."

"What do you know of family?" Brantley muttered under his breath, but not quietly enough.

The former king pounded the table with his fists, jostling the glass to his left; which was undoubtedly more alcohol than juice. If its smell was any indication.

"I will not have my choices questioned by a child!"

Brantley smirked. "You call me a child, yet you wished me to be king. To have opinions and make decisions for an entire land and its people. I cannot be both too immature to speak, and certified to rule, Father."

He pushed back from the table, his chair legs scraping along the stone floor and drowning out anything else Marcel said. His feet carried him furiously from one dark corridor to the next until he stood outside the library door, panting.

As a child he despised this room, refusing to enter unless Amelia joined him. He'd dreamed of anything but the weight of what wearing a crown meant, while she emerged the ideal ruler for Dathoviel. After the last governess had fled from the castle, tired of his antics, he had vowed to never return.

But he could no longer be selfish. Amelia had sacrificed so much for him. The power to rule had once been his, and he may still have it. . . But he needed to know for sure before he said or did anything about it. He needed answers, and they were surely inside.

He could sit on the throne as he was meant to and allow her to make all the decisions she wished. She would be in charge, and he would merely be a puppet, still free to live his own life. On his terms.

It was imperfect, but it had to be better than nothing.

~

Amelia lay awake as Alaric slept peacefully next to her. She was curled tight, giving her body the space from his it craved. Her hand slipped beneath the pillow, lifting her dagger from concealment once more. The blade glinted, almost seductively in the light of the full moon as she tilted it back and forth.

Was killing truly as simple as he described? Would the tip pierce through his flesh with ease, or would she have to use all her strength? Which part of his body would be the quickest and most deadly to pierce?

Perhaps listening closer to his inane hunting stories would have been wise.

She rolled over gently and onto her knees, facing him, the blade pointed at his chest. Right where his heart would be. If he had a heart. The pressure caused a slight indent in his skin, and he stirred. She pushed harder—her knuckles going white as she gripped the hilt. Digging for strength to press forward while simultaneously holding herself back.

His lashes fluttered and she drew her arm back, a mere moment to decide. Then his eyes opened, widening as the blade descended in one fluid movement—

Amelia awoke, bolting upwards, gasping. She looked down to the sheathed dagger clutched in her hand. The mattress next to her was empty and the sun was just peeking over the horizon.

Of course, it had been a dream. Alaric never stayed through the night.

Forcing herself to lie back, she clung to the dagger with both hands, struggling to sort reality from subconscious action. And the truth of who she was and what she was truly capable of... who she so desperately wished to be.

Pressing the heels of her hands against her eyes, she let out a groan. It was early, but not so early that breakfast had not already been served. Not that she had any appetite at the moment. What day was it? Friday? No, she had gone to the village Friday. It was Saturday. The day Olive got a break from her duties. Her coveted morning to sleep in.

Amelia threw off the covers, the faintest of smiles on her lips. She chose a simple gown she could put on alone, and steeled herself for the tongue lashing she was about to receive from her friend.

~

In the king's tower, Alaric rested back in his chair, bare feet up on the desk, re-reading the letter he'd received earlier that week.

King Alaric,

Your request for a personal audience with me has been acknowledged and accepted.
We will commence preparations for your arrival and welcome you in the springtime. I await your confirmation and look forward to discussing Dathoviel's generous offer face to face.
Hopefully a magnificent partnership between our two kingdoms shall arise.

Sincerely,
King Bartholomew of Winvoltor

The parchment was thinner and softer than what Alaric used and crinkled easily, so he made sure to be gentle. Leah, who slept soundly in his bed however, he had not been gentle with. Not that she had complained. In fact, she'd been there waiting for him to return after he'd left Amelia's room the night prior. Two women in one night was a lot to ask of him, but he was up to the task.

As Leah rolled over, the sheet fell away from her bare body, and his eyes raked over her rosy, brown skin. Slowly, he lowered his feet and stood. It was nearly time for her to wake so what was the harm in one more tryst before she had to leave for her duties.

He read over the letter one final time before carefully folding and tucking it away in his secret drawer. Later, he would inform Sebastian of their need to travel after the snow's final melt in the new year. The trip would take no less than a fortnight one way, and once there, he would give himself a full week in Winvoltor to finalize the trade details. It would be a long journey, but the rewards would be grand.

This partnership would no doubt become the most defining move of his reign.

~

Amelia traipsed through the wood, branches and newly fallen leaves crunching beneath her boots. Well, technically Brantley's old boots. They were a bit too small and pinched her toes, but she could not go traipsing through the trees in silk slippers, now could she?

The thick scent of pine and earth filled her nose and lungs, her chest expanding wide, inhaling as much as possible. Some women had a favorite flower, but Amelia had the entire forest. And though the ocean did not call to her the way moss and bark did, she smiled as the woodland floor began fading into a golden sandy beach.

It was so peaceful and comforting. Or it would have been if Olive wasn't cursing and muttering behind her.

"I don't know why I let you talk me into this," the handmaiden hissed. "And at such an ungodly hour, too!"

"It is not *that* early."

Olive gestured at the rising sun and the pale pink sky, dodging an exposed root.

"You woke me up on my *one* day to sleep in. If it's before noon it's too early."

Leaning against the nearest tree, Amelia laughed and folded her arms across her chest, watching Olive navigate the mostly flat terrain as though she were climbing a mountain.

After waking from her dream, she had needed to get out of the castle and away from Alaric, but not alone with her thoughts. With a surprisingly graceful leap, Olive landed a few feet away and grinned triumphantly.

"You were the one who refused to ride," Amelia reminded her.

She did not want to explain the dream until she fully understood it herself.

Olive blushed, looking toward the ocean. "You know I don't know how."

Amelia heard a splash. She pushed against the bark to stand, turning to face the beach. Hopefully, the sound meant kids from the village were playing again.

"Hence, the riding lesson I was meant to give you today. We shall be travelling to the village more often now and we will get there faster on horse than in a carriage."

"Plus, you told Alaric you were teaching me." Olive followed close behind. "I suppose I can't make a liar out of a queen. After dinner why don't we—"

The world went dark as two icy hands clapped over Amelia's eyes.

Olive's hands.

"What are you doing?"

Olive's smirk was clear in her voice. "There's just somethin' in the water you may not wish to see."

"Something?"

"Someone. A *naked* someone."

"Naked! Who?"

Amelia huffed, tearing at Olive's grip, but the handmaiden moved in front of her, blocking her view. Her cheeks were flushed, and yes, she was definitely smirking.

Olive glanced over her shoulder, standing on her tiptoes, neck craning as if to look over the trees rather than through them. Why could *she* look, but Amelia could not?

"It's Fredrick," Olive whispered loudly. "I know he's old enough to be my father, but... damn. I almost *want* you to see this. He's glorious. All wet and dark and—"

Amelia covered her ears. "Seems like you are seeing enough for the both of us."

Olive hummed like she was savoring the last bite of Regina's lemon trifle. Amelia rolled her eyes. Fredrick was not just old enough to be their father. He was a respected military leader. Her friend. *No*, more than that. And he didn't deserve to be ogled like this.

Amelia tugged on Olive's sleeve, eyes focused on the ground. "We should—"

Then Olive released a long sigh, her shoulders slumping. She captured Amelia's hand, mumbling under her breath.

"Come on."

The queen dug her heels in. "But you said I should not see, and I agree. Wholeheartedly."

"It's alright." Olive waved her hand. "He's out of the water now. And *clothed*."

She huffed the last word like the constable's uniform was offensive.

When they reached the beach, Amelia allowed herself to look up for the first time. Fredrick was a few feet away, buckling his belt around his hips. Despite his wet hair and their unusual surroundings, he looked normal as ever.

"My Queen!" he said sharply, nervous eyes darting between her, Olive, and the water. "It's quite early for you to be awake. And out of bed."

Olive yawned and stretched for good measure. "That's what I said when she shook me awake and dragged me from the most *glorious* dream."

Amelia felt her cheeks burn and elbowed Olive in the ribs. "Stop flirting," she hissed under her breath.

Fredrick ignored Olive's inappropriate tone like he was used to women flirting with him.

"Is everything alright, Your Grace?" he asked, worry creasing his brow.

Why did she keep getting the feeling he was keeping something from her? It was unusual, and she did not like it.

"Perhaps I should be asking that of you?"

His full lips thinned and he nodded slowly, perhaps preparing himself. He gestured to a fallen log further up the beach, asking her to join him. Olive took the hint easily and slowly slipped away. Perhaps to find a comfy patch of moss and steal a few more minutes of sleep.

The sky was beginning to lose its warmer hues and the salty ocean air stung her throat, but Amelia smiled all the same as she sat. Fredrick's elbows rested on his thighs, fingers laced.

"I have information regarding the king, and a threat he's made on your safety."

She could still picture the way Alaric's skin had dipped from the blade in her dream. It was he who was in danger, was it not?

"My safety? No, I spoke with him last night. He seemed rather calm, all things considered."

Fredrick nodded, but the tension remained coiled in his shoulders. "I overheard him and Seb discussing a plot to remove you if you continued to cause trouble for him."

She shivered.

"Oh."

"I've assigned additional protection for you, but I fear it may not be enough. So I thought of something—a plan—but I'd like your permission. Your blessing."

"Oh?"

She knew she should say something more, but her brain was busy reliving the last two days since she had helped William. In her mind she was back dancing with Alaric in the ballroom, trapped in his rough hands.

Finally, she heard Fredrick's voice again.

"Amelia."

She blinked. "Yes?"

"I believe we should organize a rebellion force," he said patiently, though he was surely repeating himself.

She gnawed on her top lip; a thin layer of skin peeling back. "Like an army?"

"Yes."

She shook her head. "No. Absolutely not. An army means battle. Death. It will not come to that. I am only helping our people."

"And taking gold from his vault."

How was he always so calm?

"Yes," she sighed. "I suppose that was a bit far."

"I thought it was wonderful." His shoulders shook as he chuckled. "But your husband has many men willing to kill and die for him. Should it come to a fight, you'll require support."

"I have no desire to watch decent and innocent men die for me."

She thought of William and Hannah and their children. Of the other families in the village, and what Alaric might do if he heard about a rising resistance. What would happen to them if Alaric became livid enough to kill her, leaving them unprotected? It all made her stomach turn and her palms sweat. There was no right answer, was there?

Fredrick reached out, covering her hand with his own.

"Please, Amelia. At least consider it."

The sharp contrast of their skin tones distracted her for a moment and she found herself leaning against him, welcoming the strength and protection he offered. Knowing she needed it, even if she did not want it. The moment she had spoken out against Alaric, a target was painted on her back.

Him aiming at it was only inevitable.

She looked out to the ocean, watching the waves dance, and was silent for a while. When she looked back, Fredrick was watching her with gentle eyes. He looked almost relaxed, like he had known she would see reason.

"You truly believe this is needed?"

"I do." He nodded. "We may never have to use it, but I would rather be overly cautious and discover I've wasted my time, than find only myself standing between you, him, and his men."

Amelia imagined that and shuddered.

"Do it," she said firmly. "I may not like it, but you are right. I will do whatever I must to avoid a battle, but if it comes to violence, we shall need all the help we can get."

September 10th, 1456

Waltzing arm in arm to the dining hall, Amelia couldn't help but snicker as Olive described in far too much detail just how well Julian's new jester suit fit.

Even seeing Alaric at the breakfast table could not banish her bliss.

As she tucked in, exchanging a smile with her brother and avoiding her father's gaze at all costs, a young page entered the dining hall.

"Your Majesty, I have something for you."

"Bring it over, Heath," Alaric drawled, ready to accept the thick beige envelope.

The young man stuttered. "For Queen Amelia."

Amelia looked up, her fingers greasy from bacon. She vigorously cleaned them on a napkin. "Thank you."

"Who's it from?" Brantley asked, leaning over to see.

Amelia beamed, hoping no one noticed how her cheeks flushed. "Caroline. She will be visiting us in a few days' time."

"Lady Caroline of Petrovia?" Marcel asked, still chewing. "Isn't she *your* cousin, Alaric?"

The king nodded, jaw tight and tone tense.

"Indeed. Why has she chosen to write to you, and not me?"

Amelia's gaze remained on the parchment. She was too excited to let him spoil this. Seeing Caroline again was a dream come true. A wonderful dream, not the kind where you murder your husband on your favorite sheets.

"We became friends when she visited for our wedding and have written one another often since."

"Does the letter say why she is coming?" Alaric asked.

"No specific reason."

"Well, we shall do our best to make her feel welcome." Marcel clapped.

"She is welcome to my rooms!" Brantley offered eagerly.

Amelia eyed him, one eyebrow raised teasingly.

"That is alright, brother. But thank you for the offer."

His crush was endearing, but Caroline was much too mature for Brantley. She was nearly Amelia's age. Perhaps a year or two younger? If anyone was going to be sharing their rooms it was going to be—

Amelia cut herself off, inhaling what remained of her breakfast in quite unladylike fashion. She looked over the letter again. The guest suites would suit her friend perfectly. She stood from the table, mind swirling, and gestured to Olive that it was time to go. There was much to do and not much time. Olive stood, but took her plate with her.

"Let's inform the staff to prepare the guest tower rooms and request Regina add another table setting."

"It's goin' to be so excitin' having Caroline around," the handmaiden exclaimed before chomping down on a slice of toast. "Perhaps Regina will make lemon trifle to celebrate our guest!"

Amelia chuckled. "Any reason is worthy enough for you to hope for lemon trifle."

When she glanced back to wave farewell at Brantley, she found Alaric's narrow, curious eyes on the envelope. They did not leave her until she was out the door.

~

With her stomach in knots, Lady Caroline of Petrovia began packing her bags. Knowing her destination helped soften the blow of the sudden move, but she was still confused.

Hopefully Amelia had received the letter in time.

Already packed and awaiting her daughter to join her, an impatient Duchess Ella stood in the bedroom doorway, arms folded. A scowl twisted her normally stunning porcelain features.

"Why have you left this to the last minute?" she scolded, failing to hide the pressure weighing on her shoulders.

"You've yet to tell me the reason we must leave in the first place."

"Those are matters you need not worry yourself with. I will stay with your uncle in Galfian, and you will find a temporary home in Dathoviel."

Caroline paused, her favorite quill set halfway into her bag. "I didn't inform them I'd be staying indefinitely."

"You won't be a burden any longer than necessary. If, you focus on finding a husband to care for and support you, of course."

Tucking a blonde wave behind her ear, Caroline refrained from rolling her navy-blue eyes. She turned, fists on her hips.

"I am a burden to no one, and I won't be forced into marrying some idiotic lord or duke or whomever, simply because I am of breeding age!"

Ella mirrored her daughter's stance. They could have been each other's reflection given the hair, eyes, and frustrated glare.

"Most women your age are already wed."

"How marvellous for them."

Ella sighed in exasperation. "If Alaric found someone to marry him, you are more than capable."

"And if I don't?"

"Lord Archibald remains available," she answered, like there were worse options.

There weren't.

"He is a fool. Not to mention my cousin. Your words are repulsive."

"*Second* cousin," Ella said, spinning out of the room. Naturally, she looked back, doubling down on her forever needed last word. "Do hurry up. We have a long journey ahead of us."

September 11th, 1456

Alaric had just finished lacing the fly of his leather trousers when a knock on the bedroom door caused Leah to shriek from the mattress. Snickering at her, and earning a beautiful glare in return, the king opened the door.

Sebastian stood at attention on the other side.

"What is it, old friend?"

The knight barely avoided eye contact with the naked woman on the bed.

"Lady Caroline is expected to arrive tomorrow afternoon at the earliest, and Queen Amelia wishes to know if you would be interested in arranging a celebratory banquet for her."

Delightfully taken aback, the king pulled on a fresh linen shirt. "If the queen wants a banquet, she shall have one. I approve of any arrangements she wishes."

Seb nodded and walked away without another word.

Leah grimaced, slipping from the sheets. "Sounds like I have a full day of work ahead of me."

Alaric moved to his mirror and attempted to tame his dark hair.

"You can blame Amelia for this one." He winked, watching her reflection re-dress.

After a few moments, she was behind him, her arms slipping around his waist. "Find me tonight?"

"Always," he promised, caressing her knuckles with his thumbs.

She pressed a kiss to his shoulder before pulling back and heading for the door.

Grateful for a moment of solitude, he smoothed back the unruly curl that always fought to rest against his forehead. Life was good, all things considered.

Leah remained his to call on. Amelia was a bother, but nothing he couldn't handle. And one of them would provide an heir eventually.

Dathoviel sat on the edge of a new dawn. A few more moves and his legacy would be established, ensuring that even long after Dathoviel had fallen or been erased by history, *he* would remain forever remembered.

All his life, he'd been bypassed. The second invisible son. Spencer was groomed for the throne. Davidson adored, then mourned. And he... well...

Alaric straightened his shirt cuffs. He would never be ignored again.

~

Caroline exhaled in relief as the carriage pulled away from Galfian, the kingdom her mother had been born into, and once again resided.

A familiar hum tickled her throat now that she was alone, blocking out the duchess's final warning to lookout for a suitable husband.

For many years, her mother complained her daughter was abnormal, but if anyone was odd, it was the fools Caroline had been surrounded by her entire life in Petrovia. Should she select any male at random to marry and procreate with? With Ella so desperate, she might not be bothered if he were less than a nobleman.

No, Caroline was not someone who could marry for anything less than genuine love—whether or not it existed. She may have grown too mature for the fairy tale books she'd left behind in Petrovia, but she remembered every word, still firmly believing love was why the earth moved. Even when reality struggled to equate to the mystical connection she longed for.

She would rather be a nun than marry someone she didn't love. Even if she did fail to believe in her father's God to begin with. A nunnery was surely a lesser punishment than a marriage of forced convenience.

Despite years of memorizing verse, she had a hard time believing an all-powerful being would allow women to be herded and paraded around for men's pleasures. Why? Because of a few anatomical differences?

She was a free woman, at least in this carriage, and the world was anything she wished it to be.

Though optimistic of what lay ahead of her, she was still unsure of *why* she had needed to leave Petrovia. How she wished Spencer had been home instead of out hunting so she could ask him. But it seemed the moment her eldest cousin had left, the atmosphere in the castle changed overnight. Ella had begun arranging a return home and telling Caroline to send word to Alaric. So excited to return to Dathoviel and see Amelia again, she'd hardly questioned the request at the time.

At first, the queen had merely been her estranged cousin's unexpected bride; a distant relative she may see once or twice in her lifetime. But the days following the wedding celebrations had given them time to connect.

They shared stories and interests, joked and laughed. Caroline had never had a close female friend before, and she cherished those two weeks, recalling nearly every day perfectly. Spencer may be the person she loved most in the world, but female companionship was different.

Caroline and Amelia had done their best to stay in contact since. They wrote letters and sent small gifts back and forth often. Their correspondence had been the sunlight Caroline needed in the strict, grey world of her uncle's kingdom. A few hours journey, and she would be home. A safe, warm home ready to welcome her with open arms.

The carriage peaked over a hill, and Caroline focused on her newfound freedom. If fate did have a fairy-tale in store for her, she'd be ready for it.

4

September 12th, 1456

CAROLINE BEAMED AS HER carriage halted in front of the castle.

While servants collected luggage, Seb assisted her out into the fresh air, the wind whipping her skirts. She did not return his smile.

Then Amelia and Olive were enveloping her in joyful hugs the moment her feet touched down.

"We are overjoyed you are here!" Amelia practically sang from pretty pink lips, her hazel eyes glittering with excitement. "Was the journey pleasant?"

The queen's hair had grown over the last year and she wore it down, like she wanted the wind to tangle it. Not at all how someone of her station *should* look, yet still magnificent. Perhaps more stunning than Caroline remembered.

"It was long but worth it."

She loved the way the queen's good mood always tended to lighten hers in their letters. In person, the effects were much stronger. Captivating, even. How had she forgotten how intense this pull was? And how could she be the only one feeling it?

She gulped when Alaric's stiff arms wrapped around her unexpectedly in what some could consider a hug. He stepped back hastily, their eyes never meeting.

Amelia directed the coachman to the stables, ensuring the horses could feed and rest before gesturing everyone to enter the castle. Seb and Alaric went their separate ways silently, while a single female servant and a pair of men carrying bags followed the women.

"We have been preparing for you since your letter arrived," said Amelia, strolling gracefully. "Tonight, we shall feast to celebrate your return to Dathoviel."

Olive nodded with zeal. "In the meantime, I shall show you to your rooms. You surely wish to rest and stretch after your journey. Leah here will help you dress."

"Welcome to Dathoviel, Lady Caroline." The female servant quickened her step to fall in line with the three women.

Caroline turned to smile at her in greeting, but one glance from Amelia had Leah falling further behind than before.

When they reached the base of the stairs, the queen paused, her smile regretful. "I have a few tasks to handle before dinner, but I leave you in capable hands."

Too overwhelmed to speak, Caroline nodded as the queen embraced her tightly for a second time. She thought the queen's hands lingered a second too long on her hips, but then she was pulling away and waving farewell. Olive had begun chattering, leading the way upstairs with Leah, but Caroline had to remind her legs how to move when Amelia disappeared around the corner, a flourish of daffodil and dark curls.

September 13th, 1456

The next morning Amelia awoke in her bed; a tangled, hungover heap with Caroline and Olive on either side.

They were still dressed in their party clothes, each sporting a lovely matted hairdo and smelling distinctly of chocolate, champagne, and sweat. When a brief knock sounded, all three women cradled their pounding heads in painful solidarity. In a silent vote involving fingertips pressed to noses, Amelia was the slowest and she grumbled as she sacrificed comforting stillness to open the door.

The tempting array of breakfast foods perched on a table in her sitting room was an almost worthy reward, but the booze sloshing around in her head begged to differ.

"Regina, ever the saint," she whispered, sliding the tray into the middle of the bed and crawling on after it. "Remind me to kiss that woman later."

"Remind me to never indulge so heavily again," Olive murmured, arms thrown over her eyes, looking like she may vomit. "Did you all hear me last night? Threatening to lick poor Julian from head to toe?"

"The entire ballroom heard you," Amelia said, rubbing the left cheek of her behind. She distinctly remembered falling out of her chair sometime throughout the night, but not why. "You made that poor man blush so hard."

"Well, he is incredibly handsome," Olive murmured defensively, peering at the tray. "Don't you agree, Caroline?"

Amelia listened closely for her answer, but the blonde on her right avoided the question entirely.

"What all did we drink?" she asked instead, her voice muffled by the pillow she was using to block out the sun.

Olive scowled, reaching for a plain piece of toast. "Wine. And champagne." She forced a bite down, staring at it with a wrinkled nose.

Caroline glanced at the tray with a single peeking eye and opted for sipping from a goblet of water.

"Can either of you hear ringing?"

"Ladies, *shhh*." Amelia lifted her finger to her lips and curled into a ball on the mattress. "As your queen, I demand silence."

Both Olive and Caroline giggled, then groaned regretfully when their brains quaked from the vibration. Amelia's own rattled around her skull.

"A wise, wise queen we have at our feet," Olive joked before passing back out, the toast still in her hand.

~

Seb stood in the center of the armory, debating with himself which defensive weapons they might need for the Winvoltor trip in the spring when the oak door opened behind him.

"Good morn' Seb," Brantley greeted brightly.

The knight did not bother hiding his surprise. "Good morning, Your Highness."

The young prince observed the swords and shields hanging on the wall, more than a dozen suits of leather armor standing beneath them. A table displaying various sized axes, and another covered in spearheads stood to his left. Quivers full of arrows lined the opposite wall, accompanied by an impressive stock of long and crossbows. Banners and flags of teal and gold hung from the ceiling, the Dathoviel crest depicted proudly across them.

He selected a sword, and it was apparent he had very limited knowledge on how to hold it.

"I hoped you could spare some time to train me?"

"As a—a knight?"

Brantley nodded. "Unofficially. I believe it would be wise to know my way in and out of a fight."

"And you ask me?" Seb's eyes widened. "Over Fredrick, or any soldier you've known longer?"

"I trust you." Brantley shrugged, not about to explain his reasoning.

"It would be an honor, My Lord." Seb bowed, unsure what had brought this on, but too grateful to have been chosen to question it. "We can begin this evening."

September 15th, 1456

Caroline listened attentively while Olive and the queen chattered along with the rattling carriage. She wasn't entirely sure what she was getting herself into by joining them on their excursion to the village today, but anything was better than remaining in the castle alone.

From her position opposite the two women, it was easy to see how close they were. Not just physically, but mentally. Laughing at inside jokes she couldn't understand, given most of their sentences weren't even finished before the next one began. They weren't leaving her out on purpose. In fact, both Amelia and Olive had attempted to pull her into the conversation on several occasions, but she couldn't shake the distance she felt.

The carriage went over a particularly rough bump, jostling the trio and nearly sending Caroline to the floor. After all, *she* didn't have anyone to clutch onto. But Amelia did. She and Olive had gripped hands, tugging one another back onto the seat, their giggling almost deafening.

Caroline righted her skirts and looked out the window, chin resting in her hand. After a moment the mirth faded away and she almost grinned, relieved she'd managed to silence them in her mind.

Then Amelia was beside her, tugging on her wrist, her eyes apologetic and her lips crooked. "I am sorry if you are feeling excluded."

Caroline's skin burned where Amelia touched her. She could barely stand it, all while wishing it would never stop. Gently she retracted her hand, sitting tall.

"It's alright, I'm just tired."

Olive shook her head. "Nonsense. We were being rude." She moved herself into the middle of the seat, ensuring Amelia couldn't return to her side. "Tell us more about life in Petrovia?"

"Oh, yes!" Amelia nodded, her hands now clasped in her lap. "Does your kingdom celebrate any different holidays than we do?"

"Uhh," Caroline wasn't sure how to answer. "I don't believe so. Petrovia isn't really that kind of kingdom."

Olive leaned forward, elbows on knees, propping her chin up with her fists. "What kind of kingdom is it, then?"

"Dark. Cold. Miserable."

Caroline said the words before she could think and blushed when Amelia's eyes widened in shock, her eyebrows dancing up her forehead.

"That sounds... unpleasant."

"No wonder you left." Olive shook her head. "Is there *anything* you miss?"

Caroline thought for a moment. "I miss Spencer and my aunt's beautiful garden. I believe we grow close to every type of flower in the world possible."

"Who's Spencer?" Olive asked.

Amelia threw her a knowing look and shook her head. "Haven't you got your hands full with dreaming about Fredrick, trying to lick Julian, and torturing Seb?"

Olive pressed her hand to her chest, mouth falling open. "I do *not* torture Seb."

"You do!" Amelia and Caroline exclaimed simultaneously.

They grinned at one another, and Caroline had to bite the inside of her cheek to distract herself from the queen's tempting lips. Instead she focused on how nice it was to finally be part of the conversation. With an inside joke of her and Amelia's very own.

Thirty minutes later, Caroline found herself seated between Amelia and a man named William at a small, handcrafted table. The cottage couldn't have been much bigger than her bedroom and dressing room back in Petrovia combined. Yet, Hannah Carpenter managed to make the little cabin feel warm and welcoming.

It was cluttered, but neat.

Tied herbs were drying on a series of hooks above the window and a basket of potatoes sat in the corner of a space clearly designated as the kitchen. Dinged pots and pans hung from a long thick branch secured over a makeshift counter, most likely built by William himself. There was a large bed pressed to the opposite wall behind them, and two smaller ones sat on either side. A wooden box with a lid, likely full of either clothes, blankets, or perhaps both, sat at the foot of each bed.

Caroline watched highly impressed while Hannah maneuvered between small children to reach for more mugs.

"Alright, that's enough. Willy, Hamish, please take your sister and the baby to the garden for a bit. And be sure to dress warm."

She placed the mugs in front of her guests as Brianna crossed her arms.

"I don't wanna go! I wanna stay here. With the queen."

Amelia opened her mouth to say it was alright, but the look on Hannah's face stopped both her and the child from continuing. She knelt down, taking her daughter's hands in hers.

"I know you are excited to see the queen. We'll call you back inside soon, alright? I promise. Why don't you go see if there are any strawberries left? What a fun treat that would be?"

Amelia nodded enthusiastically. "I do love strawberries."

The girl beamed, displaying her single missing tooth.

"I'll be back!" she cried, racing out the door after her brothers.

Then she raced right back in, snatched up her jacket and mitts, the door slamming behind her on the way out. Surely, she would be disappointed to find there were in fact no strawberries left this time of year. But at least it would buy them a few minutes.

Amelia smiled at Hannah and stood. "How can I help?"

Hannah looked as though she may collapse from shock, and Caroline couldn't blame her. It was quite unusual, but so was being here in the first place.

Had any other queen in history chosen to take afternoon tea in such a location?

"I wouldn't dream of putting Your Grace to work in my small kitchen."

Amelia scoffed and came around the table, pulling the kettle from the fire and held Hannah at arm's length.

"Your home is beautiful. Anyone can see the hard work you and William have put into it. Besides, *I* could not dream of being served by a woman recovering from illness when I have two perfectly working hands and feet. Please, sit."

William reached for his wife's arm and pulled until she fell into his lap.

"Sounds like a direct order," he chuckled, nuzzling her neck.

Caroline blushed at their free display of love. Never in her whole life had she seen her parents behave that way. Or anyone else, for that matter.

"Tea?" Amelia called, poking around the shelves flanking the hearth.

"Behind the cracked jar," Hannah answered, practically vibrating with nerves on her husband's lap.

Was she so thin because she'd been ill? Or because she rarely sat still for long?

Finally, Amelia was seated at the table once more, steam pouring from the five mugs. Whatever type of tea they were drinking smelled earthy and tasted more like dirt than herb, but Caroline sipped politely as she'd been taught, listening to Amelia bombard the couple with questions and ideas.

Olive, on the other hand, avoided her mug beyond the first taste, curiously eyeing the shelf of jars. Caroline followed her gaze, wondering if the queen had perhaps chosen the wrong one.

They shared a smirk, and then looked down at the table.

"I suppose we should start with what you two believe the village needs most, and prioritize from there."

William and Hannah exchanged a look. "With winter coming, our primary focuses are heat and food."

Amelia nodded and gestured to Olive who produced a short scroll, a bottle of ink and a quill from a satchel she'd brought. Once Amelia was settled, she began making notes, listening intently while the couple explained the troubles they'd experienced last year.

Amelia nodded when they stopped, tapping her chin with the feather. "I will ask Fredrick and a few of his men to assist with chopping extra wood, especially for the families still facing illness. William, would you mind assisting?"

"Not at all."

"I think gathering the women will be wonderful" Hannah said. "Please thank Regina for the idea, *and* for the food she sent us a few weeks ago."

"I shall," Amelia promised. "I was hoping you would be interested in leading the circle the first few times? If you are feeling well enough, of course."

Hannah beamed, nodding eagerly.

"We can celebrate new mothers, offer support and encouragement. We can learn skills from the older generations and share customs with the different families throughout the village."

Amelia grinned, taking a long drink of tea. Somehow, she didn't even flinch. Perhaps her tongue was broken?

"I imagine the final supply ship from the east will be arriving any day now?" William wondered aloud.

Olive nodded. "Yes. I'll be sure to have a fair share of the rice and spices delivered here."

"There are usually one or two passengers who decide to stay in Dathoviel," Amelia said thoughtfully. "Do we have any empty homes available?"

William shook his head. "Unfortunately no, but I can gather a few friends and have one built before snow fall. In the meantime, there is a room above the tavern."

Amelia scratched something out on her parchment, then looked to Hannah. "The church will probably be the best place for the women to gather I think. Perhaps monthly to start?"

"Yes." Hannah smiled. "Though I'm sure they wouldn't mind the tavern occasionally."

Amelia chuckled. "Let me know which nights those are, and *I'll* be there."

"As will I," Olive chimed in.

Caroline watched in awe as the queen commanded the conversation, taking precise notes as she went, all while listening attentively and gently suggesting solutions. She even poured herself a second cup of tea, surprised when no one else needed a refill.

Hannah finally picked up her mug then and sipped, nearly choking. As William smacked her back, she glanced over her shoulder at the shelf, and covertly sniffed at her drink. Her lips pursed, muffling a chuckle as set her mug aside, jade eyes glittering with mirth.

Oblivious, Amelia scratched out another few notes, nodding absently. "My personal midwife and the castle physician will continue their regular visits to the village. Can you tell me how many women are expecting children soon?"

Hannah considered. "Three I believe... no, four."

"Four," Amelia mumbled, reaching for more ink. "Very well. So, heat is taken care of. Food. Medicine. Housing. Support for those who need it."

"Sounds like you have it all figured out," chuckled William, running his left hand through his hair.

"Not quite." Amelia set the quill down and leaned close to the couple, smiling like she was about to reveal a grand conspiracy. "We still have the winter solstice festival to plan."

Hannah shook her head. "King Alaric cancelled all the festivals."

"I plan to reinstate them."

"Will he allow that?" Olive asked warily.

Amelia's teeth clicked together. "I shall talk to him. In the meantime, we can begin planning."

Hannah opened her mouth, perhaps to suggest something, when the front door banged open and a little girl stomped inside, her face red.

"There were no strawberries!" she shouted and plopped down to cry.

Later that night Caroline lay in bed, unable to sleep. She was finding it impossible to stop thinking of Amelia and how lovely she'd looked on the carriage ride home, chattering excitedly about all her plans and the things she wanted to do over the next few weeks.

Her enthusiasm was so intoxicating, Caroline heard herself volunteering to do anything she could to help before she really knew what she was agreeing to.

Now she knew.

Undermining Alaric, going behind his back, and saving people's lives. They were all worthy causes, but they also put Amelia in danger, and she couldn't ignore that. In fact, it made her feel sick, but she couldn't bring herself to talk Amelia out of anything she'd already set her heart on.

One way or another, the queen was getting what she wanted, and at least if Caroline was involved she could help Olive look out for her.

This was exactly what she'd been needing; a purpose. A passionate reason to get out of bed in the morning. Spending nearly every day with Amelia was enough to make her smile, but having something worthy to fill her time took the cake.

And if Caroline loved anything, it was cake.

September 19th, 1456

Alaric's heels click-clacked through the halls as he searched for his meddlesome wife. Nothing she had done in the village had pushed his limits before, but she'd found the last straw.

He'd made a direct ruling to absolve the festivals, and here she went, planning one behind his back. As if his words meant nothing. Perhaps it had been a good idea for him to assign Heath that special job yesterday...

Eventually, he discovered her in the library, his dark mood failing to improve despite the brightly lit space. Curled into one of three oversized chairs adjacent to the wooden staircase, she read intently—her slippers chaotically strewn before her. There was a long study table to the left of the door and floor to ceiling bookshelves lining the wall behind her. The black, navy, and beige spines were the perfect backdrop for her and her golden gown.

He cleared his throat several times before she met his gaze. Whether she'd been lost in the words, or simply ignoring him, he couldn't be sure.

"May we speak openly?" he asked.

Amelia tucked her finger against her current page as he sat next to her.

"Certainly."

He eyed the chess table between them. It had been one of the few items he insisted on bringing to Dathoviel when he'd become king. Her goblet sat on the obsidian and opal checkered top, a wet ring beneath it. He didn't bother hiding his irritation, pointedly eyeing the end table on her left. His cheeks burned when she ignored him, even jutting her chin out for good measure.

With tense fingers he set the cup aside, wiping away the offending mark with a handkerchief. He narrowed his eyes and began resetting the pieces.

"Your progress in the village is quite... impressive."

She hesitated momentarily. "Yes, I am proud of how far everyone has come. Sometimes a little help is all that is needed."

"The way I hear it, you've been offering more than a little help."

Her tone sharpened. "I have done what any queen should do. What my mother would have done."

"You wish to save them," he said as he set the white king in place. "but have you considered it might be you who needs rescuing?"

The book snapped shut, her bare feet sliding to the floor. "Are you threatening me?"

Finally. He had her full attention.

"I considered removing you once... I was furious the day you helped that farmer."

"*William*, the man whose children you nearly starved to death, is a *carpenter*," she spat venomously. "His wife is Hannah. Their two oldest sons are young gentlemen, and their daughter is the definition of sunshine. Though I doubt you give a damn."

"You give enough of a damn for us both." He turned the board so the white pieces stood at attention before her. "Care to play?"

"I had to do something for them!" she shot back, glaring at the board.

He knew she loved chess, almost as much as she hated him, and that potentially beating him at it was too tempting of an offer to decline. After a moment, she moved the third pawn forward two spaces.

"You were content doing nothing for quite some time. Was life not easier before?"

"It is easier for my people now. That is what matters to me." They continued making moves across the board, pausing to strategize. "Are you still plotting to remove me?"

Her knight took one, and then a second pawn. He paused, gazing up at her. He didn't bother asking how she knew.

"My temper drove those thoughts. Once I calmed, I tried to reason with you the night of our anniversary."

"What you define as reasoning, I consider coercion. There is no compromise with you."

Alaric removed her knight, setting his first bishop in its place, causing her to smirk. He'd taken her bait, or so he'd made it seem.

"Would a compromise of some kind bring you happiness?"

She rolled her eyes. "Do not pretend you care for my happiness."

"I care for my own. If you agree not to make any rash moves against me, I promise to focus my attention elsewhere and not contest the festivals."

Amelia must be considering his sincerity for she was quiet, capturing one bishop with her queen. He seized her left pawn with his, a sacrifice she'd made willingly for her rook. It sat strong—his remaining pawns locked in from moving forward and protecting her king.

She looked so confident, he could practically read her mind.

"You know about the festival?" she finally said, trying to keep her tone light.

She was failing.

"I know everything. It's my right to know what you've been doing. Especially when it involves our kingdom."

"*My* kingdom."

Her conviction rose as his queen slid forward, exactly where she hoped. So far, he'd played perfectly into her advantage.

"You may have your festivals, Amelia. With the added terms that no more gold goes missing from *my* private vault."

She didn't even flinch at mention of her thievery. Impressive.

"Deal."

They shook on it, hands hovering over the pieces.

"Clearly, we cannot rule as partners, but perhaps we can compromise and stay out of each other's way."

His sneer told her she'd missed something, and her eyes widened, darting between him and the board. Unsure which game she'd lost. And how.

"I do not understand."

She glanced back to the board, realizing his remaining bishop sat one move away from triumph over her king.

There was no need to move the pieces.

"Checkmate," he whispered, his grip tightening around her fingers.

. 5 .

THOUGH INFURIATED AND EMBARRASSED from defeat following the chess match, Amelia could not help her relief later that evening. She and Alaric had finally arrived at a compromise of sorts.

Obviously, she had not been entirely genuine agreeing to stay out of his way, but she highly doubted he was fully sincere either.

The queen had just changed into her riding clothes when Caroline burst through the bedroom door, her fists clenched.

"That pig headed, meddling, *scheming* woman!"

She tossed a crumpled letter into the fire ferociously before collapsing onto the chaise; fury and fear flickering in her eyes. Amelia knew exactly what her friend needed. Or at least what she needed in times like this.

"Let us walk. You look like you could use some fresh air."

Tossing over her warmest cloak from the wardrobe, the queen gestured for her to follow.

Amelia knew Caroline well enough to recognize the importance of waiting for the feisty blonde to speak first, so she remained silent as they left the castle behind, trudging toward the stable. The frost crunching beneath their boots and owls hooting in the distance were their lone companions.

A faint puff of air trailed after each breath when Caroline's explanation finally exploded from her mouth, a mile from the castle.

"If my mother mentions another potential suitor, I'll go mad."

Amelia could not help chuckling. "You can be relatively short-tempered, you know."

Caroline shot her a look.

"At least no one is pressuring *you* to fall in love or get married."

Amelia bit back a retort. Caroline needed a safe space to vent, not a reminder she had in fact already been forced into that very situation.

"Yes, well..."

Realizing it herself, the blonde sighed and looked down at her feet. "I apologize."

Amelia wrapped her arm around Caroline's shoulders and squeezed. As they neared the stables, she spoke again.

"Have you ever been in love?"

Caroline huffed out a laugh. "I doubt any man could rival my expectations of love. One knight in Petrovia fancied me. He even asked my permission before kissing me! I felt compelled to take advantage, for how often are we given a choice? Someone called for him from the guard tower and interrupted us, so it never went further. I felt foolish *and* relieved when it ended."

"Regina used to tease me when young lords would visit. I always showed little interest, and she would say love was meant to distract me from books and lessons."

Caroline shook her head. "I disagree."

"So do I. If someone is truly meant for me, they will compliment me, share a few of my interests. Challenge me, certainly, but never pull me from what is most important. I have yet to find a man capable of either."

Caroline eyed the stables with curiosity when they stopped outside the door.

"My mother assured me if I failed to find an eligible suitor, she'd marry me off to my cousin. Luckily, he's just announced his engagement to a countess. So, she wrote to ask how my hunt for a husband is going."

Amelia scowled. "Parents are meant to love their children unconditionally. To raise them to find love and passion in life and make the world a better place. Not sell them off to the highest bidder."

"Agreed."

"Did your father share similar ideals?"

"He encouraged me to be my own person. . ." Caroline hesitated. "As long as my choices sat within the boundaries of his values."

Amelia pulled open the door to the stables

"If I had a daughter, I would encourage her to love freely. If they were kind, I would not care whom she married."

"That sounds nice," Caroline said softly.

Amelia ached to embrace her again. Instead, she shoved her hands into the pockets of her cloak and gestured with her head. "I would like you to meet someone."

"Are you pregnant?"

The question shot from Caroline's mouth in a rush.

Amelia shook her head, approaching Greta, pressing her face against the mare's and inhaled deeply.

"You ask because I mentioned having a daughter?"

"Yes." Caroline blushed regretfully.

"Alaric and I are intimate only when required. We both prefer it this way. The moment I provide a male heir, the child shall have more claim to the throne than I ever did."

"And you welcome other women in his bed?"

"As long as they are willing, he may entertain whomever he pleases."

Caroline could not conceal her curiosity. "You don't enjoy any moment of it?"

"Given he repulses me, no. Have you ever, well..."

Caroline turned with wide eyes.

"My father would rise from the dead to drag me to hell's gate if I shared my body before marriage."

Amelia understood perfectly. "I was a virgin when Alaric and I met. He clearly, was *not*."

"I swear they rarely are."

"Yet we are expected to repress our desires."

Caroline slowly began to pace, passing by the stall Gus slept peacefully in.

"Alaric never mentioned wanting children. He always acted annoyed with Davidson."

"Who?"

"Alaric's younger brother."

"He never mentioned a younger brother."

Amelia selected a brush from Greta's cubby. Then replaced it when she saw *someone* had already braided *her* horse's tail. And incorrectly at that.

Damn, Nigel.

Caroline suddenly looked uncomfortable, like she had said something private.

"Davidson died as a child."

Amelia's heart clenched. "What happened?"

"My mother explained how the two boys had gone to play in the woods."

"Alone? That hardly sounds safe."

Caroline shrugged.

"It was common, but this time only Alaric came out. I remember the small casket and everyone crying.

Alaric's mother, Queen Orla died soon after. Spencer always said her broken heart couldn't heal."

"No wonder Alaric never mentioned it." Amelia reminded herself to breathe. "I always assumed there was reason behind his behavior, but never tragedy such as that. He was just a child himself."

She could not fathom what losing Brantley would do to her. Especially if she somehow felt responsible for his death.

Considering Alaric through fresh eyes, she selected a pitchfork and began adding hay to the stalls. He remained a bastard certainly, but since this afternoon's compromise, and learning more about his past, did she really know him at all? Perhaps he simply needed support and kindness? Is that not what she had told him today regarding the village? Was that not all he had asked of her since the beginning?

"I wouldn't give him any undeserved excuses, Amelia," Caroline said, as if reading her mind. "Even before the accident, he was frightening and cold."

Amelia was unsure what to say, so she nodded and changed the subject.

"Have you ever ridden?"

"No. Petrovian women travel everywhere in carriages."

"I can teach you." Amelia smiled warmly over her shoulder. "Another day when we can avoid freezing to death."

~

The storm only grew worse and Caroline was grateful they had waited. While wind whistled outside the stables, tearing the last leaves from the trees, she began to hum, the warmth relaxing her.

Watching the queen work was surprising. And though seeing a woman dressed this way was odd, it was also exceptionally attractive. Caroline inched closer for a better look.

"Forgive me, but is *this* something you should be doing?" she asked, gesturing to Amelia re-braiding Greta's tail. "I mean, isn't someone tasked with all this?"

Amelia smirked. "No offence to Nigel, but the way he stores the riding equipment gives me a headache. I do it properly when I have the chance, but he always changes it back."

"I see." Caroline frowned. "Is Nigel who you wished for me to meet?"

Amelia laughed out loud, dusting her hands off before caressing Greta's mane. "Goodness, no. He is barely Brantley's age."

Then it clicked and she felt rather foolish.

"Your horse! You wrote of her so often, I should've guessed."

Amelia grinned. "Yes, Greta, this is Caroline. And Caroline, this is Greta."

Caroline inched closer to greet the animal, her hands lifting awkwardly

"I don't think I've ever loved anything the way you love her," she confessed after a moment.

"They are easy creatures to love. And I love who I am when I'm around them. Around her." Amelia seemed lost in thought, her hand running along the horse's neck. "Greta grounds me to the earth. I am not just a woman, or a queen with her, and she is not just an animal. I believe she brings out the best parts of me."

Amelia took Caroline's hand gently, removing her glove to guide her through the movement of petting the mare correctly.

"She's softer than I expected," Caroline whispered.

"Horses are remarkably strong, yet equally gentle." Amelia's proud tone turned forlorn. "She is as trapped in this stable as I am at Alaric's side. But once in a while, we escape together."

Caroline's hand stilled beneath Amelia's. She turned to face her, voice and gaze soft.

"Thank you for sharing this part of yourself with me."

Their eyes met, and the most incredible sensation rushed through her body. It told her to turn further and step closer. To press her lips to Amelia's. All kinds of mad, impossible, beautiful things.

Her stomach tangled into delicious knots when she saw Amelia's lips part ever so slightly, inhaling short, quick breaths. Her pounding heart was so loud in her ears, Caroline could no longer hear the rushing wind outside.

Gus awoke then, neighing loudly and ending the moment. Amelia jumped back, moving to the gelding's stall as Caroline scurried to the opposite side of the stable, replacing her glove with trembling fingers.

October 21st, 1456

There was an extra special pep in Olive's step the next morning. The final supply ship had docked last night and deliveries would be made to the castle this very morning.

She intended to keep her promise to William about getting the village their share. And to help Amelia realize she could delegate more.

Olive would go down to the docks, intercept the man in charge of deliveries before he left, and split the supply before Alaric had a chance to see the amount. There would be less questions that way. But she couldn't leave the castle in the middle of the day without explanation. Well, not *again*. Regina would skin her alive, or something as equally horrible. Like threaten to never make lemon trifle again.

It wasn't worth the risk.

She'd just pop her head into the kitchen, say Amelia asked her to go down to the docks, possibly steal a slice of leftover pumpkin pie, and—

Olive froze, somewhere between a skip and a hop, mouth hanging open, hand motionless above the doorknob.

The already half open door provided a perfect view of Regina sandwiched between the counter and Fredrick. His flour coated hands were on either side of the cook's waist, their lips an inch apart. Maybe less. Definitely less.

Olive held her breath, covering her mouth in case a noise of excitement should slip out when they finally kissed. They *were* going to kiss, right? Regina's dreams were about to come true, and all over the butcher block where the best pies in the kingdom were created! This was too glorious.

Fredrick murmured something in Regina's ear, but whatever it was must have been funny. And seductive, because the cook's bronze skin blushed and she giggled, looking more like a teenager than the forty-year-old chef who liked to threaten withholding desserts. The usually pointed angles of her face softened in a way Olive had never seen before. She gave Fredrick one slow nod.

Then his hands were lifting her up onto the counter, flattening a loaf of bread in the process, fisting her thick, black hair.

It was fine. More bread could be made. Hell, Olive would even help with the fresh batch.

Regina gathered Fredrick's jacket in her fist, tugging him close, and he was *actually* groaning into her mouth. His fingers gripped her skirts, pushing them up. Then with a smirk, he stepped between her thighs.

Good *grief*, this was too intimate to be watching. And far too good to look away from. Olive squeezed her eyes shut. She should go.

Then Regina moaned and there was a clatter, like a sword belt falling to the ground maybe? Olive's eyes popped open. She *needed* to know.

Fredrick's left hand had disappeared beneath Regina's skirts, his right gripping her waist. Her head had fallen back and his mouth was latched to the skin beneath her ear. His tunic was gone, and no one would blame Regina for the way her fingers raced over the hard, scarred chest on display.

Olive could feel her breath coming from her still covered lips in hot bursts. She turned, eyes closed, mind racing. She had to get out of here. She had to—

Slam hard and fast against a wall?

Her hands fell away from her mouth as she bounced back, landing on her arse.

"I'm so sorry, miss," a deep voice said and Olive had to blink several times to make out the handsome *wall* she'd bumped into.

The color of his skin reminded her of pale butter, but there was nothing smooth about his face. He had a foreign, handsome look about him with a jagged jawline and sharp cheekbones. It was his dark eyes and tilted smile that most captured her attention. They were warm. Inviting. She could have fallen right into them like a refreshing spring on a hot summer day.

Instead she traced the path of the scar on his temple. It started at his left eyebrow and went up, disappearing into his hairline. It did nothing to deter her instant and unreasonable attraction to him. If anything, it heightened it, sparking her curiosity.

He slid the large bag of rice he'd been balancing on his shoulder to the ground easily as though it were a weightless bundle of silk. Then he was crouched in front of her, brushing her hair back, his gaze concerned.

Oh, no. Don't be ridiculously handsome, strong, *and* concerned.

That's how you get dizzy handmaidens in castle corridors to fall in love with you. It didn't help that his voice was enchanting as well. He was merely asking her name and it sounded like poetry.

"Olive," she choked out, cringing inwardly at the lack of feminine grace in her voice.

"I'm Kwan." He took her hands and pulled her to her feet. "I was looking for the kitchens. Hope you aren't hurt?"

Olive shook her head to say no. To clear it. He needed to release her so she could think clearly. He needed to *never* let go of her. He needed to pull her into his arms and—

She shook her head again.

"Deliveries are usually made to the back door."

Mentally, she smacked her forehead. What an impeccable way to thank him for coming to her aid.

He only smiled, wiping sweat from his brow and brushing back the sharp black fringe over his eyes.

"Yes, I tried, but the door was locked and no one would answer. A guard outside told me to try the front."

She eyed the bag of rice at their feet. It was half the size of her body. "And you carried that the whole way around the castle, to here?"

"I didn't want anyone to think I was a thief sneaking about," he smirked, as if making a joke only he would understand. "Could you help me find the kitchens?"

"Uh," Olive looked over her shoulder to the still half open door. She couldn't see much, but what she could see was a lot of bare skin. "Actually, the cook is a bit *preoccupied* at the moment. But I can't imagine she will be for much longer... Why don't we head back outside to the proper door? There's somethin' I must discuss with you about the rice."

He nodded and lifted the bag back onto his shoulder like it was nothing. She knew from trying to move similar bags last winter; they were *not* nothing.

"So, you're from the east, then?" she asked, trying to make conversation.

Easy, innocent conversation that didn't involve asking him if he enjoyed steamy love affairs in kitchens, or lemon trifle. Those she could ask when they were better acquainted.

"Yes. I brought my grandfather here on the ship, hoping to find a new home."

She could have twirled. They would have *a lot* of time to get acquainted. "I heard there is a room available above the tavern, though it's small."

"A roof is a roof." He grinned and she nearly melted into the floor. "I'll ask for directions when I head to the village."

"I could show you!" she offered—too fast, too enthusiastically, but he looked like he enjoyed the idea.

"That would be lovely, thank you."

She looked up, sweeping the lines of his jaw and cheekbones. Even the bags under his eyes had the gall to look attractive.

"Of course, anythin' to help."

Seriously. *Anythin'*.

"So," he said, readjusting the bag a bit as they reached the main hall once more. "What was it you wished to discuss about the rice?"

Hours later, Olive bounded up the steps to Amelia's tower, barely knocking before throwing open the door. The queen, who'd been curled up on a creamy chaise jumped at the sudden intrusion. The book she'd been holding landed on the floor with a thud.

"Goodness Olive, what is wrong?" she asked, reaching for the book.

She flipped through it, searching for her place. After a moment she tossed it against the cushion, defeated.

This was no time for books anyway.

"Where's Caroline?"

Amelia shrugged, blushing deeply. "In her rooms I suppose?"

This was also no time for questions about blushing unless it was *her* blushing. Or Kwan's.

They'd both done a fair share of it on the wagon ride back to the castle after she'd helped him and his grandfather get settled in their new temporary home.

"Well, let's go find her! I have news."

"What kind of news?"

Olive leapt forward and grabbed the queen's hands, dragging her to her feet. "I found him!"

Amelia rolled her eyes, grinned all the same. "Who?"

"The man lucky enough to marry me one day! Now let's go so I don't have to tell the story twice."

~

November passed in a frosted and icy blur.

Soon the castle buzzed with holiday preparations. Amelia, Olive, and Caroline worked around the clock, knitting blankets, hats, and mitts for everyone in town.

Miles away, teeth chattering and tugging a brown coat tighter around his torso, a man pressed on through the storm, encouraging his horse forward begrudgingly. He would rather be anywhere else, but he had a job to do. And newly coronated King Spencer of Petrovia was paying him handsomely to do it. The leather satchel across his chest held yet another letter, this one addressed to Alaric.

And for the inhabitants of the castle, the envelope contained more than mere parchment and ink, because once opened, Dathoviel would never be the same.

6.

December 3ʳᵈ, 1456

Dear Brother,

I write to inform you our father has succumbed to his illness and despair. I have officially taken his place as King of Petrovia.
This could not come at a more terrible time, but death has its own schedule. If you wish, you are welcome to travel home for his burial.
I send you strength, good wishes, and pray you find comfort in your new home.

Sincerely,
Spencer

Though Alaric was no stranger to death, his gut sank as he reduced the letter to mere shreds. The jagged pieces fluttered next to his boots, in the orange glow from the fireplace.

The pressure in his chest exploded with a roar as he swept away the contents of his desktop, cloak whipping furiously around his legs.

Viktor's voice rang in his ears. The countless speeches of what a disappointment Alaric had been to him. The whispers around the castle that something was wrong with the second born prince. How relieved the king looked as Alaric's carriage pulled away from Petrovia, bound for that dreadful foreign school.

Alaric turned to the hearth where a trio of vases sat on the shelf above. A moment later, clay lay scattered across the stone floor and ink-stained parchment.

He spun back around, aching to destroy every inch of his study, even if he had to pry up each individual floorboard with his bare hands. Blindly, Alaric hurled his chair in the direction of the door, hoping to hear it shatter. But his eyes went wide when he saw Leah cringing as the wooden legs split on contact with the door frame next to her head.

He rushed to her and captured her tightly in his arms, mumbling apologies. She held him in return, patiently awaiting an explanation to what she'd walked in on.

"My father has died," he eventually gasped.

Leah released her hold around his waist as he began pacing. "*Oh*, Ric, I am so sorry."

With fumbling fingers, he unclasped his cloak and threw it down.

"He never witnessed the king I became. A few more months! That's all I needed to prove him wrong."

Leah moved forward and cupped his elbows, attempting to steady him.

"What do you need?" she asked gently.

Without thinking, he pressed her against the wall and she surprised him by welcoming his body with hers.

"We shouldn't," he declared gruffly, though it was him who was holding her in place. "I'm far too angry."

She tipped her chin up, securing him with a sincere gaze. A few strands of hair had slipped from her loose bun when he'd pushed her back. They danced over her cheeks as he puffed out a lengthy breath.

"You won't harm me. I trust you to stop if I ask."

He easily pictured himself fucking her against this wall until neither of them could breathe or think or move.

"You should go, Leah."

His demanding tone failed to affect her.

She grasped his collar. "I will not abandon you like this, Ric."

He sought patience and calm within, but those wells were dry. Only resentment, grief, and lust remained where his self-restraint should have been.

"I cannot risk you hating me if I lose control."

He'd meant for it to sound like an order, but it escaped as a desperate plea. Certainly, she felt the same hum in the air between them that he did? Their familiar passion burned as always, but there was something dangerous and potent this time. He hardly felt safe in his own body.

"No," she whispered, lifting to her toes, kissing gently along his jaw. "Whatever you need to release, I *can* take. Let me help you, please."

He let her words sink into his mind, taking her hand securely in his and clutching the other against his chest.

"I fear no one can truly help me."

Leah studied him, looking almost as desperate as he felt. Yet, her determination was apparent. She never looked at him with sorrow like his mother had or with the same disgust as Spencer. Or their father's fear.

An upside to Viktor's death was that he would never have to see those dark, disappointed eyes again. Except in the mirror, of course. But, she would never abandon him.

"Let me at least try."

He tilted his head so their lips met, and it felt like he was inching toward the edge of a cliff. But when he looked down, it wasn't jagged, sharp edges waiting to slice him open. It was soft and polished marble. If he closed his eyes, he could slide right down into Leah's embrace, and she would undoubtedly catch him.

He had to take her, taste her, and focus on something other than the hollow pit in his stomach and the aching in his chest.

Dragging her skirts up, he guided her legs around his waist and worked open his trousers. She clung to his shoulders, whispering beautiful things in his ear; things he needed to hear almost as badly as he needed to bury himself inside her. How strong, handsome, and brave he was. How much she loved him.

He tugged the simple top of her dress down, licking and nipping everywhere.

"Ready?"

She nodded, nails digging into his shoulder blades as he positioned himself at her core and drove into her.

"I'm alright," she promised, panting when he looked up with concern. "Don't hold back."

Her permission sliced through his last thread of resolve and he snapped, pouring his anger into his thrusts, his kisses deep and aggressive. Leah held on, meeting his intensity as best she could, absorbing as much of his pain as she could contain.

And soon, his movements weren't dripping with rage anymore. Little by little they calmed. He calmed. And he watched the muscles in her face relax and her mouth fall open in a relieved sigh as he transitioned to a more familiar rhythm.

She accepted every part of him, even the dark parts everyone else rejected.

The intent behind his thrusts changed then, hopefully showing her how badly he needed her, appreciated and loved her.

Her face, her voice, and her touch were the only things that could pull him back from the brink of madness and ground him to the earth once more. Perhaps if he'd met her earlier in life, things would have turned out differently for him. He would have made different choices, invested his time and energy elsewhere. But at least he had her now.

She tugged his shirt off, her palms splaying across his chest. Her fingers hooked in the silver chain he wore around his neck, pulling him closer as moans poured from her mouth.

"It's your turn to surrender," he ordered, nipping at her earlobe.

Then he rotated his hips slightly and thrust deeper. Not harder, just... deeper.

She gasped, her head falling back against the wall and her thighs tightened around his hips. He felt her orgasm around him and dropped his forehead to her throat, following her with gasps of whispered thanks.

Calmer after release, Alaric redressed and took Leah's advice to go for a walk while she tidied the study. She was far too good for him, and he didn't deserve her, but he also had zero intentions of letting her go. If today proved anything, it was how desperately he needed her. As long as he had her at his side and his crown on his head, he could make it through anything.

Inhaling the crisp winter air, Alaric overheard the echo of clashing weapons and grunting men. Curious, he pulled the bear fur wrap tighter around his torso and followed the sound. Eyes wide, he spotted two men training with wooden broadswords a few yards from the castle. Their lack of helmets made determining their identities easy.

Ducking awkwardly, Brantley nearly failed to avoid Sebastian's blade. Then, laughing, the prince somehow managed to block the next blow with his shield. Alaric's fingers clenched tightly into fists as Sebastian congratulated the boy's efforts, voices distant but their words clear.

"You're learning quickly!"

Losing the prospect of proving his father wrong was one thing, but this—whatever this was—he would not stand for it.

Brantley had shown no interest in typical prince like behavior, but if that was changing, a simple vote by the court could end Alaric's reign.

If this was a threat, he would treat it as such.

December 5th, 1456

Understanding the pain of losing a parent, Amelia regretted the nature of Alaric's sudden return to Petrovia, but she could not deny the ease of having him away. Or the peace that settled through the kingdom during his absence. He had not asked her to accompany him, and she had not offered.

Instead, she and Caroline continued spending every hour together they could. It did not matter how often they shared each other's company or for how long. The moment they separated, Amelia missed her presence.

December 18th, 1456

The early morning hours generally graced Fredrick with solitude throughout the castle, however, he was pleased to discover Amelia examining swords in the armory. He spoke softly to avoid startling her.

"You were an admirable student once upon a time."

She turned to him, a small smile curling the edges of her mouth. "Morning, sir."

"Trouble sleeping again?"

"Have a lot on my mind, I suppose," she said wistfully.

"Anything you wish to share?"

The queen hesitated. "Actually, I have been quite tense recently; feeling emotions and having thoughts I am not entirely sure what to do with."

He nodded, knowing the feeling well. "Can I help in some way?"

"Perhaps." She selected a sword and turned to face him. "I have always felt comfortable sharing my thoughts with you, even as a child."

He grinned. "It comes with the territory. I have a daughter of my own, you know."

"You do?" Amelia's eyes widened.

"Yes. She lives in the village with her grandmother."

"I would love to meet her."

"One day." Fredrick glanced down at the sword she held. "How long has it been?"

"Since I have practiced? Too long honestly. I am unsure I will even remember how."

Fredrick grinned. "You never truly forget. Come, let's see how much you remember."

The armory was far too cramped to train in, and outside far too cold, which forced Amelia and Fredrick to duel in the throne room after Regina had chased them from the kitchens with her favorite wooden spoon.

The sun peeked through the tall, ornate windows casting a warm glow over the dueling pair. Steel clashed as their blades connected again, and again. Fredrick took it easier on her at first, but as time went on, she gradually improved, working offense to regain her footing.

The tip of his blade slid off hers as she countered his strike, tearing open the seam of her sleeve as he retracted the weapon.

"Apologies," he panted.

Amelia attempted to catch her own breath, wiping sweat from her forehead with the torn fabric. "I despise this gown anyway."

She lunged forward, taking advantage of his lowered guard.

Fredrick sprang back.

He chuckled loudly, matching her attack with a counter of his own. "I knew you hadn't forgotten everything I taught you."

"Well, you are an excellent instructor."

She dodged left.

He took a large step forward.

She spun, blocking his blow from behind.

"It helps to have an ambitious student. By the end of our lessons I was the one pleading to rest. You were relentless."

She jerked the sword over her head, blocking again.

"I lost that spark I am afraid."

Fredrick thrust the blade forward.

"You found it again, that is what matters."

Amelia brought her own down.

Clash.

"I must admit, Alaric has been acting strangely ever since I stood up to him."

Clank.

"How so?

Clang.

"We reached a compromise over the festivals with minimal fighting. In fact, we did not fight at all. Why now? Why bargain with me?"

Fredrick circled her, guard high. "Do you believe his actions are genuine?"

"I wondered, but then I realized what a mad thought."

Clash.

"It wouldn't hurt to keep your guard up."

"With him?"

Clank.

Fredrick brought his sword down, carefully hooking the necklace at her throat with the tip and tugged. The string snapped and pearls cascaded to the floor.

"With everyone, if need be."

When Amelia finally conceded the duel, they set their weapons aside and collected the pearls, which now sat in a tiny, glimmering pile at the queen's feet. Seated on the platform's edge, the thrones at their backs, she pushed away her hair, heavy with sweat and inhaled deeply.

"I missed this."

"Training?"

"Feeling like I can do anything."

Fredrick laughed. "Ah, yes. I recall that feeling well. As the years pass, I grow fonder of this sitting down part." He slapped his thighs.

"Thank you, for humoring me this morning."

"Anytime."

Amelia was quiet for a long while. "You would tell me, if I was going too far with my attempts to help Dathoviel?"

"Are you worried you might?"

"I worry I may become too focused on simply taking Alaric down. Lose sight of why I am doing it. Dathoviel is my home and I love the people, the land, our history. I cannot imagine being, or doing anything else. As I believe a queen should, but..."

"But?"

"I worry I will do whatever it takes to secure the kingdom. That I may stoop to Alaric's level in some way."

Fredrick slowly nodded. "Amelia, do you see me as a good man?"

"The best," she declared without hesitation.

"What if I told you I have taken more lives than I can count? Would your answer change?"

Her lip quivered. "You are a soldier. I understand what happens in war."

"Forgive my bluntness, Your Highness. But you don't. The wars you have read about in books, and the stories you've heard in dining halls are just that. *Stories*. Being on a battlefield is different. You stand there, weapon in hand, often face to face with your foe. You see the violence in their eyes. The fear. The desperation. You smell the blood and the sick and the dead. You hear the dying and think of your loved ones at home waiting for you, praying you return home safe. And you know this man—your enemy, also has a wife. A child. Or perhaps he is too young to have either. Perhaps he takes his coffee the same way you do. Just as you are a simple man, you recognize so is he. And you must decide in mere moments to take his life, or sacrifice yours. All because two men—who often aren't even present—crave more land or riches or ego."

Amelia's throat tightened. "What are you saying?"

"We can be good people and regret having done terrible things. But sometimes, we are put into a situation where there is no right, good choice. There is only a step forward, or a step back. I've taken lives and torn apart families—made children orphans and wives widows. I have aided the destruction of villages like the very one you strive to save. Knowing this, do you still believe me to be a *good* man?"

"I—I, do not... know. I know you are kind. That you would never hurt anyone unless you had to."

Fredrick clasped her hand tightly in his. "People are not inherently good, or bad, Amelia. The answer is not simply black, and white. You are an exceptional woman, and I am a brilliant man. Yet, we face difficult decisions daily. Death comes for all. And we have painfully little say in when it comes for us. But what we can control, is what we do with the days before."

She shuddered, gripping his dark fingers tightly.

"Do I still deserve my crown if I must do something terrible in order to save my kingdom? If it came down to it, do you believe I am capable of killing?"

She thought of her dream, the panic and fear. The rusty tang of bile at the back of her tongue. She failed when he was peacefully sleeping. But what if he was directly threatening someone she cared about? William and Hannah perhaps? Fredrick? Olive or Caroline? The truth was, his actions threatened them. Every single day he remained king.

"For the right reasons, everyone is capable, Amelia. Most people, like you and I, hold both light and darkness within. We can be both generous and selfish. We can think terrible thoughts and wish for awful things, yet we are capable of love and patience."

"And is Alaric capable of those things? Of generosity? Do you believe him capable of redemption? Of goodness?"

Fredrick sighed and rubbed his palms on the knees of his trousers. "I do not know, My Queen. And we may never know. He certainly has had enough opportunities to show redeemable qualities, yet, I've never seen a flicker of light inside him. Certain people, like Alaric, have either extinguished their light themselves or had it smothered by someone they once trusted."

"And that makes him hopeless for change?"

"I don't like to think anyone is hopeless, but I'm a hopeful man. And sometimes, hope can blind me. I've seen much in my life. Death and dishonor, redemption, and sacrifice. I believe a balance between light and dark must be maintained, for one cannot exist without the other. With Alaric, we are looking at evil. Perhaps I see a projection. A wish or justification, so I may hold no regrets in my soul over what we must inevitably do. But, Amelia... he is *not* a good man. I have looked into his heart and his mind. I have no doubts he will destroy more than he provides."

"So, if it is not about right and wrong, how can I know what to do?" Her head swam, uncertain. Fearful. "Does not everything we are taught as children preach that?"

Fredrick looked like he had much to say, but he settled for a final thought. As he spoke, she knew his words would stay with her forever.

"We all must decide for ourselves what we believe, and who we believe in. If the good, outweighs the bad. And, if it comes down to violence, what you can live with when you look in the mirror."

December 19th, 1456

Finally, the day of the winter solstice festival arrived, and those involved loaded into carriages strapped down with supplies. Despite the snow and chilled air, Dathoviel shone with life as villagers greeted them with cheers and helpful hands upon arrival. The furs Amelia had brought from Alaric's imposing private stock kept everyone celebrating warm as the bonfire's construction continued.

Caroline had never seen this many smiling faces or heard such laughter in one space before. Petrovians certainly wouldn't have been allowed to celebrate with the townspeople in their market square. King Viktor had rules about fraternizing.

Rules about everything, actually.

Here, people glowed, grinning and joking together regardless of class or color. Air puffed from the children's mouths as they raced around in the knit caps and mitts Caroline handed out. She, Regina, the queen, Olive, and a few other ladies had worked tirelessly to make enough for every hand and head in Dathoviel. The children giggled with glee, building round men from snow and falling onto their backs into the fresh white powder. Their arms and legs swung out, leaving behind angel shaped imprints.

A few feet away, Amelia supervised a cart melting chocolate. She'd all too willingly tasked herself with pouring the hot sweetness into mugs and offering the adults a splash of brandy—both courtesy of Kwan, who'd recently taken over the tavern. He'd been more than happy to help in any way he could, especially when it was Olive asking.

Caroline watched with jealousy as the dark-haired man slipped effortlessly from the crowd, hand in hand with Olive. They disappeared down the road, the handmaiden's gleeful shrieks echoing into the darkness

Minutes later, a familiar tune, soft and low, floated out from the middle of the square, and Amelia spun toward the melody. Surrounding conversations paused, attentions focused on the three men and their instruments. William gestured for everyone to gather around the now complete bonfire where couples began swaying.

As the sun set and the fire grew, the atmosphere took over. Furs were laid aside as movement and flame fought off the chill. The children abandoned their play to move closer to the music. Caroline helplessly hummed along, watching Amelia abandon the lonely drink cart to be welcomed into the middle, laughing as the children danced wildly around her.

Queen Orla would have *never* behaved this way.

Sensibilities forgotten, Amelia searched the crowd and beckoned Olive over. Grinning, she also entered the circle, dragging along a ruffled and rumpled Kwan. The villagers cheered, singing together, their feet stomping snow and bare hands clapping. The queen gestured for Caroline to join, but she stayed rooted to the spot.

Not in the mood to take no for an answer, she approached Caroline, hand extended.

"Come, join us. This is your home now."

"I've never been fond of dancing."

"This is not your typical court dancing. I promise."

Caroline glanced from the queen's simple dress to her bare, slender fingers. She looked far from regal, but never more beautiful. Willingly, Caroline placed her hand in Amelia's, biting her bottom lip as the dancing circle opened, bringing them close to the fire. Bodies spun, jumping to the music, and Caroline swallowed.

Their hands were still clasped tightly together, as if it were the most normal thing in the world, and perhaps it was. But Caroline had been cautious since the night in the stables not to touch the queen in any way. Perhaps that had been a mistake, because now the simple gesture that shouldn't have bothered her had her chest feeling tight. Did Amelia notice how damp her palm was?

If she did, she made no comment on it. Instead, she took William's arm on her right, causing Caroline to peek left where she found a grinning Hannah. They clasped hands and the rest of the villagers joined in, everyone dancing around the fire in a collective circle, singing whenever they knew the words. It was exhilarating to move her body and hold Amelia's hand for others to see.

To be included.

Eventually, the tempo slowed, and couples paired off once more. Breathless, brave, and fearful simultaneously, Caroline considered reaching out and pulling Amelia close.

Then a man lost his footing, bumping into them. Amelia stumbled forward into Caroline's awaiting arms, satisfying her craving to press their pounding hearts together, but only for a moment. Amelia apologized, stepping back and Caroline could have groaned in disappointment.

All eyes focused on the man and Amelia. He was wrinkled, short in stature, and his narrow eyes flickered with intoxication. He dropped to his knees; lips full of slurred, accented apologies in a quick foreign language Caroline didn't understand.

"Please forgive me," he finally blubbered in Amelia's native tongue, but when she responded, she did so in the rapid dialectic he'd been speaking before.

The queen patted his arm with a soft smile and a comforting tone despite the hot, drunk breath Caroline could smell from where she stood.

"Fredrick!" Amelia gestured for the constable's help, guiding the older man to rest by the frozen fountain. Barely able to stand, he slumped against the small stone wall.

Kwan strode up before Fredrick could; his own narrow eyes stern, but tone gentle as he rubbed the older man's shoulders.

"Ojii-chan, I think it's time for bed."

The barman received a string of what could only be curses in response.

"Is he alright?" Amelia asked.

Kwan faced the queen with a nervous bow. "Apologies, Your Highness. I should have been watching him more closely. My grandfather is infamous back home for his lacking ability to handle his drink. I'll get him home safe."

"And I'll assist you." Olive winked at her friends as she and the barman tossed the doddering man's arms over their shoulders.

Smirking, Amelia turned around. Caroline's nerves turned violent, immediately fluttering in her stomach when they stepped together.

"That was kind of you."

"We have all drank and stumbled one time or another." Amelia smiled. "Let us dance!"

Caroline shook her head, amused. "Aren't you tired?"

"I may be, but I shall not allow my feet or heart to notice, yet."

The queen pulled her back into the crowd, the slow tune fading into a brighter one. Arms raised, they danced fervently, and soon enough, Caroline relaxed into it. She forgot about the eyes surrounding them. They stepped out, together, out again and again. Their footsteps left imprints in the snow, as they held their skirts away to kick, meeting in the middle.

The next time the music paused, they stood nose to nose.

"We must take a brief rest!" announced a younger musician, wrestling away his uncle's flute to enforce the break time.

The older man argued his way into the tavern while the crowd hummed and dispersed—some irked, others grateful to rest their feet. As if a spell had broken, Caroline jumped away and headed for her post. Children were already lining up, hoping to replace lost mitts or stray hats. Disappointed in herself, she crouched down to assess her remaining supply, trying to focus on her work. Amelia had returned to her cart, but Caroline could feel her gaze. She wouldn't turn around though. Not until her skin had stopped humming from the queen's touch.

December 20th, 1456

After a well-deserved late morning in bed, the ladies climbed back into the queen's carriage, having promised to return and assist with clean up. An odd service for members of nobility, but Amelia now prided herself on being the odd queen. On the way down, Olive recounted the three various times she'd enjoyed Kwan's body the night before.

And she remained in the village for a fourth, leaving only Caroline and Amelia riding back to the castle later that afternoon. Seated side by side they fell into easy conversation, discussing whatever crossed their minds and never veering away from topics many considered inappropriate to discuss.

Amelia shook her head in amused disbelief, listening intently as the carriage jostled over the uneven road.

"Please, tell me you did not truly ask him that?"

"I'm afraid I did. Poor Spencer, trying to explain to twelve-year-old me, why he didn't bleed once a month."

Caroline released a laugh, covering her mouth with her gloved fingertips, and recalled the blush that stained her beloved cousin's teenage face. Amelia's eyes sparkled with delight, unable to contain her laughter. The carriage went over the now familiar bump in the road, their respective shoulders and thighs brushing as they attempted to remain in the seat.

Even through the many layers of skirts, the momentary connection burned Caroline's skin in the most delightful way. She glanced to where their bodies had briefly met, half expecting to find embers between them. The tingling sensation traveled down her shoulder, to her chest, stomach, and up from her thigh. It met, churning low in her gut. Lower.

Amelia's gaze captured hers, her pupils momentarily dark before she blinked a few times and cleared her throat.

"It is a shame you were not better prepared."

Caroline rolled her eyes. "My parents focused more on lecturing me about the importance of heaven than matters of reality, like what changes my body would go through."

She sensed Amelia's hesitation. They agreed on many things, but religion was a rather large topic they disagreed on. Or so it seemed.

"It is no secret the church can have an agenda. My relationship with God is my own, and is not dictated by an offering plate or the approval of a man in robes."

"I respect the relationship you have with God," Caroline said gently. "I never intend to make you feel negatively by stating my distaste for the whole idea. At their cores, all religions send a similar message. Be kind and love others. I don't need to attend mass to understand all we need to know about life."

Amelia nodded in understanding. "Some find comfort in a pew, others in the forest, or the water. I believe if we live with kindness and love, we are closer to God than any man or woman sitting weekly in a confession box."

Caroline clasped Amelia's hand in hers, gentle enough to be friendly. Yet, the air hung thick between them with something deeper. Unsteady heart pounding in her ears, she gazed at Amelia's mouth; her pale pink lips parted. She wasn't going to be able to pull away this time. She—

Hooves clattered outside. A barking command from the driver had the carriage jolting to a stop before the castle. Feet scrambled above their heads as the driver clambered down, and by the time Fredrick opened the door to greet them, the queen had returned her hands to her lap. Both women exited the carriage silently and parted in separate directions.

Avoiding each other proved successful for the duration of dinner as well, despite being seated together. They focused their attention on others; Caroline conversing with Olive and even entertaining a few sentences with Seb when she felt desperate.

At the head of the table, Amelia concentrated on Fredrick, sharing their progress in short, coded sentences. Whenever she caught herself gazing at the queen, Caroline would take a sip of wine and force her eyes elsewhere. But soon her ears were buzzing from the alcohol and she was forced to stop. Instead, she chose to poke at her untouched cake, watching the silver fork gleaming in the candlelight.

When the meal ended, Amelia bid a general farewell to the table and left alone, seeming desperate to escape. Caroline watched her go silently, heart sinking.

It was only when she was alone in the glittering dining hall that she headed to her tower, quite aware another sleepless night was ahead.

~

Amelia rolled over, willing her mind to quiet, but knowing it was useless. She should have been tired. Constantly attempting to stifle this undeniable desire for Caroline was beyond exhausting.

Since her arrival in Dathoviel, it had become increasingly difficult to ignore the physical and emotional responses she inspired.

Amelia knew she could no longer ignore the truth. If the carriage ride had not transpired today, what happened at the festival had proven enough. Then there was the night in the stables, and all the small moments in between. Not to mention the letters.

Throwing off the quilts, she surrendered her bare feet to the cool stone floor and slipped on her warmest robe. She would go to the kitchens and hope warm milk still worked to calm her. Or she could go to the library and read until the sun rose.

Whatever she did, she would *not* go to Caroline's tower.

Despite the mantra, she took a tentative step left, lacking control over her body, feeling the pull toward the woman haunting her thoughts. With a stomp she turned towards the west wing, tiptoeing along. Male voices trickled out from the armory, catching her attention a few minutes later. As she passed, she quickly glanced two guards inside; one affixing arrowheads to new shafts, the other staring out the window.

"I heard the husband killed both women. Appears they were more than friends."

"Are you saying they—"

"Can't be certain, of course. Word's swept from one kingdom to the next. I heard the husband came home and found them in bed together."

"Together? I can't imagine it!"

"Can't you?"

One guard chuckled.

"If I found out my wife shared our bed with a man, I wouldn't hesitate to kill him. But a woman? I haven't the faintest idea what I'd do."

Both men fell silent, and Amelia moved along carefully. If love is what she felt for Caroline, it must be a blessing. Surely, she would not have received these feelings by accident. Bypassing the kitchens, Amelia changed her course for the chapel.

The torches remained lit within, illuminating the aisle just enough. She approached the cross, hands clasped, head bowed, and took a deep breath.

"Heavenly Father. You know best the truth of my heart, and the path laid out before me. I once asked you to protect my heart from the king. Are these emotions for Lady Caroline a punishment for that request? Or a reward for the virtuous work I have been doing? If this love is not meant for me, I humbly request you illuminate my true path and remove it. If it is genuine. . . I ask for your blessing and continued protection forward. For I know our journey will be trying, should my feelings be returned."

With a whispered amen, Amelia left the chapel, her body feeling quite heavy as she returned to her tower. One way or another, she would learn the truth regarding Caroline's feelings for her. And she would do her best to accept whatever answer awaited.

. 7 .

December 21ˢᵗ, 1456

THE WOMEN'S CIRCLE FOLLOWING the winter solstice festival was the busiest Hannah had led. The ladies gathered in the tavern, for it was warmer than the church, taking over the small round tables and pushing them together in a jumble that drove Kwan mad.

Bless him. He only smiled from behind the bar and kept the wine flowing, blushing and politely deflecting any flirtatious comments. When he joined her and William for dinner that evening, she would have to tease him about Olive. They'd grown quite serious it seemed.

Hannah sat quietly amidst the eager chatter absorbing information the queen might need in the future. Today the topics were less about struggles and more about the festival.

Who had snuck off for a tryst during, who had ended affairs, and what the new year might hold. All while trading Yule recipes and passing newborns around. It was almost too loud, but she basked in the hum of voices, knitting a simple blanket for the newest addition to their village.

When the once loud conversation to her left hushed, her ears perked up, straining to listen over Brianna and baby Winslow playing at her feet.

"It's just a rumor," an older woman with grey hair stated, her voice thick with dismissive displeasure.

"Have you ever heard of such a thing?" whispered another, her excited gaze focused on the trousers she attempted to repair.

The women gathered closer; Hannah included, though her eyes did not sparkle with conspiracy or interest like the others. Instead, they flashed with concern.

A third woman spoke.

"My cousin lives in the castle, you know. She spotted Lady Caroline sneaking out of the queen's tower one morning."

Hannah attempted to protest, but the second woman cut her off.

"Can you imagine?"

The eldest woman's eyebrows furrowed. "No! There are laws against it!"

"Not in our kingdom." Hannah reminded them sternly.

The three women turned, fear and embarrassment on their faces. Everyone was aware of her and William's loyalty to the queen.

"Hannah, even you must admit the queen and Lady Caroline looked *close* at the festival."

"It's no one's concern what Queen Amelia does in her private hours. Our concerns should remain on all she *has* done, and continues to do for us."

The older woman narrowed her eyes. "Imagine a kingdom with two queens! It's not done."

Hannah set her knitting on the cracked wooden table and fixed the woman with her best glare. "Just because it hasn't been done, doesn't mean it can't be done, Laurel."

"I do not support it." Laurel tossed her grey hair. Her wrinkled skin showed age and wisdom, despite her typical immature behavior.

"Luckily no one asked you," grumbled Hannah's sister Margaret from where she leaned against the bar.

Laurel huffed indignantly, her chest puffing out. "If we allow this to happen, who knows what shall come next? Those kinds of people are sick. They need help."

"The sick person who needed help was me," Hannah said, jaw sore from grinding her teeth. "I had prepared to leave my children behind, but the queen took pity on William. She helped me heal, sent us aid and food, for our sick and starving." Hannah addressed the group collectively. "Her doctor heals our loved ones; her midwife delivers our children. We must support our queen as she supports us."

"Indeed," Beatrice said proudly.

She tossed back her wine like it was a shot and waggled the empty glass at Kwan, requesting more.

Uncorking another bottle, his wide eyes shifted back and forth between the arguing women. He was probably wondering if he needed to break all this up. Hannah sincerely hoped it wouldn't come to that.

A middle-aged brunette with light brown skin nodded. "Hannah's right. Besides, having two queens *could* be fascinating. It's not as if the king serves us well."

Agreement and curiosity hummed throughout most of the circle, and when Laurel stormed out no one stopped her. As the topic faded, save for a few disgruntled mumbles, everyone moved on to helping Maria plan her summer wedding.

Hannah wondered if Julian knew his eldest daughter was engaged as she abandoned her knitting, bringing a whimpering Winslow to her breast. Ignoring her calls to leave Kwan alone, Brianna requested the barman put her on his shoulders. He laughed, tossing down the rag to lift her.

Later in bed, surrounded by the snores of their sleeping children, Hannah contemplated the queen's potential relationship with Lady Caroline. Imagining them sharing a bed, similar to her and William now. She rolled over to face him, admiring the sharpness of his nose and the dip in his chin in the dim candlelight while he sketched.

They'd known each other their entire lives, yet he still took her breath away. Sensing her gaze, he set aside the drawing of their future home, dusted the charcoal from his fingers, and rolled to face her.

As he listened to her dramatic retelling from earlier, his eyes grew wider by the minute.

"I mean, who cares what the queen does in her private time?" she finished with a huff.

William sighed. "I'm afraid a great many people will. Other kingdoms may quarrel with the idea of two women being together at all. Never mind sharing a throne."

She didn't bother telling him she could understand the queen's attraction to Caroline. Though she loved him and was content at his side, she sometimes wondered what it would be like with a woman. She wasn't ashamed of these urges and fantasies. Actually, they fascinated her, but she had decided a long time ago that they were for her, and her alone. A woman deserved to have one secret, right?

"What's *your* opinion on the matter?"

Resting on his back, William tucked his hands behind his head. "I've heard stories of terrible punishments for men engaging in relationships with each other. Not many about women. When I was young, my father explained how men from his land sometimes took the body of another to dominate. To take something, whether it be power, wealth, or even his wife. To think of it as a demonstration of love is foreign to me."

"Some men take from women too," she murmured.

Nausea assaulted her senses as the memory of rough hands around her wrists, hot breath on her face, and hay cutting into her back rushed in. She squeezed her eyes shut and hugged herself, focusing on her surroundings to pull herself back to the present.

She started with the scent of dried herbs from the kitchen and the sound of her husband's even breath. Forcing her eyes open she started counting the boards that made up the room. And when she could feel her own body again, she released her arms to caress the plain bed sheets.

William must have read her mind, remembering the day he'd nearly beat his uncle to death for trying to take what wasn't his. Drawing her in tightly, he stroked her arm, pressing her ear to his chest so she could listen to the steady beat of his heart. They rarely talked about the attack these days, but she took comfort in the way he ensured to never ignore or brush her memories aside.

After a few minutes her breath evened out, and she relaxed into the mattress.

Only then did William begin speaking.

"The very question of how women would engage in lovemaking warrants some consideration," he wondered aloud, attempting to bring her back to the lighter end of their conversation. "Would it even be possible?"

Hannah lifted onto her elbows to gaze down at him. "Of course. Back before our wedding night, I may have craved you inside me, but lack of penetration never hindered pleasure."

"Shall we experiment?" William grinned, fixing her with loving, understanding eyes. "Only if you feel safe."

"I always feel safe with you," she whispered, caressing his face. "But, we mustn't wake the children."

His lips quirked as he ducked beneath the blankets, and it wasn't long before she needed a pillow to muffle her moans.

December 22nd, 1456

The gentle knock at Amelia's door had her glancing away from the ties of her trousers. She quickly laced the fly, rolling up the sleeves of her blouse and prayed whoever it was would not chastise her for wearing men's clothing.

She would *not* be training with Fredrick again in a gown. It was too frustrating.

Opening the door revealed Caroline—both a simultaneously relieving and nerve-racking sight. The scent of lilacs was unmistakable, and it was then that Amelia decided she did in fact have a favorite flower.

"Good morning." Caroline smiled her signature small smile.

Would her lips taste as sweet as they looked?

Amelia bit down on her tongue as a reminder to compose herself and respond properly.

"Good morning."

There. That was a reasonable, innocent response.

Caroline beamed. "I was wondering if you wouldn't mind joining me for a walk. It's looking to be a surprisingly warm day, and I'd enjoy your company."

Amelia coughed, clearing her throat. "I would love nothing more, but unfortunately I have arrangements this morning with Fredrick. He's agreed to assist me in becoming skilled with a sword again."

"Fascinating! You know Spencer taught me how to duel when we were younger. He always did have a terrible time saying no to me."

Of course he did. How could anyone say no to that face? Those eyes. That perfect—

"With Petrovia being focused on their military, that does not surprise me."

"Yes, I was never as skilled as I'd have liked to be, and once my father found out, he instantly put a stop to the lessons."

"How did he find out?" Amelia asked, though she was certain she knew the answer.

Caroline rolled her eyes. "Alaric snitched one day to get back at me for beating him in a duel."

"I should have guessed. My father ended my lessons as well."

The blonde hesitated, bottom lip between her teeth. "Would you be opposed to me joining you?"

Amelia gulped, a blush creeping up her neck.

"You wish to observe?"

"To also train perhaps..."

Inside she was losing her mind, but outwardly she managed to look calm and composed. A talent most queens had, especially those married to men like Alaric. However, it wasn't wrath or frustration that had her reeling. Though perhaps it was frustration of a different kind. Training with Caroline was not a fantasy she had previously indulged in, but the mental images her imagination was presently concocting certainly made it one now.

"Let us go ask Fredrick if he minds."

Amelia stepped left in the abandoned classroom Fredrick had converted into a training space, and ducked, attempting to ignore the rapid rise and fall of Caroline's heaving chest as the blonde stepped forward, nearly striking her with a well-placed jab.

Her slippers were silent on the golden carpet as she retreated, grinning, her guard up. For a woman who had not wielded a sword in many years, Caroline could certainly hold her own. Ignoring how Caroline's neckline seemed to have fallen lower since they began, Amelia drew her gaze up to the blonde's burning eyes. They looked darker—an almost navy blue.

Amelia watched the way her long elegant fingers gripped the hilt as she blocked Amelia's final and distracted attempt for triumph.

It seemed the harder she tried to ignore Caroline and the affects her presence created, the more difficult it became. Yet somehow, she did not hate it. She liked the way heat pooled in her cheeks, *and other places,* when they had accidentally brushed hands or their eyes lingered on each other a moment too long.

That was how they had been for a while now. Close but not touching. And with each passing day, the ache for more was becoming unbearable. Occasionally, Amelia glimpsed the same longing in Caroline's gaze, but it was most likely the reflection of her own desires. The chance of having the person you yearned for return the same feelings was rare. Even rarer in someone like Caroline.

Fredrick clapped his hands a few minutes later, rising from the desk he'd been leaning against. "My apologies, Your Highness."

Amelia looked away from her dazzling opponent, grateful for the moment of reprieve. "Of course, Constable. We have taken much of your time today. Thank you."

"Yes, thank you, sir." Caroline crossed her arm over her chest, sword still in hand. "It felt good to hold one of these again."

"You did well, Lady Caroline. I hope you join us again soon?"

"So long as the queen doesn't mind losing again."

Her eyes flicked to Amelia and she winked.

"Ha! I clearly let you win. How else was I to inspire your confidence to return?"

In all honesty, she had lost fair and square. Her panting and dripping sweat was proof enough.

Fredrick bid them farewell on his way out the door, chortling all the way down the hall. Amelia reached for Caroline's sword to replace the weapons in the stand next to the door, and their fingertips brushed.

A spark travelled up her arm, spreading beneath her skin until it registered deep within her body. Caroline coughed, nearly jumping back. She wiped the sweat from her brow, giving a small curtsy before she began backing away.

Had she felt it too? Or was she running for another reason?

"Well, this was lovely. Thank you for letting me join."

"Y—you're welcome," stuttered the queen.

"See you tonight at dinner."

"Yes, see you—"

She was already gone. Should she chase after her and apologize? For what she was uncertain, but somehow an apology felt needed. Unfortunately, the only plausible scenario ended with visions of kissing her in the middle of the hall, which was obviously out of the question.

Head shaking, fingers trembling, Amelia returned the swords to their home, ensuring to lock the door on her way out. Where could she go? What should she do? She needed a bath, but dinner was hours away. Surely it could wait. A ride wasn't out of the question, but it wasn't the solution for *this* particular brand of tension coiling tighter inside her with every second.

She turned right toward the library.

Once inside, she ensured this door was locked too before heading for the stairs; her gaze locked on the highest shelf. She knew exactly what books awaited her there, for she'd read nearly all of them. But today, she searched for one in particular.

Amelia could still recall the blush that stained her mother's face when the merchant from the east had presented it to her and Marcel.

A gift of gratitude for continuing trade with his colony, he had said.

As a young princess, Amelia had not understood what the fuss was about a simple book until years later when she had come across it in her mother's room, tucked away in the drawer next to her bed.

She had never seen a book with illustrations like that before. She had flipped through the pages with wide eyes and a pounding heart. The words were in a language she had yet to learn, but it was not long until she had convinced Brantley's governess that he must know the dialects of their most valued trades partner. So, she learned, absorbing every moment of the lessons. Afterwards, she would slip away to her tower, translating the page she had torn from the middle of the book. Occasionally she would touch herself to the images on the opposite side.

One day, when she was nearing her twentieth birthday, Olive discovered the page while making Amelia's bed. Initially, it had been embarrassing, but Olive quickly explained pleasure was nothing to be ashamed of.

"It's completely natural," she had promised. *"It's actually good for you, they say. It can clear your mind, help you sleep..."*

Amelia's heart rattled against her chest as her hand closed around the crimson spine. Was she really going to do this now? With sunlight beaming through the windows and across the very spot she stood? She had only ever touched herself at night and in bed.

Hoping to avoid making a mess of her favorite chaise, Amelia opted to sit on a lower stair and opened the book in her lap; feeling the familiar tingle as she turned the pages. Certain sections explained the basics of pleasure or the way men's and women's bodies worked. Other's detailed locations and techniques where touch could bring said pleasure to one's partner. *Or oneself.*

And then there were the drawings. Talented illustrations of various positions and anatomy and intriguing intimate moments.

Before she knew it, the book had tumbled to the floor, the laces of her trousers were open, and her arm had slipped down. She gripped the railing with her free hand, the other rubbing—teasing, and wondered how the skin just beneath Caroline's collarbone would feel under her tongue.

Would all parts of her taste the same, or would it depend where she licked? *Good God.*

She recalled the navy shade Caroline's eyes had turned during their duel. Was it a similar shade when she touched herself? Did she do this sort of thing? Was she... was she doing it right now? Skirts pushed up with her fingers between her legs, head tossed back against her pillow, perhaps? Craving a touch other than her own?

A moan tore from Amelia's lips as the lust built inside her. No longer burning embers begging to be stoked, but a raging wildfire absorbing every thought and intention in its path.

Her ribs and abdomen clenched, her knees wanting to come together, but she hooked the toes of her boots on either side of the railing and tightened her grip. Her fingers moved faster and faster, imagining what sounds Caroline might make. If she cursed or screamed as she came, or if—

Amelia cried out and released the railing to cover her mouth as pleasure crashed through her hard and fast. Panting and shuddering, she allowed her fingers to slow until she was too sensitive for any touch. Then she lay back on the stairs, breathing deeply and threw her arm over her face.

December 23rd, 1456

Amelia had wished to decline Alaric's request for a personal audience following his return to Dathoviel. Breakfast had already been uncomfortable enough with Caroline refusing to meet her eyes yet again, and she was exhausted. Alas, an afternoon nap would have to wait.

The man who entered the throne room seemed different than the one who had left days ago. Without his crown and confident airs, she hardly recognized him. His beard had grown out, and he bore no fur cloak on his currently slumped shoulders. Instead, he wore a simple tunic and tan linen trousers, no leather pants in sight.

He took his seat next to hers, running his fingertips over the worn, golden velvet coating the arm of his throne chair. Moonlight bounced off the snow outside, basking them in silver light from the left, as warm orange flames flickered shadows from the torches on their right.

"I trust all stayed well in my absence."

"Of course. We did not expect your return so soon."

"Petrovia is no longer my home. There is nothing left for me there."

"What of your brother?"

"I fear he hates me just as my father did." The king looked up, sadly. He was genuinely hurting. "I know you look on our marriage with sorrow, Amelia. But you were not the only pawn in play that day. Our fathers made a deal for their sole benefit. Mine was as pleased as yours, to rid himself of the burden he believed me to be."

Her eyes softened. "I am sorry about your father."

"He's not the first family member I've lost," Alaric dismissed gruffly.

"You mean Davidson?"

LET IT REIGN

His gaze hardened before quickly slipping back into grief. "I couldn't save him. I still recall how small his body looked in my father's arms..." Alaric took a deep breath, perhaps mustering a great deal of courage. "I understand we shall never be close, but I've been reminded of the importance of family. With your permission, I wish to seek out quality time with Brantley. It's too late for Spencer and I, but perhaps I can find a brotherly bond with him."

Recognizing his fragile state, she struggled to object. "The decision is his."

"Thank you."

Speechless and uncertain what to do next, she gingerly stood, clamping down on her empathy.

"I will tell Regina to bring you some leftovers, shall I?"

Her instincts screamed to run, but somehow, she managed to keep her feet at a calm brisk pace as she exited the throne room.

The door shut behind her before he could answer, blocking her view of him. If she had looked back, she would have seen his posture straighten and the sorrow melt off his face into a dark menacing smile.

~

Triumphant, Brantley turned the page, finally discovering what he'd been searching for all along. It was so simple it almost hurt. All he needed was a vote... or rather, to *win* the vote. He would gather the court and announce he wished for his throne after all. He would have to be convincing. Perhaps he could think of far-off places and dream of strange foods and exotic women while using words like 'decree' and 'duty'. And maybe if he succeeded, he could also convince himself.

Alaric found him that way, huddled over the long table, transferring notes to a spare sheet of parchment in the library. Realizing he had company, Brantley closed the book, concealing his parchment beneath it, hoping the movements appeared innocent enough.

"Alaric. I'll be out of your way in a moment."

The king lifted his hand. "I glanced a ravine full of deer this morning. I hoped you'd join Sebastian and I on a short hunting trip. It may be an opportunity for us to bond."

Brantley eyed him, uncertain. "Seb will be joining us?"

"If we're going to bring back enough meat for a Christmas feast, we'll need a third pair of hands. I plan to depart in a few hours, camp overnight, and return Christmas Eve."

"Does Amelia know about this?"

He nodded. "She approves."

In the year and a half since Alaric arrived in Dathoviel, they'd exchanged perhaps ten words. There was definitely something going on; Brantley could smell it in the air. Something the king was plotting. Perhaps against Amelia? Would Alaric try to turn him against her? Of course he couldn't. But perhaps he could play along and overhear or observe something useful about the king. Something that would help steer the court in the right direction.

"I'll prepare Gus then."

"Wonderful."

~

Leah watched Alaric stride into his study, his footsteps light. He was whistling, hopefully because he knew she would be waiting for him.

He stopped in the door a moment, observing her perched atop the important papers strewn across his desk. His face split into the wide grin he reserved only for her. She knew her body read like a forbidden book, open for him, desperate to be caressed. To have each page turned with deliberate attention to detail.

He sauntered toward her, already removing his belt.

"Did you miss your king?"

"More than you know."

He cradled her face in his hands. "Is it me you missed, or my body?"

"I could ask you the same question," she teased, letting her fingers lightly trail across the front of his trousers.

He was already hard for her. To be fair, she was just as ready.

She relished every moment as Alaric's mouth slipped from her lips, down her chin, and beyond. He made quick work of the simple dress, capturing her breasts, nipping her collarbone. Despite his insatiable appetite for sex and attention, she knew she had the strength to rule not only Dathoviel, but him as well.

Grasping her hips, he tugged her to the edge of the desk; wrinkling the papers beneath. Her dress cascaded to the floor, leaving her body bare. His fingertips danced upward in slow circles, searching her thighs, spreading them open. She knew he would bring her pleasure without needing to ask for it. He always gave generously in the bedroom.

Sinking to his knees, the king's face disappeared between her thighs. She ran her fingers through his hair, gripping the roots tightly.

His tongue swept up, drawing slow, gentle licks against her. Inside her. She hissed and whimpered, holding him in place until her hips adopted a mind of their own. When she heard him grunt she released her hold, but didn't stop her lower body from jutting forward against his mouth.

"I definitely missed you," he breathed, speaking directly to her core.

He gripped her waist roughly, latching his lips and teeth to the inside of her thigh. Her head fell back.

"I missed your mouth," she panted her hips snapping forward in search of his tongue.

"I missed your skin," he growled, fingertips digging into her calves.

His left thumb found the heel of her right foot and he pressed, running his smooth thumbnail along her arch. The sensation shot up her leg, settled in her pelvis and she gasped.

"Promise me you won't go away again."

He looked up, tongue darting out to his lips, his mahogany eyes almost feral.

"I promise."

They both knew it was a lie, but she took it. His left hand moved to grip her thighs next, his right roaming toward her center again. Two fingers dipped into her as she returned his mouth to where it belonged, and her body thrummed—begging for release.

"Worship me," she whispered, rolling her hips against him. "Worship your future queen."

~

Wrapped tightly in warm clothes later that evening, Amelia spotted a note someone had slid beneath her door. She was just on her way out to bid Brantley farewell, but she paused, noticing Caroline's familiar script in her trademark blue ink. The queen's gut sank, gloved fingertips smoothing the parchment, scanning the words a few times before her brain truly understood them.

Amelia,

I am not feeling well and have decided to stay in my tower today. Wish Brantley well on my behalf, will you? And please stay away for now should I be contagious. Your health is of the utmost importance.

-C

Amelia carefully refolded the parchment and tucked it into the top drawer of her cherry-wood vanity. Was this an answer to her prayers from the other night? She truly hoped not. Though, given the control she had lost yesterday, perhaps space wasn't the worst thing for them.

Descending the tower stairs, Amelia tied her pale blue scarf and decided to respect Caroline's request for at least two days. She could use the free time to find a gift for her.

If all they could be was friends, she vowed to be the best friend she could be.

Once Gus was comfortably but efficiently loaded with food and blankets, Amelia embraced her brother tightly in farewell. She still felt uncertain about this trip, but he assured her it was necessary.

Alaric—dressed in furs and a large hat—rode in on Celestial. The mare's black body contrasted sharply against the falling snow, her impatient copper horseshoes tapping along the cobblestones.

"Are you men ready?"

Brantley pressed a kiss to Amelia's cheek, sensing her nerves. "I'll be alright. I trust Seb."

She turned to the knight. "Bring him home safe."

It was both an order and a plea.

Already astride his horse, Harlow, Seb dutifully bowed his head in respect. "You have my word."

Brantley lifted himself into the saddle. "I have a plan to share with you when I return," he whispered. "Refrain from any drastic actions until I explain?"

Confused and curious, Amelia nodded. She hugged herself tightly against the chill, watching them disappear into the early evening light.

8

December 24th, 1546

THE KITCHENS PROVED INTOLERABLY warm right before meals, so Leah always retrieved hot water for Caroline's bath before dinner. Even if it was when things smelt the most delicious. But today was Christmas Eve and Caroline had requested her bath before breakfast. Apparently, Amelia had the same idea, leaving Leah with the unfortunate pleasure of crossing paths with Olive.

Not even the scent of cinnamon sugar and fresh bread could improve her mood upon seeing the handmaiden approaching the hearth. Each balancing two heavy buckets, they bumped into one another on their way out the door, neither prepared to surrender being first. Steaming water sloshed across the floor and soaked their simple skirts.

Scalded and furious, both released a string of curses and rounded on the other.

Quite aware of their rivalry, Regina glanced up from the pie crust she was cutting into strips, her paring knife pointing at them both, one eye on the large batch of eggs she was cooking.

"Ladies, if you brawl in my kitchen again, I *guarantee* you'll miss dessert tonight."

No one dared piss Regina off on a normal day, never mind when her famous apple pie was on the line. Christmas would be devastating without it.

Olive huffed in defeat, and stepped aside, careful no more water spilled from her buckets.

"Apologies, Regina, I was in a rush." She sneered as Leah passed her. "Though I suppose no one has more to do than *her*."

Leah froze, glaring over her shoulder. If the bitch had something to say, she should get it over with.

"What's that supposed to mean?"

"Well... you're the main maid for the king, and now Lady Caroline. You must be exhausted runnin' from one tower to the next."

Leah's ire reached its boiling point, her grip tightening on the handles.

"Shut it, Olive," she warned, tongue feeling heavy. "Not like *you* haven't been sneaking out to the village at night."

"So, what if I have?"

Perhaps missing pie this year would be worth getting to dump scalding water over the blonde's head.

"Who's the lucky man this time? Or are you whoring yourself to the whole village hoping one of them will sweep you away come spring?"

Olive stalked forward, a menacing glint in her amber eyes, but Leah refused to back down. She focused on maintaining her smirk the way Alaric taught her.

"As if the king will ever give *you* anythin' more than a few minutes in his bed before tossin' you back out to fetch him more tea."

"You have no idea what you're talking about!" Leah screeched.

Regina's knife clattered to the counter. "That's it! You two, out, right now."

Both women scurried through the door like scared mice, silent until they were out of the cook's earshot. The sun had yet to rise, leaving the stone corridors dim, save for the glowing torches.

"It doesn't have to be like this, you know," Leah eventually said. "We could work together and rise above our stations."

Olive wasn't buying it.

"You have time to be my friend too? Aren't your hands full with the king's cock?"

Leah stood tall.

"Don't worry. I can multitask."

The handmaiden snorted. "Oh, I bet."

Teeth bared, Leah raced to the front. She blocked Olive's path, ignoring the water splashing onto the floor. "You're going to regret choosing to be enemies over friends."

"I'll be sorry when the chickens begin layin' golden eggs, perhaps. Or when you become queen."

Olive's laugh echoed as she disappeared around the corner and all Leah could do was stand there bristling, buckets still in hand.

"When I become queen," she whispered. "you'll be the first one tossed out of my castle."

~

The aroma of a simple, yet delicious breakfast awoke Brantley come morning, long before the sun. He hadn't slept well on the freezing ground and accepted the steaming coffee Seb offered with relief.

It was refreshing to be outside though. He'd never been away from home before, and part of him dreaded returning. Even with the prickling at the back of his neck from Seb's continuous, watchful eyes, and the sudden kindness Alaric was showing him. It was almost off-putting how often the king smiled at him, like he desired something only Brantley could provide.

Already dressed in furs and leathers, Alaric looked up from his own mug, smirking across the fire.

"Are you up for a hunt of your own today?"

The two men had stayed up late, regaling tales for him of the various escapades they'd gotten into during their youth. Brantley had enjoyed himself immensely, high on testosterone and tales of adventure. He'd never felt so included before. Like one of the men, rather than the only boy at court.

"Indeed. I wish my father had come. He could use an outing like this."

"Well, we'll bring him along next time." Seb lifted his cup and smiled.

"Next time," Alaric agreed, sipping his coffee.

Seb handed a tin plate over. It was far from Regina's cooking, but it looked like a glorious meal all the same. *Man-feed,* Seb had called it.

"The sooner we capture dinner, the sooner we can head home," said the knight.

"Precisely," the king set his mug aside and rubbed his hands together, warming them. "Brantley, would you be willing to scout the location I showed you on the map last night? Sebastian and I will take down camp before joining you."

Brantley looked up from his plate, mouth full. "You trust me to go ahead alone?"

"You will merely be. . . observing. Should explore while you can, yes?"

Brantley scarfed down his remaining breakfast and stood to straighten his vest, proud to be considered responsible enough for such a task.

Seb watched the boy climb onto his horse, trapped by his promise to the queen, and his duty to the king. He disapproved wholeheartedly, and there was something in his gut telling him this entire trip was wrong. But he couldn't leave Alaric to dismantle camp alone. And as much as he wanted to object, the words were trapped in his throat.

Moving quick, he disassembled the tents and loaded them back onto the sled, ensuring to leave enough room for the meat.

As long as Alaric remained in sight, he could ensure the prince's safety.

~

Amelia noticed the deep furrow in Olive's brow while she poured the second bucket of hot water into the tub, muttering under her breath. Normally she liked to bathe in peace, but seeing her friend distraught meant no peace would be had until she got to the bottom of why.

"Would you like to talk about it?"

Olive's jaw clenched. "Talk about what?"

"Whatever has you so upset?"

"Leah."

"What did she say this time?"

"Honestly," Olive set the bucket upside down, using it as a seat. "I was the most vulgar in the conversation. She just angers me so."

Amelia sunk deeper into the water, surrendering her knees to the chill air so her breasts and feet could be warm.

"I promise you, I don't care about her relationship with Alaric."

"No, it's got nothin' to do with that. She thinks she's better than everyone, always has."

"Well, she did manage to land herself the role of king's mistress. That is normally reserved for women with title. So there is *something* special about her."

Olive's nose wrinkled as she moved from the pail to sit on the edge of the bed.

"And she's been beyond insufferable ever since. The way she looks at you... I don't like it."

"How does she look at me?"

"Like she wants your head on a platter."

Amelia cleared her throat. "Perhaps, but she isn't in a position to harm me. I am more than protected, and even if she tried, what would be her happy ending? Becoming queen?"

They both laughed.

"Imagine." Olive waved her left hand, the other wrapped around her ribs.

Amelia watched the rippling water steady around her limbs, her giggles fading. In a strange way, she understood Leah. Though they were vastly different women, they shared common goals.

"I do pity her sometimes," she admitted.

"You aren't serious?"

"Well, we cannot entirely fault her, can we? Both you and I long for change. We wish aspects of our lives were different. That we had more power, more freedom."

Olive's eyes softened, *barely*. "I suppose."

"We may not like her personality, but she's simply a woman praying for change."

"I see your point, I do. But she doesn't have to be such a bitch about it."

Amelia dipped her knees back into the water, sacrificing her toes instead. When were they going to make a tub where she could submerge her entire body at once?

"Perhaps she could use a friend? She must be lonely, especially when Alaric is away."

"If you're suggestin' *I* befriend her..."

"No, no. I wouldn't ask that of you. But perhaps in the new year I can reach out to her. Many wives and mistresses are friends in other kingdoms. Plus, we have the added benefit of not being in love with the same man."

"Yes, well, let's get through Christmas first, shall we?"

Amelia tipped her head back into the water, soaking her hair as Olive stood to reach for the soap.

"We shall."

The handmaiden took her seat on the stool behind the head of the tub, lathered her hands, and began to massage Amelia's scalp.

"I must admit something."

Amelia nodded, encouraging her to continue.

"I'm also a little cross with you. Ever since Caroline arrived, we've spent less and less time together just the two of us. Aside from my required duties, we hardly speak. And now you're considerin' making time for *Leah* of all people?"

Amelia's heart sank and she tipped her head back, making eye contact. "You are right. I have been a terrible friend when you have been nothing but supportive to me. I am so sorry. I thought you were wrapped up in Kwan, enjoying new love. But I should not have assumed. Please forgive me."

Olive squeezed the queen's fingers in reassurance.

"Of course, I forgive you. It's just so clear you and Caroline share somethin' special."

"You and I took our first steps together, Olive. We've grown together. Caroline *has* become important to me, but I have room in my heart for you both. I promise."

Olive nearly relaxed.

"There is one more thin' on my mind..."

Eyes closed and almost at the point of ultimate relaxation, Amelia sighed happily. "Mm-hmm?"

"Do you recall how the children used to have class in the tavern because nowhere else was big enough for them all? Perhaps we could build a school."

Amelia's eyes shot open. "*That* is a wonderful idea!"

"Imagine the impact a full, proper education would have on our kingdom. If every child knew how to read and write? If they could learn at their own pace and explore what interests them? What could it mean for future generations? For our society?"

Amelia pondered the idea. "I would be curious to find out."

"Perhaps if we gave these children a better chance, we'd have fewer desperate people like Leah."

"William would be the best person to discuss the build with."

Olive beamed and stood. "I'll talk to him next week. Now lay back and relax. I have a few finishin' touches to put on your gown before you can dress."

"I can bring in someone new to make my gowns. You need not continue taking on that responsibility."

"Nonsense." The handmaiden waved her hand. "I've grown to enjoy it, truly."

"Very well. And Olive?"

The handmaiden paused at the door. "Yes?"

"Thank you for being honest with me."

"I won't hide my feelin's from you again," she promised.

~

Wrapped in her favorite pale pink robe, Lady Caroline took a seat at the small desk situated beneath her window. Early afternoon sunshine poured in, warming her skin. She glanced longingly back to the lavender and cream bedspread, but her mind raced. There would be no more avoiding. She considered her options, nails drumming on the smooth wood.

The tapping increased as anxiety deepened in her chest, weighing her down. Her feet craved to walk familiar steps down to the garden. To lean her head on

Spencer's shoulder and listen to the soothing gruff of his voice. He would know exactly what to say and what she should do.

Lips pursed, she reached toward the selection of quills and ink pots, selected a fresh piece of parchment, dipping the tip of a white feather quill into blue ink.

My Darling Spence,

How I miss you.
I hope you received my last letter and condolences in regard to your father's passing. I know you told me to remain in Dathoviel, but I ache to think of you going through this alone. Remember when speaking was simple as heading downstairs to our garden bench? We would discuss anything on our hearts and minds. Only you could understand what weighs on me now.

You recognize the pressure I face finding a suitable husband. I always doubted I would find someone to equal my wild ideals. But I realize now, holding the myth of true love on such a high pedestal was a way to protect myself. From disappointment, and from the truth. I do desire to share my body, soul, and heart with a partner for the rest of my life. To receive the same in return. Not just from anyone though, and here lies the problem.

The focus of my desires is unnatural to the expectations of society.

You would know what to say Spence, and would tell me what I must do. You would remind me to be my truest self. Perhaps, I shall return to your side sooner than expected. For now your father is gone, so is his request for my mother and I to leave. Should I uncover the courage to send this letter and it find your hands, know I send it with love and gratitude.

Forever your faithful cousin and friend,
Caroline

Setting the quill aside, she scanned the letter. Should she burn it? Send it? Her fingers began to drum once more on the tabletop. She reached to the far corner of the desk for an envelope instead of the candle, but fate decided for her. With a quick, accidental knock of her arm, the ink pot spilled, seeping into the paper.

She dashed to grab a piece of cloth to stop the spread, but the ink had already absorbed the words she'd written. Disappointed, confused, and concerned this may be a sign she ought to heed, Caroline yanked the curtains closed and found her bed in the dim. For a moment she wished she believed in God. If she did, she might have prayed for guidance.

~

Alaric packed snow onto the remaining embers and checked the position of the sun.

Brantley had yet to return, and he seized the opportunity. Climbing onto Celestial, he turned her in the direction the prince had gone, passing Sebastian who was busy tying equipment onto the sled.

"I fear the snowfall will begin soon. I shall go find the boy before his tracks disappear."

It was an absolute statement with no room for disagreement.

"I'll be right behind you," the anxious knight called after him.

Alaric followed the horse tracks a few miles into the trees before eventually spotting Gus and the tall oak he was tied to. Brantley must have gone ahead on foot. Alaric armed himself with the bow and quiver attached to his saddlebag, following the footprints north. Sebastian would arrive any minute—he must act now.

Keeping to the right of Brantley's tracks, he slid from Celestial's back, quickly secured her to a tree and crouched low, moving silently through the forest.

He knew the deer had moved on, because he'd scared them away last night while the others had slept. Still he stalked, hunting as if the meadow were full. His eyes scanned every inch of the snowy tree line ahead of him, imagining how confused the prince must have been when he discovered no game. Probably why he'd gone ahead on foot, with hopes of sneaking up on the unsuspecting prey.

Just as the king did now.

Alaric glimpsed Brantley's navy cloak as the boy gazed up at the trees, a carefree smile on his face. Snow danced around him in the wind, and Alaric hesitated.

A twig snapped further ahead and they both looked toward the sound. A brave fawn had returned, but she quickly spotted the would-be hunters and turned to dash back in the direction she'd come. Brantley lifted onto his toes to watch.

A skilled archer and hunter, Alaric rarely missed. He was fast, and his arrows even faster. With practiced fingers he loaded an arrow, aimed, and let it fly. It sliced through the air, finding its target with precise ease, sinking deep into flesh.

Flesh. Not hide.

Brantley's body fell to the ground with a sickening thud.

~

Seb clutched Harlow's reigns as she raced through the snow, his heart beating hard and fast along with her gallops. He could only pray the two sets of tracks he followed would last.

Soon, he discovered both Gus and Celestial tied in the trees. Distressed, Gus drug his hooves through the ground, attempting to break free.

Hands shaking, Seb secured his mare to a tree of her own and attempted to approach the furious gelding. He reared up, kicking and Seb backed off, looking around, trying to listen. Aside from Gus, everything else was still in the forest.

Too still.

"Brantley!" Seb shouted, breaking the chilled silence, his breath ghosting into the air. "Where are you?"

"Here!" Alaric called out in return.

His voice came from a few yards ahead and Seb took off running. He entered a small clearing and his heart stopped, unable to comprehend the sight before him.

There was *so much* blood. And somewhere off to the side, Alaric stood stoically, his longbow in hand.

"Dear God, no!" Seb collapsed to his knees next to the prince's body, tugging his cap from his head, paying no attention to how his feather now hung limp or the way the red tainted snow soaked his trousers. "Your Highness! It's alright. It's going to be alright."

The terrified hazel eyes of the young boy pleaded up in haunted silence. Slowly his mouth opened, but no sound came out. One of Alaric's arrows had struck above Brantley's collarbone, silencing him. It was too late to save him. The prince only had moments left.

Seb's throat stung and he fought back tears a moment before letting them fall anyway.

Furious and sick, he turned to the king.

"Take a deep breath, Sebastian," Alaric said, far too calm for the situation.

His false name had never stung so deeply.

"*Christ* Alaric, what have you done? Tell me this was an accident. Tell me you didn't bring the boy out here to..."

He couldn't say it.

Desperate to comfort Brantley, Seb laid his hand on the prince's shoulder, willing him to hold on, knowing it was pointless. Brantley had stopped shaking, his body surrendering to the cold. To death.

"I ensured we didn't lose everything."

Seb shook his head, eyes narrowed on the king. "He is no threat to you! He wants nothing to do with the throne."

"You've been teaching the boy to fight!" Alaric spat. "What did you think would come of it? Only a matter of time before his sister, and *your* training inspired him to take my crown. This is as much your fault."

Seb swallowed, reaching for the prince's hand. A million apologies on his lips, all unworthy of being spoken.

"How do you plan to escape answering for this?"

Alaric's lips curved into a menacing smile. "This is hardly the first time I've faked an accident, Sebastian. It is the first time I have a loyal witness to back up my story, however."

"I won't lie for you."

Alaric stepped over Brantley as if his body were a bothersome log in his path. Seb's instincts screamed to flee, but Alaric was too quick.

The king reached a gloved hand out, gripping the front of Seb's jacket and dragged him to his feet. Helpless, the knight's heart clenched, terror and confusion waging an inner war. He ached to lash out at Alaric, but he knew better. They were far from evenly matched in hand-to-hand combat. He would surely lose.

"Oh, you will lie to the queen, her father, and to anyone else who asks."

"And if I don't?"

The king sneered. "You should know better after all these years. Of course, I'll tell them it was your arrow. You're the one covered in his blood after all..."

Seb's hands clenched into fists. "I knew you were a bastard, Ric. But this is unforgivable."

There was a dull thud behind the two men. They turned toward it, seeing Brantley's once outstretched arm now resting in the crimson snow. Seb shook free of Alaric's grasp and knelt beside the prince once again, his trembling fingers hovering over the boy's chest.

He'd promised to keep him safe.

Devastated, the knight captured the prince's hand between his, feeling the weight of the icy limbs. Though his eyes remained open, there was no denying the truth.

Prince Brantley of Dathoviel, was dead.

~

Amelia stood in the kitchens reviewing Christmas packages Fredrick would deliver to the villagers, a quill tapping against her chin and parchment scroll in hand. Blankets, food, a bit of gold for each family, and handmade dolls for every child. She'd even pulled her and Brantley's schoolbooks for the tavern classroom that would soon be replaced by a proper schoolhouse.

Amelia paused counting, her eyes shining when she spotted Caroline in the doorway.

It felt like weeks had passed since the last time their gazes had met.

"You are out of bed! Are you feeling well?"

Caroline nodded, looking around the busy kitchen. "Perhaps we could talk somewhere quiet for a moment?"

"Of course."

Amelia set aside the quill and parchment next to a giant cake adorned with mint leaves and powdered sugar, following Caroline to the nearest room with a door, which she shut. A large table sat in the middle, surrounded by empty chairs.

"First, I wished to say I needed time to think."

"About?"

Caroline took a long, deep breath. "There is something you must know about me."

Amelia opened her mouth to interrupt, but shouting from outside the door put an immediate stop to the conversation. Shouting did not happen often inside a castle unless a baby was born or war had been declared. The queen rushed to the door, threw it open and looked for the culprit. She spotted Kwan pacing the corridor, calling for her.

She waved him over. "What is it? What happened?"

He grabbed her hands, his composure broken and all decorum gone. He stuttered over the English words and slipped into his own language, knowing she would understand him all the same.

"My Queen. You mu—must come now. It's your brother."

It hurt to breathe, like her lungs had forgotten their purpose. With Caroline on her heels, Amelia sprinted out of the kitchen and down the hall. As she approached the entrance, she saw Gus standing outside, head hanging low. His saddle was empty.

"Brantley!" she cried, her slippers becoming drenched as she dashed into the snow, slipping on the ice. Where was he? Was he hurt?

There was no answer.

Alaric stood far back, something akin to sorrow plastered on his face. Then Seb stepped into view, a body wrapped in blankets in his arms. The scent of blood was thick in the icy air. All eyes focused on the knight, and what he carried. Olive, who must have heard the shouting, appeared in the doorway.

"What's happenin'?" she demanded, falling silent when her eyes settled on the scene. She reached for Kwan and he pulled her close.

Amelia lifted the blankets, revealing the prince's stony face.

Seb's lip trembled. "My Queen—I am so, so sorry."

Her eyes turned hard and she slapped him, a sob violently ripping from her throat. Unable to speak or scream, Amelia stumbled back, head shaking in horror. Caroline reached for her, but not quickly enough. Knees buckling, Amelia collapsed to the icy ground, her heart shattered.

9

December 25th, 1456

THE CHURCH BELLS RANG hollow throughout the kingdom as everyone prepared for a funeral instead of a feast. Christmas had become a grim day in Dathoviel and would remain so for many years to come.

Tearfully, Olive struggled to pin rosemary into Amelia's hair.

"Are you sure you don't want the veil?" she whispered.

The moment Brantley's body entered the castle, so had a need for hush.

"Yes," Amelia said, her throat stinging. "I see no reason to hide. We are all mourning."

A timid knock interrupted them, and the queen gingerly nodded to let whoever it was in. Marcel stood on the other side, dressed head to toe in black. The circles under his eyes were proof he had slept poorly.

"Sad day," he said, breath escaping with a shudder.

With puffy tear-stained cheeks, the former king opened his palm and presented Amelia with the mourning ring. The silver band was stamped with a cross on the outside and Brantley's name within. Amelia clutched it protectively against her chest as though it were a rare and precious stone.

Marcel could not muster the strength to speak again. He nodded, squeezed her shoulder and left the room, his echoing sob trailing after him. As Olive retrieved their cloaks, warmers, and scarves, Amelia slid her brother's ring onto her finger. It rested above the one she'd been given following her mother's death. Numb, her eyes remained focused on the two bands until Olive took her hand, gently guiding her arm into the sleeve.

When they met Caroline in the entrance hall less than an hour later, she was comforting Marcel with an awkward hug while he wept against her shoulder. Alaric stood at the open door, eyes downcast, arm outstretched. Amelia refused to acknowledge him and moved to the casket. As requested, the lid was sealed, but she only needed to close her eyes to recall how Brantley had looked drained of life. The image would be etched into her memory forever.

Grim, solemn music drifted back from the front of the line. Placing her hand over the cross carved into the wood, she signaled to the riders. With somber nods, they alerted the horses hitched to the cart, and the procession began down the hill toward the village.

In Dathoviel, when someone in the royal house died, the family would parade from the castle to the church for the final memorial service and burial. Usually, the villagers would look on from their doorways, blow kisses and send healing wishes.

Today every member of the kingdom mourned the beloved prince. Dressed in the warmest clothing they possessed, the villagers left their homes to gather behind the procession. William, Hannah, and the boys joined first. Brianna, who had scurried ahead, clasped Amelia's gloved hand in her own. She could not speak, but the gesture warmed her heart.

One by one, the village banded together, and with each new family that joined, Alaric was pushed farther and farther away until he stood at the end of the procession. Even Seb left him behind.

As they reached the church, Caroline and Olive gathered around the queen. Few words were exchanged as the mourners congregated inside. They watched as heavy-eyed pallbearers carried the casket from the cart to the platform where it would sit before being taken to the family tomb. There, Brantley would rest alongside their mother.

Amelia did not bother restraining a single, blinding tear as the ceremony commenced. Clasping Caroline's hand tightly, she let her head drop to Olive's quivering shoulder. The ache in her chest weighed her to the pew, drowning out the priest and turning the surrounding sobs into a distant hum. Not even Caroline's voice could break through. She longed for the chill, dark solace of her tower where she could wail and break things. Where she could privately mourn without all these sympathetic eyes focused on her.

By the time Olive managed to shake Amelia from her trance, the church had emptied and Brantley's body had been removed.

December 29, 1456

The castle remained in a cold, quiet state of grief for days.

Alaric has started taking his meals in his tower when the dining hall began to feel unwelcoming. But it wasn't until Leah refused to see him, that he was forced to consider he may have gone too far by killing Brantley. Outwardly he appeared unaffected, but internally his conscience begged to repent. Instead, he channeled his guilt into resentment, suppressing the humanity clawing at him from within.

As he strove to move on from the whole thing, nightmare hauntings of Davidson returned, no longer banished to a corner of his mind.

The chill of death around a small body in a forest and young life fading from innocent eyes haunted him. Forever reminding him of a flickering candle submitting to the snuffer. The visions began torturing his waking hours as well. Then one night the dream changed. Davidson was no longer a lifeless body lying on the ground. He was a small boy with flushed cheeks and crystal blue eyes running through the woods.

"Chase me, Ric!" he called, laughing.

Alaric followed into the thick forest. Searching. Listening. He glimpsed Brantley. No, wait. That wasn't right. . . His head whipped around, heart pounding. He searched desperately for one. For both.

Teeth grinding, he raced forward, the soft earth giving way under his boots, threatening to swallow him up. The trees closed in, their branches reaching for him like claws.

Then silence.

Alaric froze, spotting his brother leaning against an oak tree. The oak tree.

"Davidson? Are you alright?"

Davidson scoffed, sounding strange—more mature. "How old would I be now?"

Guilt tugged at Alaric's heart, his hands shaking.

He would have been the same age as Brantley—or rather the age Brantley had been.

"I'm sorry I couldn't save you."

The child laughed, jabbing at the tree above. "Save me? What lies do you tell yourself about that day?"

"I tried to stop you, but you wouldn't listen, so I ran for Father."

"Stop lying!" the boy shouted.

He was Brantley again. Then he wasn't.

"Remember, Ric. Remember what really happened. What you did to me."

"To both of us." Brantley's voice was unmistakable.

Alaric refused to look up, chest compressing his lungs. His head pounded as memories fought against the mental door he used to lock away the terrible things he did.

He couldn't open it. He wouldn't.

"I had to ensure they didn't forget about me!" he shrieked, hands tearing at his scalp. "With father, I could never compete with Spencer. But you changed the dynamic of our family, our kingdom. I deserve to be remembered!"

"And so, you shall," Davidson sneered.

He lunged forward. Only he wasn't alone.

"As the king who kills brothers," spat Brantley, his tunic drenched in blood, hands reaching for Alaric's throat as Davidson tackled his legs and sent him to the ground.

Alaric awoke, violently kicking the tangled sheets from around his legs, clawing at his neck. The ghosts had not returned with him.

Panting, he rubbed his hands over his face before reaching across the mattress for Leah. But he was alone.

January 20th, 1457

New Year's Day came and went without Amelia realizing or caring. There was no talk of the throne or love, or anything at all.

Her brother was gone, and she was foolish to believe she could take on Alaric and win. She had failed all of them. The pity and disappointment were clear in Olive and Caroline's eyes whenever they sat with her, explaining the villagers understood her absence. But she hardly heard their voices or tasted the food they brought.

Even the Saint Valentine's festival failed to spark her attention.

The handmaiden continued visiting the village, overseeing the build of the school. Whenever she left

Amelia's side, Caroline would swiftly appear in her place, often reading aloud or humming a tune meant to be comforting. They strove to ensure she was rarely alone with her thoughts, which proved both annoying and a blessing, as Amelia could hardly stand her own company. Especially in those brief, solitary moments when the tears could not be stifled any longer.

January 29th, 1457

Racing up the steps, clutching her pale green skirts, Caroline found Olive outside Amelia's door, head in her hands, back pressed against the wall.

"I'm sorry I'm late."

The handmaiden looked up, eyes tired and heart heavy. "No worry. She's sleepin'."

"Any improvement?"

It was the same question they asked without fail whenever they met in the hall. It never got easier to hear the unchanging answer. Still, they asked, hopeful for any sign Amelia would return to them soon.

"Not today."

The now familiar ache behind Caroline's breastbone tugged as Olive slipped past.

Hopeful to avoid waking the queen, Caroline turned the handle quietly and tiptoed into the room. A precious part of healing the heart was sleep, and it could not be interrupted. Or so Aunt Orla had always said.

Sleep to heal your heart, water for your body, nature for the mind, time for spirit, and passion for your soul.

Quietly, Caroline crossed the lounge to the untouched tray Regina had delivered hours ago. Taking a small plate, she arranged half a sandwich and a trio of cookies before pouring Amelia a chalice of water. She carried both into the bedroom where the queen lay curled in the center of her mattress, a cream knit blanket draped across her legs.

Setting the food and drink on the nightstand, Caroline reached out, gingerly bringing the edge of the blanket over Amelia's shoulder. She couldn't help staring, nor could she help sweeping away the dark hair from her beautiful face. A face she hadn't seen smile in too many weeks.

Time for spirit. Yes, Amelia simply needed more time to grieve.

Caroline's gaze drifted to the window where the stable roof peeked over the edge. She'd speak with Olive about slowly introducing fresh air to Amelia's routine after this cold snap. If they planted the idea slowly and gently, perhaps the queen's dazzling smile would return sooner.

Grief was a tricky beast, but Caroline could be tricky too. Anything to help the light return to Amelia's eyes.

~

"Hannah, this bread is enchanting," Olive moaned.

Impulsively, she took another slice from the platter between her and William.

At her side, Kwan chuckled behind his hand, eyes glittering. His elbow rested on the table next to his empty soup bowl. Seeing this, Hannah refilled it, nudging him to eat more. She patted the heads of each of her older children as she passed. They were seated on the floor together playing a game. The baby was in his cradle, sound asleep.

"Thank you. It's William's grandmother's recipe."

William nodded proudly. "She was a hell of a baker. Just like you."

The domestic compliment did not go unappreciated. Hannah took pride in her home and the food she put on the table. Man and wife leaned in to kiss, and after a few moments Kwan cleared his throat. They pulled apart blushing.

"If you'd like, we can take the kids and let you two be alone. . ." He smirked.

"Oh, nonsense." Hannah waved her hand dismissively. "You already watched them last week. Between wrestling with the boys and Brianna shadowing you, you're no doubt growing tired of them."

He scoffed lovingly. "I'm quite used to little ones. My sister had a brood of her own. In fact, I quite miss it."

Olive gazed over from her own bowl, spoon halfway to her mouth. This was the first true mention of his past she'd heard. He typically evaded questions or mentions of his life before Dathoviel.

Not that she terribly minded his distraction methods.

William looked equally stunned, though he managed to cover it with his coffee cup. "So, Uncle Kwan, is it?"

The two men chuckled. Meanwhile, Olive and Hannah shared a look conveying mutual surprise.

"Are you interested in having children one day?" Hannah asked, at neither Olive or Kwan in particular, leaving space open for both to answer.

He dropped his gaze to the table once more, picking at the wooden edge with his thumbnail.

Olive blushed, needing to fill the silence. "I'm not sure, honestly. I hadn't considered it would ever be an option."

Kwan shifted in his seat.

William's spoon scraped the rim of his bowl.

"How is Amelia doing?" he asked, changing the subject like the true hero he was.

Olive shrugged sadly. "Sometimes I swear she's improving. She sits up, eats, even looks out the window. Then other days I go into her room and the covers are pulled over her head, her dinner still untouched from the night before."

Hannah nodded. "Finding happiness is a struggle during winter, even under ideal circumstances. Perhaps with the spring she will rise."

"I hope so." Olive reached for her mug, but didn't lift it to her lips.

Under the table Kwan's hand found her thigh and he squeezed gently. Her gaze met his, finding comfort and a warm smile. She leaned close, pressing her cheek to his shoulder.

So, he didn't want kids? Or he did? Was it too soon for them to discuss such things? Or was it better to know now, before their relationship became even more serious? She clearly already loved him. Not that she'd said it.

Then again, neither had he...

"Well." William stood, his chair legs scraping on the wooden floor. "I think it's time for dessert."

"Oh, yes!" Hannah clapped as he went to the counter to retrieve a dish covered with a square of fabric. "Maria asked me if I would make her cake for the wedding, so I tried a new recipe. Let me know what you think before I let the bride taste it?"

Olive straightened in her chair, suddenly quite distracted from thoughts of pitter-pattering feet and tiny faces with Kwan's eyes.

"You don't have to ask me twice."

William set the sweetest cake in the middle of the table, a thin drizzle of icing across the top in a simple, yet elegant design. Olive could already smell the lemon zest and her mouth watered. Kwan reached for the bread knife, making quick work of slicing four portions of cake. Eager hands reached forward, taking their serving. Soon the room was full of pleased groans and nodding heads.

"Wow," the barman said, swallowing. "I'm sorry Hannah, I can't possibly think of anything else to say."

She beamed. "I'll take speechless as a fine compliment."

Olive's eyes were closed, savoring the sweet tang of the second to last bite. "Maria will love it."

Licking his fingers, William smirked at his wife. "Has anyone told Julian yet? About the wedding?"

Olive shook her head, cringing slightly. "The last time we spoke, he didn't seem privy to the information."

William nodded. "Someone's going to have to tell him. I have a feeling Maria won't."

"And we all know why," Kwan said, leaning over and stealing the final bite from Olive's fork, ignoring her gaping mouth and subsequent death glare. "He's going to hate Francis."

The ladies nodded. Francis was quite attractive, but that was all he had going for him.

"Do fathers ever like their son-in-law's though?" Olive asked, eyeing the cake.

Hannah noticed and slid the plate closer to her.

"My father accepted William."

He laughed "Eventually."

"My hopes aren't high for Julian *ever* accepting Francis." Kwan leaned back in the chair, arms crossed. The tan vest he wore pulled tight across his chest.

"Well, I'm not telling him," Olive finally said, brushing her crumb covered fingers against her skirt.

"He'll find out eventually." Hannah waved her hand. "Oh, Olive, Maria was wondering if you'd help her with her gown."

Olive grinned and lifted her mug. "Anything for the bride."

The still air of the empty pub filled with Olive's slow exhale, as her hands submerged into the rapidly cooling dishwater Kwan had abandoned. He'd invited her upstairs to join his bath, but she'd elected to finish cleaning the glasses. The faster they got this done, the sooner she could rest.

With the piercing tension in her shoulders fading and her eyes fluttering closed of their own accord, she wasn't sure how much longer she could remain standing.

LET IT REIGN

She'd promised to help tidy the bar in preparation for an inevitably busy evening, but she was just *so* tired.

She must learn to stop volunteering herself for everything and anything. To say no more often.

She loved Amelia with her whole heart; however, the additional care on top of her regular duties and the constant travel between the castle and the village was wearing on her. Mentally, emotionally and physically.

And perhaps she had somehow fallen asleep standing up behind the bar, because before she knew it, the stairs to her left were creaking and Kwan was making his way to the main floor. Perhaps she would leave this to him after all and sneak upstairs for a brief nap?

She turned to look, her sluggish mind working to piece the words of her request together. But at the sight of him, all thoughts halted. His hair was damp and ruffled from his bath, and the water droplets that remained on his bare chest were trailing down his abdomen in a quite delicious and distracting way.

She allowed her eyes to drag over the permanent black ink residing over his left pectoral and across his shoulder.

If she was honest, she was still as mesmerized by it now as the first time she had seen it.

He moved toward her across the pub floor, winding through the tables one by one and taking down chairs as he went. Still in the bucket, her hands seemed to come back to life as they watched one another. She gripped the rag and reached for the first dingy mug from the stack next to her.

She traced the raven's wings which expanded from his left nipple, over and down to his bicep. In her mind she circled the curves of the full moon on his shoulder, various parts of her body flooding with desire. Even as her feet and lower back begged for rest.

He'd only set half the chairs before slinking behind her and pressing his damp front to her back. His arms wound around her waist, pulling her in, encouraging her to lean on him. Rely on him.

"I can see the exhaustion in your eyes," he whispered, pressing a kiss atop her head. "I can also see the desire. Tell me, to which am I to respond?"

Her hands went still in the water once more, but her grip on the glass and rag were tight.

"One at a time, if you please."

He hummed affirmatively in her ear, hands drifting to cup her elbows a moment before running up to her shoulders, massaging the knots away.

"A good man would pull you away from this bucket, carry you upstairs to bed, and watch over you 'till you fall asleep."

She almost whimpered when his hands slid down her arms once more, but they caressed lower, past her forearms, into the water.

"And what kind of man are you?" she teased, voice quivering.

His touch was familiar now and comforting. She allowed her spine to melt against his warm chest, her head falling back to the curve of his shoulder, her forehead resting against his throat.

He swallowed, somehow stepping closer.

"The kind who knows it's wise to quench your desire completely, so when you rest, it's peacefully and fully satisfied."

His long fingers stroked slow patterns across the backs of her hands and knuckles—teasing the insides of her wrists. Then her body was tingling, the soreness and weariness sliding temporarily behind a wall of arousal.

The glass sank to the bottom of the bucket with a dull clank as she released it and the rag, tilting her face up to leave slow, lazy kisses along his jaw. He pressed his thumb into one pressure point on her hand, then the next, and she released a low moan, the knots in her shoulders forgotten.

Instead, the lower ones had her attention. Had her thighs rubbing together, arching her spine, and pressing her arse back.

His touch should be outlawed. It wasn't safe for him to be going around freely in this world with these hands.

"So you're not a good man, then?" she taunted breathlessly.

She must have pressed against him again because he let out a low groan, shifting to nip at her right earlobe.

Then his boots were scuffing against the floor and he was turning her around to face him, his wet hands gripping her waist, his thumbs pressing just above her hipbones. And something had happened to her knees, so she clung to his shoulders, trying to pull him down, her mouth searching as the water from her sleeves dripped down his back.

"Not at the moment," he growled.

There was no other way to describe his tone. Or if there was, she couldn't think of it. She couldn't think much of anything as his tongue slid between her teeth.

They kissed for less than a minute, hands turning desperate, lips turning violent.

"Take me upstairs?"

They practically raced, feet pounding on the creaky steps, then skidding to a halt on the brightly lit landing. She reached for his trousers, hooking her fingers in the waistband, and tugged, narrowly avoiding falling into his tub.

He tripped forward into her, his laugh gusting over her face as they tumbled back onto his bed.

He dragged her skirts up, bunching them around her hips, rolling their bodies side to side slightly to release them from beneath her. When he stilled over her, she felt his length. Every inch of it. And she shuddered, unable to stop herself from lifting her hips and rolling against him. There was friction and pressure, but it wasn't enough.

Her fingertips found the edges of his damp hair, combing it back from where it had fallen into his face. It was getting a little long, but she liked it. She liked everything about him.

"I need you."

"You'll have me," he promised, sitting back on his heels for a moment to pop open his trousers.

Then he was back, leaning over her, their bodies pressed dangerously close. His lips moved from her mouth, across her chin, and down the length of her throat to her collarbone. Wrapping her legs around him, she whimpered from how tightly their bodies were pressed together, how easily he slipped inside her.

She sighed.

He groaned.

He hooked his hand behind her knee, pulling her leg up, lifting her hips to meet his steady thrusts.

"You feel so fuckin' good," she murmured, burying her face in his neck and littering his skin with kisses.

"*You* feel so fucking good."

She saw the love in his eyes when he pulled back, capturing her gaze. Could he feel hers in the way she held him close?

One day they would say it, but for now...

"Tell me I'm yours," she whispered.

His eyes flickered over her face almost nervously, but his pace didn't slow. In fact, his thrusts increased, and he shifted his weight to one arm so he could dip a hand between them, finding her clit.

"You're mine."

She arched into his touch, overwhelmed by the relentless sensations coming from everywhere.

"And you're mine?"

She said it almost like a dare, but he only chuckled, leaning in close, nipping at her ear.

"I'm yours."

She clung to him as the rising pressure in her core sprang free. She was white hot bliss erupting beneath him. Around him. He kissed her, swallowing cries, curses, and moans, capturing everything about her essence in this moment.

His thrusts stuttered after a few moments, and when his trembling faded, he broke the kiss, panting heavily against her neck. He was covered in sweat and would surely need another bath before the pub opened this evening.

She protested when he slipped out of her and he quieted her by pulling her close, slipping her leg over his hips, and tucking his arm beneath her head.

She wanted to ask what he thought about kids and their future together...but her eyes were heavy and her mind foggy.

"Sleep, Olive," he said, pressing a kiss to her forehead.

And she did.

~

Amelia remained still on her mattress, eyes closed. There was the weight of a blanket over her and drool dried at the corner of her mouth.

Who was in the room with her this time? Olive perhaps? No, Olive had been holding her hand when she fell asleep, and it was still daylight out. She was not alone, for there was the sound of pages turning and steady, even breaths coming from the far side of the room.

Her heart ached for so, so many reasons, and she clamped down on each of them. One. By. One. Eyes shut tightly, she willed the tears not to fall. If there were even any left at this point.

How many days had she spent crying in this bed?

Then the book shut with a hollow clack, and her companion stood. Their slippered feet scuffed lightly across the floor as they approached. Then there was a dip in the mattress by her ankles from where they sat, and the faint scent of lilacs helped her easily identify Caroline.

"You're awake," she whispered.

"Yes."

"Are you hungry?"

"No..."

Caroline sighed. "Can you look at me, please?"

Amelia held her breath, forcing the muscles in her face to relax. She started at her chin, working to her eyelids. She imagined the creases in her skin softening, her lids slowly fluttering open. And then finally, her body followed her mind's command, and she was peering at Caroline.

She had never seen the beautiful blonde so sad. No, sad was the wrong word. *Torn*. As if she wanted to do something, but was unsure how to ask permission.

Amelia attempted to smile meekly, but it surely appeared as a grimace of sorts. "I am sorry. I know I should be feeling better by now."

"Not at all." Caroline shook her head. "You need time to process, and I understand that. I respect it. But..."

"But?"

The skin around Amelia's ears prickled with heat and embarrassment.

"I'd like to try something today. If you're open to it."

"Wh—what did you have in mind?"

Gracefully, Caroline folded her hands in her lap, sitting tall. She kept her face perfectly straight as she said, "I want you to scream."

Amelia balked. "Excuse me?"

"I know it sounds strange, but I've been watching you for a while now, and I think it's worth a try. It might help you release some of the tension you have built inside."

"Screaming?" Amelia heard the disbelief in her own voice. "You want me to scream? At what? At who?"

"At me, if you'd like. Or into one of your pillows. I could ask Regina to bring up some water and prepare you a bath."

"You want me to scream into my bathwater?"

Caroline nodded. "If you'd like."

"This is mad." Amelia shook her head. "You have gone mad."

"Indeed, I have." Caroline turned to face her more, her leg coming up on the bed, bent at the knee. "I've gone entirely mad sitting here watching you suffer. Seeing your pain. I know I can't fix it, but I thought maybe we could try something new today. If it doesn't work, no harm done, but if it does, if it helps even a little, then maybe I'll be one step closer to having you back."

Amelia's gaze flicked between Caroline's bright blue eyes. Perhaps there was some truth to all this. There was no denying the heaviness in her chest and the tightness in her lungs. The way her lips were taut from lack of use.

"Alright," she said, sitting up. "Tell me what to do."

Caroline beamed and scooted further onto the mattress. She positioned herself against the footboard as Amelia shuffled her skirts around, settling against the pillows. A few moments later, they were sitting cross-legged, facing one another on opposite sides of the bed. Caroline's hands were flat on her knees, where Amelia's flopped uselessly in her lap.

"I suppose it's best to start with your eyes closed."

Amelia followed her instruction immediately, but after a moment she popped one eye open, staring at her. "Where exactly did this idea come from?"

Caroline only smiled. "Let's just say my aunt was a bit... eccentric. She believed a lot of strange things, had a lot of curious books, and kept very detailed journals of her various... *experiments*."

"Experiments?"

"Today let's focus on the screaming."

Now both of Amelia's eyes were open. "So she screamed like this?"

"Yes. When you're married to a man like Viktor—and *you* actually are, the need to scream comes often. However, she often told me everyone could benefit from it, especially women. Men can find release in it as well, but they aren't silenced in the ways we are. They have other ways of expressing themselves."

Amelia considered that for a moment. Her father had his alcohol. Brantley had—well, he once had nature. Alaric hunted and Fredrick had those curious sunrise swims. Even William got to hit things with a hammer every day, which she could only assume was therapeutic in its own right. Meanwhile, she and most of the women she knew were expected to sit quietly, speaking only when spoken to, and even then, usually ignored.

Most of her life she had been ignored. Silenced. Interrupted and talked over. It was not proper for her to show any level of frustration or anger, or grief aside from slow, silent tears. Only crying was socially acceptable, and even then, it was hardly tolerated for long. Once tears were deemed unworthy or annoying, they were quickly categorized as hysterical or weak.

She pressed her eyes closed once more and took a long, steadying breath, her lips parting and shaking as she inhaled.

"Alright. I am ready," she said after a few moments.

"Would you like to scream alone first? Or would you feel more comfortable if I screamed with you?"

Amelia gnawed on her top lip, considering. "Together sounds best."

"Very well."

Her eyes were still closed, but she felt Caroline moving closer to her. When their legs touched she inhaled sharply. If Caroline noticed, she said nothing. Instead, she reached for the queen's clenched hands and opened them, palm up. Then she lay them gently on the inside of her knees.

"I feel strange."

"I know. It will get easier," Caroline promised. "I'm going to count slowly, and your job is to just breathe. When I get to five, I want you to reach deep into your gut and draw up everything you've been hiding away. Guilt, rage, grief, fear. Not only for Brantley," she stuttered over his name. "About anything weighing you down. You won't get everything out today, but a step in the right direction is still a worthy start."

Amelia nodded. "I will try my best."

Caroline grazed her thumbs over Amelia's palms softly, perhaps absentmindedly? She cleared her throat then and pulled back, and it took all the queen's self-control to refocus on her breath and not open her eyes.

"Oh," Caroline said gently, almost a whisper. "You should know, crying is perfectly normal."

"More crying? I thought this was supposed to help."

"Often when the body releases tension like this, well. . . I don't understand everything about the practice. I just know I often cry, and my aunt almost always did."

"Very well. I am prepared to cry."

Caroline cleared her throat again. "One. . ." Amelia inhaled deeply. "Two. . ." And exhale. "Three. . ." Inhale. "Four. . ." Exhale. ". . .five."

Amelia inhaled the deepest breath she could, imagining Brantley's cold, dead face. Remembering every disgusted and disappointed shake of her father's head. The pitying looks she had received at her mother's funeral. Alaric's smirk and his voice, and the way he snatched the coins from her the day she helped William.

She already wanted to cry.

Caroline must have been holding her breath, waiting, because she squeezed Amelia's wrists, coaxing her on. Their hands were clasped again. Amelia squeezed back, her fingers wrapping around Caroline's forearm. And then they both let out blood-curdling screams, the sounds reverberating through the entire room. Her face was surely bright red and her throat stung, but she kept screaming until every last ounce of air had left her body.

She gasped, gripping Caroline tightly.

"Again?" she choked out.

"Again."

This time Caroline counted to five quickly, but that was okay. Amelia was ready. She had a better idea of what she was doing this time.

Her second scream was even louder, and she felt Caroline flinch under her firm grip, but neither pulled away or opened their eyes. They just held on tighter.

Instead of gasping this time, she coughed. A fit of coughs, really. They shook her chest and shoulders, and she doubled over for a few minutes, her head light and dizzy. Then the tears came, pouring down her cheeks faster and harder than any tears she had cried before. They were big and hot and soaked her sleeves. She whimpered, releasing Caroline then and drawing her knees against her aching chest to hug herself tightly. She wanted to crawl into a dark hole and never return. Her spine protested the next wave of despair, threatening to snap, but there was no stopping it.

"It hurts," she sobbed.

"I know." Caroline moved beside her, wrapping her arms around Amelia's shoulders. "It's okay that it hurts. You're safe with me. Let it go, Amelia."

And she did. She cried and cried until she could not breathe or think or speak. And then she cried some more.

Eventually, her body stilled and she could only sniffle quietly. Tentatively, Caroline released the hold she had around her, but she returned a moment later, a glass of water in her hand. She forced Amelia to take it, and since her throat was on fire, the queen accepted, gulping the liquid gratefully.

With her forehead resting on her knees, she turned to look left, her eyes meeting Caroline's. She reached over with her free hand, capturing Caroline's fingers in her own and without thinking, brought them to her lips. She pressed a quick kiss to them in thanks, clutching tight, tethering herself to something solid other than grief and despair.

Caroline remained silent, returning the pressure and nodding proudly, the smallest of smiles showing.

. 10 .

March 27th, 1457

AS THE SNOW MELT for the final time and the earth began to wake, Amelia sensed an awakening of her own.

She had yet to take the time to understand exactly what changes were happening within, but the pain eventually dulled into a quiet, familiar ache and she became accustomed to the emptiness of the castle.

The birth of a foal, and Olive's insisting she take in at least an hour of fresh air, dragged Amelia from her tower and into the stables.

Amelia went to Greta immediately, nuzzling her face against the soft brown hair. Tears trickled down her cheeks.

"I am sorry I was away so long." A soft neigh from behind caught her attention and she turned to see Gus, her heart breaking. "Oh, poor boy, you must be so confused."

She brushed away her tears, but more appeared in their place.

"I tried to explain what happened," a familiar voice said.

Amelia jumped. Caroline stood in the doorway, smiling. "You did?"

Caroline went over to him, patting his nose. He seemed familiar with her and welcomed the touch. "I figured they would be lonely without the love and attention they're used to. And someone needed to keep Nigel on his toes."

Amelia took Caroline's hands and wrapped her in a hug.

"Thank you. You cannot know what this means to me."

Caroline was quiet as they embraced, her breath silent like she was holding it. When they pulled apart, she inhaled a deep breath, her eyes cast nervously to the floor. As if she were ashamed, though Amelia couldn't imagine why.

"Sadly, I couldn't take them out, but Nigel assures me they are well exercised."

"I shall have to thank him."

Caroline's gaze remained uneasy when she looked up. "Would you still be willing to show me?"

Amelia's eyes glowed for the first time in months. "How to ride?"

She glanced from Gus to Greta, hoping Caroline would understand she was not ready for anyone else to ride him. She could not very well take his sister and leave him behind though. Greta probably would not like having someone else ride her, but it was better than not going at all.

"It can wait for another day if you aren't ready," Caroline suggested gently.

"We should go." Amelia headed to the rack of saddles. "I'll take Gus though."

Caroline beamed. "Certainly."

~

Leah nestled against Alaric's bare chest, rejoicing in the feel of his hands and the warm water lapping at her ribs.

Tilting her head back, she searched out a kiss as he gripped her hips, sliding her closer to him in the tub. She released a soft moan, her toes curling as he spread her thighs open.

Her back arched in response when his right hand skimmed lower, fingers slipping inside her. Then his left hand came up, cradling her throat, keeping her head on his shoulder. Meanwhile, his tongue and teeth attacked her earlobe.

How lovely it felt to be back in his arms.

The last few weeks his moods had slowly improved, and she once again felt safe around him. Of course, he would be leaving for Winvoltor any day now and though she craved to accompany him, he'd made clear his wishes of keeping her away from King Bartholomew. She'd wanted to ask why he was doing business with the northern king if he was such a terrible man, but she knew better than to ask.

"Will you miss me when I'm gone?"

His tone was gruff as his right hand pulled away, his finger leaving her. As if she needed reminding how it felt to be without him.

She turned and straddled him, ignoring the water splashing to the wooden floor beneath the tub.

"I'll be miserable without you," she declared, straightening the tangled silver chain around his neck.

He brought her close, hands clasped possessively on either side of her face.

"I'll need you to keep an eye on Sebastian while I'm away."

This surprised her. "You aren't taking him to Winvoltor?"

"No." He shook his head. "Ever since Brantley's accident he's been acting strange. I will be taking a significant group of guards for protection, but I fear he won't be at his best. It's better for everyone if he remains here."

"I'll keep him company," Leah promised, pressing her chest to his. Just one roll of her hips and he would be inside her, but she needed reassurance first.

"And when you return, you will name me queen?"

Alaric inhaled deeply, patiently. "This trip is incredibly important, as you know. King Bart is extremely wealthy, and his gold mines will surely make us rich. *If* he accepts my offer."

Leah didn't appreciate his tone, but played along for the moment. She would do whatever she had to. It was the only way she knew how to live.

"What will you offer him?"

"The men in the village," said Alaric. "I will guarantee King Bart enough workers for a new mine. Any gold they uncover, he will retain a cut of. The rest will come to us."

Leah sat back on his thighs, shaking her head. "You're talking about slaves, Ric. Amelia will never allow it."

He tugged her close, tongue painting a line between her breasts, fingers caressing her lower back and hips. Her body began to melt and she cursed it, but it was his words that had her fully surrendering.

"By the time she learns of the plan, it will be too late. And *then*, my darling, you will be crowned. Even if it means Amelia is in the first wagon to Winvoltor herself."

She opened her mouth to speak, but he gripped her waist and sheathed himself inside her. Cursing, she circled her hips, taking him in deeper and imagining if being queen would feel this satisfying.

~

As they rode peacefully through the countryside, Caroline struggled to focus her gaze on anything other than the woman next to her. Not even the glorious rolling hills and budding flora were as enticing as the way the wind danced through her long, dark hair, turning it more untamed than she'd ever seen it. Caroline's fingers twitched, craving to reach out, so she tightened her grip on the reins. It would do no good to discuss serious matters such as love or lust today and risk scaring Amelia right back into her tower.

"I believe the dress is holding me back," Caroline admitted when they stopped near a rushing river for the horses to drink.

Thin chunks of ice floated south; a reminder of just how cold winter had been. Still in Gus's saddle, Amelia gestured at her own skirts with distaste.

"Now you understand why I prefer to wear men's clothes for riding."

"I do."

"Perhaps Olive can tailor you something if you wish to continue riding," the queen suggested, leaning over to stroke Greta.

Then she stretched, spine arching, arms long as she reached to the sky. Caroline bit her tongue, feeling warm and forced herself to focus on Greta's mane rather than the long line of the queen's neck as she tilted her head side to side. The horses lifted their heads, bumped noses, and once again began trotting away before Caroline realized Amelia's stretch had been out of necessity. Beneath her heart pounding in her ear, her own muscles were begging for rest.

"Could we stop soon? I'm growing fairly sore."

Amelia thoughtfully scanned the surrounding area, shading her eyes from the high afternoon sun.

"If you can hold on a little while longer, there is a striking view of the mountains just over that ridge. We could have lunch there."

"I can make it," she agreed, her heart hammering upon seeing Amelia's smile.

~

Amidst the rhythmic hammering and squeaky wheelbarrows, Olive relished the warm breeze ruffling her skirts. It was wonderful being outside without boots and blankets wrapped around her. Her eyes settled on Kwan, leaping like a bird from branch to branch as he climbed through the rafters of what would soon become the schoolhouse, gathering measurements on a parchment scrap William had requested. Apparently, he could move splendidly both in, and out of the bedroom.

He tossed her a grin over his shoulder before assessing a way to get down. She watched anxiously as he teetered off the edge of a beam and executed a series of graceful leaps before landing on the opposite side of the structure. Then he wrapped around a post and slid, his feet thudding to the muddy ground.

From behind her, William let out a low whistle.

"Impressive, mate! Where'd you learn those moves?"

Shrugging, Kwan avoided four curious eyes. "Same way anyone learns, I suppose. Practice."

Yet another secret he didn't wish to divulge.

William changed the subject. "I believe we'll be able to begin the walls next week. Long as the wind stays calm."

Olive gazed at the roof, imagining how it would look completed. "I can't believe how well this is goin'."

Kwan gestured to the surrounding villagers. "Community is a powerful force."

"That it is." William clapped the barman on the shoulder. "I'll see you both later?"

"Indeed. Bring Hannah by for a drink this evening if you wish. On the house."

The sun had already begun turning the carpenter's cheeks pink, yet his blush was evident.

"Last time Hannah and I indulged, we received a *surprise* nine months later. The woman can't keep her hands off me."

"Yes," Olive chuckled. "You must be utterly helpless against a woman half your size."

The men exchanged a knowing look before William headed off to help a villager kneeling next to her tipped wheelbarrow. Meanwhile, Kwan captured Olive in his arms, hugging her back against his chest.

"When must you return to the castle?" he asked, nuzzling against her hair.

"I won't be needed again for a few hours."

He smirked, his tongue flicking against the curve of her neck. She shuddered, her toes curling.

"And how would you wish to spend those hours?"

"You could tell me how you learned to use your body in such tempting and curious ways."

He stiffened behind her.

"Olive," he warned.

"Yes?"

She tried to sound teasing, but this game was growing tired for the both of them. He sighed, his head falling against her shoulder, but at least he kept his arms around her waist.

"Please understand, I'm not maliciously keeping secrets from you. But there are certain stories I'd rather stayed in the past."

She refused to pout, so she kept her eyes on his hands, his fingers laced with hers, gripping tightly. "But why?"

"Knowing them may lead to you hating me, and I can't risk that."

She turned to face him, wrapping her arms around his torso. "Kwan, don't you realize how I feel about you?"

There, she'd finally said it. Kind of.

"I know." He nodded. "I feel the same way about you."

"And don't you desire to know every part of me? Because I ache to know you. Body, mind, and soul. Past, present—and God willin'—your future."

At first, he looked speechless, so he pressed his lips to hers, savoring the moment, or buying himself time. Either way, she had no choice but to relax into his hypnotizing kiss.

Eventually, he pulled back, eyes dark and chest heaving.

"You truly wish to know everything?"

She nodded, caressing the length of his scar, starting at the thinnest point beneath his eyebrow. "Everythin', like how you got this, and all your other scars. Why you chose to ink a raven onto your body and about your childhood. I want to know all the stories, because our stories make us who we are."

"If I tell you the truth, you must promise not to tell a soul. Including the queen."

"You have my word," she promised, smoothing the dark hair she'd ruffled during their kiss.

He pulled her down the quiet street, leading her toward the tavern and onto the back porch.

As if unable to control himself, he pressed her against the door, boxing her in with his arms. She surrendered to his next kiss for mere moments, almost forgetting. Then she pushed against his chest, eyes firm.

"There's no distracting you today, I see?"

She smirked. "Imagine how close we'd be if I knew everything about you."

His knee slid between hers, coaxing her legs apart until she could feel his thigh pressing against the spot her desire pulsed.

"Imagine how close we'd be if your gown was up and my trousers were gone," he hissed in her ear, his tongue darting out to taste her skin.

"Kwan."

She'd meant to sound chastising, but she practically moaned aloud in broad daylight on the porch where anyone could turn the corner at any moment. The sun was beaming down on them, but it was his body and the memory of it that had her flushed and breathless. He chuckled, teeth now grazing beneath her chin.

"Yes?"

She yearned for bare skin and simple sheets—for him. And he knew it. A quiver shot up her spine as his teeth grazed across her bottom lip. In response, she rolled her hips against his thigh, desperate to find the right amount of pressure at the perfect moment, but it was no use. Her head fell back against the door, and she huffed, frustrated.

"Please just tell me your secret so we can go upstairs."

He wrapped her long braid around his hand and tugged, luring her head to the side.

"As you wish." He submitted, teeth finding her clavicle, the sensation forcing her to grip his elbows to remain standing.

Apparently if he was going to tell her certain things, he was going to do it his way. Very well, she could be attentive and moan at the same time.

"I'm listenin'."

In fact, she'd never listened so intently before.

"I've explained how I came to Dathoviel to protect my grandfather from certain dangerous people. The ones who kept him drinking and passing out money."

"Yes," she said breathlessly.

Her eyes shut tight as he pressed her tighter against the door and hooked her knee up by his hips. The lower half of his body snapped against hers and she gasped.

"Well, when I overheard the last trade ship was departing, I knew we must escape, though I hated the thought of leaving my sister behind. However, she was safer without me under her roof."

Another snap of his hips. Then a roll. Her heart was thundering and she chanced a look up to make sure it wasn't storming. The blue sky glinted back at her as her head fell against the door.

"Why was she safer?"

His tongue and teeth moved up the other side of her neck.

"You see, some rather important people were hunting me, and if they found me, there would be no one to help my family."

Olive's eyes flew open. "Hunting you? Why?"

He ran his thumb over her lips, gently coaxing her eyes shut once more. She couldn't help but surrender.

"I had a habit of. . . *borrowing* things that weren't exactly mine. And failing to return them. In fact, I'd often sell them to help feed my sister, her kids, and pay for doctors who swore they could cure my grandfather. At least from here I can send her gold when I have any to spare. Honest gold."

This time her eyes opened slowly. "You were a thief."

"A very good one, most of the time." He buried his face at her throat, avoiding her reaction. "It's behind me now, but certain skills remain."

"Like being able to leap across the schoolhouse beams?"

He nodded. "I'm also an excellent climber and I can handle myself in a fight, if required."

"And so, you thought telling me you did what you thought you must, to protect your family would make me walk away?"

He shrugged, finally standing, but still refusing to meet her gaze. "I'm a very wanted man in two different kingdoms, love. Our future could prove tricky, given how much you wish to travel."

Olive captured his face gently, caressing the hard ridges of his cheekbones.

"I appreciate your honesty. As for our future, let's continue takin' all this one day at a time. You make me happy, and I don't wish to lose that."

"So, you'll share a drink with a former thief?"

She grinned.

"I enjoy your whiskey kisses."

He reached behind her to unlock the door, and they stumbled inside. Then he was pulling her behind the bar, tugging her close, hands sliding lower and lower.

"I have one more confession," he admitted, voice thick.

"Oh?"

"Last night, I dreamt of bending you over right here."

He eyed the long wooden bar, gaze practically on fire.

"You did?"

He nodded and looked back at her, lips parted, teeth gleaming. "And I can't seem to banish the thought."

The unrequited desire low in her gut suddenly bloomed and her breath hitched. The same image clouded her thoughts.

"Well, we'll have to do something about that."

~

Seb marched nervously toward Alaric's study, tugging at his once coveted armor. What more could the king possibly want? Had he not given his soul and sanity already?

The leather vest pulled tight across his body, compressing the air from his chest like a coiled snake preparing to snap his ribcage. Even his custom boots were no longer comfortable and the sword belt around his waist hung heavy despite the lack of weapon sheathed there.

Once he'd dreamed of being a decorated soldier, but now every stitch in the leather was a reminder of each drop of blood Brantley had left in the snow. The patches on his shoulders mocking him for every lie he'd told. Every crime of Alaric's he'd looked away from.

He'd been nothing but nervous and sick for months, hardly eating or sleeping as guilt gnawed away. And though he remained at the king's mercy, all fantasies of friendship had deteriorated the moment he'd been forced to lie directly to Amelia's face. Seb decided then things must change. *He* must change. Something that could never happen while standing at Alaric's side. So, he'd been counting the days until the Winvoltor trip, dreaming of escape and fresh starts.

"You wished to see me," Seb announced himself from the open doorway after a brief knock on the frame, hands moving behind his back.

The summons Phillip handed him moments ago was still clutched in his fist. Alaric gestured towards the empty chair across from him at the chess table.

"Come, join me."

"No, thank you. I'm not one for chess, as you know."

Alaric's eyes narrowed with displeasure as he made a move against his invisible opponent. "I'll be departing in the morning."

A white knight was removed from the board.

"I notice you say *I* and not *we*."

"I wish for you to stay and watch over the queen. As you know, I will be taking a large group with me. Leaving Amelia unprotected in her current state would be unwise."

As if protecting the queen was ever Alaric's priority. He was pleased she'd imprisoned herself in her tower, but he needed her to stay there, preferably forever. Seb could read between the lines.

"If that is your wish, I shall honor it."

As if he had a choice.

Playing both sides of the board, Alaric paused mid-reach over a black pawn, turning in his chair to face the door.

"Shall you ever forgive me for what happened in the woods?"

Seb's fists tightened, nails digging into his palm, crinkling parchment.

"Never."

Alaric sighed. "Sebastian, you don't understand what it's like to have so much at risk. To fear losing it all. I did what I must to keep the crown on my head. The armor on *your* back. Don't forget, you wouldn't be here without me."

"I remember." Seb stepped back, hand on the knob. "If you require nothing else, I shall go."

He stomped down the corridor, kicking himself. How could he have ignored Alaric's darkness so long? The charm, promises, and smooth lies were all manipulations. Tactics. And it seemed they worked beyond women he wished to bed, to men he hoped to control. The king was undeniably intoxicating and his talent for reading the desires of others didn't hurt. Nor did his ability to grant the wishes of anyone whose loyalty he wished to earn. There was nothing genuine about Alaric, except his thirst for power and control. And the fact he would clearly go to any lengths to secure them.

But the spell was broken for Seb. He saw through it all now, prepared to steal his power back. Alaric had taken advantage of a young boy, but Seb was no longer a child. He must stop believing he was nothing without Alaric. Yet, he would never be *anything* if he remained in the shadows. He just needed to decide who he would be outside of it.

~

Within an hour, Amelia and Caroline lay side by side, a blanket between them and the grass. Their slippers were tossed to the side in a haphazard pile, their skirts lifted to their knees so their skin could absorb the sun's warmth. They had devoured the food Regina packed them, and were now watching the clouds pass silently by the mountain tops; a light breeze promising spring had truly arrived. Outwardly, everything was still and peaceful.

Amelia watched the horses grazing in the distance, her heart torn in two different directions. On one hand, being out here made her miss Brantley more than ever. On the other, it was hard to ignore the fact she and Caroline were alone. This ultimate privacy could not be wasted.

Amelia sighed softly and rolled onto her stomach, reaching out to toy with the bud of a flower. She could do this. She could be brave. Saying she loved Caroline was hardly as terrifying as taking on Alaric. Right?

"It's lovely to see you smiling again," Caroline said, though her eyes were elsewhere.

"I needed this. I have wanted to come out often, but I thought it would hurt too much." She inhaled, bolstering a great deal of strength. "I wish to thank you for staying by my side."

Caroline finally turned to meet her eyes, but her gaze remained guarded. What was she hiding?

"You're welcome, but there's no need to thank me. Support is what friends are for."

Amelia flinched at the word *friends,* though it was far from an insult.

"Death is funny, is it not?"

Caroline turned her face back to the clouds, jaw tight. "How do you mean?"

"Does anyone truly live how they want? Love who they wished to love? Or do we all take our final breaths praying for more time? For another chance?"

"Regrets, you mean?" Caroline whispered, her bottom lip between her teeth.

Amelia dragged her gaze back to the grass, but only for a moment. She could not help staring, caught between how beautiful Caroline looked and how terrified she felt.

"Do we not owe it to ourselves to make life as remarkable as possible? To accept the gift of life and utilize every aspect of it? To live and love, unafraid?"

Caroline closed her eyes for a moment.

"You don't appear afraid of anything."

When she opened them they were darker, a deep sea of navy beckoning Amelia closer. Her heart skipped a beat.

"I am afraid all the time," she admitted. "Will I defeat Alaric peacefully? Am I capable of leading Dathoviel the way I wish to? Will I ever find a love like my parents?"

Amelia let her hand rest atop Caroline's as her voiced drifted off in the wind. Her fingertips moved gently across Caroline's knuckles impulsively. This was it. Her chance to be honest and brave. So why did she feel like vomiting?

Caroline's chest was still, like her breath was trapped somewhere inside. She must have seen the torment in her eyes, because she covered Amelia's hand with her own. They were so close Amelia could taste the chocolate cake Caroline had devoured during their lunch. So close that when Amelia exhaled, it was the same air Caroline drew in.

"What is it?" she asked softly. "I know I'm not Olive, but you can still tell me anything."

Amelia inhaled deeply, leaning closer. One final test to see if either would pull back, lean in, or remain perfectly still. Perhaps she could kiss her, and if it went poorly pass it off as a joke.

No.

If she was going to kiss Caroline, it had to be real.

"I am also afraid I have fallen in love with someone who may never love me in return."

"Whom have you fallen in love with?" Caroline sounded fearful.

Amelia hesitated only a moment, though it seemed a dozen decades passed. Her heart was pounding, her palms sweaty. *Do not vomit.*

"You," she finally whispered, a great weight leaving her body. It was out there, on the wind. She could not take it back, but she did pull away, providing Caroline space to process.

"You—you love... *me*?"

Amelia focused on the blanket beneath them. "I know it is completely mad. I prayed God would take my love if I was not meant to have it. But it remains, and I am here, and you are there. I do not wish to die one day with regrets." Their eyes met. "I, Queen Amelia of Dathoviel, love you, Lady Caroline of Petrovia."

Caroline sat up, dragging Amelia with her. "This is unbelievable."

There was a lump in Amelia's throat growing with each moment that passed. Soon she may not be able to breathe or speak.

"I understand if you do not return my affections."

"But I do." Caroline cupped her face gently. "I loved you from the first moment I saw you in a white gown, your wild curls dancing along to music that was far too loud. And I fell deeper in love with every letter you sent. Then in trousers, standing in a barn piling hay in the stable. And every moment since."

Amelia's hands wrapped around Caroline's wrist, heart ready to burst from her body. "You love *me*?"

"Yes," Caroline sighed. "and you love me."

Amelia brought her close, their foreheads pressed lightly together, their noses brushing. "May I kiss you?"

"You may," Caroline nodded, though it was her lips that captured Amelia's first, pressing their bodies together tightly, surrounding her, pulling her down into a current she was pleased to drown in.

And there on the hill with two horses and God as their witness, Amelia and Caroline relished the moment, celebrating who they truly had been all along.

11

March 28th, 1457

AMELIA HAD GROWN USED to waking with a mournful ache in her chest, but today Caroline's presence in her bed eased it. Inching across the sun-soaked duvet toward blonde curls and soft curves, her fingertips met Caroline's sleeve in slow strokes.

"Morning," she whispered, praying her touch would not break the spell

Caroline's timid eyes focused on the roof of the canopy, breath shallow. Her gown was rumpled from sleep and her cheeks pink with nerves.

"How are you feeling?"

"Like I could dance down the halls."

Caroline tilted her head to the side hopefully.

"No regrets?"

"None."

And then Caroline beamed brighter than the sun and Amelia could not help leaning in to press their lips together.

"I'm glad you stopped us last night. I don't think I could have," the blonde admitted.

Amelia blushed too, remembering her struggle to keep her hands from slipping beneath Caroline's gown once she'd locked the bedroom door behind them. She was not confident she could resist such temptation again.

"If you're willing to be patient—"

Caroline pressed her fingertip to the queen's lips. "I've waited for you my entire life. What's a few more weeks?"

"I think it will be closer to months, unfortunately."

Feigning an eye roll, Caroline playfully huffed. "Oh well, that's far too long."

She made to leave the bed, but Amelia pulled her back. They fell into a heap against the sheets, both giggling. Amelia leaned in, losing herself in glittering crystal blue before Caroline's lids fluttered closed. Desperately she captured the queen's mouth with hers. Fingers dove into curls, their chests pressed together, and Amelia's hand had just begun itching to slip under those rumpled emerald skirts when someone interrupted them with a knock on the door.

Smoothing her hair down, she moved to answer it while Caroline jumped up and endeavored to shuffle her gown into place. When the queen opened the door, her mood plummeted straight to hell.

Seb gulped and bowed. "Your Highness, I apologize for the early morning intrusion."

"What do you want?"

He did not flinch at her tone, but the guilt was clear on his tired face.

"I've been asked to inform you the king is departing today. He says if you wish to bid him farewell, now is the time."

Surely, this was a joke, or perhaps a test?

"Tell my husband I could not possibly care less." Amelia wrapped her hand around the door, shutting it as she spoke. "*Bon voyage* to you both."

"Actually," the knight called through the wood. "I'm to remain here with you."

Right before the door clipped his nose, she yanked it wide open. "Explain."

His eyes were on the floor, hands behind his back. He rocked forward on his heels once, then squared his shoulders. But he still did not look up.

"Alaric requested I stay with a handful of men to guard the castle and provide you protection in his absence."

Amelia scoffed. "Interesting he would choose you for such a task when you've shown how incapable you are of protecting one boy."

The door rattled as she slammed it shut, the lock clicking into place with finality.

~

Despite the queen's scorching words, Seb rejoiced from atop the east guard tower as the travelling party faded into the distance.

Would Alaric slip into familiar habits while away? Betrothal certainly hadn't stopped him from bedding every woman possible, but perhaps Leah was where he would draw the line? Or did lines exist for Alaric at all?

Certainly, when it came to friendship he didn't care. And the more Seb looked back the more he realized, the king had never cared for him.

A perfect example was their trip from Petrovia to Dathoviel nearly two years ago. They'd given the horses a night to rest at the inn between the two kingdoms. And there, in the common area after dinner, Seb had seen a woman—the first in many years he'd openly shown interest in.

"Go talk to her," Alaric encouraged over his mug. *"Introduce yourself."*

Seb shook his head, sinking deeper into the burgundy armchair and turning his gaze to the fire. It didn't help. The flames were the same color as her hair.

"We depart in the morning."

"You don't need to marry her, Sebastian, and who's to say she wants more than a night with a knight?" He chuckled at his own joke. "Besides, how long has it been?" Unwilling to admit his virginity, Seb had stayed silent. Alaric leaned across the table. "If you don't take her to bed, I will."

That was the thing about Alaric. He was no one's friend.

"Don't you think you've had enough the last three days?" Seb asked, watching the prince stand and roll up his sleeves.

"This trip is my stag, Sebastian! After I marry the princess, I'll be stuck making love to some aristocratic brat. I deserve to enjoy myself before we arrive."

Alaric had apologized to him the next morning for sleeping with the woman. But looking back, he'd been far from genuine.

"I only wish to make you the best man you can be," he had said.

Growing up, Seb believed it was them against the world, and that he owed Alaric his loyalty. After all, he'd likely be dead without him.

The night Alaric had caught him stealing food from the castle kitchen in Petrovia as children, could have been his last. But instead of outing him to King Viktor, he'd convinced the cooks to let him lend a hand with serving meals. How does one repay such a debt?

You couldn't, but you could lose your soul trying to.

But with the king gone, Seb could begin his search for a new beginning. Once he'd released the past, including telling Amelia the truth about Brantley.

March 30th, 1457

"I see the fresh air yesterday treated you well," Olive said, helping Amelia out of the bath and into her robe.

"Yes." The queen floated blissfully to her vanity with a content sigh. "Caroline joined me. I believe she may need some riding clothes if you have time."

Olive nodded and began combing through her wet hair. "You should ride daily if it makes you so happy. Or do you smile because Alaric has left?"

Amelia fidgeted with the navy sash at her waist.

"Actually, my mood has to do with a secret I've been keeping from you."

Olive's hands froze. "Please tell me you're not bloody pregnant."

"No!" Amelia waved her hands. "It has to do with Caroline."

"Oh, Christ!" Olive pinched the bridge of her nose for a moment before resuming her battle with the tangles. "Don't scare me like that. What about her?"

Their eyes met in the mirror and Amelia took a long, deep breath and turned around, making eye contact.

"Caroline and I—we are—well. We are in love."

The air hung heavy for a moment.

Olive paused and came around to face the queen, leaning against the vanity, piecing together the relationship she'd witnessed unfold. Amelia's nervous eyes followed her, waiting.

Finally, Olive grinned.

"So much makes sense now," she chuckled. "This is wonderful!"

Amelia gaped. "You approve?"

"Is there a reason I shouldn't? You are finally in love. I'm surprised you didn't realize sooner that men weren't your style."

"A relationship with two females was not an option I considered plausible. So, I locked the truth away and refused to let it cross my mind."

"You two are great together. Anyone can see you share somethin' special."

Grinning, Amelia jumped up and they embraced tightly.

"Your support means everything to me."

"I will always support you," Olive promised, telling herself the tears teetering on her lids were from the hair currently filling her mouth and eyes, not her bursting heart. "As long as she makes you happy, I'm happy."

"She does make me happy, truly."

Olive's smile wavered a moment and she pulled back, needing to see Amelia's face when she asked this. "How will it work though? Given you are married and all. I may support you, but I have a hard time imaginin' the court will, and I don't see you being able to keep this secret for long."

"We shall struggle, I know. To convince the court I can rule without a king is one thing, but with a woman at my side..." Amelia seemed to have purposefully avoided similar thoughts, and was set to continue. "For now, I wish to enjoy an Alaric free castle, the woman I love, and the company of my dearest friend."

Olive lifted the comb once more, setting aside the impending trouble for a later day. She'd just gotten the smile back on Amelia's face. Surely, they could have today before it was stripped away again.

"Then we'd best get you dressed."

~

Julian was many things.

Father, daydreamer, court jester, and a pacer, especially when stressed. For someone with a calling to entertain and make people laugh, he stressed often. It came with raising five daughters' solo, especially when one of them was Maria.

His eldest was as feisty and as radiant as her mother had once been, and while she didn't cause trouble on purpose, it seemed to follow the young woman wherever she went. That particular skill she had inherited from him. Lately, his stress had little to do with fatherhood, however.

As he was hardly noticed by others in the castle outside of performing, he heard and saw nearly everything behind the scenes. And this particular afternoon, Julian was struggling to focus on anything other than what he'd overheard Leah gossiping about while folding laundry.

So, pacing back and forth inside the library and toying with the frayed edges of his grey jacket was where Olive spotted him.

"Do you need help?" she asked softly from the doorway.

Her attempt to avoid startling him failed. He nearly jumped out of his skin at her voice, but he forced a smile, smoothing his dark hair back with sweaty palms.

"Oh, hello, Olive. Just preparing for my next performance."

She smirked, and if he hadn't known her so well, he would have taken her teasing to heart.

"No offence, Julian. But judgin' by the look on your face, the routine may not be as funny as you hope."

He glanced away a moment. Her plump cheeks and golden waves always reminded him of the drawings of angels. Not that he believed in such things. Not anymore, anyway. He had a hard time believing in a God who would take a mother from her young children. Take his wife and soul mate from him.

Olive, however, could be trusted. If he could tell anyone this, it would be her.

Unable to meet her warm eyes thanks to his nerves, he compromised with staring at the shoulder seam of her chocolate coloured gown.

"I overheard some troublesome things this morning. From Leah."

Her eyebrows shot upwards as she crossed her arms. "Well, out with it."

Once Julian began talking, it was always difficult to stop.

"Last week the king ordered his guards to build large wagons for transporting goods to Winvoltor, but he didn't take any with him when he left. And today, Leah was gossiping about Alaric removing Amelia and becoming queen herself. I also believe Seb is hiding something, though he's always been difficult to read. Normally he's stuck to the king's side, yet he remains here."

Olive sighed, appearing half overwhelmed, half relieved.

"What could the transport wagons be for?"

"No idea, but Alaric is clearly planning on moving large quantities of something."

Olive huffed. "Surely Leah knows, though I doubt she'd tell us."

"She does enjoy talking, but she would not betray him knowingly."

"What *precisely* did you hear her say?"

"That Alaric promised she would be queen before harvest."

"Christ." She stomped aggressively toward the third window on the wall to his left and leaned against the sill. "What are we to do?"

He shrugged. "Now you see why I pace."

Olive nodded, her foot beginning to tap against the hardwood floor.

~

The information churned inside Olive until after dinner when she could speak with Amelia in private.

Well, mostly private.

"We must do something about Leah." Caroline chimed in from the sitting room sofa once Olive had dropped onto the chaise, having finished recounting her conversation with Julian.

Amelia wavered in front of the fireplace, one hand on the hearth. "Harming her in any capacity would hurt Alaric. He would retaliate, and I cannot risk that."

"Not even after Brantley?" Caroline asked boldly.

Her mouth snapped shut when the queen's eyes flashed in her direction.

"I will not stoop to his level. Who knows how low it truly goes."

"How do we know we can trust the jester?" Caroline tried again after a moment. "He could be spying on us for Alaric. He is probably out for himself."

"Julian is a reliable man," Olive countered, eyeing Caroline with a friendly warning to back down.

Caroline scoffed, as if such a thing existed. "We don't need a man's help. We need to stick together."

"He's intuitive, and he knows about what goes on in the castle. He even expressed he's suspicious of Seb."

"Being observant doesn't make him trustworthy."

Amelia pondered, chewing at her thumbnail. "I would like to talk with him. I see no reason why we should not give him a chance."

~

Within the hour, Amelia and Caroline were face-to-face with Julian. Olive stood to the side. They had chosen to use the stables as a gathering spot, ensuring no one would overhear, aside from the horses. The queen searched the jester's eyes for any devious intention.

She found none.

"I wish to ask where your loyalty lies, and I will need your complete honesty."

Julian nodded, bowing slightly. Not at all offended. "My loyalty and duty, Your Majesty, belong to my daughters, myself, and you."

"What proof can you offer the queen?" Caroline demanded from where she stood at Gus's stall, stroking his mane absentmindedly.

Julian's tone remained calm. "I was born and raised in Dathoviel. I have served the court for many years, as my father did before me. I hold no respect for a man who treats women the way I've seen King Alaric behave. If you cannot believe my words as a man, perhaps you can find truth in a father's plea. Let me help you save our land and protect anyone he wishes to harm in the future."

Amelia again searched his eyes, her instincts wishing to trust him. After a moment she extended her hand. When he bowed to kiss it, she stepped closer and took his, shaking it the way a king might. The way a friend would.

"Having you on our side is a blessing indeed. Please keep your eyes and ears open for any information you believe I may need."

"Of course, Your Grace."

A new alliance had been formed and a new ally gained, but the queen felt empty as Julian and Olive departed. Already her connection with Caroline was showing strain. She ached for yesterday morning when the sun beamed over already warm sheets and their bodies were pressed close.

Instead, they stood silently side by side in the stables, watching Greta contest for the final carrot against her brother. Their hands would brush if one reached out, but neither did.

Their relationship may still be in its infancy, but Amelia knew she must set boundaries for this to last. At least she and Alaric had always been blunt with each other. She hoped for the same with Caroline, albeit in a far more loving and respectful manner.

"I wish to discuss expectations with you," Amelia said, repressing a stutter.

Caroline glanced over. "Certainly."

"We have no idea what the future holds, but ideally, I assume you wish to stand at my side when I am named Dathoviel's sole ruler."

Caroline paused. "I would."

"I doubt the court will name you queen alongside me..."

"I expected."

Amelia continued, hoping to thaw Caroline's cold stiffness. "Should we succeed in securing the throne, I will always value your opinion on matters and hear you out."

"However?" Caroline turned to face her, clearly sensing the hesitation in the air between them.

"I understand the way you view the world, but I cannot tolerate your blatant disrespect for my male friends simply because you struggle trusting them. I have known Fredrick and Julian my entire life and I would not entertain their support without believing their additions were valuable."

Caroline remained quiet for a long time. When she finally spoke again, her shoulders had softened.

"I never intended to offend you."

Grateful, Amelia captured her pale hand, bringing her knuckles to her lips. "I do not bring this to your attention to shame or change you. Your beliefs and misbeliefs are your own, and you must work through them in your own time, as we all must. Your suggestions are welcomed, but I request you not pressure me to adopt them."

Caroline brought their bodies close, their noses brushing. "Thank you for your words. I promise to strive to remember them moving forward."

Amelia rested her forehead against Caroline's as Greta crunched away at the half carrot she had won and triumphantly settled into the hay for a long nap behind them.

"And I promise to show patience while you try."

March 31st, 1457

Seb stood in the hall the next morning, his cap crushed in his hands, fingertips nervously running over the feather. He knew the queen would be inside the dining hall sharing breakfast with those she trusted. Understandably, he'd been excluded. He was the last person she wished to see, but she had a right to know the circumstances surrounding Brantley's death. And what Alaric had planned for her people in Winvoltor.

Finally, the doors opened and Amelia strode out, followed by Caroline, Olive, Fredrick, Kwan, and Julian. Their eyes met instantly, but she appeared set on ignoring his presence, stepping around him gracefully. The others followed her example.

"Your Majesty. May I humbly request a few moments of your time?"

The group froze at his audacity to address her directly.

Amelia turned slowly to face him.

"I have no desire to hear more lies, *Sir Sebastian*."

Her use of the wrong name cut deep, but he wasn't giving up. He moved forward quickly, knowing his opportunity was fading. Julian and Fredrick both stepped up, blocking his view, though neither met his eyes.

"Please, just a few moments. I have information. There are many things you must know."

"Stay away from her," hissed Caroline, eyes flashing indignantly at him.

He hung his head. "Your cousin is a terrible man and because of him, I've done terrible things, including standing by his side in silence."

Amelia gently motioned Julian aside to face Seb herself. "I will listen."

"Nothing I say will bring you peace," he warned. "Though, it may bring you closure."

Olive crossed her arms, her tone impatient. "Go on."

Kwan stared unblinking at her side.

Seb took a deep breath. "Alaric has commissioned transport wagons to be built."

"We already knew that," Julian said haughtily.

"But do you know why? Do you know why he left yesterday?"

"No," Amelia answered. "Can you tell us?"

"Alaric has gone to speak with King Bartholomew to arrange for a portion of the gold he mines in exchange for workers. He plans to take every able-bodied Dathovielian man and send them to the mines—as slaves."

Amelia shook her head again. "King Bart was once friends with my father. He would never agree to something horrific as that."

"Power can turn even the best men dark," Seb sighed knowingly.

A long pause followed.

"I understand now," the queen said, her eyes focused on a tapestry behind Seb.

Caroline looked concerned. "Understand what?"

"Why Alaric allowed us to feed and clothe the villagers. Send doctors to heal them. We have been creating him stronger, healthier slaves."

"My god," Olive whispered and turned to Kwan. "Imagine Hannah and the children watch William get dragged away. I can't take it."

He wrapped his arm around her silently, jaw set tight.

"So, we fight him!" Caroline exclaimed, fists clenched. "Fredrick, you've been training the villagers."

He sighed. "We are going to need more than a few farmers and merchants dressed as would-be soldiers to win a true battle against Alaric."

Amelia couldn't seem to disagree with the constable. "The court will listen to *this*. They must."

"One can hope," Kwan said.

"I thank you for bringing this to my attention," Amelia said stepping closer to Seb.

His stomach lurched. There'd be no going back after this. "There is one more thing, if I may."

Amelia's flushed face drained instantly.

"Regarding my brother?"

Shame washed over him.

"I wished to tell you as soon as we arrived back at the castle. Alaric threatened me, and I'm ashamed to say I submitted to those threats."

"Did he kill Brantley?" Amelia's face resembled stone, but she couldn't hide the tremble in her hands.

"Yes. I let him out of my sight, allowing Alaric the opportunity. When I found them, it was too late."

Amelia reached for Caroline's hand, clutching it desperately. "Give me one reason why I should not have you executed."

Alaric would have him killed when he learned there were no more secrets.

"I cannot."

After a moment she said, "I won't do it."

He stared wide-eyed. "You must desire something in retribution?"

"Only honesty when you tell me where your loyalty lies now?"

Seb placed his cap back on his head, bringing a clenched fist to his chest.

"With you, My Queen."

. 12 .

ONCE THEY WERE ALONE in her tower, Caroline led the sobbing queen over to her bed and steadied her in her arms.

Stifling Amelia's overpowering need to mourn Brantley's murder would only increase its hold, so Caroline kept watch, saying little and stroking the queen's dark hair as they both processed. She would be Amelia's quiet, safe place in this fresh storm of grief.

Eventually exhaustion won out and Caroline monitored the creases in the queen's forehead, and around her mouth. She recalled the months Amelia had spent nearly comatose following the funeral. And she did something similar to praying it wouldn't happen again.

By the time Amelia awoke, dinner was being served and both women were famished.

"I can request for Regina to bring us a tray?" Caroline offered as the queen rose, stretching.

"No." Amelia buried her face in the curve of Caroline's neck. "We ought to eat with our friends."

Caroline tensed. "I cannot imagine ever calling Seb a friend."

"I am not ready to trust him completely either. But if he remains on our side, he shall be a fine ally to utilize. No one understands Alaric better, and he knows we will be watching him closely awaiting any mistake."

"I only wish to keep you safe."

Amelia smiled in response and squeezed her hand before placing a soft kiss on her lips.

"I know."

Caroline watched the queen slide open the drawer of her nightstand and reveal a sheathed dagger.

"Where did you get that?"

Amelia took her time answering, admiring the beautiful weapon.

"Alaric gifted it to me on our anniversary."

"An odd gift?"

"I thought the same at first, but it became comforting. At least I would have the means to defend myself if he ever crossed a line."

"And now, knowing the truth regarding Brantley?"

Amelia tested the blade's sharpness with the tip of her finger. "I had a dream once, where I attempted to end Alaric's life, but failed."

"And now?"

"Now, I'm ashamed to admit, I fear being unable to control myself when I see him again."

"No one would blame you," Caroline said gently, meeting her beside the bed.

She took the queen's wrists in her hands, holding the dagger with her. Amelia didn't look away from it.

"Death is forever. If I took his life for Brantley's, it would not bring him back. And what would that make me? Could I live with that version of myself?"

Caroline struggled to answer. "His presence is poisonous. I doubt anyone would mourn him."

"Leah would. And Spencer, perhaps?"

"Doubtful. They hate each other."

Amelia remained focused on the glinting blade.

"Is vengeance a worthy reason to kill?"

"Some would say yes."

"His death would also protect my people."

"But?"

"Even with him dead, the law will stand. Dathoviel requires a king and his spot will simply be filled by another. I must *prove* my worthiness to rule. The courts must believe in the power of a queen's reign."

Caroline's short temper had always been an issue for her growing up. But she had not realized how short until comparing her reactions to Amelia's. Her willpower was inspiring.

Caroline slid closer, took the dagger and set it aside. Then she captured Amelia's face with both hands.

"This is your fight and your kingdom. Whatever you choose, I will stand at your side."

Amelia rested her forehead against Caroline's. "Thank you."

April 1st, 1457

As Amelia rode to the village, a warm breeze danced through Greta's mane and the wisps of fallen hair from the loose bun resting against her neck.

The square was alive. Villagers delivered fresh water to the fountain with pails from a newly dug well. The colorful banners of the open market waved invitingly above two men at a nearby cart who were arranging handmade jewelry to sell. They chatted quietly, standing close, smiling at one another as if they shared a secret. Down the road, the doors to the tavern stood open, welcoming anyone interested to join the clinking glasses and merry chatter within.

Olive definitely deserved a medal for maintaining progress in her absence.

"My Queen," William called from behind her.

Amelia turned to where he waved from the tavern door.

"Afternoon," she greeted brightly in return.

He set aside the tools he had been using to repair the shutters, approaching as she dismounted from Greta's back. His gaze swept over her trousers and shirt, grinning.

"That is quite a practical choice for riding."

"Why, thank you. How are Hannah and the children?"

"All's well." He hesitated, eyes turning sad for a moment. "You've been greatly missed around here."

"I was away far too long."

William bowed. "Is there anything I can help you with today?"

"Actually, yes. Have you been training with the constable?"

He hung his head. "Hannah asked me not to."

Amelia waved, excusing him from the guilt.

"Please, no shame. I only ask because I must speak with Fredrick, and I hoped you could show me where the camp is."

"They have moved deeper into the forest. Allow me to saddle a horse and I'll happily escort you."

Within the hour, Amelia and William reached the training grounds and observed the energetic groups of men and women spread throughout the grassy clearing.

Around twenty villagers trained in weapons, either dueling with wooden swords or shooting arrows at targets hanging high in the trees. Another twenty or so threw daggers into marked hay bales spread various distances or practiced tying knots. The third group was positioned further back by the small camp of tents. Half participated in hand-to-hand combat, while the rest performed strength and endurance exercises supervised by Fredrick.

Opposite the tents, a woman in leather armor with dark skin blew into a horn. Strikingly beautiful, she stood confidently atop stacked hay bales, her dozens of tight black braids secured away from her face with a band.

Surely this was Fredrick's daughter.

At the sound of her horn, weapons dropped and the groups rotated stations. It was clean, organized, and precise.

Fredrick looked up, spotting the queen, and shouted off a few quick orders to keep the fighters moving before climbing onto his horse. As he neared, Amelia saw the proud, youthful fire in his eyes.

"Your Highness! I was unaware you would be gracing us with a visit today."

They clasped hands tightly.

"Forgive the surprise, Constable. This is an impressive operation."

Fredrick lowered his chin in appreciation. "We have just under sixty men and around thirty women."

"Wonderful set up, sir," William commented. "Perhaps when this is all over, you can wrangle my children into order."

"I heard the new school may need an instructor or two," Fredrick laughed. "Have you come to join us, William?"

"Ah, unfortunately not sir."

"Excellent." The Constable nodded. "The village couldn't bear to have their most talented carpenter out here in the forest."

"How old is your daughter now?" Amelia asked Fredrick.

He beamed proudly, gazing toward the woman shouting orders to the groups below her. "She will cross into her twenty-fifth year with the harvest."

He glanced toward the fighters before turning back to Amelia. "So, what brings you here?"

Her resolve faltered. "The castle has been rocked with unfortunate news, in the form of a confession from Seb. Alaric knows what we have been planning. He did not intervene, hoping to keep us distracted while setting his own plans into motion."

"I was aware he looked to create a trade deal with a northern kingdom," Fredrick admitted sadly. "But since I've heard nothing else."

Amelia paused, and her eyes shifted to William, not wishing to worry him unnecessarily. He read through her hesitation.

"I'll just go say hello to Eloise, then."

Once he was out of earshot, Amelia let her shoulders slump.

"Alaric plans to trade King Bartholomew our men to work in his gold mines. In return for the slaves, Alaric will receive a cut of their findings."

"And this is the trip he recently departed on?" Amelia nodded.

"Seb also admitted the truth regarding my brother's death. Alaric murdered him, fearing Brantley would reclaim the throne."

Fredrick rippled with fury, hands turning to fists around the reins.

"Does anyone in the castle have physical proof? A letter or a journal?"

"Not that I am aware."

His eyes glazed over, thinking long and hard. Eventually, he turned back. "We will hold him accountable for this. In the meantime, I'll increase your protection detail outside of the castle guards Alaric knows."

"You know someone you trust to protect me?" she followed his gaze to Eloise who was now crouched and speaking with William.

"I do."

April 2nd, 1457

With the taste of Regina's blueberry pie still on their tongues, Amelia gathered her most trusted in the throne room. Caroline stood next to her, Seb and Julian flanking Olive, while Fredrick completed the circle.

The queen clasped her hands, praying her voice sounded stronger than she felt.

"It is time to set aside our differences and work together. We do not have to like everything about each other, but we must agree to a common goal. A focus for tomorrow and every day that follows."

The others nodded in response. "Yes, Your Majesty."

"We shall move as a unit," Amelia continued. "Making decisions unified, and aligned. I wish to take our kingdom from the broken shell Alaric created and restore its true greatness. Should we succeed, this will be a joint effort and a joint victory."

"We are at your service," Fredrick promised.

Both Julian and Seb murmured and Olive swayed in agreement.

"Where do we begin?" Seb asked.

Amelia's tone shifted. "You know about the training camp in the village, I assume?"

"Yes. Constable Fredrick is doing very well."

The two men exchanged polite, but strained glances.

Amelia nodded. "I continue to pray we avoid bloodshed and will not require an army to defeat Alaric, however, I understand the importance of reinforcement. You are tasked with covertly questioning the loyalty of the remaining guards and soldiers at the castle. Those on our side will report to the camp and assist Fredrick."

Fredrick bowed in thanks. "The help would be most welcome."

"What of the men loyal to Alaric?" Seb asked.

"We cannot risk them spoiling our progress in any way," Amelia said. "For the time being, house them in the dungeon, but keep their conditions comfortable. They have not broken any laws by siding with their king."

Seb's approval was clear from his expression. "I'll begin tonight."

Amelia turned to Olive. "Will you inform Regina their meals are to be delivered to them?"

"Of course."

Beaming, Amelia laced her fingers together. "When this comes to an end, they will be granted the opportunity to re-evaluate their allegiances."

"And, how may *I* be of service?" Julian asked, foot tapping.

Olive placed a reassuring hand on his elbow.

"Please remain my eyes and ears throughout the castle," Amelia answered. "Listen when people talk. See who may become our ally, or who we should be wary of. Relay any information you uncover immediately."

"You have my word," the jester guaranteed.

Amelia clasped her hands. "If we are to take Alaric down without war, we need physical documentation for the court. Proof he has been bleeding the land dry, and his plans with King Bart."

"I'll find what I can," Olive volunteered.

~

The castle at night was quiet, save for the crackling torches and the faint padding of the handmaiden's slippered feet as she floated through the dim hall toward Alaric's tower.

His study seemed a logical location as any to begin. Lone candle in hand, she gingerly climbed the steps, noticing the office door was ajar as she reached the landing. Warm orange light glowed through the crack, and her stomach sank.

Someone had beaten her inside.

Silently, Olive slipped from her shoes and moved forward on bare feet to peer through the narrow opening. Leah stood before the fire holding a stack of parchment, tossing sheets and scrolls one by one into the flames. Any evidence she sought in this room was quickly turning to ash.

With a shuddering breath, she stepped into the darkest shadows around the corner, extinguishing her candle. Somehow, she must trick Leah out of the room before every page was burned. Shoes still in hand, she tossed one towards the staircase with all her might. As desired, the clattering echoed against the stone wall before landing out of sight with a thud.

Leah gasped, her head poking through the door a moment later.

"Who is it? Who's there?"

Heart pounding in her ears, Olive watched her duck back into the study, only to reappear, candelabra in hand. Descending the staircase slowly, Leah called out again, receiving only silence.

Olive's stomach lurched and flipped.

Christ, that was close.

She slipped into the room. A quick sweep informed her the remaining parchment was most likely useless. Still, she grabbed a bundle, hoping Leah wouldn't notice it missing. And that she wouldn't vomit from the nerves coursing through her body. Fleeing back to the shadows, Olive clutched the documents to her hammering chest as Leah rose over the stairs, her weary and confused features illuminated by the candelabra. She peered into the shadows, taking one step toward Olive's location.

Struggling to swallow the lump in her throat, Olive pressing flat against the wall. She held her breath.

Luckily, Leah returned to the study, seemingly satisfied. The door locked behind her with a thud and a sharp click.

Creeping past, Olive searched for the landing in the pure black. Now barefoot, she raced triumphantly down, taking two at a time. Her breath stayed locked in her lungs until she was far from the king's tower.

April 3rd, 1457

The sun was just peeking through the trees as Fredrick emerged from his tent, pinecones crunching beneath his boots. He stretched and surveyed the training grounds. Everything was right where it should be, and as usual he was the first to rise. Though, Eloise would wake soon enough. He tugged his shirt from the line where it had dried overnight and slipped it over his shoulders, heading toward the fire pit.

Just as he'd brought the flames to life and was considering which path to take to the beach for his morning swim trotting hooves could be heard in the distance. He shot up, instinctively reaching for his sword. Then, he remembered.

He was expecting company today, just not this early. A dozen men appear through the trees, stopping just outside the camp, awaiting admittance. Wonderfully surprised at the group's size behind Seb, Fredrick climbed atop his horse and rode forward to meet them.

"Good morning, Sir Sebastian."

"Please, call me Seb," the knight requested nervously.

"Very well." Fredrick observed the newcomers, most whom he'd trained himself. "We're grateful to have the extra hands. Though I warn you, Eloise isn't as pleased as I am. But with time I'm sure she will warm up. Come on, I'll show you how things have been working around here."

A few hours later, the soldiers had found spots throughout camp to aid in training or constructing the private armor and weapons station. With things running reasonably smooth, Seb and Fredrick took the opportunity to sit together outside the constable's tent and admire their progress. They sipped steaming coffee from tin mugs, eyes on the men and women filtering around their posts. Fredrick broke the surprisingly comfortable silence first, his curiosity strong.

"So, Sebastian is not your true name?"

Seb sipped; eyes closed for a moment as if allowing the drink to return him to life.

Judging by the dark circles beneath his eyes, the young man hadn't slept.

"I was very young when my parents and I arrived in Petrovia. Until his death, my father told me how our people fled our kingdom of sand and heat in search of safety. They had a leader much harsher than Alaric. Seb, is native to my homeland. It means '*God of the earth.*' I always thought it meant I would do something impressive with my life. That I would reach my parent's expectations. After all, they went to Petrovia hoping I *would* have a better life."

"Did they adjust well to the new kingdom?"

Seb stared into his mug. "After my father died, it was hard for us to make it on the streets. We had no real home or money. One night my mother told me to sneak into the castle and bring back food. They wouldn't miss it, she'd said. And she was right. I'd never seen so much food before, some just wasting away. When I returned to her side, she had already died."

"How old were you?"

"Six? Maybe seven? We didn't celebrate birthdays. We were just grateful for every new day. Or, I was after that."

"So how did you go from the streets to a knighthood?" Fredrick asked, riveted.

"Sneaking into the castle proved easier than you'd think. I was thin and quick. I studied the guards from afar. Knew their routines, and when the door to the kitchens were left unoccupied. A few months after my mother's death, Alaric found me. He didn't demand to know who I was or what I was doing. He just asked if I needed a bath and new clothes."

Fredrick couldn't help sounding surprised. "He was kind to you?"

"I thought so. Truthfully, he saw and seized the opportunity to use me. I was so grateful for his help I pledged my loyalty to him. He swore to make me a knight one day when he became king."

"And that's why you stood by his side for so long?"

Seb nodded. "He took every opportunity to remind me I was nothing without him as a way to keep me in line."

"So, what changed? Why join us now?"

Their gazes met as Fredrick refilled their mugs. "I realized there is no line Alaric won't cross for what he wants. He has no compass directing him between right and wrong."

"Do you think we have a chance?" Fredrick eyed the camp. "To beat him?"

Seb followed his gaze. "I'd hoped our numbers would be greater, but you've done a fine job here."

"Remember, battle is the last resort. The queen still believes it's avoidable."

Seb nodded. "A noble notion, certainly."

"Mm-hmm. A potentially impossible one as well."

"Yes, I fear the same. I imagine she and Olive are currently discussing if the handmaiden found anything last night to incriminate Alaric."

"He wouldn't be stupid enough to leave anything out in the open."

"She's betting he's too arrogant," Seb said, seemingly hoping for similar things.

"Well," Fredrick inhaled. "I'll be the first to admit she's been underestimated since birth. There's no precedence for an Amelia without Brantley. She married Alaric to protect him. There's no telling what she'll do to avenge him."

Guilt covered Seb's face. "Whatever consequence Alaric receives will not be enough."

"Our army may be small." Fredrick waved his hand. "But I believe they require a name all the same. An official title to present Amelia with."

"Agreed."

Both men considered potential labels for a few moments. Finally, Fredrick smiled.

"The Queen's Order."

Seb grinned and they clinked their mugs together, sealing the deal.

"The Queens Order, it shall be."

13

April 6th, 1457

JULIAN HAD NOTHING TO report the next few days.

Never before had castle life been so tedious. Leah was rarely seen, and the most significant change was Lord Marcel gathering the male servants for horseshoes on the lawn every afternoon. He clearly still felt his son's absence; however, he'd abandoned the bottle and thankfully begun bathing again.

With each passing day battle loomed, seeming inevitable. Julian had observed Caroline striving for patience while Amelia warred with herself, both praying for a miracle that never came.

Just that morning Fredrick's note had arrived, inviting everyone to the Queen's Order presentation that evening. He and Seb seemed to be working well together, which was a relief, as was tonight's event. At least it was something to do.

But Julian was still frustrated. He patrolled corridor by corridor, room by room, his ears and eyes open for *anything*. Ultimately, he ventured outside.

It proved even duller—at first.

After a quick stroll around the grounds, he heard a woman cursing outlandishly in the distance.

"Fuck this!"

Grinning, Julian spun and strode toward the sound. His cheer faded however, as he entered the tree line and an arrow whizzed past his ear. He dropped to the ground intuitively, covering his head.

"What the hell?"

"My thoughts precisely," said the woman from above him, her long braids swinging back and forth like a glorious raging curtain. Her rich brown complexion was a similar shade to the acorns he'd collected as a child.

"Do you typically shoot arrows at strangers?"

"Do *you* typically walk right in front of targets?" Her midnight eyes flashed with frustration as she dragged him to his feet, then pointed.

He followed her finger to the bullseye.

"I admit milady, I did not see that."

She scoffed. "Don't bother with those fancy words around me."

Tossing her hair and grabbing the arrow from the dirt, she headed back to her invisible firing line.

Julian followed close behind her where it was hypothetically safest. "Who are you?"

Side-eyeing him a moment, she lined up her next shot.

"Who I am is not your concern. If you must, think of me as the woman with excellent aim... *Normally.*"

A craving he'd believed to have gone dormant forever burst to life, and he quickly tried to clamp down on it. Why had she suddenly reawakened this part of him? Aside from the fact she was clearly remarkable.

"So, you missed? You weren't aiming for me?"

She lowered the bow, eyes narrowing on him. "Be glad I'm having an off day, or your pretty face would have an arrow through it."

Julian stepped back, hands raised—more for her benefit than his. He recognized a dangerous woman when he saw one, though it took a lot to terrify him. His daughters ensured that. Still, he registered her compliment.

She found him pretty. He could work with that.

"Are you always this cross, or just during *off days*?"

Ignoring him, she aimed again. Her arrow slashed through the air, practiced and flawless. She smirked triumphantly as the arrow sunk deeply into the target, tearing the center of the canvas. Her own personal artist's signature.

"Appears my good luck has returned."

He must know absolutely everything about her.

Not for himself, no. But for the queen. Yes. To ensure she wasn't a threat.

"Have you lived in Dathoviel long?"

"Since birth." Her tone was clipped as she aimed again.

"How have we neglected to meet before today then?"

She threw him a glance over her shoulder. "You've enjoyed the pleasures of castle life while my grandmother raised me in the village."

"I split my time between the village and the castle, actually."

"Well, we must run in different circles."

"Did your grandmother teach you to shoot?"

"No. My father."

"Would I know *him* perhaps?"

She released another arrow into the bullseye, sighing. "If I tell you what you want to hear, will you fuck off?"

"If that's your wish."

Swinging her bow over her arm, she focused in on him. "My father is Constable Fredrick. I've been entrusted with protecting the queen. Satisfied?"

No. Sadly, he would never be satisfied again having met her. Not until he made her cry out in pleasure, and even then, he'd just ache for more.

"You're Eloise?"

"I am."

He should have known. Only the constable's daughter could look and shoot like that.

"Lovely to finally meet you. I'm Julian, the court jester. You should join us for dinner tonight."

"That won't be necessary. I won't need to join your mad circle of anarchy to keep Amelia alive."

Julian's gaze widened in shock. "Why do you say that?"

Eloise groaned. "Why do *you* to ask so many questions?"

"Talking *is* my profession."

"Clearly," she sighed. "Let's just say, the royal family and I don't see eye to eye."

He wasn't the slightest bit surprised she had issues with authority. There didn't appear to be a submissive bone in her body to the untrained eye. Every move she made was deliberate. From the curve of her lips, to the crease around her eyes, and the flex in her hold on the weapon. So controlled she might snap at any moment. And once given consent, he'd be honored to tug her safely over that edge.

"How so?"

"My father is one of the greatest soldiers Dathoviel has seen. He trained me early. Sword in my hand before a doll type childhood."

"Go on," Julian encouraged gently, testing her compliance.

She plucked her handmade target from the tree and wrapped it in cloth to cover the markings before sliding it over her back by the linen straps it hung from. Her bow and quiver went on next, and she headed straight for the castle, showing no intention of waiting for him to follow. His long legs matched her pace easily, eyes transfixed on the ends of her braids, just grazing her well-muscled shoulders.

She spoke, oblivious to the way her beauty tortured him. Which was alright. His cravings were his responsibility to control, not hers to worry about.

"My father requested retirement a few years back. He wished to live a normal life in the village, but King Marcel refused, saying he was too greatly valued. My father explained *I* was available to take over, and they even tested my skills. Ultimately, we were rejected. The trials the former king put me through were for his own entertainment and never serious."

"So, the queen is not the only woman Marcel has underestimated."

"Well, he is a pompous ass."

Tough to get going, but once wound she didn't seem to hold back. How perfect.

"Yes, he is."

"My opinions of Alaric are lower, for the record."

He met her fire with calm.

"You might become fond of Amelia if you got to know her properly. You two share many similar opinions."

Eloise scoffed. "A mutual dislike for the men who undervalue us does not guarantee friendship any more than differing opinions creates enemies. Besides, if that was the case, every woman in the kingdom would be the best of friends."

"I suppose you have a point."

Eloise stopped short outside the gate and faced him, mere inches between them. He inhaled the lemongrass oil on her skin, practically tasting it.

"After her victory—should I do my job well and she survive, Amelia will turn out the same as the rest. Selfish and greedy."

"Excuse me for saying so, milady, but you're mistaken. She will make an excellent ruler. You've seen the changes she's already made in the village."

Eloise stepped even closer, eyes challenging, subconsciously testing him.

"You truly believe this little rebellion will succeed with a handful sized army? One she *isn't* even willing to dispatch, mind you. And a group of servants as allies? The king has fearful, loyal men by the hundreds and comes from a heavy military kingdom. Or have you lot forgotten about his older brother and *their* massive army? Who's to say he won't call for support?"

He was getting nowhere with this beautiful, bitter creature, but he could be patient.

"Just give her a chance. You know better than anyone what it is to be a woman needing someone to believe in her."

"Alright!" Eloise conceded, eyes aimed to the heavens.

He would have serenaded her if he weren't afraid of how she'd react.

"Alright?"

"I promised my father I wouldn't leave her side, so we may as well start with introductions. As long as you don't call me *milady* again."

Her first limit.

"After you, Eloise."

Her name slid off his tongue as he swung open the gate, guiding her through and ensuring his hand hovered behind her back, not touching her just yet.

No, that first touch was one he would savor.

~

"We'll have to meet Seb soon." Caroline turned from the window to Amelia.

Looking stunning in new navy trousers and a tight gold blouse, the queen glanced over from her vanity, eyes terrified.

"I cannot do this."

"I imagine you'll have to say a few words, but otherwise tonight should be fairly simple."

Amelia shook her head. "No. Say we win the battle with Alaric. I will still have to face the courts. And how can I with blood on my hands?"

Caroline went to her, taking her trembling fingers as she knelt next to the stool the queen was perched on, emerald skirts pillowing around her.

No one could blame Amelia's resistance. Dathoviel's desirable land had not been soaked with blood for many decades, so she lacked experience with the true process of war. She didn't understand the duty behind it, but Caroline had been raised to appreciate the glorious clash of iron and steel, even as a Lady.

Men like Alaric would never just sit and talk. Like Uncle Viktor said, *one could not barter with the devil.*

"I understand why you won't kill him yourself. Why you wish to take this kingdom back with your people's love and respect."

"And how can I, while burying those whose support I call on?"

"Revolution is messy," Caroline shrugged sadly. "Every member of your army volunteered, wishing to fight, defend their land, and their families. I know you don't like it, Amelia, but honor *can* be found in war."

The queen's shoulders sagged and for a moment it looked like she might cry. "I should never have allowed Fredrick to create this Order."

Caroline lifted Amelia's chin and straightened her crown, gazing into her eyes softly.

"Your people wish to stand with you. They know this is their opportunity to show Alaric they are not his to use. You are wise to consider all possibilities, but remember, if you dissolve your rebellion, far more lives will be lost and families torn apart."

"I know that!"

As soon as the fire ignited in Amelia's eyes, she smothered it, murmuring apologies and pulling Caroline close.

"It may be time to ask for more help," Caroline whispered against her neck.

"There is no one left in Dathoviel to ask."

"We could look outside the kingdom."

"What do you mean?"

Caroline pulled back, wiping away the few tears trailing down Amelia's cheeks.

"Spencer has boundless resources and manpower at his disposal."

"What man would side against his own brother?"

"Spencer would."

Amelia's teary eyes narrowed, almost teasing.

"I thought you were against asking men for help?"

"He is my one exception. Please, consider it at least."

Amelia's lips pursed and Caroline couldn't resist kissing them, feeling the stress slowly ease from the queen's frame.

"I will consider it," she promised softly.

A knock swiftly ended the conversation.

"May I come in?" Julian called.

"Yes." Amelia turned as his head appeared through a crack in the door. "Is everything alright?"

Julian's eyes flickered over their intimate embrace, but he didn't comment.

"There's an Eloise to meet you. Fredrick sent her to be your guard."

Amelia nodded. "We will be right down."

~

Eloise had chosen her seat across from Amelia as the kitchen staff laid out platters of buns and bowls of steaming stew between them. Regina's freshly baked bread never failed to inspire hunger, and soon plates and mouths were full.

Once bellies had been satiated enough for discussion, the queen turned to Eloise.

"Fredrick must trust you greatly for sending you to me."

"I'm his daughter, after all."

Eloise's tone was closer to indifference than annoyance, but her lack of warmth was noticed by all in the room. Julian coughed at her side, perhaps embarrassed as Caroline glared, but Amelia only tilted her head to the left.

"I cannot thank you enough for everything you and your father have done for our kingdom. For me. I am honored that you shall be the one protecting me."

The queen did prove likeable after all. How annoying.

"You're in capable hands," Eloise promised. "According to my recent marksmanship evaluations, I would be the highest-ranking knight in our land—had I been born male."

Amelia nodded in understanding. "Is that what you desire? To lead our soldiers?"

"God granted me sharp sight, quick reflexes, and strong lungs. I only desire to utilize these skills and serve a greater purpose."

Amelia folded her hands on her lap as a servant cleared her plate. She thanked him with a kind smile.

"Lady Caroline and I were just discussing potentially visiting Petrovia. Would you be willing to accompany us?"

Eloise considered many things in a moment. The first of which was how utterly mad the queen must truly be.

"The current reigning monarch is Alaric's eldest brother, King Spencer." Caroline leaned forward, her disapproving lips pulled thin. "We are hoping he will align with us."

Eloise shook her head in disbelief shooting a look at Julian from the corner of her eye. This had to be a joke, right? Some kind of initiation?

"Was my father aware you had a death wish before he sent me to protect you?"

Julian tapped his boot against hers under the table warningly. She ignored him.

"Excuse yo—" Caroline began.

Amelia's hand rose in a calming manner.

"She is free to speak," the queen said. "King Spencer is aware of Alaric's true nature. Lady Caroline believes he will side with us. I am unsure, as I have not spoken with him personally but, Petrovia may be our best hope. If we fight Alaric with our current numbers, everyone will be slaughtered."

Well, the queen wasn't a completely fool then. Her honesty and guts would serve her greatly as ruler, should she survive, of course. Which they absolutely wouldn't at this rate.

If the rumors circulating the village were true, Alaric would destroy them anyway. They may as well die fighting.

"If I am going to risk my life for you," Eloise said. "I request something in return."

The queen nodded without hesitation. "If it is within my power to grant, I will do everything I can to make it happen."

Eloise inhaled deeply. *This* was the only reason she'd agreed to her father's request.

"Years ago, my father requested a retirement from service, but he was refused. Should we survive, I require your word he will spend his remaining days in peace."

"Consider it done."

Eloise's fists released. She hadn't been aware how tense she was until that moment. "Thank you."

The queen's eyes turned roguish. "Though, his absence will leave quite the hole in our military force."

"If he does not have someone in mind, I shall recommend his replacement."

"Why not you?"

Eloise blinked. "You would appoint me the new constable?"

"Yes, or any title you prefer. You need not answer now. Either way, I would be honored to knight you officially."

"I have your word, Queen Amelia," Eloise stood and offered her hand across the table. "and you have my loyalty."

~

Amelia had apparently made her final decision a few minutes before Seb arrived at the castle to collect her. No one was more shocked than he to hear about tomorrow's departure for Petrovia.

Unable to hide his shock, he escorted her into town, Caroline, Julian and a beautiful dark-skinned woman in tow. As if she were hoping to put him at ease, the queen swiftly explained all he had missed the last few days while staying at camp.

"Do *you* believe going to Petrovia a wise move?" Amelia asked, her horse trotting next to his. "Because you do not appear confident in my choice."

He kept his eyes ahead, surprised she cared about his opinion.

"I've seen the hate between the brothers first hand. I cannot guarantee Spencer will help, but I doubt asking him will gain you an enemy."

She nodded, looking a little unsure herself. "That will have to do. We are running out of time and options."

~

They reached the village as the sun slid from sight. A large bonfire crackled and burned, the scent filling the quickly cooling air. Torches glowed in a wide circle, beckoning everyone inward as the light from nearby homes and shops aided in illuminating the square. Villagers watched from open doorways, some impatient—others anxious.

As she slid from Greta's back, Amelia waved to William and Hannah. Dressed in her nightgown, Brianna smiled broadly from her father's shoulders.

Where the market carts usually resided, men and women of various heights and creeds stood at attention, their new armor shining. Fully geared with weapons, the freshly trained soldiers had been split in two sections, each made up of five rows, most ten strong across. It was an impressive sight, even if their numbers were lower than a typical army.

Fredrick stepped forward from the left to greet Amelia, offering his arm as she approached him. She accepted it, grateful her hands had stopped trembling.

Seb, Julian, and Caroline followed, while Kwan guided Olive over to Hannah's side. Eloise shadowed her father, gazing intently at the Order. Perhaps checking their formation.

"Fredrick, this is remarkable," Amelia said, feeling winded.

He beamed proudly, his white teeth flashing in the torch light. "Your Highness, may I present you with, the Queen's Order."

Surely rehearsed, every soldier saluted, then bowed in her direction.

"Long live Queen Amelia," Seb called from behind her.

The Order members followed his cue.

"Long live Queen Amelia!"

Their unified echoing cheer hit her square in the chest. Powerful was an understatement.

Holding back tears, she climbed atop the ledge of the fountain, hand on the constable's shoulder momentarily for balance. She surveyed the group and the hundreds of expectant eyes locked on her. The speech Caroline had helped her write in preparation burned in her cloak pocket, but she left it there.

"Thank you, to each and every one of you standing before me this evening. We gather because we share the common goal of taking back what has been stolen from us. I do not take lightly your choice to volunteer for your kingdom. You are strong, proud Dathovielians who saw the opportunity to take your lives into your own hands once more. To purify our land of an ill-appointed ruler and restore power where it rightfully belongs."

"Here, here!" hollered a man from the front row.

Amelia continued with a smile, confidence flooding her with each word. "I received testimony that King Alaric is responsible for Prince Brantley's murder. But that is not all. It has also been discovered he plans to trade our strongest men as slaves to Winvoltor. He views us all as nothing more than pawns on his chessboard."

"He must be eliminated," someone bellowed from the crowd.

Amelia raised her hand. "I wished to avoid bloodshed at all costs, but King Alaric threatens to destroy us from the inside out, and so we may need to fight."

"We will fight," a woman proclaimed from the left.

Steel clanged as the soldiers roared in agreement, swords banging against shields.

"We depart in the morning to call on more forces from our neighbours in Petrovia, and I hope you will join me."

"We shall," Fredrick declared, and most Order members nodded their endorsement.

Amelia took a deep breath.

"You all know the legend of King Dathos, for who we are named. He saw the beauty and promise of this land when everyone condemned it as unholy and uninhabitable. The sickness that tragically wiped out the indigenous tribe who first made these hills and forests their home, has returned in Alaric. Like a plague, he threatens your homes and lives. King Dathos fought off any potential tyrants with fair fighting. Surrendering soldiers were welcomed into our kingdom in exchange for their service and loyalty. As a result, Dathoviel amassed a great army. But he was not alone in garnering a large military force. Many men saw what he had taken and made fruitful, and they wanted it for themselves. My great-grandfather and a few men managed to survive the three long summers of the Great War, but they became a minor military power once again. Not unlike us here tonight. But Dathoviel was never again invaded! We had earned the respect of the surrounding kingdoms, and the surviving enemies told stories of the bravery that flows through our blood. We must remember that glory is not equated by our numbers. And only one cure is needed to eradicate sickness, not thousands!"

Scattered roars and whoops came from the group and the surrounding villagers, with Brianna's brothers perhaps the loudest of all. Hannah did not bother trying to quiet them for William was stomping his foot and hollering right along with everyone else.

Amelia beamed, the warmth of support bolstering her. The energy was contagious. She saw the sword hanging sheathed on Fredrick's hip and wordlessly requested it.

She had done this once before as a child during a training session when she had grown tired of the wooden swords and wished to know the unapologetic weight of a true weapon. At the time it had been taller than her, but tonight she knew she had the strength.

He passed it to her with a proud smile and a murmured, "Well done."

She gripped the hilt, thrusting the blade through the air over her head.

"Dathoviel is *our* kingdom! It belongs to us. The Queen's Order will heal and cleanse every last trace of King Alaric from our land. Tomorrow, we rise!"

The village exploded with celebration, their excitement deafening.

The revolution had begun.

. 14 .

"I ESTIMATE THREE HUNDRED men and women. I'm prepared to ship them by summer's end," Alaric said, fingers steepled beneath his chin.

It was late in the evening, but he'd nearly won.

Winvoltor's pale skinned, golden-haired monarch jumped from his chair with glee. The ornate wooden desk between them rattled as his rather large gut bounced off the edge.

If one could measure a person's wickedness, King Bart would rank as the cruelest ruler in the eight Northern Kingdoms. He'd become the wealthiest and most feared through many dastardly alliances, and anyone who wouldn't cooperate, swiftly met the tip of his sword. He'd never met a foe he couldn't conquer, or a tempting offer he could refuse.

"And your queen is supportive? Her father always struggled to see the *correct* way of doing things."

"My queen knows her place," Alaric assured him.

"Well," Bart extended his thick, fat fingers. "seems a firm handshake is in order. I'm pleased to finally partner with Dathoviel."

"The pleasure is ours."

Alaric wasn't about to question his luck. Fate had dealt his cards, and he deserved this.

After a night indulging in drink, a seven-course meal, and a few unique substances, Alaric decided to enjoy the scenery and take advantage of the rare game Winvoltor offered. He would still arrive home a full week earlier than estimated, and Leah would be so pleased with a fur coat no other women in Dathoviel could possess.

He'd send word in the morning of his success and haste return with a request to hurry along the transport wagons. Perhaps if they could deliver the villagers early, Bart would agree to a higher cut. Alaric had ensured their original agreement remained low enough that Winvoltor's vaults would hardly notice the mild depletion in hopes of negotiating a higher percentage in the future.

With everything going his way, nothing could stop him now.

~

Julian entered the crowded pub, eyes scanning the tables for Eloise. He'd hoped to wait longer than a single day before approaching her again, but she was leaving in the morning, so he had no choice. He still knew too little about her to have the confidence he preferred when talking to a woman like her, but desperate, last-minute times and all that.

He looked past the laughter and celebration of the couples snuggling closer than usual as they prepared for separation. Possibly forever. Olive was tucked behind the bar, whispering to Kwan, her arm around his waist. His eyes widened before he gestured to a man on his left, tossed over the towel he had thrown over his shoulder, and tugged the handmaiden upstairs.

Julian watched them, gut twinging with longing. That was all he wanted, and for some mad reason, he wanted it with Eloise.

Finally, he spotted her gracefully striding toward a table of Order members, two mugs in each hand. She sat with ease, passing the drinks to her seated companions. Her head fell back as someone made her laugh out loud.

Gods, she was stunning.

He watched, practically entranced, as she lifted the mug to her lips and smiled against it, testing the first sip of beer before drawing in a longer taste. She licked the foam from her dark lips, and in that moment, he'd never been more jealous of an inanimate object then he was of that mug.

Deep breath.

She's not yours yet. She might never be.

Still, he could picture himself one day grabbing a free chair, dragging it next to her, flopping down, and wrapping his arm around her shoulders. Pressing a kiss to her temple and earning himself a smile. He could also picture vomiting all over his shoes and scaring her away for eternity. So, the confidence wasn't all there.

Deep breath. Don't be intimidated. Just go sit down. They weren't exactly friends, but he was an honorary member of the Order. He belonged here.

An odd pull coiled at the base of his spine, propelling his feet forward. He wasn't running, but he wasn't moving at a typical pace either. A purposeful stride, or a confident march perhaps was the best description he could hope for.

When he got close enough, he reached out, touching her bare elbow. It was barely a graze, but her head spun, arm pulled back like he'd stung her. Her narrowed eyes softened for a moment over his face before hardening like a mask. But she didn't look away.

So. . . there *was* a glint of something beneath the steel. And if he was patient enough, he might get to see more of it.

"Come to tell some jokes?" one man at the table laughed.

He elbowed the soldier beside him, causing the man to splutter alcohol everywhere.

"Hey everyone!" another called. "The Fool's here to grace us with his *talents*."

Julian narrowly avoided flinching. No, he didn't think he'd like to sit at this table after all. Eloise continued to stare, her expression guarded, perhaps keeping important thoughts tucked away.

The first man continued, goading Julian for a poem or a song. He pounded his fists on the table in a rhythm meant to inspire the other patrons to join in his aggressive chant of "Dance, Fool!"

But when Maria's name crossed the second man's lips, along with some crass suggestions, Julian broke. He made to lunge across the table, but Eloise was already standing, her chair clattering to the wooden floor. Her fist connected with the second man's jaw, snapping his head back. Blood pooled at the corner of his mouth, dripping from his nose, and Julian's head spun. He had to look away, so he looked to Eloise. She might as well have been on fire as she spat curses from her exquisite mouth to the table.

"—and keep your fucking mouth shut!" she finished, whipping around to grab Julian's wrist, right where his tattoo ended.

Her touch pierced his skin and shot up his arm. She dragged him outside, Fredrick racing behind them down the stairs. Julian waited for him to chastise his daughter, but it never happened.

"Are you two alright?"

Eloise was seething. "I *told* you Jameson was a cad. I demand he's released from the Order. Tonight. *Now!*" She dropped Julian's wrist, aiming back inside. "In fact, I'll do it myself."

Fredrick put a hand out to stop her, his expression firm but understanding. "I'm certain you already took care of that. It's doubtful he'll be reporting for roll call in the morning."

"Don't you want to know why I hit him?" she challenged.

Fredrick tilted his head to the side, almost amused. "Have you ever hit someone who didn't deserve it?"

"No."

"Do you *want* to tell me what happened?"

"No."

"Then perhaps we should all retire for the evening," Fredrick finally looked toward Julian. "Are you staying in the village tonight or returning to the castle with Amelia?"

"No sense waking my girls at this hour," he answered.

The look on Fredrick's face as he looked between Julian and his daughter was near devilish. Then Regina appeared in the doorway and he let out a long, clearly fake yawn and stretched.

"I'll stay behind for now, but I'll see you when the sun rises."

Julian could have kissed him in gratitude. Instead, he clenched his sweaty palms behind his back. To be alone with Eloise was all he'd wanted, but now what? He hadn't actually thought this far ahead.

Fredrick pressed a gentle peck to Eloise's cheek and gave her shoulders a squeeze before slipping back into the pub. Julian glimpsed the constable sweep Regina into his arms and their slanted kiss before the door shut, blocking them from view.

Julian grimaced uncomfortably when he realized Eloise had been staring at him. No, glaring.

Was she displeased because of the encounter inside, or because she'd been left alone with him? She turned on her heel, heading north to the trees.

"Mind if I walk with you?"

She glanced back at him, contemplating. "If you must."

He jogged to fall in step beside her. "I wouldn't want to go wandering alone without my fierce protector."

She didn't return his smile, but at least she had stopped scowling.

"I may have acted a bit rashly," she admitted as they entered the forest. "I have a low tolerance for assholes."

"And I thank you," he said gently. "For reacting at all. I've grown used to their taunts, but when they bring the people I love into it... Let's just say, you beat me to the *punch*."

A sound almost like a chuckle escaped her lips as she dodged a low-hanging branch.

When they reached the beach, she stopped. He watched her eye the star splattered sky and the water reflecting it. He itched to feel her skin beneath his fingers and wondered if her kiss would still taste like the beer she'd sampled earlier. But he didn't dare reach out again.

"I'm sorry for the things those men said to you," she said after a few moments. "And about your wife."

"My wife?"

Did she mean Maria?

"Well, whoever she is, she doesn't deserve being spoken about like that. No woman does."

He looked upward, following her gaze across the constellations.

"Maria is not my wife," he assured her.

Her lips pursed. She looked down at the water.

"I told my father Jameson couldn't be trusted. Someone who thinks the way he does cannot be relied upon. Not in battle or ever."

"I'm surprised he didn't listen. You and your father seem close."

Eloise's shoulders rose, then fell, like she was taking a deep breath. "Yes, we are. Though. . . I hadn't the slightest inkling he was courting Regina."

Julian laughed.

"I don't think courting is what they are doing."

Her glare was meant to freeze his soul no doubt, but it only encouraged him.

"Well, I'm not interested in naming it anything else."

"Don't tell me you're against their relationship?"

She looked out over the water again, the toe of her boot digging into the sand. "I'm not against it. . ." She sighed. "It's just that my father hasn't been with anyone since my mother died. Of course I don't want him to be alone forever. I guess I just never took the time to imagine him with someone else."

Now it was Julian's turn to stare at the water. He chose the spot where the half-full moon reflected on the rippling waves.

"What about you?"

"What about me?"

Their eyes met. He thought she would look away eventually, but she didn't. So he didn't either.

"Are you currently courting?"

Her eyes widened. "That's a very personal question."

"Yes. Will you answer it?"

"It isn't really any of your business." she scoffed and looked away.

In fact, she turned right around and began walking back toward the trees. It took him almost a full minute to follow, sand filling his shoes with every quick, sloppy step. How was she able to move so swiftly across the sand when it was taking everything in him not to fall on his face?

"I didn't mean to offend you," he called, hoping she would hear him and stop.

"You didn't offend me," she shot over her shoulder. "I am not so delicate I could be offended by a simple, although intrusive question as that. What kind of girl do you think I am?"

She'd stopped long enough for him to catch up. The moon was slipping behind a cloud so he could only make out the profile of her jaw, which was set tight. If he could see her eyes, no doubt he would be able to see her nerves. Was she trembling? He had to blink at her hands twice to confirm she was. And there was no way she was breathless from her smooth walk up to the forest. He bothered her. Hopefully, in all the right ways.

"I don't believe you are any type of *girl*. You, Eloise, are a woman. One who knows exactly what she wants, I'd bet."

"What I want?"

He stepped sideways, guiding her to turn and face him. The clouds parted and the moonlight finally cast over her confused features.

"Yes. I know what *I* want, and it's you."

"For what exactly?"

He almost chuckled. Oh, so, so many things.

Testing, he took one step closer to her, still ensuring they didn't touch. He wanted her to initiate contact this time.

"Everything, Eloise. I want absolutely everything with you."

She gaped at him. "Are you drunk?"

"Not at all."

"Mad, then?"

He smirked. "That's debatable, but no. Not regarding you."

"So what?" She flung her hands around. "You're declaring your love for me randomly on this beach? We met this morning, and frankly I'm unsure if I can even stand you."

"Not love, no."

"So lust then," she challenged, her leather vest tightening as she crossed her arms. "You just want to take me to bed? That at least I can believe."

"I would very much like to take you to bed, yes," he nodded calmly. "but not for only one night, if that's what you're thinking."

Her eyes narrowed. "Speak plainly, jester. Right now. Or so help me—"

"I want you in bed, Eloise. And up against that tree and down in this sand, and behind a tapestry in the castle and in the middle of the damn square on a Sunday just as church is letting out, if you'd allow it. I want you in every way possible, in every location possible. And I'd like if you wanted the same."

His hands were clenched into fists at his side, using every ounce of control he possessed not to grab her and kiss her senseless. Her mouth hung open, eyes just blinking. Then her lips started to move, open and closed like she was trying to form words but couldn't.

After a fumbling moment that felt like a thousand years to him, she grabbed the front of his tunic and tugged, wrapping her free arm around his neck.

She inhaled in a quick breath, drawing it right from his lungs, pulling him close roughly. He knew he needed to be in control. To guide her through this and get a grip on himself, but he was out of practice. And it was far too easy to be swept away by those lips and those fingers. There was no use fighting it, and for a moment, he considered surrendering *to her* fully. He had the ability. But that wasn't what she needed. She needed him to provide her freedom. To lift the weight of the world from her shoulders.

And then he felt the beginnings of her submission.

A slackness to her jaw, the buckling in her knees, and the press of her chest against his. And he heard her moan travel from the depths of her belly, up and out through her mouth. When her breath ghosted over his lips, he reached around and pulled her close, his tongue running over the edges of her teeth, seeking admittance. When she granted it, his own knees almost gave out, but he held on.

He held on with everything he had.

April 7th, 1457

Leaving the kitchens behind and reaffirming his grip on the basket Regina had packed him, Fredrick squeezed her trembling hand in his, dragging her close so he could press a kiss to her forehead. Her bronze skin wrinkled with fret over his departure.

She wanted him to stay, but she would never ask. He couldn't let Eloise face whatever was about to happen in Petrovia alone. And she understood better than anyone. After all, she'd begged him to release her own son from the Order when she'd found out he joined.

Neither spoke as they made their way toward the main castle entrance, the sun just beginning to rise outside the windows.

"Regina," he began, clearing his throat.

But a gruff sound from the left interrupted him. Lord Marcel, still in his pajamas, was stomping toward them from a nearby corridor. His cheeks were flushed with anger, and his hands clenched into fists.

"Constable! What the hell is going on?"

Fredrick sighed. He'd really been hoping to avoid this.

Instinctively he stepped in front of Regina, tucking her behind him. It was doubtful Marcel would physically lash out, but there was no telling if he'd returned to his drinking.

"My Lord."

Marcel swore again and shook his fist. "I demand to know what the hells going on!"

Fredrick stopped his compulsive bow halfway and straightened. He owed this man nothing, including respect.

"I'm afraid it's not my place to explain."

Marcel sneered. "I doubt Amelia's hysterical explanations will make any sense. If you cared about this kingdom and its inhabitants, you'd chain her up somewhere until we can bring in proper help."

Fredrick stood tall. "Your daughter is a brave, intelligent woman. If you speak against her again, *you* will be the one tossed away in chains."

Regina let out a low gasp and tugged on his sleeve, warning him. He ignored her. This fight with Marcel was decades in the making, and he was tired of staying silent.

"Who the hell do you think you are?" Marcel bellowed, jabbing his pointer finger into Fredrick's chest. "I may no longer be king, but I'll be damned if I let someone like you speak to me this way."

Fredrick could feel the vein in his temple pulsing. "To which part of me are you referring? My title? My power? Or my color?"

Marcel jabbed him once more. "You know precisely what I mean. If I had it my way, you would never have been allowed to rise through the ranks. But, Diana always had a soft spot for things like you. You might as well have been a broken black horse she could fix up and show off."

"Lord Marcel!" Regina exclaimed. "Have you forgotten yourself?"

"Shut it, woman."

Fredrick's blood boiled. He moved forward, stepping into Marcel's bony finger, bending it back.

"One more word, Marcel. Give me a reason, I beg you. I've wanted to knock sense into your pathetic, intolerant, narrow-minded drunk ass since the day we met."

"Fredrick, don't," Regina gasped, fingers grazing his armor, trying to pull him back.

She was only trying to protect him, but he was done being afraid of Marcel. He stepped forward again.

"One. More. Word," the constable dared, knowing how terrifying he looked glaring and looming over the former king.

Marcel tried to return the glare, but he didn't have it in him. In less than a minute his arm had dropped and he was backing away.

"You know nothing about me," he said weakly.

Fredrick refused to back down. He was too far gone in his anger for himself and Amelia. For Eloise. For everyone he'd seen Marcel look down upon the last thirty years. He and Diana had been friends, so her death had devastated him, like everyone else in the kingdom. Having lost his own wife, he could sympathize with the man to a degree, but not in a way that excused his abhorrent parenting and slanted nature.

"I know you had a wife who only saw the best in people. She lived to offer anyone worthy a chance to reach their full potentials. I know she saw greatness in you, and that you tried and failed to live up to it. I know her death drove you to madness because without her, you were nothing. Everyone knows that is why you abdicated, Marcel. It wasn't your hate for politics. It was because you were nowhere near man enough without her guiding you. You failed Diana. You failed Brantley. And now you're failing Amelia."

"Enough!" Marcel bellowed, but there was no fire in his gaze.

He was no longer angry, but desperate to avoid the truth.

"You have a choice, Marcel. One last chance to be the man Diana hoped was inside you and the father your daughter deserves. To open your mind to the world in front of you and see how people who look and act differently than you aren't a threat. If you don't, I guarantee you will lose everything."

This time Fredrick reached for Regina, jaw so tight he feared his teeth might shatter between the grinding and the heavy impact of his boots against the stone.

The only thing that kept him from turning back and breaking the former king's nose was the familiar visualization of rolling ocean waves and Regina's warmth at his side.

~

The first thing Eloise noticed upon waking the next morning was how calm she felt. The second was the taste of sea salt on her lips. Third was the sand digging into her hip.

She had fallen asleep on the beach?

It had happened before, so it wasn't the most alarming discovery. That title she reserved for the awareness of a body shifting at her side. A warm, snoring, distinctly *male* body. A *shirtless* male body. The steady rise and fall of his warm chest beneath her palm was evidence enough.

Eloise bolted up, all the way to her feet. She clutched desperately at her torso, both surprised and relieved to find her clothes on and everything in place.

Nothing had happened.

Her sudden exit from Julian's embrace had roused him and he was easing up, blinking around the beach.

Gazing up at her, he shielded his eyes from the sunrise and moved to stand.

The memory of his words and lips from last night, and the way she'd felt had her stepping back.

"G'morning," he said, voice deep with sleep.

She traced the dark ink on his arm, distracted by it. "Morning."

A thick, black vine curled around the length of his arm, starting at his wrist and up past his bicep. Between the leaves, five different flowers were spaced evenly on the vine, each a shade darker than the last and slightly larger.

She'd seen many men shirtless the last few months as she'd trained the Order. None of them had tattoos. In fact, she couldn't think of anyone born and raised in Dathoviel that had one, particularly no one that lived in the castle. Such things weren't tolerated in court, but then again, Julian did have one foot in, and one foot out of castle life. If anyone could get away with something like that, surely the court jester could.

"Sleep well?"

She scoffed, hoping he hadn't noticed her investigation of his arm. "I would have slept better in a bed."

His eyes flashed with lust and she took a second deliberate step back. She'd stepped back because she wanted to step closer and lose herself in his kiss again. To feel his arms around her and her chest pressed tightly against his.

She must get away from him. She had to—*shit!* She needed to find her father. And deal with the sand in her braids. They were leaving in a few hours, and she still hadn't packed.

"I recommended a bed." Julian smirked. "And a few other places if I remember correctly. You said no."

She could have screamed from frustration.

"Can you put your shirt on, please?"

He chuckled, dropping his inked arm from above his eyes, and bent to retrieve the folded navy fabric from the sand. She'd used it as a pillow, apparently.

He stood once more and tugged it on, lips quirking, eyebrows dancing on his forehead.

"Is this where you tell me last night was a mistake, and you don't know what you were thinking? That it can never happen again?"

Part of her brain begged her to say yes. To banish every memory and forbid him from mentioning it. Instead, she listened to the other parts of her body. The parts that didn't care how quickly their relationship was developing.

"No. I mean. . . nothing happened that needs forgetting. I regret nothing."

Surely his grin was brighter and wider than the entire ocean at her back.

"That's marvelous to hear."

"Yes, well." She looked toward the trees. "I need to get back now. There's still a chance I can beat my father to the stables."

He stepped out of her way, gesturing to the path leading to the village. "I'll find you at send-off."

She halted as she passed him. "You aren't going to follow me?"

"There's something I must do, and I'd prefer no witnesses."

"Oh," her eyes narrowed at him, but she forced her legs to move forward. "Alright."

As the ground beneath her feet turned from sand to moss a series of cheers carried on behind her.

She laughed. Julian's joyful whooping as he splashed in the water carried her back to the village.

~

Amelia yawned behind her hand as she and Caroline descended the tower steps. The blonde chattered eagerly, looking vigilant despite the lack of sleep from last night's celebrations.

"It will take two days to reach Petrovia," she said briskly, her coral pink skirts swishing as she talked more to herself than the queen. "There is an inn situated a few miles beyond the halfway point. It should have sufficient beds to accommodate most of us."

And what might happen if there were not enough beds. . .

Amelia distracted herself with tugging at the cuffs of her blouse as they selected the corridor leading to the main entrance. The Order had been instructed last night to meet outside there at sunrise with their horses—if they had them, and any belongings they wished to bring.

"Are you still planning to ride lead with me?"

"Of course." Caroline grinned. "As long as you're still comfortable with me riding Gus? I can always share the carriage with Olive otherwise."

Amelia nodded, a small smile on her lips and a faint twinge in her heart. Leaving him behind felt unjust, not to mention cruel. Caroline riding him meant he would remain at Greta's side.

"He seems to like you."

Caroline blushed. "I'm still a little nervous riding him, but knowing you'll be close by helps."

Their fingertips brushed, both simultaneously moving closer despite the vast hallway. Amelia eyed an alcove to the left. She considered dragging Caroline into it for a moment of privacy before hundreds of eyes were on them, but the heavy footsteps coming up behind them had her pulse racing.

When Marcel's sharp tone cut through the air, she froze, heart sinking. Her hope of leaving Dathoviel without him knowing had been foolish.

"Amelia!"

Slowly, she turned.

"Yes?"

He huffed, looking rather scruffy, open robe whipping behind him and hands flailing as he gestured to the front doors. His eyes swept crossly over her riding clothes, but he prioritized other transgressions first.

"I overheard a guard saying something about you being gone for a few days? I asked Fredrick, but he. . . was unwilling to share your destination."

"You heard correctly."

His cheeks flushed red. "Where are you going? And why is your travelling party so large?"

She did not have time for this.

"Father, please try to understand what I am about to tell you."

"Understand what? *Where* are you going?"

"Petrovia."

His eyes nearly popped from their sockets. "What?"

"I intend to speak with King Spencer regarding Alaric, and request his help. We have come to understand Alaric intends to enslave our strongest and healthiest men to Winvoltor as slaves in exchange for gold."

A part of her had wondered if he had known all along, but to her relief he looked justifiably appalled.

"If you have proof of this you can present it to the court," he barked.

"If I had proof of it, I would have already done so. It seems Alaric's mistress knew we were privy to the information and destroyed any evidence. All we have is our word against his, and it is no secret how thickly he lines the justice's pockets."

"And what do you think Spencer will do?" He scoffed, gesturing at Caroline flippantly in her cousin's place.

The back of Amelia's neck burned. Of course, he wouldn't believe in her now. Why would today be any different?

"Well, someone must try something. Alaric cannot be allowed to continue ruling our kingdom."

His eyes narrowed, scolding. "It's not that hard to be a wife. To turn a blind eye and simply enjoy the blessings God granted you at birth."

"It is if you have a soul."

He waved a finger at her. "This has gone too far. You must relinquish this fantasy of life without Alaric. He is your husband and your king. You *will* submit to this fate, Amelia. You must."

Her body quaked with energy and rage. He had no idea what he was talking about, but perhaps it was time he did.

"I *must* do nothing but stop the madman you brought into our home. Mother would be so ashamed of you."

His face turned purple.

"Leave her out of this!"

"When are you going to wake up and accept she is gone? A fact you should be grateful for, because I doubt she would take kindly to you endorsing the man responsible for killing her son!"

The blood drained from Marcel's face.

"Brantley died in a hunting accident."

Her eyes stung, and she let the tears flow, not caring what he thought of her. "Have you ever known Alaric to miss a target?"

He shook, unable and unwilling to process the news. So, she watched as he did with it what he did best. He locked away reason and acceptance in a box, far from his heart and mind. Whatever he had left to feel turned to resentment and he directed it her way.

"That is some story you've concocted to justify hating your husband, and I won't stand for it, Amelia. It's sickening. Can you not let your brother rest in peace?"

"He will never find true peace until Alaric pays for what he has done."

"And you believe Spencer will make him pay? What do you think will happen, Amelia? Do you plan to seduce him and ask him to kill his brother for you?"

Beside her, Caroline bristled, but she held back, giving Amelia the space to stand up for herself.

"I have more to offer than my body, Father."

He ignored her.

"I'm calling the counsel into session. What you're doing is treason!"

He could if he wanted to, but she and the Order would be long gone before they could gather and make decisions. He had no power over her, and judging by the despair in his eyes, she knew the fact was not lost on him.

She had watched him wither away from a crown, from life, into a bottle and books and denial. He was just a lost old man. And despite how badly she wished he would love and understand her, or even *see* her as worthy of his time, he never would. And she could not force him to. It was not her job to save him. To make him care. Love between a parent and a child should not be this hard.

As her father, he should have been the first one at her side. But he wasn't. All he was now, was the last thing standing between her avenging Brantley's death and saving her people.

"Brantley died alone and cold, far from his home and the people who loved him most. He was murdered, Father, and I intend to make the man who did it, pay. One way or another. Since you will not help me, I must look elsewhere for support." He opened his mouth to interrupt, but she stepped forward, glaring at him. "No. You will never silence me again. I am doing this, and you will remain here in Dathoviel and keep our kingdom safe. *That* Lord Marcel, is a command from *your* queen."

He balked, and she spun on her heel, refusing him the chance to recover. Whatever he said next, if he said anything at all, was to an empty, echoing corridor.

~

Hannah watched with bright eyes as Olive and Kwan embraced for a third time, stalling.

The majority of the traveling party were already perched in their saddles or riding in one of two large wagons. There were only a few stragglers who'd slept in or were still saying their farewells, Olive included.

"Perhaps I should stay with you," the handmaiden said, bottom lip quivering.

Kwan shook his head. "We both know you can't. This lot would fall apart without you."

He pulled her against him tightly, and Hannah turned to look at William. He wrapped his arm around her shoulders, keeping her close. She was so thankful he had not joined the Order.

"We'll take good care of him, Olive," he said, clapping Kwan on the shoulder. "Between your trip, and the tavern and the kids, you'll both be so busy there will hardly be time to miss one another."

He smiled, trying to simultaneously comfort them both.

"Yes," Hannah chimed in. "You'll be home before you know it."

The handmaiden nodded, stepping back towards the queen's carriage. She was now the last Order member with her feet still on the ground. Kwan reached around her for the door handle and pulled it open before helping her onto the step.

Then he wrapped his free hand around the side of her neck and kissed her hard. Hannah's own cheeks heated from the intensity, and William whooped, encouraging the display.

"Maybe I ought to come with you," Kwan suggested once he'd pulled back. "If you'll truly return soon, what harm will it do the village to be without their drink a few days?"

It was clear Olive wanted to say yes. "You're needed here, just as I'm needed there. Your grandfather needs you."

She slipped into the otherwise empty carriage, and Kwan shut the door, neither looking happy.

He blurted out his next words as if he hadn't properly thought them through.

"I love you, Olive."

Her eyes widened. "Oh Kwan, I love you too."

He smirked, teetering on the step. "Yeah?"

"Yeah." She nodded and grabbed his collar.

They shared one last kiss through the window between teal curtains as a trumpet sounded from the front of the convoy of horses and wagons. It was time.

Begrudgingly, Kwan stepped back, moving next to William, never taking his eyes off Olive.

~

It was time.

At the front line, Amelia's ears were ringing, both from the trumpet and her argument with her father.

Her fingers gripped the reins roughly, and Caroline briefly reached over, caressing her knuckles.

"Scared?" she asked gently.

Amelia nodded, thinking of her father. "Among other things."

Caroline's lips pursed.

"I'm here to listen when you're ready to talk."

Amelia smiled gratefully, turning her palm up momentarily to grip Caroline's hand.

"I wish I could kiss you right now."

Caroline licked her lips and pulled back, looking to her own reigns. "That would be nice."

Before Amelia could respond, she felt a tapping on her boot. She gazed down to find Brianna beaming up at her, a tattered bouquet of wildflowers in her hand.

Margaret stood nearby, her watchful eyes focused on her niece. "Please excuse the intrusion, Your Highness. Brianna insisted on bidding you farewell."

Amelia slid from the saddle and crouched so she could be at the child's height. She held her hands open.

"Are the flowers for me?"

Brianna nodded eagerly and thrust them forward.

"The purple ones are to bless your journey, and the white ones are to protect you in, Pe—Petrovia."

Amelia took the flowers, many of which had dirt still attached to their roots and held them to her chest.

"Thank you for your generous gift, Brianna."

The girl watched with wide eyes as Amelia selected one of the white blossoms and shortened the stem. When she secured it into the thick braid hanging next to Brianna's ear, the girl grinned.

"And this is to keep you and your family safe. You'll look after them for me while I'm gone?"

"I will. I promise." Brianna nodded eagerly.

Amelia rose.

Quickly, the child wrapped her arms around Amelia's legs, squeezing tightly. The queen smiled, embracing her in return, her own chest expanding with pleasant overwhelm.

When Margaret finally pulled Brianna away, the queen was fighting back tears. She climbed into the saddle once more, tucking the flowers into her satchel bag.

With a quick look over her shoulder, she found Fredrick's eyes and nodded. He mirrored her gesture and pressed one last farewell kiss to Regina's hand before he began calling out commands to the Order members surrounding him. Eloise followed his example a few rows back, looking both ready and exhausted.

Amelia turned back to face the horizon. The warm orange and pinks of sunrise were slowly fading away into a pale blue.

"Shall we?" Caroline asked.

"We shall."

15

Near midday, the sun beat its hottest and brightest over the Order. They'd been making excellent time, but it was clear from everyone's wavering demeanors that the initial excitement was wearing thin with each passing hour.

Surrounded by a chorus of complaining and cursing, Fredrick coaxed his steed forward. Once he reached Eloise's side, she greeted him with a confident smile and a nod, her new armor glinting. The small shells her grandmother had carved into beads clinked at the ends of her braids, perfectly timed with her horse's trots.

"How's the Order holding back there?"

Fredrick grinned mischievously.

"Most have never ridden this long, so there's much groaning."

"They'll sleep well tonight, which is good. They shall need it. We have a bit further than this to go tomorrow before reaching Petrovia."

He watched her assess the horizon and their surroundings multiple times, her eyes always returning to Amelia. The queen rode just ahead, flanked by Caroline and Seb; the three occasionally chatting quietly.

"I'm very proud of you, Eloise."

She glanced back to him, a faint smile curling the edges of her lips.

"For?"

"How seriously you're taking all this. Overcoming your dislike for the queen."

A light chuckle escaped as she straightened her reins, readjusting her position in the saddle.

"I admit, she's not *as* terrible as I originally thought."

"What changed your mind?"

When Eloise looked up, her gaze crackling with nerves.

"She's agreed to allow your retirement when this is all over."

"Ah," Fredrick nodded, lips pursed. "I see now."

The world made sense again. This was never about the queen or Alaric, or even Dathoviel. How foolish he'd been to think otherwise.

Their eyes met.

"See what?"

"You've been going along with all this for me."

"You're surprised?"

"I had hoped you'd moved on from your obsession with making Marcel pay."

"Never." She looked back to the horizon.

"He's not even king anymore. Please release this vendetta."

"I won't. I must see his face when Amelia names *me* Constable." She grinned. "Imagine! He always looked down on you for your skin color, Father. Now a *woman*, with the same skin, will be leading his former army, protecting his daughter as queen. It's too rich."

There was a long pause while Fredrick worked to gather his thoughts. Truthfully, he was grateful to have a daughter who loved him so much. But she hardly had a life of her own.

At her age, she should be distracted and passionate about things that made her heart beat faster. That consumed her dreams. Not his fate, which had been sealed long ago. Still, he knew he wasn't the one to tell her to live her life differently than she wished. Not only would she have not listened, but quite like her mother, she would have only dug her heels in and fought harder.

Still, he *could* make suggestions, couldn't he? Inspire her to look beyond this cause.

"One day I'll be gone, Eloise. Where will you channel your energy then?"

As expected, she wasn't interested in hearing his subtle warning.

"Oh, Father, we both know you'll live forever."

The greying hair above his ears said differently.

"You will need to find someone else to give all this attention to. Or perhaps, you could focus it on yourself for once."

"You speak as if I'm unhappy."

"I know you're content with your life," he said gently, sensing a snap coming from the way her eyes narrowed. "But don't you think maybe there's something else out there? Something you're missing?"

"You know I'm not the marrying kind if that's what you're talking about."

He knew better than to suggest that again.

"You don't need marriage to be happy, Eloise. But have you considered perhaps needing someone, or something more than me? What about Julian? You two seemed to get along last night at the pub."

She looked away. "I don't like thinking about life without you."

"I know, darling." He reached across the space between them, and took her hand, pressing her fist to his chest. "But remember, I'll always be with you and you with me. Right here."

She nodded, blinking back tears.

"We'll discuss this more when we return to Dathoviel."

He sighed in relief. That answer was better than any he'd heard before.

"Agreed."

~

Everyone knew Amelia wished to press on to Petrovia, but as they reached the town that was barely a town, the piercing spikes in her lower back and her companion's weary faces proved the final leg of their journey must wait till morning.

The innkeeper, an older woman with thinning grey hair, had no qualms with sharing her life story. She served the sizeable crowd a hearty dinner, chattering throughout the first course about how her husband had run off to a faraway village. Everyone devoured the stew gratefully, longing for a bed and silence, but no one perhaps more than Caroline.

It had been the longest day of her life. Every muscle and bone in her body ached, begging for her bed back in the castle. Her soul was devastated as she realized this inn was a far cry from the luxurious sheets and lavender scented pillows she was used to. Whatever bed she was given tonight would not satisfy her needs.

Of which she presently had many.

Since last night her heart had been pumping unyielding desire through her bloodstream. And now, sitting across the table from Amelia, her body finally still, she felt the full force of the pulsing ache.

She watched with hawk like focus the way Amelia's fingers gripped the spoon. How her lips closed around each bite, lids fluttering as she savored the meal.

Finally, their eyes met. Amelia's next bite froze in mid-air on the way back to her tempting lips and her eyes turned questioning, as if to ask Caroline what was wrong.

How she'd love nothing more than to drag her from the table and capture that pretty mouth with her own. One might imagine the craving to kiss would subside after a few sessions, but if that point was possible with Amelia, she'd yet to reach it.

Since last night at the presentation a fire had been growing inside her, stoked by every glance and accidental hand brush they'd managed to covertly execute. But now she was fit to burst, and it took all her strength not to stand up from the bench she shared with various Order members and beg the queen to take her right here.

Whatever that meant.

She'd heard other ladies talk that way, and though she wasn't entirely sure if it were possible for two women, it seemed right to think it. She would love nothing more than for Amelia to take her body and do as she pleased with it. And then allow Caroline to do the same in return.

Mind swimming with images of what that would look like, inspired by the things she'd heard and read, she squirmed. Her thighs pressed together and short breaths escaped her barely parted lips. Amelia seemed to notice *that* at least, for her eyebrow raised ever so slightly with silent questions.

Heartbeat now pounding between her ears, Caroline bit down on her lip, forcing the answers to stay inside. Why had she chosen to sit here rather than next to Amelia? If they were closer, she could reach under the table. Perhaps caress her thigh or run her fingertips along the inside of the queen's wrist. Anything to make her skin flush so they burned at the same degree.

Caroline was so tightly wound that when a hand touched her shoulder, she yelped. She broke free of Amelia's gaze, glancing quickly to Seb who sat next to her, looking genuinely concerned.

"Are you feeling unwell?" he asked slowly, as if he were repeating it. Perhaps he was. Until a moment ago, she'd been unable to hear anything but her racing pulse and tormented thoughts.

"Actually, I believe I should lie down."

Aroused and embarrassed, Caroline stood and headed around the table. Amelia's eyes remained locked on her as she reached the innkeeper.

"Ye alright, miss?" the older woman asked, interrupting herself. "Needing a refill?"

"Just directions to my room, please."

The woman unhooked a metal key from a thick ring around her hips, the rest jingling as she stepped closer to place it in Caroline's hand. "Up the stairs, turn left, fourth door on the right."

Caroline risked one last glance at Amelia, half hoping she'd follow.

How was she supposed to sleep in this strange place with her body fit to burst? *Uncomfortably*, that's how.

~

Amelia accepted her bath water cooling quicker than she preferred as a sign to rest before morning came. She certainly didn't want to move, but this tin tub wasn't getting any comfier, and if she lay here any longer, thinking of how Caroline had looked at her during dinner, she may go mad. Water pooled at her bare feet as she stepped across creaky planks, hoping to avoid alerting Eloise in the next room. She dodged an exposed nail and reached for the closest towel; a shabby looking thing she seriously considered not touching at all.

This was all part of the journey.

A quiet knock startled her and she hastily dried her body before slipping on a thin cream robe. With a quivering hand, she grasped for the dagger stowed in her satchel.

"Who is it?"

"It's me." Caroline's hushed voice carried through the keyhole. "Hurry."

Relieved, Amelia flipped the lock, opening the door a few inches. "Eloise is next door," she hissed.

"Then we best be quiet." Caroline, dressed in a mauve robe, slipped through the opening. "I couldn't sleep knowing you were all alone."

"I have grown fond of waking at your side," Amelia admitted.

"So, you understand why I couldn't last the night without you."

Amelia set the dagger aside, linking their fingers. "You are not used to riding so long. You must be exhausted. I *would* like you to stay, but—"

"Sleep is the last thing on my mind," Caroline whispered, blowing out the candelabra on the nightstand boldly.

The flames became smoke, casting the room in darkness save for the silver pooling moonlight across the bed. Powerless, Amelia melted into her arms.

"I am open to hearing alternative suggestions."

Caroline looked away nervously.

"I hoped you'd reconsider sharing yourself with me, tonight, rather than waiting until Alaric has been dealt with. The anticipation of our first time—*my* first time—is torture."

Amelia's head swam with visions of skin and tongues and moans filling the air.

"I had hoped we could marry first."

Caroline paused, perhaps searching for composure and patience. "I don't wish to pressure you, but I had to ask, or risk lying awake, tortured, and regretting my silence. I've craved every inch of your skin against mine since our first kiss."

"And you choose the most dangerous night of all to seduce me?" Amused, Amelia shook her head. "We have never had less privacy."

Caroline caressed Amelia's cheek with the backs of her fingertips.

"I know it's... inconvenient. If I could've ignored it, I would have."

"But you cannot control it?"

"Watching you last night as you addressed the Order...your body alive, eyes on fire, and your voice so commanding. It drove me mad. I want to taste your power on my lips and feel the strength beneath your skin."

She brought Amelia's hand to her ribs, her heartbeat pounding beneath the pale pink fabric and flushed skin.

"Caroline..."

"If you refuse, I promise not to utter another intimate word until our wedding night. But, if you desire it, my body is yours to rule, here and now."

Passion coiled low in Amelia's belly, burning from the inside out. Her left hand lifted, resting on Caroline's throat, holding herself steady. Caroline's lips parted and her head fell to the side, blonde waves pouring down her back. Then Caroline's hands slid down, kneading Amelia's hip. Her behind.

The queen's world went dark.

Her chest contracted as she traced the curve of Caroline's neck with her tongue, everything below her hips clenching. Everything above pounding at a tantalizing rhythm.

They slowly pulled apart, chests heaving. Their kisses and touches had already caused Caroline's robe to loosen and open enough for Amelia to rake her eyes down into the shadows of her cleavage.

Her tongue and teeth ached to follow.

"What do you want."

"All of you," Caroline whimpered.

"And you shall have me," Amelia brought Caroline's wrist to her lips, sucking the sensitive skin and earning a series of moans in reward. "But remember, we must be as quiet as possible."

Caroline nodded, clamping her lips together tightly.

Amelia's robe cascaded to the floor first, then she coaxed Caroline's down next.

Within a few moments, they both stood naked.

"You're the most beautiful sight I've ever seen," Caroline whispered, her cool fingers clasping Amelia's hips.

Anxious to please and be pleased, Amelia guided her beneath the blankets, seeking Caroline's lips and finding her hand clenched into a fist between their bodies.

"How can one filled with such intense desire, be so nervous?" she teased

Caroline gnawed her trembling bottom lip. "I fear failing to please you."

Amelia recalled the fear she had felt on her wedding night, even with *the* book.

"In many ways, this feels like my first time as well. You can start by touching me the way you find pleasure when you are alone. I shall express what I like or prefer."

Caroline's teeth clicked together, avoiding eye contact. "But... I... wish to taste you."

Desire spread to Amelia's toes and they curled in response.

"First, I must reward you. For your bravery and loyalty, patience, and understanding."

Amelia coaxed Caroline's legs open with light caresses, tempting out a lifetime's worth of forbidden desire. Her lips dropped over Caroline's exposed breast, kissing softly. She gazed into Caroline's darkening eyes.

Her fingers slipped down ever so *slightly*, ever so *slowly*, and Caroline yelped, head thrown back as a finger slipped inside of her.

"Amelia, please—"

"More?"

Caroline nodded vigorously, her hand clapping over her mouth when a second finger slid in. "Oh, God."

"Is this what you need?" Amelia teased, teeth nipping at a spot between Caroline's breast and shoulder. She found her clit with her thumb, and pressed. "Because *this* is what *I* have wanted since you stepped out of the carriage all those months ago."

Amelia dragged Caroline's hand away, devouring the sounds spilling from her lips. There was nothing hesitant or gentle about this kiss, unlike so many others before. Tongue diving into Caroline's mouth, her free hand laced through blonde curls, holding tight. She might float away otherwise.

Caroline soon began to writhe, gripping Amelia's shoulders, curses and pleas pouring from her mouth.

When her boneless body relaxed against the mattress, Amelia gently removed her fingers and tipped Caroline's head towards her, capturing satisfied sighs with slow kisses.

The familiar low clenching of desire returned as Caroline's tongue slipped between her teeth, searching for its mate.

"May I?" she whispered, pressing onto her elbows.

Feeling bold, Amelia nodded, rotating to her back, hips lifting off the mattress in anticipation. She watched as Caroline's dark glittering eyes disappeared between her thighs. She knew from the book what would happen, but the sensations would be new. Alaric had never bothered with this. Not that she had wanted him to.

Then she felt Caroline's lips on the inside of her knee, all the way up her thigh. Instinctually her legs tried to close, but Caroline wouldn't allow them. Then Amelia felt her tongue against her core, *testing*, curious, and all thought was purged. One hand fisted in the sheet, the other she tried to keep gentle in Caroline's hair. It was no use.

Her legs shook, her hips wanted to snap upward, but she held back—at first. The first time her hips rose, Caroline lost her rhythm, gulping for air. They both giggled, locking eyes for a mere moment before Caroline disappeared once more. This time she found Amelia's clitoris faster, her tongue moving more confidently, and the queen whimpered when she felt Caroline's groan rumble through her. Into her.

Amelia knew words were leaving her mouth, but she was not sure what they were. They must have been encouraging, because Caroline's tongue sped up, curling, and rolling.

Something familiar was happening inside her, but it was *more*. An intensity she'd never experienced alone. Then the coil within her core snapped, her grip tightening, hips bucking like an untamed stallion.

The darkness behind her lids flashed white. Somehow, she managed to turn her face into the pillow, and bit down on it, as Caroline left a trail of heated kisses from her stomach to her chest.

Please let Eloise be a deep sleeper.

April 8th, 1457

The Order made it to Petrovia in record time the following day, the setting sun greeting them as horses and riders reached the high iron gates. Amelia's eyes swept over the tall dark castle just beyond. Even outlined by the flaming orange sky, it was a stark, grey, and intimidating contrast to Dathoviel.

In place of simple wooden homes and children playing in the village square, Petrovia had stone walls covered in crawling ivy and fully armored guards marching in sharp battalions. She could not see any signs of a village, though surely there was one. Suddenly, meeting and dealing with the man ruling this well-oiled, cold kingdom seemed like a terrible idea.

Her hands ached to jerk Greta's reigns round, but backing out now would ensure Alaric's victory. Her people would suffer, and both she and Caroline would surely meet death.

Turning to Seb, she nodded for him to announce their arrival as rehearsed.

He spoke with the three men standing guard who appeared surprised, but pleased to see him. Moments later, the gates opened, and the Order was welcomed inside the kingdom. Upon reaching the front steps, servants appeared to guide the horses to the stables for a well-deserved rest, and the party was directed to the Great Hall by a quartet of uniformed guards.

The castle buzzed with energy as the servants did their best to accommodate the unexpected guests over the next few hours.

While the Order took space in the barracks, Eloise and Fredrick selected quarters on either side of Amelia's temporary rooms.

Caroline led her and Olive to the tower she and her mother had once occupied while Seb remained with the Petrovian guards to briefly explain why they were there and organize an audience with King Spencer immediately.

After everyone had a chance to eat and bathe, they collected in the Great Hall again. Strapped into a formal gown, Amelia tugged at the lace on her collar, already missing her riding clothes, as a new guard with bright red hair led her and Caroline to the throne room. Seb and Eloise followed but were ordered to wait as they reached the heavy redwood doors.

Eloise's objections fell on deaf ears.

"She'll be safe," Seb promised.

Amelia wondered if he was right as the door shut behind her.

The guard bowed toward the throne. "Your Highness, I present Queen Amelia of Dathoviel."

King Spencer stood, a warm smile on his handsome face. "It is a pleasure to meet you." They bowed in mutual respect to each other before he opened his arms to Caroline. "And it is so wonderful to see you again, dear cousin."

Amelia watched their embrace, observing not the slightest trace of Alaric in Spencer's demeanor. Despite the silver cape hanging across his broad shoulders and tall stature causing him to resemble one of the stone towers surrounding his castle, he seemed open and welcoming.

Yet she sensed he could turn to iron if provoked. Everyone had a limit, and when reached, there was no telling what could shift about a person. Herself included.

Caroline turned, drawing her attention back to the present and gestured for Amelia to join them.

"Spence, we do apologize for the unannounced visit. Amelia and I have urgent matters to discuss with you which couldn't wait."

"This castle is your home. You may come and go anytime." He gave a toothy grin before turning his attention to Amelia. His features shifted from boyish excitement to a man ready to discuss business. "Just how may I be of service?"

He gestured to a few nearby chairs. Amelia noticed he chose to sit *with* them rather than at his throne. Certainly not a choice Alaric would have made given similar circumstances. As he dismissed the guard who clanked away, Amelia sat, digging deep for bravery.

"We have come, Your Highness, to request your help regarding Alaric."

Spencer nodded, unsurprised. "I often wondered how long it would take for someone to put an end to him."

"I regret to admit I nearly allowed him to destroy my kingdom. He was well on his way to starving my subjects to death before I stepped in. Recently we have learned he plans to sell them into slavery and intends to have me killed so his mistress may become queen. There is also the personal matter of my brother, Prince Brantley, who he murdered."

Spencer's fists clenched. For a moment, the iron within quivered, but just as quickly, his stoic expression returned.

"And what is it that you seek?"

Amelia clamped down on her nerves. "I desire to rule my kingdom without his influence."

Caroline leaned in. "You know better than anyone, Spence. He must be stopped. We don't have the numbers to take him on ourselves and he won't step aside without a fight."

Spencer clapped his hands against his thighs as if they'd just decided what to have for dinner and he was the cook. Amelia could even picture him rolling up his sleeves, but he only tugged at his burgundy cuffs.

"Very well. Alaric has angered a great many people in his life. No one would doubt an assassination attempt. Where is he now?"

"Winvoltor," Amelia explained. "When he returns, we believe he will begin taking the men from the village. Whom he intends to sell to King Bartholomew for slaves in his gold mine. *If* the king agrees to his terms."

"Oh, that bastard won't hesitate. We've long considered going to war with him. However, he can buy many allies, and I'm not in the business of making enemies I don't need to. If Alaric gains his favor, he will become unstoppable. We must act quickly."

~

Late that evening, Caroline slipped from her old familiar bed and crept past the door to her mother's suite where Amelia slept. She loved her life in Dathoviel, but the Petrovian gardens would forever hold space in her heart.

Right in the middle of iron and stone, beauty and life bloomed in colorful glory. The garden had been her aunt's doing, and Caroline could only assume Spencer had taken on the responsibility now.

As she strolled through the ornate arch and dodged the white peacocks, the blossoming apple trees and sweet smelling rose bushes embraced her. Memories from her childhood of chasing Spencer and being chased by him were so clear.

"It's lovely seeing you home again."

She'd sensed him behind her before he uttered a word. They were synced, despite the five years separating them. She turned, grateful to share a private moment with him again. He was a simple man here without his cape and crown. Light from the moon and flickering torches bounced off the pond between them, capturing the angles of a nose broken one too many times. It sat crooked on his otherwise perfect face, a moniker of his tendency to start fights, and finish them. She'd always found the scarred, crinkled skin endearing.

"You've done well keeping the garden growing, Spence."

"This is the one place I can truly think," he admitted, fingertips caressing a nearby vine. "Plus, tending to it has helped keep my mind off missing you."

She found a stone bench and patted a spot next to her. "Sit and talk with me a while?"

He joined her, sliding his arm around her shoulders. His tone turned pained. "I've missed you. We didn't even get to say goodbye."

"Mother wouldn't wait until you returned from hunting so I could."

"I never got a proper explanation from my father, but it seems he is the one who told your mother she must go. I'd hoped you would return after he passed, but you seem quite happy now."

Caroline gnawed at her bottom lip. "You are my truest friend."

"I always will be."

"And we've always been honest with each other."

"We have."

"I've been aching to tell you something for many months now."

His dark blue eyes sparkled mischievously. "I believe I know your confession. And I must say, you've no reason to fear sharing it."

"Oh?"

"You're in love with the queen."

Her face warmed. "You—how did you—"

He pulled her close. "I knew the moment I saw you together. The look in your eyes. I've only ever seen you look at cake that way."

He chuckled and she glared.

"You're not funny."

"It's a little funny." He nudged her shoulder. "Honestly, I knew in the way you supported her. The way *she* looked at *you*."

"You're not at all surprised?"

"It was only a matter of time before you realized what I had long ago." Of course, he would know her better than she knew herself. "Is she kind to you?"

"She is. I challenge her, and she does the same in return. We differ in opinions on much, but we respect one another. Neither of us fears speaking our minds."

"That's all I need to know."

She leaned into him, her head tucked beneath his chin.

"You don't know what your support means to me, Spence."

He paused for a long moment.

"Have you thought about what you'll say to your mother?"

Her gut lurched. "I've been avoiding thinking about it."

"I can't imagine she'll take it well."

"No, neither can I." Her eyes fell to her lap. "You're truly supportive, though?"

"You and Amelia will experience enough adversity once your relationship becomes public. You don't need that same negativity from me."

Caroline wrapped her arms around his neck. He squeezed her tightly in return.

"Thank you."

"Once Alaric is dead, and she takes the throne, what will you do?"

She pulled back, shrugging. "I know she will make room for me."

Spencer pressed a kiss to her hair, nodding, trusting her. "I love you."

"And I you," she whispered gratefully.

April 9th, 1457

Morning came too quickly. Especially for Eloise who'd spent most of the night patrolling the hall outside of Amelia's suite.

By breakfast, King Spencer had prepared a trio of his best guards to head for Winvoltor with instructions to find Alaric and carry out the assassination. It wasn't the best plan, but she couldn't think of a better suggestion, so she kept quiet.

With any luck, the guards could dress as civilians and stage it to look unconnected to both Petrovia and Dathoviel. Amelia seemed grateful for the help, but a greater guarantee of success certainly wouldn't have hurt.

Just hours before the guards were set to depart, Jacob—the Petrovian constable; a tall, pale man with ginger hair, escorted a cloaked visitor into the Great

Hall. Spencer and Amelia met them warily. Eloise stood at the queen's side, arrow at the ready.

A moment later, the man's hood slid back to reveal Julian's face. He looked disheveled and exhausted, as if he'd taken the full journey from Dathoviel without stopping. Lowering her weapon, she quickly snapped her mouth shut, unsure when it had fallen open.

"I bring word," he said, voice raspy as he addressed the queen. "Though you won't enjoy it."

Amelia took a steadying breath and approached the jester, guiding him toward Spencer with a comforting arm around his shoulders. "Let us hear it all the same."

He caught his breath, eyes dragging over Eloise almost longingly before he forced them back to Amelia and Spencer.

"I managed to intercept a letter from Alaric. He is returning early to Dathoviel. Whatever your plan is for him, you have only days now."

Amelia turned to King Spencer. "And no idea where he will be. He could already be on his way back."

Spencer crossed his arms and cracked his neck. "Well, Your Highness. Seems a new plan is in order."

. 16 .

OUTSIDE THE KING'S STUDY, an impatient Eloise strained to listen through the door, sneaking glances through the keyhole. Spencer and Amelia were inside, seated on either side of his desk, papers piled between them.

Someone cleared their throat behind her, and she jumped, her braids nearly whipping them in the face as she spun around.

"Seb!" she hissed as the knight stepped back, hands raised defensively. "What are you doing?"

She wasn't disappointed Julian hadn't come to find her yet. She *wasn't*.

"Caroline was worried. She sent me to see if they were getting along without her. How's it going in there?"

"They've been pouring over maps and flipping through treaties for hours. Sounds like they're pulling apart every law of their respective kingdoms."

He nodded, leaning against the wall. This gave her the opportunity to study him. They'd yet to converse, and had certainly never been alone together, but he seemed harmless. Considering his loyalty had been aligned with Alaric just a few months ago.

"I can't imagine working out a plan to defeat Alaric being easy."

"Not one that keeps the queen's hands clean and protects everyone involved, while being executed in a timely manner."

He nodded.

They fell into a comfortable silence the next few hours, occasionally sharing a sip from Eloise's flask.

Around dinner time, the king and queen's voices raised so loudly eavesdropping became pointless. For a moment, Eloise and Seb fought like children over the keyhole, each wanting a peek inside, but thanks to a well-placed elbow, Eloise won. She watched the queen's fists pound against the oak desk, which was now strewn haphazardly with crumpled parchment, weighted maps and decrees unrolled across the floor.

"You are talking about an ambush!" Amelia shouted.

The flame from the candle beside her flickered.

The king tugged his already unkempt locks into an even wilder state.

"We have no other choice!"

After a moment of heated glaring, they both collapsed into their chairs, defeated.

By the time Eloise's flask was empty and her stomach was growling, servants had appeared to light the torches.

Seb yawned and cracked his neck. "How much longer do you think they'll be?"

Eloise had taken a seat on the floor across from him. She shrugged, head resting against the stone wall.

"Hopefully not much."

"Perhaps I can assist?" Fredrick said from down the hall.

Both Eloise and Seb sighed in relief.

The knight gestured to the door. "Please."

Eloise clambered to her feet, allowing her sore muscles to relax when her father put his arm around her.

"They will be grateful to see you."

Fredrick knocked confidently on the door. "I'll do what I can."

It swung open, revealing an exhausted queen and a relieved looking king.

"Constable," Amelia sighed. "Please come in."

"You two better join us as well," Spencer said over the queen's shoulder.

Eloise and Seb didn't need telling twice.

~

Everyone had gathered in the throne room an hour later.

Julian stood to the side, observing Amelia, Caroline, and Spencer muttering to one another on the thick, carpeted platform as the clock struck midnight. Fredrick and Seb chatted as well, in a vaguely calmer fashion.

On the queen's left, Eloise looked ready to pounce.

He simply *must* speak with her tonight.

Spencer stepped forward, his booming voice reaching around the vast room. "Your patience is appreciated. Queen Amelia and I wish to share our plan with you now, understanding its risks and imperfections. Unfortunately, given the news of Alaric's haste return, we've been left with minimal time and even less options."

He offered the floor to Amelia who clasped her hands together tightly as she faced the crowd.

"As a red herring to remove Alaric, King Spencer has declared war upon Dathoviel."

Irate gasps sounded from the Order. Spencer stepped forward again.

"My brother will fight to defend what he believes is his. With the help of Petrovian troops, he won't stand a chance against the Order."

Amelia nodded.

"We agree Petrovia will temporarily conquer Dathoviel, securing it away from Alaric—should he survive the battle we have planned. At the earliest opportunity, Spencer will relinquish his claim to our land, allowing you to appoint a new ruler through vote."

"The intention, of course, will be to rename Queen Amelia as regent," the king said.

"And if he survives?" someone demanded from the sea of faces.

"My court will charge him with treason, and he will be dealt with accordingly."

Everyone murmured, some displeased, others excited. Amelia flushed with guilt, examining the carpet until Eloise tapped her shoulder and shook her head, whispering. When Amelia looked up, her face was like stone.

"I assure you, we have discussed every possible avenue. More than anyone, I wished for different terms. No one will be forced to fight. If you wish to return home, do so with my favor and understanding."

Spencer gestured to his right.

"Seb has agreed to intercept Alaric on his return to Dathoviel. From there, he will attempt to lead their traveling party in our direction, where we will be awaiting them."

"When will this be happening?" Julian called from his spot against the wall.

Eloise's gaze locked on his and he met her with a similar intensity.

"The morning after next—if my estimations are correct," Spencer answered.

The crowd shuffled anxiously.

The possibilities of failure were endless, but what other choice did they have? They certainly couldn't waste another day arguing.

"We're all with you 'till the end, Your Majesty," Fredrick promised.

~

The last-minute feast was meant to raise spirits, and for the most part it was working. Eloise watched as food and wine was greedily consumed by everyone in the castle. Well, almost everyone. Amelia had retired to bed early, appearing not to have much of an appetite. Caroline left not long after and even Spencer, who should have been hosting, was scarcely seen.

Unable to stomach another bite, Eloise bid her father goodnight and slipped outside. She took the rock path Caroline had described earlier, following it until she reached an elegant floral arch. Stepping through, she kept her gaze focused, hoping to find Julian without too much trouble. After the announcement, he'd managed a quick request in her ear as she'd exited the throne room.

"Meet me in the gardens just after midnight," he'd said.

So, here she was, without the slightest clue what she was doing or what she would say when she saw him.

Countless stars littered the night sky and the partially full moon painted the blooms and bushes in a cool glow. She discovered him seated, leaning against an apple tree. His left knee was up, elbow propped on it, hand covering his mouth. He'd rolled the sleeves of his tan tunic up, tattoo on display once again. When she looked back to his face, his eyes were drilling into her. The air between them tightened, but she didn't turn away. The corner of his mouth lifted.

He'd been appearing in her dreams frequently since leaving Dathoviel, and occasionally when she was awake. Between her many obligations as Amelia's protector and second in command of the Order, her mind chose to devote its rare free time to recalling the way his hands had felt on her body and how his tongue had darted out to taste her skin. It had been pure torture.

Their night at the beach had been fairly innocent, but that didn't stop her imagination from playing an agonizing game of '*what if*'.

She'd imagined seeing him again from the moment he'd waved goodbye outside the castle, his other arm around Regina. But now she felt uncertain. She wished he would decide what the next step would be. To say something and take the decision out of her hands. She was tired of making the hard and fast decisions. It was exhausting.

"I've been looking for you," she said.

His hand fell away—his handsome, intoxicating grin on display. It felt inappropriate given the gravity of the day behind them, but that only made her more grateful for it.

"You've found me."

His eyes followed her movements as she sat next to him, legs folded beneath her. Not so close they touched, unless he stretched out his leg.

"Thank you for coming to warn us about Alaric's letter. I dare say you saved this little revolution."

He hesitated. "I've decided to join the battle."

Her heart lurched and she cursed it.

"Is this one of your jokes?"

"I have much to lose if Alaric wins. Therefore, I must protect it."

He rubbed his hands down his thighs, over his knees, and back up.

"What do you have to protect?"

"Five daughters." A peal of laughter tumbled from his lips, he gestured to each of the inked roses on his arm. "Isn't that mad? A court jester with his very own circus."

Slowly the gears in her head spun until they locked into place.

"Maria is your daughter then?"

He nodded. "The eldest."

"And their mother?"

His face fell and he rubbed at the back of his neck. She shouldn't have asked.

"The same illness that took Queen Diana took my wife as well."

There had been so many lost that winter. Eloise could easily recall the hours she and her father had spent stabbing at the frozen ground, willing it to move so they could bury the dead.

"It nearly took my grandmother."

"My youngest was just a few months old at the time," he mumbled quietly as if lost in thought.

Eloise's eyes turned sharp.

"You must return home, Julian. War is no place for someone like you."

His knuckles popped. "Just because I'm not a soldier doesn't mean I cannot fight. What's one more body on the field to you?"

She hadn't meant to offend him. Truthfully, having him there would be incredibly distracting, and she already had her father to worry about.

"I've no doubt you're capable. I simply believe someone with so much to lose, should not risk it so carelessly."

His eyes were hard and dark when he looked at her. "There are nearly a hundred men and women inside prepared to risk everything for the people and land they love. Even more from Petrovia planning to fight in a battle they might not even believe in. At least I have something worth fighting for."

"Hence why you must return. I lost my mother as a child. I couldn't stand it if something happened to my father too." His eyes softened and his hand twitched, like he wanted to reach for her but couldn't. Wouldn't? "Your girls need you. Go home, Julian."

She watched the stubbornness ease from his shoulders slowly as he let out an almost relieved sigh. He hadn't truly wanted to fight.

"You're right, I was being foolish."

Eloise placed her hand on his shoulder and he almost jumped. His pupils dilated and she inhaled sharply, though neither pulled away.

"*Well,* you are the fool."

He snickered. "Court jester is only part of my identity, but I appreciate the wordplay."

She pulled her hand away, then inched closer to him instead. And she didn't bother hiding it. "Tell me about another part."

He shifted, his leg moving nearer in response to her advance, a breath of space remaining between them. Perhaps to see if she would take the opportunity and pull away?

"Losing my wife taught me many things, like not waiting to tell someone how you feel. No matter how mad it might sound."

"Oh?" Her heart was stuttering in her chest.

"I genuinely believed I could never feel this way again, but I do when I'm with you. I hoped to do this slower and give us time to get better acquainted, but there is a genuine chance we may never see each other again. I thought that night on the beach was potentially farewell, but we've been given a second chance in a way. As unfortunate as the letter that brought me here is."

"What are you asking?"

Was he asking something? Had she missed it?

"I'd like to have you."

Eloise blinked. "Have me? Do you mean court me? Or bed me?"

"Both." He chuckled, raking his hands through his hair. "And a million other things, but we must start somewhere."

Her skin prickled at the implications behind his words. She felt warm.

"So, that night before I left, it was all because you wanted... what? A taste in case I died?"

His lips pursed and she couldn't stop staring at them.

"When you explain it like that, it's not quite so romantic. Do you not want to have me?"

Yes. She looked down at her hands resting in her lap. He wouldn't be her first, but he would be the first who counted. The first she'd chosen for no reason other than simply wanting to.

"You may be a fool, but I'd be a liar if I said no."

Finally, he reached for her, dragging her close.

Their skin warmed where it met and she sighed, surrendering against his chest, and he groaned into her mouth. Perhaps the loveliest sound she'd ever heard. His hands trailed down her arms, gripping her waist, pulling her into his lap. She felt his back hit the tree, keeping them up. Then his fingers were on her hips, holding on. The only way they could be closer was having him inside her.

As his lips found a spot beneath her chin she imagined what it would be like to be naked with him.

Then he was pulling back and panting, resting his forehead against her collarbone. She could have kept going, never stopping.

"Wow," he whispered, the tip of his nose brushing against hers. "That was better than last time, wasn't it?"

She wouldn't dignify that foolish question with an answer. Of course it was.

His gaze flamed and he rolled his hips upwards against her. She felt his cock, and against her best wishes, she whimpered. She hated herself for it, but it couldn't be helped. She ached for him.

"I need to hear the words, Eloise," he said.

His voice was strained, like a bowstring about to snap. He was challenging her, needing assurance and consent.

"You can have me."

And then she was on her back in the dewy grass, her hands pinned against the earth and his body was pressing against hers.

His left eyebrow lifted, teasing. "Still so sure?"

She lifted her hips again, relaxing her wrists and surrendered.

"Positive."

He grinned and lowered himself over her, finding her lips.

~

The hem of Spencer's silver cape swept along the marble floor as he moved through the quiet corridors. He sighed gratefully in the silence that most of his guests had retired for the night. Hopefully the decisions made today were the right ones, and when the time came, he could face Alaric. And end him.

Their brotherhood was strained at the best of times. Aggressive and violent at the worst. When his parents doubted how Davidson died, Spencer had known the truth. He'd known the moment Alaric was born that something was off about him, and he'd never been proven wrong.

A glimpse of movement down the corridor to his left, lilac perfume, and unmistakable humming distracted him from his thoughts. Caroline met him beneath the painting of roses and silently took his arm, resting her head on his shoulder as they walked.

"Planning the attack couldn't have been easy on you," she said softly after a few minutes.

"I wish there was another way to end Alaric's tyranny, but we must act before more innocent lives are lost."

"How did you convince Amelia?"

He rubbed the back of his neck with his free hand. "It was no simple task. She's rather. . . *diplomatic*, your queen. I'm surprised she asked for my help at all. Though, I doubt the idea was hers alone."

Caroline's grin was quick and small. "If you couldn't help her, who could?"

"I believe she wants her kingdom back, but I worry she won't always do what it takes to keep it. Especially if it means putting her morals on the line. A leader must be willing to sacrifice everything for their people."

"She believes taking Dathoviel forcefully will make her unworthy of it. No better than Alaric. After all, he too does whatever it takes."

Spencer nodded. Solutions were never as clear as he wanted them to be. "Killing Alaric to save hundreds isn't right, but what else can we do?"

Her feet paused and she turned toward him. "I believe in you both. You'll always do what's needed in the end."

He squeezed her tight, her cheek pressed to his chest, praying for the will to do what needed to be done.

~

Unable to stand the thought of her empty bed, Caroline slipped beneath sheets already warm from Amelia's body. Sensing her awaken, she wrapped her arms around the trembling frame she'd craved all day. Hoping the queen would return to sleep, she gently caressed her dark tresses, letting a comforting tune hum from the back of her throat.

What *would* happen to their relationship when Amelia became sole queen? Would the subjects ever accept two women together? Or would she be forced to follow one step behind Amelia, never an equal?

She nuzzled into Amelia's neck, pressing soft kisses to her skin.

"I wish we could remain here forever," the queen whispered desperately.

"What a lovely thought." Caroline sighed as Amelia's fingertips toyed with the sleeve of her robe.

"I am due to report to Spencer's side after breakfast. Seems we have important *war business* to handle."

"It's still night. You have many hours before breakfast."

But the queen couldn't rest in this state, could she?

"You truly believe he can be trusted?"

"Yes. I trust him with my life."

Amelia sat up, reaching for her brush from the nightstand, working through the knots in her hair.

"What about the lives of the Order?"

Caroline grimaced. "You've been able to trust Seb, but not Spencer?"

"I just have a feeling something terrible is going to happen."

Caroline shivered. Not liking the sudden chill of Amelia's absence in her arms, she moved closer. "That's natural. Though controlled and small in scale, your kingdom still faces war."

"Even after agreeing with Spencer, I hoped there was a better way. That I could think of one, but, I have known all along what needed doing. If I had been brave enough to take matters into my own hands, none of this would be happening." She choked on the final words. "Brantley would..."

Caroline reached out. "You mustn't blame yourself."

"But I do."

Their fingers entwined, and Caroline let her forehead rest against Amelia's. Her eyes fluttered shut, their lungs competing for the air residing between their mouths. Countless emotions washed over her in a confusing concoction of fear, love, despair, lust, regret, and desire.

The slow, primal potion spread as Caroline slid her leg over Amelia's, drawing her closer. They both needed an escape.

"I can't help recalling the last time I had you alone in a dark room."

The queen inhaled sharply; her exhale stuttering out across Caroline's lips. She seemed welcome to the distraction.

"What do you remember?"

"My mind craving your presence. My body desperate for another taste of your lips. My soul aching, as if a piece were missing. And my mind anxious to know if I'd succeeded in memorizing every line of your body."

"Such poetry," Amelia teased. "Did you read that in a book?"

"I've read many books about love, but none encompassed the truth. Not even my own words are worthy."

The queen's eyes turned curious. "When did you know you felt differently for me than anyone else before?"

Caroline caressed the tip of Amelia's nose with hers. "Your wedding day. Though, I would have fallen for you at any first encounter. My mother had been pressuring me all morning to keep a sharp eye out for suitable men. But I watched you all night. Surely anyone who noticed thought I was mad."

"So, love at first sight?"

"It wasn't until we began writing letters that my feelings and my understanding of them became clear. By the time my uncle ordered me out of Petrovia, I missed you so terribly it hurt. Not that I told anyone. I refused to admit it to myself unless I was dreaming. How rare is reciprocated love between two people? Two women no less? Well, I suppose it mustn't be any rarer, but it can't be the easiest path."

"Yet, you still came to stay with me?" Amelia asked eagerly.

"I took the chance you would welcome me, and I had resigned myself to friendship at least. Anything more than ink and parchment."

Amelia caressed Caroline's face, no space existing between them now. "Thank you, for coming back for me."

"When I stepped out of the carriage that first day, everything I'd hidden came flooding back to me. I did not realize any one day that I loved you. But that first day in Dathoviel, I remembered I had loved you all along."

Their lips met desperately, but somehow their hands remained calm. Like their bodies were warring with saying more or falling back into the mattress and never speaking again. Amelia pulled back first.

"The first time I felt your lips against mine, I was lost in the nerves. The night we made love, I was captured by lust. Tonight, I wish to be more intentional. To run my fingers through your hair and notice every strand. To feel the excitement quaking through your muscles as we come together."

Caroline stiffened in anticipation when Amelia lay her back, touching and tasting gently. She melted, absorbing every sensation and sound. Amelia's lips moved shamelessly from her mouth to her cheek, then to her earlobe and the spot beneath. She found the hem of Caroline's robe and let her fingers slide under it, kneading Caroline's thighs, coaxing them open.

Caroline swore, her knees parting and the queen slid between them. Rolling against her. She bunched the fabric of Amelia's nightgown in her fist, trying to pull it up, craving flesh on flesh.

"Oh, God."

Amelia chuckled against her throat, leaving a trail of open mouth kisses. "Was that a prayer? Or a curse?"

"Both." Caroline's breath escaped in short, shaky pants. "Do you think he heard me?"

Between them, wild fingers opened laces and pushed aside sheer fabrics.

"If God sees all, perhaps we should give him a performance to remember?" Amelia whispered, a roguish smirk twisting her swollen lips. "For if we are damned, we must make it worth it."

Caroline paused, panting.

Personal beliefs aside, she respected Amelia's religious choices, and her words were pure blasphemy. "I know being together feels right, but does it also feel wrong?"

"Wrong?"

"You are a married woman who believes in heaven. And hell."

Amelia's eyes turned from lustful to grateful.

"The first time in my entire life I have felt right is with you. Loving you is the closest sensation to what I imagine heaven might be. Someone, somewhere decided love like ours was flawed and sinful, despite the bible never truly denouncing it anywhere within its pages. I know it was simply their fear tainting the way they saw love. And their hateful beliefs will never carry more weight than how I feel for you, or who I am inside. They could have just as easily decided that men and women were too different to be compatible and outlawed their love."

It was almost too good to be true. "You no longer fear for your soul?"

"My love for you is no temptation from the devil. If damnation is my fate, loving you will not be the reason behind my undoing. If anything—it may save me." Caroline's heart battered against her chest, hoping to find Amelia's and lay with it forever. "I shall never return to pretending I'm not precisely who I was born to be," Amelia swore.

"And who's that?"

Caroline felt the smirk across her lips as Amelia pressed her into the mattress.

"A strong, passionate queen, in love with you."

17

April 10th, 1457

BY BREAKFAST, THREE MEN and two women had relinquished their weapons, respectfully leaving the Order. Amelia blessed their return to Dathoviel with gratitude, understanding, and Julian as their escort.

At noon, the remaining members of her army and any willing Petrovian soldiers gathered in a large clearing just beyond the castle.

A light breeze spread the scent of pine, sweat, and damp earth. Amelia prayed the rain that visited overnight would stay away until after the battle tomorrow. With Spencer at her side, she watched General Jacob and Fredrick discuss each soldier's strengths before assigning them to one of three groups.

Selfish relief flooded her as one by one, many members of the Order were sent to the second or third wave.

A young man with dark eyes and light hair stepped forward for his placement interview, and her heart clenched as he was assigned to the front-line minutes later. Fredrick assured her everyone had volunteered, but where others looked proud to fight, this boy appeared terrified. He couldn't have been much older than Brantley.

Well, then Brantley had been...

Before he could step back, she moved forward, capturing his attention.

"Your name is Heath?"

He trembled, unable to meet her eyes. "Yes."

"Thank you for joining us," she said, keeping her voice hopeful.

He moved closer as if to shake her hand. Instead, he grabbed her by the wrist, swung her around, and pressed the sword to her throat, holding her against his chest. It happened so fast.

Amelia gasped, the cool blade biting into her skin. It was clear from the way the boy vibrated against her that he lacked confidence.

Everyone stepped forward to defend her. Eloise had drawn an arrow, setting Heath in her sights as she moved in slowly. Behind her, Spencer narrowed his eyes, hand on the dagger at his hip. By now everyone knew his skill with throwing blades.

The others awaited word to attack.

Amelia attempted to raise her hands, hoping it would hold them, but Heath's arm was secured strongly around her.

"Stay away!" He tugged her tighter against his chest. "I *will* kill her."

She gulped beneath the blade. "We can help you, just explain why you are doing this."

"King Alaric said he'd lost faith in Sir Sebastian, so he asked me to join the rebellion and inform him of your every move. He said I would be rewarded, and he needed me."

A man stepped forward from the group to their left. "Release the queen, Heath. This isn't like you."

A quick glance showed both men shared similar physical features.

"The king promised he would spare you. Joining the Order is treason, Finn. He's going to kill everyone the moment he gets the chance. But, if I found a way to kill her, he swore you wouldn't be harmed."

"You can't trust him, brother."

"I'm not a child anymore! He chose me. She's dangerous. See how far her lies have taken us? Look where we are."

Amelia's skin burned, the blade's pressure intensifying. She could practically taste her own blood in the back of her throat.

Helpless, Finn turned to the Order. "Please do not attack, I beg you. He's just a child. He doesn't understand the weight of his actions."

"He's far from a child." Seb moved forward, eyes and voice soft. His hands were raised, showing he was no threat. "Heath, Alaric does not care about you. He knows how to manipulate others into doing his bidding."

"Shut up, you traitor!"

Seb took another step forward. "I did betray Alaric. But what I will regret for the rest of my life is that the prince—a young man like you—had to die for me to see the king is incapable of love and loyalty."

"It's true," Spencer said. "He will turn on you the moment you're of no use to him."

Heath shook his head. "No, I have the king's word."

Seb's next steps were undetectable. "I recognize the look in your eyes. It's stared back at me from the mirror almost my entire life. I promise you don't need him."

Fredrick held his hand out, requesting the sword. "Come on, lad, I trained you myself. I know this isn't what you want."

"You know nothing!" He turned to Finn, jerking Amelia with his movements. "We need to go."

Fredrick stepped between them; the lines of his face hard. "Whether you live or die is your choice, mate, but if you kill our queen, everyone will attack. Eloise has an arrow aimed at your back right now, and she won't miss."

Amelia felt Heath shudder, his tears soaking her collar. "I was only trying to save you." he choked in his brother's direction. "You're the only family I have left."

"I know." Finn moved forward quickly, grasping the young man's elbow.

The sword clattered to the earth as Heath released it, and her.

Amelia fell next to it, knees weak.

Eloise rushed to her side, covering her body protectively with her own as Seb captured Heath. Fredrick knelt, mud staining his otherwise pristine uniform. He lifted the queen's chin, examining her wound.

"A few drops of blood in comparison to what could have been." He sounded relieved. "You're safe now, Amelia. He will be punished."

Eloise nodded. "There's banishment, or—"

"No." Amelia grasped the constable's arm. "See no harm comes to him. I cannot say I would have acted differently in his place."

"You are foolish if you believe this is over," Eloise scoffed. "You cannot allow his freedom. Use this to set an example."

"No. I cannot prove Alaric right, and have them think me wicked." Amelia turned to Seb. "Lock him away until the battle is over. We will arrange a fair trial for him back in Dathoviel."

"Yes, Your Grace." Seb bowed and escorted Heath inside with a trio of guards.

"You've got to be fucking joking," Eloise hissed through gritted teeth.

She ignored the warning look from her father.

Spencer also came to kneel beside Amelia, sliding his arm around her and lifting her to her feet.

"I agree with the queen. We cannot risk him going to Alaric and warning him about the battle. Having him behind bars is the safest place for everyone."

Finn hesitated on the sidelines as Amelia regained her footing. "Your Majesty, I wish to offer my thanks. Sparing my brother's life is a debt I know not how to repay."

Amelia smiled faintly, gripping Fredrick for support. "Heath and I agree on one simple truth, sir. There have been enough brothers lost to Alaric's bloody hands."

~

Before Spencer and Eloise had even escorted Amelia back to her tower, word of the attack spread throughout the corridors, kitchens, and out back to the gardens where Caroline had been collecting roses for the funeral wreaths they would no doubt need the next few days.

Though she and Olive heard the news separately, they met on the staircase. With their skirts hiked up, they raced to the queen's room.

"What did you hear?" Caroline demanded, taking the stairs two at a time.

Olive was right on her heels. "Only that there was an attack."

They reached the landing as Spencer appeared in the hall, shutting the door behind himself. Caroline's heart clenched at the sight of his hunched shoulders and pale expression. Olive strained to look around his broad frame.

"Is she in there?"

"Is she alright?"

"What happened?"

"Who did this?"

"Was anyone else hurt?"

Spencer had no choice but to interrupt them gruffly. "Amelia is inside. She's alright, though not unmarked. Eloise is tending to her wound."

"Wound?" Olive screeched.

"How bad is it?" Caroline demanded.

"I'm sure she'll explain everything. Excuse me, ladies." He moved past them and down the stairs.

He obviously needed consoling, but Caroline couldn't follow. With her heart torn in two directions, she threw one last glance at his retreating back, then followed Olive through the door.

Eloise was balanced on the edge of the bed, carefully cleaning a cut on the queen's throat. It didn't appear life threatening, but panic bloomed in Caroline's chest all the same. Her hands clenched over her abdomen and she rushed forward.

"Are you alright?"

Amelia took Caroline's hands and held them to her face as Eloise shifted away, giving them room. Neither thought to hide their intimacy.

"A bit rattled, but alive."

"She was quite brave." Eloise sounded almost impressed.

Caroline turned to the dark-skinned woman at their side. "Aren't you supposed to protect her?"

Eloise's mouth popped open, ready to retort, but Amelia shook her head.

"Everyone did exactly as they were supposed to. If she had reacted differently, I would probably be dead."

"No one should have gotten that close to you. What even happened?"

Before the queen could answer, Eloise raised the cloth and bowl she'd been holding. "If I finish cleaning your wound, I can give you privacy to explain."

"Yes, of course." With a thin smile to Caroline, Amelia turned back.

Olive stood in the corner wringing her hands as the queen hissed whenever Eloise dabbed the green salve across her wound.

Everyone remained silent until the bandage was secure around Amelia's throat, and the door shut behind Eloise with a tense click. On cue, the two remaining women surrounded Amelia. The scent of the strong ointment failing to detour either of them from wrapping her in a tight hug.

"They said you were held hostage," Olive whispered. "That you were almost killed?"

Caroline listened intently, air trapped in her lungs, as the queen recounted the experience.

"It all happened so fast," Amelia concluded. "Fortunately, I was not alone."

"I imagine his punishment will be harsh," the handmaiden said.

"As it should be! Spencer will see to it," Caroline declared, white knuckles gripping her coral skirts.

Amelia shook her head. "Spencer agreed to hold the boy until after the battle when he can face trail. We cannot afford to lose focus now."

Caroline bit her tongue, a million objections poised on the tip of it. Now was not the place or time to push. Instead, she wrapped her arm around Amelia's waist and drew her close, thankful today hadn't ended in tragedy.

~

Olive had brought dinner upstairs so Amelia could continue resting that evening. After devouring the steaming roast and potatoes with zeal, the queen surrendered to the trauma she had experienced and slept.

Many hours later, she woke alone; the room coated in darkness. She stretched and instantly regret it as the cut at her throat stung. After trying and failing to go back to sleep, she decided to search for the kitchens, somehow starving once more.

Lost in thought, she maneuvered through the halls, the hem of her powder blue robe sweeping along the marble floor. The candle she held flickered with each breath, casting shadows on the walls surrounding her.

Voices from the left caught her attention so she followed the sound, keeping her feet quiet. As she grew closer she recognized Spencer's voice.

"—protection at any cost," he was saying.

Ducking into the shadows, Amelia narrowly avoided Eloise as she headed back towards the tower, no doubt intending to guard the queen's door.

Spencer was less distracted. "I see your flame," he called. "Lurking in the darkness will not protect you."

When Amelia stepped into the light, the king relaxed.

"Apologies if I frightened you."

He replaced his knife into the hilt strapped to his thigh. "I've been quite tense since this afternoon," he admitted, eyes downcast.

"I understand."

Then he was looking up, his face so similar to Alaric's, and yet his eyes were like Caroline's.

"Amelia, I must apologize for not reacting quicker in your defense."

"You did the right thing under the circumstances."

"If you insist," he said, though the wariness remained in his voice. "I'm just relieved Caroline wasn't there to witness it."

"As am I."

He gestured for her to follow him to a marble bench resting a few feet away. It seemed to have been placed there for anyone wishing to admire the portraits hanging on the walls. Neither Spencer nor Amelia paid them any mind as they sat.

"You wish to tell me something?"

"I wondered if hearing a bit of family history would further put your mind at ease."

"Regarding?"

"Your concern I may fail to end Alaric's life out of love for him."

Amelia clasped her hands in her lap, a sad smile on her lips. "I do not mean to offend you especially since you have done nothing to prove yourself untrustworthy."

"And yet, you doubt."

He was so much like Caroline. Outspoken, honest, and straight to the point. It was as refreshing and overwhelming in him, but luckily, she was used to it.

Alaric was just as bold, now that she thought about it. Must be something in the Petrovian water.

"I understand the bond between siblings. It cannot be simple, taking the life of someone with whom you share blood."

Spencer looked away, his gaze on a painting, but not truly focused on it. "Any hope for connection died many years ago when he killed our youngest brother."

Had he truly just blurted that out like it was common knowledge?

"Caroline shared a little of the story. She hinted her suspicions, but never gave any facts."

"She was quite young when it happened to truly remember the fighting, and the weeks my father forced Alaric to remain in his tower as punishment for his... *carelessness*."

"You sound quite certain Alaric was responsible."

"I saw the guilt in his eyes. Not sorrow or regret. Just—guilt. And relief. It was sickening."

Because he seemed so familiar, she ached to reach out for his hand, to comfort him. Because they were practically strangers, she held back.

"So, what do you believe happened in the woods that day?" she asked. "If—if you wish to share details of course."

He considered for a moment, then turned toward her, legs uncrossed, palms open.

"Davidson loved climbing trees, but he had a condition you see. His bones were weak, and Alaric knew the risk of taking him out alone."

"Do you think he pushed him?"

"Alaric said he fell, but I doubt it. Either way, he left our brother there alone in the woods. He said he'd come back to the castle for help, but by the time my father found David's body—or what was left of it—it was too late."

Amelia felt a metallic taste at the back of her tongue and pressed her lips together, palms against her stomach.

"What was left of it?"

Spencer shuddered.

"The animals found him before my father did."

"I am so sorry."

"I always knew Alaric was capable of many things, and none of them good."

"And your father?"

"He could never admit it, but his greatest focus became getting Alaric out of Petrovia at any cost. It took nearly fifteen years, but we were finally rid of him for good."

Amelia's stomach churned. "Where he became Dathoviel's problem. Your father honestly believed shipping him off to my kingdom was the wisest choice?"

"When your father came to Petrovia for help with your military, mine hardly knew what he was agreeing to. Rather, he hardly cared. Marcel explained he needed a successor. Preferably someone to marry you and keep you in line. I imagine my father believed the power of being king would calm Alaric's wickedness."

Spencer's eyes fell to his hands before he continued.

"I cannot bring either of our brothers back or repair the damage done to your kingdom. But I can help you stop further destruction. I would be lying if I didn't admit that taking Alaric out is as much about vengeance for me, as it is justice for you."

Amelia searched his eyes. There wasn't a single trace of malice or contempt directed her way. She and her kingdom *would* be safe in his hands.

"I believe you, and I trust you. We will do this together."

He nodded and smiled.

Amelia knew there was little chance of sneaking back to her room without Eloise realizing she had left it.

Sure enough, when she reached the landing, Eloise was pacing outside her door, arrow resting in the bow, ready for aiming at any moment. Her shoulders were tense and the leather armor she wore glowed in the torchlight.

"Your Grace!" Eloise exclaimed, fingers tightening on her weapon. "You're not in bed?"

Their eyes met, ones appalled and the other apologetic.

"I was speaking with King Spencer."

Eloise slung the bow over her shoulder, slid the arrow in her boot and crossed her arms. "May *I* speak frankly with *you*?"

"You always do." Amelia failed to hide her smirk.

"It is my job to protect you, keep you safe. You asked my father for this protection because you fear for your life. And given the attack today, you have a right to.

Putting yourself in danger by walking through the castle unprotected, sneaking about, and not informing me you've left bed makes it difficult to keep you alive."

Amelia's indignation faded. "You are correct. I apologize."

Eloise's shoulders relaxed slightly.

"There is one more thing, to clear the air."

"You have my full attention."

"If you and Caroline wish to keep your relationship secret, you might consider refraining from interacting in public. At least for the time being."

Amelia's eyes widened. "You know?"

"The walls at the inn might as well have been made of paper, but, her behavior today solidified all other suspicions."

"You almost sound like you approve?" Amelia asked timidly.

Eloise shrugged in response. "Who am I to tell a queen—or anyone else, who to love? Not everyone in the kingdom will share the same indifference or support, so be mindful. You are already a woman trying to rule without a king. The target on your back isn't getting any smaller."

"Or making your job easier."

"Precisely."

Amelia folded her hands. "Very well. Consider your request heard and validated. I appreciate your counsel, and thank you for your loyalty and discretion."

"Certainly."

"Do you mind if I ask *why* you are supportive?"

Eloise sighed.

"My mother was fair skinned, like you. When she and my father met there was much. . . talk. Threats. They were not allowed to marry, but after two decades, the cruelest villagers finally left them alone."

Amelia reeled; the weight of all the information she learned tonight sitting heavy on her shoulders.

"I had no idea."

"It helped he spent most of his time in the castle," Eloise continued, her eyes glazed over. "But the glares and the whispers were never truly absent, and they never married."

"And that is why you support my love for Caroline?"

Eloise stopped. "I support love. The love that gave me life, and so many others. If you and Caroline are meant to be, then I have faith you will be, regardless of what anyone else does or says."

"Thank you."

Eloise nodded, fiddling with her bow as Amelia headed towards the bedroom.

"I do have a favor to ask," Eloise declared suddenly. "Regarding the battle."

"Yes?"

"I'd like you to remove my father from the plans. From the field."

Amelia glimpsed desperation in the usually serious dark eyes. "I do not understand."

"I cannot risk losing him."

"I see." Amelia gnawed at her bottom lip, torn. "Your father's absence certainly puts us at a disadvantage. But, you have my word he will not be expected during the fight."

"And you have my gratitude." Eloise tipped forward in a bow.

"How will you convince him to stay behind?" Amelia asked softly.

"I'll handle that part. King Spencer has already agreed and will inform Jacob to make the necessary changes in the morning."

"You thought of everything I see."

Eloise nodded, opening the bedroom door and gestured her inside.

"Thank you, My Queen."

Their gazes met for the briefest of moments before the door shut. Perhaps after all this they could be friends. If they survived, of course.

April 11th, 1457

The bright, warm weather and singing birds were clearly ignorant to the impending battle as the grey clouds from previous days parted to reveal a pretty blue sky. It was refreshing and unnerving.

Spencer had done his best to gage Alaric's journey home based on the letter Julian had provided. But nothing was guaranteed. They had no choice but to pray the king's estimation was correct.

As the sun reached its highest point, Seb prepared Harlow for their trip, rehearsing the false news from Dathoviel he would share when he intercepted Alaric on the road. Hopefully it would lead the king towards reinforcements only Spencer could provide.

Where the Order would be waiting.

Amelia passed through the open doorway of the vast Petrovian stables, heading for Greta just as Seb finished with Harlow's saddle.

"Good afternoon, My Queen," he greeted, watching her pass Gus a carrot from the pail next to the trough. "Are you feeling well?"

"As well as possible, I suppose." She met his gaze. "Are you nervous to see Alaric?"

He paused his arrangement of the reins. "Terrified."

She nodded. "If we succeed tomorrow, I want you to know I would never have been able to do this without you, Seb."

He tipped his hat toward her; the feather drooping in a bow of its own. "I look forward to witnessing your coronation."

Amelia remained quiet until she finished saddling Greta.

"Would you like company to the border?" she asked, swinging herself into the saddle.

He smiled, straightening the final saddlebag. "I would."

Once outside the gates, the mares fell into an easy trot beside each other. It felt like a lifetime had passed since they'd last been alone together. But her words the morning she finally stood up to Alaric remained clear in his mind.

Amelia must have caught his pensive gaze. "Mind if I ask what you are thinking?"

"You once questioned why I stood next to Alaric. Even though it was clear what a horrible leader he was."

"I remember."

"I never agreed with the choices he made, but I stayed loyal because I was afraid that without him, I would be nothing. For many years I felt I owed him my life, and therefore I let him control me."

"He still controls us," the queen said, jaw tight. "His actions brought me here, risking the very lives I'm attempting to protect. He has made me into something I never hoped to be."

"I know the feeling well."

Both riders fell quiet for a few moments, Greta and Harlow's hooves against gravel the only sounds until the queen spoke again.

"What do you think of Spencer's plan?"

"His intentions to ambush Alaric, you mean?"

Her eyes hardened, proving his suspicions that she disapproved.

"Yes."

"I believe it's necessary. By allowing him to live, we risk the lives of everyone. Including ours. We have a right to protect ourselves and the people we care for."

She nodded. "I suppose I need more time to wrap my mind around the justification of taking his life. Unfortunately, I seem to be running out of it."

"Forgive me for saying this so bluntly, but could you forgive yourself if we didn't end his treacherous ways, and he killed Caroline or Fredrick to harm you? Or any of the families in the village? One life in exchange for many is justifiable, don't you think?"

Her shoulders slumped, normally regal posture gone.

"Yes. No. I... I do not know. I hate being forced into this. I wanted a choice, and I have none."

"It seems to me, women don't have much choice when it comes to their lives."

She gave the slightest hint of a smile, glancing at him from the corner of her eye.

"You noticed, have you?"

He brought Harlow to a halt, facing her. "If we do this, Amelia, it will be the last terrible thing we do because of him."

~

After hours of searching through her aunt's former dressing room, Caroline finally discovered the ring. Spencer's first genuine smile of the day beamed as she pulled the wooden box from the back of a false bottom drawer. Set inside the gold band was a black tourmaline stone her aunt had believed held protective properties. If anyone needed protection and grounding going into tomorrow, it was Amelia.

"I can't believe you found someone who lives up to all those fairy tales," Spencer said, his arm slipping around her shoulders.

Caroline blushed.

"When Alaric is gone and this is all over, she will be free to marry whomever she chooses. And I hope she chooses me."

"I have no doubt she will, dear cousin."

Caroline shook away thoughts of what she did have to worry about—like her mother—and brought the ring closer, inspecting the inscription inside. It was Latin, so she hadn't the slightest clue what it said. Perhaps Amelia would know? She bounced from left to right, as nervous as she was gleeful.

"I don't know if I can wait, Spence. I think I'll ask her tonight. In case..."

His eyes softened. "You fear one of you might not make it tomorrow?"

"It would be foolish not to at least consider the possibility."

He grimaced, but quickly replaced the expression with a comforting, flashy grin. "Then you best get proposing."

That evening as they dressed one another for dinner, Caroline and Amelia discussed anything but the battle. Even when they peeled back the queen's bandages to check her wound. Whatever that salve had been, it was miraculously healing. She would have a scar, but tomorrow she'd likely be able to let her skin breathe.

Once laces were tied and hair had been brushed, Caroline took Amelia's hand.

"Join me for a walk?"

"I would love to."

The queen glowed in her sunshine colored gown as Caroline led her to the gardens.

"I wish to show you my favorite place in all the world," she explained as they walked through the arch and into the bushes and flowers.

"It is beautiful," Amelia whispered, settling onto a bench beneath a flowering tree. "We can create a similar space for you in Dathoviel if you would like."

"I would love that."

Heart hammering between her ribs, Caroline slipped in beside her. Taking Amelia's left hand, she reached into her skirt pocket for the ring. It felt heavy and hot in her palm.

Amelia leaned in close, and Caroline welcomed the kiss, aching for connection and reassurance.

Breathless and grinning, they pulled apart, but Amelia seemed to sense her nerves.

"Are you alright?"

"I have a question for you."

Amelia caressed her cheek with gentle fingers. "You are safe with me. Ask me anything."

Caroline's eyes drifted closed for a moment, relaxing into Amelia's touch.

"I love you more than words can describe. I cannot imagine going back to life without you."

The queen smirked, her fingers toying with the ends of Caroline's curls. "Why do I feel you are about to ask me to make love to you out here?"

Heat spread across Caroline's cheeks and down her throat, disappearing past her flushed neckline and into her gown. It was now rather difficult to think of much else.

"What makes you say that?"

"I am learning how to recognize that look in your eyes."

"Not what I had in mind. . . this time." Caroline opened her palm to reveal the ring. "Queen Amelia of Dathoviel, will you allow me to stand at your side when you become queen? Will you love me, and allow me to love you in return? Will you—will you be my bride?"

Amelia's eyes widened.

"You are proposing!"

"I am." Caroline giggled. "We can't make anything official, but my heart belongs to you. And I believe yours to me. Once you are free from your bonds to Alaric, and if you're willing to remarry, I hope to become your wife."

The ring slid onto Amelia's finger with ease, as if it were made for her all along.

"Yes, of course. Yes. Yes," Amelia cried.

Wiping each other's tears away, bringing their lips together. And in that moment, everything faded away, for love was love, and there was nothing more powerful.

. 18 .

April 12th, 1457

SEB'S EYES STUNG, STRAINING to keep focus on the horizon, but as the sun rose, his resolve faltered. He'd camped all morning atop this hill, awaiting a glimpse of Alaric's travelling party.

At least he could lean against this tree.

His lids fluttered closed, just for a moment as he tipped his head back against the trunk, loose bark tangling in his dark greasy hair. Surely, he looked as terrible as he felt. He certainly didn't smell great, though that could *potentially* be blamed Harlow. With a discouraged sigh, he reached toward his bag, praying some food remained.

As he bit into the apple, juice dripped down his chin and he wiped it away, forcing his gaze back to the ridge. What if he'd chosen the wrong location to observe the road? Perhaps Spencer's estimations were incorrect after all. They could have missed Alaric completely.

Hell, he might already be back in Dathoviel, loading men into wagons.

Hunger forgotten; Seb's gut churned. There were too many variables to this plan. He didn't even want to see Alaric. Why the hell had he volunteered for this? Maybe he should—

He leapt to his feet, the apple rolling away, forgotten in the grass as the sound of clopping hooves and the low masculine hum of voices grew closer. Turning to Harlow, he slung his empty satchel across his chest.

"Alright, girl. It's time."

She gave a soft snort, gobbling his discarded apple as he climbed into the saddle. His spine and hips protested, but he ignored them. Finally, the king's carriage crested over the hilltop, surrounded by knights on foot or astride decorated steeds. No doubt Alaric would be inside, protected from the heat while everyone else baked.

The assembly of men seemed unhurried, but Seb still raced into the valley, coaxing Harlow from her gallop as they approached the first group of knights. These men had weapons and would surely use them should they suspect Alaric was in danger of any kind. To show he was no threat, Seb brandished a white handkerchief from his pocket and waved it in the air.

The man in front was already reaching for his sword. "Sebastian! What the hell are you doing?"

Seb tugged on Harlow's reigns once more, grateful when she came to a stop. It took a few moments longer for the travelling party to halt.

"I must speak with the king immediately."

The man peered at him through his visor before lifting it. "About what?"

Seb would recognize that smug face anywhere.

"Just let me through, Phillip. We don't have time for your games."

"You may address me as General, now."

A moment of bitterness washed over Seb. Of course, Alaric would name this idiot his general. Seb had lost himself that honor knowingly, but the punishment still stung.

"Congratulations," Seb said through clenched teeth. "If you won't let me through, please bring the king forward. This is an emergency."

Phillip signaled to the men behind him, and a few moments later, Alaric exited the carriage. As he approached the front, Seb dismounted and displayed his lack of weapons. The king needed to trust him completely, and fast.

"Sebastian!" Alaric spread his arms in welcome. "Leah was supposed to tell everyone I would be arriving early. Is everything alright?"

Seb stammered, as rehearsed. "I—I come with terrible news, from Dathoviel."

Alaric's eyes narrowed sharply. "What news is this?"

"The rebellion I discovered in the woods many months ago stormed the castle last night. The queen has been captured and is being held hostage. They plan to ambush you when you arrive. I escaped and rode all night, hoping to find you before you reached the border."

Alaric hesitated, perhaps searching for any signs of deception. It felt like moments stretched to minutes.

Finally, the king clapped a hand on Seb's shoulder, jostling his weak knees.

"Even now, you prove loyal to me. Seems I didn't waste years of friendship on you after all." He turned to Phillip. "We must detour to Petrovia. My brother may not join the fight, but he should grant us a few men to strengthen ours."

"Yes, sir!" The general nodded, eager to please.

He turned to the man on his right, shouting orders for the change of directions.

Meanwhile, Alaric's fingers dug into Seb's shoulders, squeezing, holding his gaze tight.

"We'll teach those peasants once and for all their true place in my kingdom."

~

Eloise watched from the base of the stairs as Amelia and Caroline stole a moment of Spencer's time amidst the hustle of final preparations. Despite the clear intentions behind the quick-footed servants rushing back and forth through the hall, Caroline couldn't seem to disguise her glee. Though she sure looked odd dressed in trousers.

Battle was no place for layers of heavy skirts.

"I hoped you would be the one to marry us?" Caroline requested hopefully, so high in love she practically sang the words.

"After the battle of course," Amelia clarified a slight more firmly.

Spencer wrapped them both in a simultaneous hug. "I would be honored!"

After a moment, Eloise cleared her throat, hoping to remind them what today was.

"We must get moving."

Spencer released the two women and saluted her. "Yes, sir!" he proclaimed, blue eyes sparkling.

Then he strode forward and swept her into his arms, clearly possessed by excitement. She yelped as he spun her around to the melody of Caroline's clapping. Both she and the queen were laughing so hard they had to lean against one another for support.

"What has gotten into you people?" Eloise demanded once her leather boots landed safely on solid ground.

She patted her head, ensuring the twists and braids were still secure. Battle was also no place to have hair in one's eyes.

"Don't shoot me," Spencer pled, winking before sprinting down the corridor.

Amused and shaking her head, Eloise turned on the two women. "Judging by your expressions, we're attending a ball this afternoon. Not facing battle."

"We're keeping spirits high," Caroline shot back, her eyes losing a few degrees of sparkle.

It was a wonder she didn't stick her tongue out like a petulant child.

Though clearly in love, the queen proved to have a bit more logic. "We should head to the armory and dress."

Hands clasped, the pair practically bounced away in the opposite direction Spencer had fled moments ago. *Shit*, is that what love did to people? If it was, she might need to steer clear of the jester.

Her body tingled as she allowed herself a moment to recall their night in the garden, but she quickly squashed the memory down. There was still one thing left to do before she finished suiting up herself.

~

As expected, King Spencer's armory put the one in Dathoviel to shame, both in size, with its high ceilings, large windows, and beautifully organized inventory. Each item in the lemon and leather scented room gleamed from hours' worth of cleaning and polishing. Dust wouldn't have dared settle here.

Amelia had successfully found suits of armor for both herself and Caroline next to the double doors. In fact, they had been created especially for them, she realized upon reading the note attached.

"It's Olive's handwriting," the queen said, holding the slip of parchment to her chest a moment. "The Petrovian blacksmiths work fast."

The iron breastplates, golden gauntlets, and feather adorned helmets fit as if they'd been crafted from an exact mold of their bodies. Fastening the teal cloak across her chest, Amelia had never felt so powerful. Helmets in hand, they moved further into the room to select their weapons.

"What should we choose?"

Amelia surveyed the tables, glass cabinets, and display cupboards lining the walls.

"I am not entirely sure. Despite our abilities to engage in combat, Spencer wants us out of sight. After all, he is the one *attacking* Dathoviel."

"Let's start at the swords," Caroline suggested.

Preparing for the worst, they selected a pair of perfectly balanced swords before moving onto a case housing more unique items. Amelia chose an appropriately sized war hammer, small enough she could wield it, but not so unimpressive it would fail to do damage.

Caroline was filling a quiver with silver-tipped arrows when Spencer entered the room, also dressed in a fine suit of armor. His crimson cape hung from bronze fasteners, the colors a match to the Petrovian flags and banners hanging around the room. His breastplate displayed quite a few scratches, but he wore them well. A sheathed broadsword was belted at his waist and his trademark blades were strapped to his thighs.

"Nearly ready?" he asked.

Amelia nodded. "You still desire to end Alaric's life yourself, yes?"

"Yes."

"Then you should take this." She slipped her dagger out of her boot. "It pains me to part with it, but I have dreamed too often of it being the tool to avenge Brantley's death."

"A handsome piece," Spencer observed.

"Alaric gifted it to me on our anniversary. If this battle must end with bloodshed, let it be Alaric's. And let it be with this."

The king nodded, slipping it into his own boot. "Would you care to join me in the chapel for a final prayer before we depart?"

"I would." Amelia nodded.

"I'd like to come too," Caroline said, surprising them both.

~

After preparing a breakfast tray for her father in the kitchens, Eloise carried it to his room. The coffee sloshed over the side of the clay mug as she climbed the stairs, and when she paused outside his door, her quivering hands rattled the silverware. She could do this. Her fist rose to meet the door, knocking three times.

"Good morning," she called.

"Come in, darling!"

As she entered the room, she spotted his armor standing at attention on the mannequin in the corner. His handcrafted dagger had already been extended into its spear form, and his bed was made.

She found him seated beneath the window, slipping on his boots. His chest and back were bare, his dark skin littered with scars. As a child, she'd been proud of those marks. Jealous even. To her, each symbolized a moment of heroism. A time he'd cheated death.

She was all grown up now though. No one, not even the great Constable Fredrick could continue on forever. He might look rock solid from a distance, but she'd stopped believing he was invincible when her mother died. And she'd been trying to save him ever since.

She eyed the ring of keys lying on a table to her right, ensuring he wasn't watching as she swiped and pocketed, and set the tray in their place. He always had everything just so.

Biting back a wave of nausea, Eloise knelt before him to finish lacing his boots.

"How did you sleep?" she asked.

"Well, considering. You?"

"Well enough."

He glanced towards the tray. Only up close could anyone detect the wrinkles around his compassionate brown eyes.

"That's quite the selection. Did I miss breakfast? I thought it was still early?"

"It is." She stood, hands clasped behind her back. "I feared you would be hungry later, and I didn't want you to go without."

"I am capable of feeding myself, you know. I'm not quite so old yet."

"I know."

She couldn't help wrapping her arms around him when he stood, squeezing tightly. The keys were like lead in her pocket. He caressed her back, holding her close, tucking her head under his chin, her cheek pressed to his chest. She always felt like a child again when he did that.

"By this time tomorrow, we could be on our way home," he whispered.

Selfishly, she allowed her eyes to close. Letting his comfort warm her in this moment, knowing it must end.

"Yes, we can hope that's true."

He squeezed her shoulders, his hands always so large. He'd taken many lives with them, but they never scared her. He'd always kept her safe, ensuring she lived a long, happy life. It was time she returned the favor.

The floorboards creaked beneath his boots as he moved to the tall mirror next to the bed, slipping a plain linen shirt over his torso. Eyes fixed on his back, she silently shifted towards the door.

"Is the Order prepared to depart?" he asked. "Have you checked on the queen yet?"

"It's all under control."

She exhaled, lips trembling, her hand wrapping around the knob. This was her shot.

"Of course, it is. You're going to make a fine constable, Eloise. I know it."

A lump caught in her throat. "I have a confession."

"Oh?"

"You know that jester?"

Fredrick smirked and reached for his coat. "Yes? He genuinely seems to fancy you."

"Well, we kissed. More than once."

The rest he didn't need to know.

Their eyes met in his reflection. "Well done, daughter."

"Damn fool thought to join the battle," she ranted. "Risk his life, leave his daughters behind. But I managed to convince him to return to Dathoviel."

Fredrick smiled, his eyes returning to the buttons on his jacket. "I see. Well, I'm sure his daughters are grateful to you."

"I fear you won't be so easy to convince."

His grin shrank. "What do you mean?"

"You won't be joining us on the battlefield today, Father. Queen's orders."

He turned to look at her, eyes frozen wide. "Why do I not believe you?"

"Just promise me you will stay here, please," she pleaded, throat tight. She clutched the keys, cursing the tears forming at the corners of her eyes.

"You know I can't do that, love. I took an oath. Not just for our kingdom or the queen, but for you as well. I must be at your side."

"I was afraid you would say something like that."

She met his eyes for a moment, taking in the sight of him, heart hammering against her ribs. She felt sick.

"Eloise..."

"Forgive me, Father."

Before he could react, she turned the knob, backed out of the room, and slammed the door shut, all in one swift movement. She heard the tray clatter to the floor as he searched for his keys. The click of the lock as she trapped him inside told him exactly where they were.

He began pounding on the door.

"Eloise, let me out of here this moment; that's an order!"

She rested her forehead against the wood, the sensation from his fists vibrating through her bones and she surrendered to the burning tears trailing down her cheeks.

"I must keep you safe."

"You will need me on the battlefield!" The banging stopped, and his voice cracked, heavy and thick, like it hurt to speak. "Please... I cannot lose you too."

She hadn't heard him so desperate since the day he'd begged her mother's lifeless body to open its eyes.

"That's why I must do this," she whispered, palm pressed to the door, wishing she could embrace him one last time. "I can't lose you either."

"Eloise!"

The door rattled as he once again began pounding, but she had already set the keys on a nearby ledge.

"I'll send someone to release you the moment this ridiculous battle is over," she promised, trying to sound strong, forcing herself not to look back.

~

Not unlike the Petrovian armory, Spencer's personal chapel surpassed the one in Dathoviel.

Twice the length, and double the capacity, it more closely resembled the church in the village. Countless lit candles were perched throughout the space, acting as the primary light source. They surrounded a bronze cross placed front and center, overlooking the communion station. The space was breathtaking, and coupled with the familiar aroma of frankincense, Amelia welcomed the wave of calm cresting over her.

Spencer marched straight to the front, bowed slightly, and crossed himself before partaking in a sip of wine and breaking off a piece of bread. After a moment of silence, he dropped to his knees, awaiting the women to join him. Amelia took communion while Caroline simply knelt between them. Finally, Spencer spoke.

"Heavenly Father, we ask for your blessings and protection today. We ask you keep Seb safe while he is with Alaric, and that you watch over the men and women fighting for justice today. Giving them sure feet and strong arms. I also humbly ask for your safeguarding of Queen Amelia, Lady Caroline, Eloise, and myself. You created Amelia to do incredible things for her people. Today we ask for your assistance in providing us the path she needs to achieve her destiny. For she will serve you through a fair and just reign."

Overwhelmed by his kind words as Spencer fell silent, Amelia continued the prayer.

"We kneel before you this morning to thank you for bringing us together. Each of the souls before you have experienced heartbreak and loss. We know the pain of being left behind. We head into this battle with memories of our fallen loved ones on our lips, and the promise of justice in our hearts."

"For Dathoviel," Caroline whispered.

"And Brantley," said Amelia.

Spencer cleared his throat. "For Davidson."

Eyes closed and heads bowed, they joined hands.

"Amen."

~

King Alaric sat, arms crossed and scowling in his carriage. Seb sat across from him, looking at the golden fields as the road ahead split over a great, rushing river—the left bridge led to Dathoviel, the right road to Petrovia.

The carriage shifted as it turned, taking the bumpier option, the vastness giving way to lush trees and rolling hills. Alaric's fists clenched tighter. Having to ask Spencer for help was the last thing on earth he wanted to do. He could imagine the smug look on his older brother's pretty face as he explained why he'd left his kingdom and queen unprotected with a known rebel force being built against him.

If only those filthy peasants had given him one more day. They'd all be locked into wagons on their way to Winvoltor and far away from his throne. He could only imagine what they were doing to his castle...

He thought of Leah, and his heart skipped a beat. Hopefully she was safe. If any of those bastards touched one hair on her head—

Sebastian cleared his throat. "Perhaps we should head that way?"

Alaric followed the knight's pointed finger, gazing out the window. The worn trail would lead them off the main path through the forest and across an old battlefield. It hadn't been used since his grandfather was king, and it was hardly the smoothest ride, but it always proved quickest.

"I suppose you're right."

Alaric stuck his head out the window and barked an order to keep heading left.

As they approached the tree line, the castle towers peaked over the treetops and a familiar dread settled in his gut. Most people returning home were flooded with memories of comfort and happier times, but not Alaric.

Petrovia may have birthed him, but he was his own man.

He owed them nothing. He—

The carriage halted then, jostling the two men inside. Alaric and Sebastian exchanged a look, silence stretching painfully between them. It was an odd place for bandits to attack, but with the way his day was going, it would have hardly been a surprise.

The roof rattled. A few horses whinnied in fear as bodies thudded to the ground around them, including the coachman who'd been seated above them. Alarmed, Alaric leapt from the carriage, sword drawn and eyes focused on the tree line. There were no bandits. Just wailing, bleeding men on the ground at his feet, and more soldiers riding in from the back to help.

"What the hell is going on?" Sebastian demanded from behind him, sword drawn.

Alaric shook his head. "I don't know. Do you see—"

A streak of arrows arched through the sky, raining over the men as if they'd been fired simultaneously from the forest depths.

This was no small group of bandits robbing them. This was a carefully organized attack. And he knew exactly who was behind it.

. 19 .

COMFORTED BY THE STRENGTH of Greta beneath her and unnerved by the weight of the helmet on her head, Amelia observed the rows of soldiers awaiting orders. Her gut clenched as she toyed with the reins. She would *not* run back to the castle.

Caroline must have sensed her distress because she reached out, encouraging Gus to move closer to his sister. Amelia gripped the pale outstretched hand with her own and kissed Caroline's knuckles, grateful for the grounding moment. To their left, Eloise cleared her throat. Her features were neutral, as if she wore a mask.

The thick covering of trees acted as protection for those positioned in the first wave from the empty clearing ahead. Optimistic, Spencer had explained the land was used in previous battles and would serve them well. But despite the lush emerald grass and abundant foliage, there wasn't a single hint of life. No birds chattered away from the branches above their heads and no deer dared to graze lazily. This land was where many had come to die, and whether or not they succeeded today, it pained Amelia that blood other than Alaric's would be spilled.

Seb's words returned to her, and she forced herself to sit a little straighter, a bead of sweat trickling down her temple. She searched the horizon for sign of anything. Had Seb intercepted Alaric in time? Was he able to convince him to take the alternative route?

Was he even still alive?

So much of today relied on Alaric's blind cooperation, and if he saw through Seb for a moment, it would break the entire operation.

But fate was on their side it seemed.

The distinct sound of clomping hooves broke the frozen silence of the clearing, and Amelia held her breath. A few moments later, the outline of Alaric's carriage and closest guards entered their line of sight. More would be arriving any minute. They must act quickly.

On her right, Spencer signaled to his general it was time to begin. Eloise did the same with the Order members assigned to her.

The first wave crouched, awaiting the moment their targets were in prime position. Not so close they could spot the attack coming, but near enough they couldn't turn and run. A man with white blonde hair rode lead, men on horseback and foot flanking him, surrounding the carriage. He clearly sensed something was wrong because he paused in the middle of the field, fist raised, bringing the others to a halt.

"Now!" Spencer shouted.

"Fire!" Jacob ordered.

A streak of arrows shot forward from the first row of raised longbows, descending over the carriage in a dark shower. A fair few reached their targets. The coachman was one of the first to fall as he had no shield to cover with. A few of the guards on foot managed to duck out of the way to Amelia's secret relief.

Then Alaric jumped from his carriage, sword drawn, head wildly sweeping back and forth as he assessed his surroundings. The sight of him made her stomach drop. When Seb appeared next, Eloise sighed.

"He's alive, thank God."

She glanced back at Amelia, clearly aching to be part of the action.

"Judging by the disbelief on Alaric's face, Seb lied well."

The rest of Alaric's men had arrived, their numbers double of what a typical king's travelling party should be. But they were no match for the Order and Spencer's men.

"Again," bellowed the general, and a fresh streak of arrows shot into the sky.

The first wave of bowmen withdrew as the second wave of fighters charged forward to meet the advancing guards. Alaric was shouting, but Amelia was too far back to make out his exact words. Swords were drawn. Blades clashed. Blood stained the grass as bodies met the earth.

Amelia glanced away, sick. She thought she had known what she was getting into, but just like Fredrick had warned—the sound and the smell, and the reality of it all was nothing like the stories she'd heard at court. It was much, much worse.

Was she cut out for ruling a kingdom if she couldn't stomach even a small-scale battle? She glanced at Caroline for reassurance, but she appeared terrified as well.

"Seb is coming," Spencer announced, pulling her attention back.

Harlow raced toward them through the field, kicking up dirt as Seb's blade sliced through the air. He stopped before them, unharmed. Thankfully every member of the Order knew his true intentions. Caroline surprised everyone by speaking first.

"Welcome back."

"Thank you." He bowed in her direction.

Spencer clapped a hand on his shoulder, looking impressed. "You did well."

"It is good to see you, Seb," Amelia managed to choke out, thankful to have his warm eyes to look into instead of the death unfolding behind him.

"You as well, My Queen."

"Where is Alaric?" Spencer asked, rapidly scanning ahead.

"Hiding." The knight pointed to the carriage. "Behind there."

"Very well." Spencer slid his helmet on and snapped his horse's reins.

Eloise followed him onto the battlefield with the rest of the third wave. "Stay here," she ordered to Caroline and Amelia, her visor now lowered and obscuring most of her face.

As if they needed reminding.

Seb glanced at the retreating backs of their friends, then to the queen. "Shall I remain here and act as guard for you?"

"No." Amelia shook her head. "Help them end this quickly, please. And be safe."

"As you wish." He nodded, guiding Harlow back into the fight.

Caroline squeezed Amelia's hand as the queen finally let her tears fall.

~

Out on the battlefield, the stench was far from pleasant, and it grew fouler each minute. Eloise shot with accuracy and pride, trying to take deadly aim only when necessary. Some of these men were true Dathovielian's just following their king. Arrow after arrow launched from her bow, taking out opposing soldiers left and right.

This was what she was meant to do.

She eyed a man headed for Spencer and captured him in her sights, arrow primed for the attack. She pulled back, the string taut, and exhaled, both eyes glued to her target.

One, two, th—

A dirty, blood covered hand grabbed her leg. She shrieked. There was no time to reach for the reins and save herself as she was pulled down and pinned beneath an equally filthy body. She eyed the dagger clamped between her attackers' teeth, heart hammering in her throat.

His once white uniform jacket was stained and torn, his face cut and bloody. He dragged her helmet roughly from her head; the edges scraping her skin and tugging on her braids. The shot she'd aimed at him a minute ago had been intended for his heart, but her arrow protruded from his ribs instead. A painful injury, surely, but nothing that immobilized him. Especially with the help of adrenaline.

Her own pulsed through her blood as she thrust her arms forward, attempting to shove him off. He grabbed her bow and pressed the arrow rest against her throat, then trapped one of her arms beneath his knee, eyes filled with hate and disgust. She choked against the pressure of her own weapon, trying to remember a logical way out of this position.

The dagger dropped from his mouth to his hand. "What a waste of a pretty face," he hissed, drawing the blade back, prepared to end her life. Just as she'd attempted to end his.

Surely, she knew him, they came from the same kingdom, but beneath the dirt and rage, it was hard to tell.

Abruptly, a blade erupted through his chest, spattering her face in his blood. She could taste the rust on her tongue. The pressure on her throat released as he fell to his side next to her. Dead. Quickly she rolled away from him, spitting, grabbing her bow and loading an arrow at once. Then she saw the spear sticking out of his back. The spear that could only belong to one person.

She gazed up, terror and gratitude flowing through her simultaneously.

Fredrick stood in the midst of war, chest heaving as though he'd run a great distance. He wasn't supposed to be here.

Yet without him, she'd be dead.

"Father!" she shouted, pushing back onto her feet.

She dashed to him, wrapping her arms around him as close as their armor would allow.

"A servant released me," he explained quickly.

Battle was no place for lengthy discussions.

"You were supposed to stay inside where it was safe." She shook her head. "Thank you for saving my life."

"It's a father's duty and honor, to protect his daughter."

He hugged her tighter; an instant comfort amid hell.

Battle was also no place for hugs, but she couldn't be bothered to care at this moment.

"We must get you out of here," she said, looking for her horse.

He didn't respond.

Her heart stopped as his body turned rigid in her arms. She struggled to support his weight as he gripped her gauntlets, collapsing to his knees.

"Eloise," he gasped.

She followed him to the ground. "What—" her voice faltered as she spotted the arrow lodged in his lower back. Right through his armor.

She couldn't look for his attacker, though they must be close. She wouldn't take her eyes off him. A wound like that...

She'd taken that shot herself many times today. Unless he received immediate aid... even then...

He caressed her face. "My darling, run."

"No!" Her head shook frantically.

She should be on guard, wary of the weapons around them, but they only had a minute left together. At most.

Crouching protectively over his body, she snapped the arrow in half so he could at least lay back.

"I love you, Eloise."

She pressed her forehead to his as his eyes closed. "I love you."

His last breath fluttered over her face, and she let out a blood-curdling scream against his chest. Not of fear or despair, but a warning. A battle cry like no other.

She lunged for her bow, loading two arrows at a time. They flew with the sharp accuracy only a vengeful daughter could have. It was unclear which of Alaric's men had taken her father's life, or who she knew personally, but it mattered little now.

Every single one of them could die.

~

Alaric looked over as Phillip slid from his saddle and took cover next to him behind the carriage.

"What the hell is this?" the general shouted over the clamoring and grunting around them. "I thought we were here for help from your brother. Not to be fucken ambushed by him!"

Alaric peered around the carriage wheel. Spencer was closing in. He ducked back as a chilling scream ripped through the air. He didn't dare look to see where it came from.

"Appears Sebastian lied to us. I should have known. Where is that traitor now?"

"I'm uncertain, Your Highness."

"Well, if you find him, don't kill him. Do what you must to capture the bastard, but ensure I am there to observe his final breaths."

Phillip grinned menacingly, displaying every crooked tooth.

~

Amelia jumped at the scream ringing across the field.

"What *was* that?" Caroline asked, clinging to Gus's reins, eyes wide with fear.

"It sounded like Eloise, but I cannot be sure."

Heart pounding, the queen urged Greta outside the protective cover the trees offered them, eyes searching the battlefield. It was impossible to recognize anyone.

"Was it her? Is she alive?"

"I do not see her," Amelia called back inching closer, guilt tearing through her aching ribcage. She should be down there with them.

How many lives had already been lost? *Had* that been Eloise who screamed? Or one of the members of the Order perhaps? It had definitely been female and—

"Amelia!"

Caroline's sudden terrified shriek and Gus's stressed whinny had the back of the queen's neck prickling. She turned and gulped. A man in torn and blood-stained Dathovielian armor was clutching Caroline to his chest, a sword pressed against her throat. Her sword. The queen froze, fear clawing at her insides.

The sight was too similar to the way Heath had held her. Everyone had reacted calmly when she'd been captured, and she would have to do the same now. This man stood wide; twice the size of both women, so hand to hand combat would be a last resort. Whatever he wanted, he could have. Anything to keep Caroline safe.

He seemed to follow a similar line of thinking, sneering at her as he flicked his head to the side. It did nothing to move the dark hair plastered to his pale forehead by blood and sweat.

"Easy there, Your Grace. I don't want to hurt the lass. I'm here for you, but I will if I'm forced."

Keep him talking. Distracted. Maybe someone would come to help. Dammit. Why had she sent Seb away?

"What is your name?"

"That's none of your concern," he spat.

Her chest threatened to burst at any moment, but she resolved to stay calm. He could not to see her fear. "How can I help you?"

His thick, split top lip curled into a chilling grin. He gestured with a jerk of his bearded chin for her to dismount.

"Imagine the reward King Alaric will bestow upon me when I deliver the head of his treacherous bitch wife."

Carefully, eyes locked on the weapon he held, she climbed down. Her war hammer hung from the saddle, but it was too large to grab covertly. Her sword remained at her hip, but if she reached for it, she risked him slitting Caroline's throat. She should have never given Spencer her dagger. Quickly, Amelia assessed his stance, praying Caroline would know to run the second she could. The man appeared desperate, and she bet he wouldn't be unable to pass up any opportunity she offered.

"Release her unharmed, and I will go with you quietly."

Wide with terror, Caroline's eyes shot silent objections at her.

Slowly his arm dropped from Caroline's throat, gesturing for Amelia to come closer. "Let's go find the king, shall we?"

Breathing heavily, Caroline shuffled back towards Greta as the man reached for the queen's arm. He hissed triumphantly, and just because he could, he backhanded her across the face. The shock buckled her knees, and the force of his meaty fingers sent her to the tall grass. She put pressure to her cheek and the stinging cut he had made.

Laughing maniacally, he tugged her back to her feet and faced her toward the battlefield. Her instincts screamed to fight, but she repressed them for now. She must get him away from Caroline.

He gripped her elbow, and she winced, her gauntlet digging into her skin.

Assessing the space between them and the surrounding treeline she tried to think of the next right move. She *could* get free of him, but it would probably cost her a dislocated shoulder or broken arm...

Then a sickening crack made her jump. The man released her with an agonized shout, stumbling into her and bringing them both to the soft earth. With great effort, Amelia shoved his heavy body off her desperately and reached for her sword, the tip pointed at his face. But he was too busy sobbing and clutching his legs. Legs that were clearly broken.

Amelia looked up.

"What should we do with him now?" Caroline huffed, the war hammer dropping from her shaking hands.

~

In one swift movement, Spencer leapt from his horse and drew his sword.

"Come on out, brother!" he called.

After a moment, Alaric stepped into view. There wasn't a drop of blood anywhere on him. He rolled his shoulders, cracked his neck, and lowered into a fighting stance. Their eyes narrowed as they met, sizing up the other as they had many times before. Two brothers.

Two kings. Meeting amidst the slaughter, both aware only one would make it out alive.

A step to the left from one was a step to the right for another; perfect reflections, almost like they were dancing. Whatever move they chose, it must be something neither had used on the other before. Having grown up training together, this scene was familiar. Spencer already knew his brothers favored attacks, common defensive strategies, and evasive moves. But of course, Alaric had the same information about him. They'd always been closely matched in swordplay, but it was the hand-to-hand combat Spencer excelled in. If he hoped to win and do so quickly, he needed Alaric to drop his sword.

"Care to explain the meaning behind all this?"

Considering their current position, Alaric looked and sounded quite smug. He rotated the weapon in his hand, its blade glistening in the sun.

"You had your chance to prove worthy of a crown, and you've failed."

Alaric took another step closer.

"Who are you to decide my successes and failures?"

Spencer countered, stepping back and to the left, keeping himself at a distance. "I'm the man willing to end your madness. Something I should have done long ago."

He lunged forward, but Alaric met him on beat, their blades connecting in a piercing clash. The battle continued around them, but their focus stayed on each other. Alaric's sword sliced through the air. Then Spencer's.

Their childhood flashed before his eyes.

"You're a big brother now, Spencer," Orla said, her golden eyes exhausted from birthing the newborn infant as Spencer—a child himself held his new baby brother. "It's your job to take care of baby Alaric. Love and protect him."

A second connection clanged, the tremor vibrating up the king's arm.

Alaric was a boy, stomping on ants who dared crawl through the open door to the kitchens. He'd grinned brightly, waving Spencer over with a chubby hand.

"Look, Spence! Look what I can do." After a moment, he'd dragged Alaric away, trying to explain he had no right to take the insect's lives. "But they're smaller than me. They're not important."

Alaric took two steps forward, causing Spencer to leap backward, the blade narrowly missing him.

A small casket was presented to the kingdom. So small, Spencer believed he might have been able to carry it out of the church himself. His mother sobbed at their side and his father sniffled away tears. And there was Alaric, stony face next to them. Bored.

"Poor child," someone had said. "Imagine what this will do to him."

They were too evenly matched. Their movements too practiced and familiar. This could go on forever.

"Enough!" Alaric shouted, sinking the blade into the earth with a forceful stab. "Let's finish this."

"On your feet!" the Petrovian general shouted. "Alaric, release him."

Teenagers now, Spencer gazed up into his brothers' furious eyes; so dark they were almost black. Like death. He could feel the pressure of Alaric's hands at his throat. The haze that came before unconsciousness. Spencer repeatedly slapped the leather mat they'd been training on, unable to shout.

"You're done, Ric." A guard grabbed the young prince by the collar and Spencer sat up, coaxing oxygen back into his lungs as Alaric was dragged away.

Spencer's sword clattered to the ground as well.

"As you wish, brother."

Their hands turned to fists, and initial swings were thrown. Some punches managed to be blocked or avoided. Most connected. Spencer's nose broke—no surprise there. In turn, Alaric's rib cracked. Both spit blood, wiped sweat from their brows, and kept fighting.

A kick to the kidneys finally had Alaric on his knees. Heaving for air, Spencer rushed forward to take the advantage. His arm wound around his brother's throat, choking and holding him in place.

"He is your brother!" Viktor shouted from his throne. "And the only one you have left. You will attend the feast tonight."

"No," Spencer spat. "I will not celebrate his birthday just to show off for the dozens of people you've invited. I'm tired of the lies. You're not fooling anyone, not even him. He knows you're afraid of him."

Viktor's voice boomed as he pounded the armrest. "I fear no one and nothing!"

Spencer reached for Amelia's dagger.

Alaric's eyes widened when he saw it, clearly shocked. He hastily scanned their surroundings. "What happened, dear brother? Did my wife seduce you? No longer the *virgin* king of Petrovia?"

"No, brother." Spencer sneered, his bicep flexing and pressing against Alaric's neck. "All she had to do was ask."

"Where is she?" he coughed, tugging at Spencer's sleeve.

"Somewhere safe."

He felt the resistance of nature pulsing in his blood. Holding him back. Ensuring this was what he truly wanted. He was a warm-blooded man, more than capable of killing. He had done it before in battle, but this was different, and he would be lying to himself if he thought otherwise.

"Remember what I said, Spence." His mother had clutched his hand, her final breaths shuddering from between her lips. "Look out for him. He needs you to guide him back to the light."

Then her hand had slipped from his, eyes shutting for the final time.

A tear escaped. He'd failed his mother and both of his brothers. All he wanted was freedom from this responsibility—this burden. The pain he'd been holding on to all these years.

"This is for Davidson," he whispered, teeth gritted and jaw locked. In his grasp, Alaric froze. "And mother, and father, and all those you've ever harmed. Or would have if I didn't do this."

"Do it, you coward," Alaric dared, voice cracked from the pressure on his windpipe. "See if you can."

Spencer shut his eyes, a silent sob escaping his lips as his heart broke one more time. He plunged the silver blade into the side of Alaric's throat and yanked, severing the carotid artery.

Blood was dripping down the hilt and over the sapphires when he opened his eyes once more. Alaric's stony face stared up at him, utterly lifeless.

~

The longing sound of the horn came from the middle of the battlefield—a call to stop fighting. The battle had ended, meaning one, or both of the kings had died.

A chill swept through Amelia as she glanced away from the knot she was tying around her attacker's ankles.

"Amelia," Caroline gasped, hand outstretched.

Amelia clasped her fingers and stood, eyes intent on the slow-moving bodies across the battlefield. And the bodies that didn't move at all.

Two horses approached through the sea of soldiers, one with a rider, the other bare. Spencer looked a little worse for wear than the last time she saw him, but he still breathed. As they came closer, Amelia realized the second horse did have a passenger of sorts. A lifeless body hung across its back, the trademark leather boots unmistakable.

It was over.

20

SEB FOCUSED ON THE quivering feather attached to his quill without fully registering its presence. His boots, caked with blood and dirt felt heavy, as if they might pull him deep into the earth. The parchment in his other hand had crumpled under his grasp. He blinked a few times, focusing once more on the names.

Sorting the dead was never an easy task, and he hated having been the one assigned to it.

Initially, the job had been appointed to Eloise, but once they'd learned of Fredrick's death, Seb and Amelia had ensured she was devoid of all post-battle responsibilities and returned to the castle alongside the constable's body.

With the Petrovian general at his side, Seb supervised the customary stripping of the bodies.

Cataloguing recovered weapons, armor, and valuables as they went. These would return to Dathoviel, as Spencer said his vaults and armories were well stocked. Amelia didn't want the spoils, but no matter which monarch took them, they still needed sorting.

On the side of the field, a trio of high ranking Petrovian guards had rounded up the surviving men who'd fought for Alaric. Spencer was asking them one by one where their loyalties lay with Alaric now gone. With both eyes on the dead and one ear on the living, Seb shuddered at the sound of Phillip's voice. Of course he'd survived.

"*I* am a general!" he shouted. "Release me at once."

"I will do no such thing," Spencer said evenly.

His clothes were stained with his brother's blood, eyes swollen from exhaustion. How desperately he must wish to return to the castle and wash the memory of battle away. Seb certainly desired to scrub every last speck of death from his skin.

Phillip continued, struggling against the rope tied around his hands. "You can't treat us this way. We were defending our king."

"Hence why you still breathe." Spencer folded his hands, turning to address the remaining survivors. "You shall each be presented with three choices, gentlemen. Either, return to Dathoviel with your allegiance pledged to Queen Amelia, or remain in Petrovia under my watchful eye. Either way, you will be assessed, ensuring your loyalties no longer lie with the fallen."

"An—and the th—third option?" stuttered a knight from further down the line.

"Banishment, of course."

"So, death," Phillip spat. "You'll send us off with nothing and expect us to live?"

Spencer narrowed his eyes. "I expect you'll see the error of supporting my brother and return home to your families."

~

That evening, after everyone had shed their armor and bathed, Amelia tucked Caroline into bed with a promise to return soon and went downstairs to Spencer's study.

She poured over the list of names Seb provided, struggling to remain stoic.

With Spencer and Olive on either side of her, they began arranging proper memorials for those who perished. The number of dead *was* lower than it could have been, thanks to Spencer's swift action. But it was still higher than Amelia wished.

As her eyes settled on Fredrick's name, whatever strength remained fled her body. A sob tore through her, and she turned to Olive who welcomed her trembling body with open arms.

"I promised Eloise he would be safe."

"I know, I know," Olive soothed, caressing the queen's hair.

Amelia gratefully accepted the embroidered handkerchief Seb passed her, wiping her eyes and nose before clutching it to her chest.

"Have you seen her?" Olive asked, glancing between Spencer and Seb.

"She won't leave his body," the knight whispered wearily.

Spencer had his arms crossed over his chest, hugging himself. "She isn't holding well."

No one could blame her.

April 13th, 1457

The day following the battle was tireless and devoid of joy. Though victory had been achieved, no one wished to celebrate. On the second morning, Alaric's body was laid to rest in his family tomb. Spencer oversaw the sealing of his casket, but no ceremony was held.

Fredrick's funeral was a grand function, however. Nearly every remaining member of the Order attended and paid their respects, and many chose to speak in his honor. When time came for the official eulogy, Eloise struggled to stand. Even with Spencer and Amelia's help, she was unable to make it to the pulpit. Seeing the desperation in her eyes, Amelia took her place, uncertain if words alone could pay tribute to the man lying before them on burgundy velvet.

His eyes were closed and his hands had been folded peacefully over his ribs. His uniform was pristine, adorned with medals and a teal sash. Amelia clutched the edges of the marble podium, her knuckles turning white. She shared a look with Eloise, shaken by the genuine sadness in her hollow brown eyes. As silent tears streaked down Eloise's dark face, the queen inhaled deeply.

"There is much to be said about Constable Fredrick, and I know more will be spoken of him in the days to come. Perhaps you knew him well, or perhaps you were never given the pleasure of seeing his bold smile. Of hearing his boisterous laugh. He was truly a man who loved to laugh. I remember a time—I was just a young princess then, desperate for someone to look at me and not laugh when I said I would be queen one day. Sure, Fredrick chuckled, but in the same breath, he handed me a wooden sword and said, '*Well, then you best learn to fight, little one.*' And from that day on, he took it upon himself to train a hopeful princess into the woman you see before you. He was always there to support me. I know I'm not the only one Fredrick took under his wing and inspired. He was a glorious man who died protecting his greatest treasure, his daughter. And I know he wouldn't have wanted it any other way. And I pray, wherever his soul has travelled, he is somewhere laughing and smiling over us."

After a quick prayer Amelia retook her seat, and Eloise gripped her hand in silent gratitude, their mourning rings clinking together.

April 15th, 1457

Duchess Ella travelled to Petrovia as quickly as she could. Clearly, Caroline needed reminding of her place in the world, and that armor and weapons were not items meant for a Lady.

With a long, confident speech prepared, she entered the drawing room where her daughter awaited, back to her, amidst vases of lilacs, plush furniture, and the typical crimson drapes that hung throughout the castle.

When Caroline turned from the window and their eyes met, it became clear something had changed within her daughter. She glowed, looking as if she'd aged a decade in months. She stood tall; her smile the most genuine Ella had seen since she was a child.

Could she have finally found a man to marry? Even with the horse riding and sword wielding?

"My darling daughter, I am so pleased to see you."

They embraced tightly and Caroline's first words were muffled by Ella's shoulder. "I apologize you were not given a proper welcome, mother. Everyone's had their hands quite full these last few days."

"No harm. I know my way around."

They pulled apart. "What brings you to Petrovia?"

Ella squeezed Caroline's fingers tightly. "I knew I must come as soon as news of the battle reached Galfian. Is it true? Did Alaric truly perish in the fighting?"

"Yes."

"And what does his death mean for Dathoviel?"

Caroline pursed her lips as if she were uncertain. Though it wasn't clear if her uncertainty lay in lacking knowledge, or willingness to share.

"Queen Amelia shall announce in a few hours our plan to depart in the morning."

"Will power revert to her father then? Until they can find a new king for her to marry?"

"No." Caroline tucked her hands behind her back—a familiar image, signaling a fight between them was about to begin. "She intends to rule alone."

Ella's eyes widened so quickly the strain hurt her head and her mood plummeted as the familiar tension they commonly shared returned.

"I don't understand."

"She won't be the first woman to rule without a husband. There've been others."

"Not in our lands."

Caroline did not waver as she crossed her arms, lips pursed into a thin line. Her beaming smile was long gone.

"There *is* a first time for everything, Mother. Amelia was destined for this."

Disgruntled and defensive, Ella threw her hands into the air. She was used to her daughter's defiance, but it seemed now she had a friend with mutual ideals. No doubt they'd been getting into all kinds of trouble.

"Why can children not just leave things alone? You're all so quick to turn your back on tradition."

Caroline sighed, her feet carrying her toward a table where maps and instruments were spread. Several books lay open and she picked up the nearest one, examining the spine as if it would give her the words to respond.

"The history you glorify, Mother, is not without its share of black days. If life continues on the same, how will we ever achieve progress?"

"Progress comes at a price."

Caroline looked up sharply. "As a woman, you *must* feel the unbalanced, stifling ways of life. How can you not desire change as badly as I do? If not for yourself, then at least for me?"

"Roles and expectations between the sexes exist for a reason." Ella crossed her arms, then uncrossed them upon remembering duchesses were too dignified for such an action. "Men protect and provide. Women take whatever they bestow upon us and make it greater. It is an honor to be a woman."

"I agree, but it's not that simple. It never has been."

"Why can you not allow things to run naturally?"

Caroline dropped the book, leaning against the table, her fingers curling around the carved edge. Ella nearly demanded she stand up straight, but held her tongue.

"There is so much more to being a woman, *a person*, than arranging flowers, birthing children, and smiling at the correct times."

Indignation coursed through the duchess's veins. "So, in your eyes, I'm a failure as a woman? Any woman who takes pride in her home, in her children, and wishes to serve her husband is lacking?"

"No, of course not! If those things truly brought you joy and fulfillment, that's wonderful. The point I'm trying to make is some women want something different. And they should be allowed to go after that without fear of being ostracized—or murdered. There are even men who desire a life without dominance and power and the weight of providing for their families. No one is saying the traditional ways are completely worthless. But it's time you realize they aren't the *only* ways. That those of us who crave change aren't attacking you, or aiming to destroy anything you've worked for. We only wish to find joy and live out our days doing what we love. With the people we love..."

Ella strained to ignore the tugging between her ribs. She heard the near desperation in her daughter's voice. The desire to be heard and understood. She thought of her own parents and how strained their relationship had been. But unlike *her* mother, she wasn't wrong about this. Admitting she was mistaken would mean admitting things she wasn't ready to deal with, so she dug her heels into the plush carpet, head shaking.

"I knew allowing you to be tutored alongside your cousins was a mistake. You learned things you didn't need to know. Heard ideas not intended for your ears."

Caroline pushed away from the desk. Her hands clenched into fists. A long, tense moment passed between them. Then she forcefully exhaled, fingers spreading.

"I am grateful for my education. What I learned then, and during my time in Dathoviel has helped me see the world more clearly."

"And *what* do you see?"

"Women must step out of the shadows. Voice our ideas and opinions. Have them be heard and taken seriously. As you said, we have the ability to take what men provide and transform it into something beautiful. A man catches a fish and a woman turns it into a delicious meal. But what is to stop the woman from fishing and the man from cooking? Imagine if all men and women worked together based of their personal strengths."

"They do work together, but that doesn't mean each shouldn't understand what seat at the table is theirs. You cannot go around rearranging things, Caroline. That will only lead to chaos."

"You're mistaken, Mother. As queen, Amelia desires to make positive change. I believe in her, and myself. You should see the impact in Dathoviel already. The village thrives, when before her people were starving and dying."

"Could those changes not be done with a king in power?" Ella challenged.

Her arms had crossed again and this time she didn't bother uncrossing them.

"With the right king, but Alaric was not that man. Dathoviel is Amelia's kingdom by birthright. She should not have to share it with someone unless she wishes to. It should come down to character, desire, and aptitude. Not gender or biased entitlement."

"Where you have come from is not so terrible, you know." Ella's eyes narrowed, her cheeks warm and flushed. She must deflect and distract—not only

Caroline, but herself as well. "You have more opportunities than I did as a young woman. You at least learned to read."

"That's precisely my point!" Caroline exclaimed. "Knowing how to read shouldn't be a privilege, Mother. Education should be granted to all. Each new generation *should* be an improvement on the last."

"And what would that look like to you, may I ask?"

Caroline only smiled. She'd been waiting for this question it seemed.

"Boundaries being tested and prejudices re-evaluated as needed. There should be innovation, new laws made and passed. Lessons learned from the suffering instead of increased compliance and tolerance. The education I received would not have been given to me if Aunt Orla had not advocated the importance for noble girls to learn to read. Even if it was so we could better communicate with potential husbands. Imagine if all girls, regardless of class and color, were given books. What could that mean for our kingdoms and beyond?"

"You're speaking about more than books!" Ella shrieked, the space between her eyes beginning to pound. "You're talking about unbalancing the order between genders and classes. People need order. They need *rules*."

"The world is changing. It needs to."

Ella's throat stung as if she'd sucked on a lemon.

What *if* she'd had the space to voice her opinions, rather than have them silenced growing up? How might it have felt to have Charles respect her ideas? Perhaps implement a few instead of brushing her off? How had she never allowed herself to ask these questions before? When had she turned from a fierce young woman herself into one compliant in nearly every aspect of her life?

"You look at the world through the strangest eyes," she observed quietly.

Caroline took a deep breath as if bolstering a considerable amount of courage. The hard lines of her shoulders softened and slumped, the fire fading from her eyes.

"There's something else I must tell you, and I may as well do it now."

Ella's heart hammered against her ribcage.

"Yes?"

"Amelia and I are in love."

A heavy weight compressed Ella's chest.

"What did you say?"

"We're engaged to be wed, and Spencer has blessed our union."

Ella felt sick. Helpless. This couldn't be happening. Not to her. This was too far.

"Is this a statement you two are making for your cause? A joke? Because if so, no one is laughing."

"It's neither. We are simply in love, like any other two people blessed to find one another. The ceremony is tonight."

"Tonight!" Ella clapped a hand over her heart, sinking into the nearest chair. "If your father was alive, this would kill him."

Caroline knelt before her, renewed patience in her eyes. And a hint of desperation. "All my life, you've hoped I'd find love and marry. I've finally done that, Mother. I implore you to see my happiness. To feel my joy and share in it. I understand you wished my love was directed at a man, but my heart belongs to Amelia. And hers to me."

Ella clutched her daughters' hands tight, heart aching. "How did I fail you for you to end up this way?"

"Mother, I—"

"Really consider what you're saying, Caroline," she pled.

"I have, and what I am- *who* I am- was not caused by anything you did wrong. Or right. It has nothing to do with you. I'm me. I always have been, and I always will be. You can't fix me. I'm not broken. All you can do is choose to love me, Mother. Or walk away. . . and lose me."

Ella's stomach lurched as a sharp stab pierced her heart right through the middle. She tore her hands back. Caroline's hovered in the air for a moment, fingers reaching. Then slowly they slipped down into her own lap. Eyes stinging with a wave of tears, Ella bit back a sob.

"How can you say such unfair things?"

Caroline did not bother controlling or hiding her tears. They poured from her eyes in a devastating trail, falling to Ella's skirt.

"How can you look at me and see something wrong, just because I'm different than what you've always pictured me to be? I'm your child. Your love for me should be unconditional."

"I do love you."

"Then choose me!" Caroline choked. "For the first time, see me for who I am and love me. Not in spite of anything, not ignoring certain pieces of me. All of me. Exactly the way I am."

Ella's lip quivered. "Caroline, please. . ."

"This is a chance to think for yourself, Mother. To consider your thoughts and where they come from. If they are actually yours, or what you've been told to think by the people around you. Could you truly turn your back on me simply because I love a woman?"

Ella flinched.

Slowly she pushed her mind to process. To sort through the ideals and notions whirring violently through her head. Beliefs she'd grown up believing were true and necessary. What thoughts *were* hers? What values did *she* truly hold? Would they be different had she not grown up in a castle? Not been raised in a loveless home? Charles had not been a stern husband, exactly. But he'd been stubborn and opinionated. Which hadn't left much room for her to think.

Desperation gripped her ribs. Looping and curling like a needle and thread, pulling tight until she feared it might snap and her body would crumble.

This was not the kind of mother she hoped to be. She didn't want Caroline to fight for her love, to feel like she needed to earn it.

She'd grown up that way, and it was exhausting. Never being enough and knowing that no matter what, you would fail. No, all she wanted to do now was cradle Caroline in her arms and apologize for all of it.

But could she? Or was it too late?

Ella swallowed and blinked, attempting to focus on her daughter's tear-streaked face.

Ella smiled faintly. "I will need time to adjust, sort out my own opinions from years of teaching... But I do not have to understand everything about your life and your choices, to love and support you. It is *your* life after all, and as long as you are happy and loved, that is truly all that matters."

"You—you do support me?" Caroline sounded both suspicious and relieved.

"All a mother wants is for her daughter to be safe and happy. I cannot say I necessarily like it, but I will always pray your future is long and bright. In time, I hope rest comes."

Caroline's shoulders sagged with relief, her forehead falling to Ella's thighs. "Thank you."

Caressing her daughter's cheek, she pressed a kiss into her golden hair. Her daughter would surely face more foes regarding her choices, but Ella swore to never again be one of them.

~

That evening, after Ella had departed back to Galfian, Amelia called the Order back to Spencer's throne room. There were new faces, but far too many missing ones.

Her heart broke once more, but she stood tall, flanked by Caroline and Spencer.

"Thank you for accepting my summons," she called. "I cannot promise you Dathoviel will never face war again, but I swear, as your queen, I will do everything my power allows to keep you, your neighbors, and your loved ones safe. Dathoviel is our home, and tomorrow we will return a few souls lighter, but stronger as a whole."

No cheers or chants followed, not that she had expected or wished for any. There were a few salutes and bows of respect, but the air in the room was thick. She sought out Seb in the crowd as his words came back to her. The battle *would* be the last horrible thing she ever did because of Alaric.

~

There was nowhere else in the world Caroline wished to marry Amelia than the garden.

With the sun drifting low on the horizon, they met Spencer beneath the sweeping branches of a large oak tree, hands clasped like equals. Partners, now and forever. It was all she'd ever wanted, and yet her heart pounded so loudly she hardly heard the melody drifting from the minstrel a few feet away.

Her gown glowed in a pale pink shimmer, drifting softly to her bare feet, the hem dancing around her ankles in the floral air, which she inhaled deeply as it grazed the exposed skin of her neck and collarbone. Amelia wore a crisp white blouse and flowy, high-waisted cream trousers. Where Caroline had a crown of roses set around her curls, Amelia wore her hair in a thick twist down her back, baby's breath weaved throughout.

It was a lovely, lustful sight to say the least.

Caroline's lower lip slid between her teeth, willing it to still as she wiggled her toes against the dewy grass. Amelia smiled warmly at her.

Was it absolutely forbidden for them to kiss before Spencer declared them officially married?

Olive, who'd been following a few paces behind with a glorious bouquet in her arms, joined Seb on Spencer's left. She took a moment to pin one of her blossoms to his uniform, their supportive witnesses.

A year ago, Caroline could never have imagined this moment would be real. Yet, as Amelia clasped her hand, nothing felt more destined. She pressed her eyes closed, only opening them when she felt the backs of Amelia's fingers caressing her cheek.

Oh, please let the ceremony be quick.

Spencer grinned as if he could read her mind. The wink he shot her from his unbruised eye confirmed that he'd at least guessed. Forever reliable, he jumped straight into his speech.

"Before me stands two remarkable women. Strong, capable, and brave. In the short time I've seen you together, I've watched you love fiercely, unapologetically, and without fear. Shall you move forward through life, hand in hand, leaving the world a better place than you found it, and spreading love wherever you go. I am honored to bless your union." He handed over the first ring. "Caroline, do you devote your heart and future to Amelia?"

"I do."

"And do you swear to support her, inspire her, and remind her of your love every day?"

Amelia released Caroline's hand for a moment to swipe away the tear creeping toward her chin.

"I do," Caroline choked out.

Her heart was threatening to burst.

"And Amelia, do you devote your heart and future to Caroline?"

"I do."

Spencer sniffled, clearing his throat. "Do you swear to support her, inspire her, and remind her of your love every day you share?"

"Every day," she promised, her thumb running across Caroline's knuckles, pulling her closer.

Behind the queen, Olive wept. Chuckling silently, Seb passed her his handkerchief, which she immediately blew her nose into rather loudly. Her cheeks burned red and her eyes flashed apologies under the weight of everyone's amused gaze.

Giggling, Caroline slid the simple silver ring onto the queen's finger with a surprisingly steady hand before graciously accepting her own. The weight of the band felt like a warm embrace she never wanted to end.

"From the moment you entered my life you have been one of my biggest supporters," Amelia said, pressing a soft kiss to Caroline's hand. You kept me going in my darkest time, and reminded me happiness could survive heartbreak. You inspire me to become the woman I was born to be. To unapologetically embrace my truest nature. There is no word worthy of describing how thankful I am for you and I will spend the rest of our lives searching for it, but for now, *love* will have to do."

Joyful tears spilled down Caroline's cheeks.

"I knew the first moment I saw you that we were meant to share our lives together in some way. My heart longed for what it wanted when we were apart. And when we reunited, I knew it was you I loved. Then you said you loved me too, and for the first time I finally felt like I belonged on this earth. The universe took a strange path to bring our souls together, but I intend to keep us that way."

Spencer coughed, struggling to remain composed.

"As King of Petrovia, I have the power to grant you two wed. And I do this now with pride. You may seal your declarations and promises with a kiss."

Caroline tilted her head to the side and pulled Amelia in tightly, their lips meeting. Her fingers dove into Amelia's hair as the queen's arm curled around her, gripping her hip.

She hardly heard their friends clapping and cheering over the pounding of her heart, hardly felt the tears streaming down her cheeks.

This was her happily ever after.

~

Father,

I pray things are well for you in Dathoviel. By the time you receive this letter, we will most likely be on our journey home. I am writing to inform you that Alaric perished in a fight with King Spencer. His body is to remain here, as it has already been committed to his family's tomb.
When I return we will sit down and discuss how to move Dathoviel forward, and whether or not you still wish to hold a seat in court.

Sincerely,
Amelia

The sound of smashing glass and splintering wood carried through the corridors as Leah unleashed her grief in every unlocked room she could.

Despair coursed through her blood as she reduced the intercepted letter to shreds, tossing them into the fire in Alaric's study.

Finally, she collapsed to her knees before the hearth; the cinders turning her apron black. Her chest and shoulders were heaving, her blood burning. Clutching her stomach, she forced herself to take deep, steadying breaths, inhaling the scent of smoke and ash.

Amelia believed she had won, but the battle was far from over.

Leah had been promised the throne, and Ric's death changed much, but not everything. The only thing standing between her and the throne now, was the queen.

Once the court learned of Amelia's conspiracy against Alaric, Dathoviel would surely be taken from her. After all, it was hard to wear a crown without a head.

Leah got to her feet and moved to Alaric's desk, her desk now she supposed, and gathered ink, parchment and a quill.

Spencer may prove tricky. . . but she would figure that out if the time came. She'd made Alaric fall in love with her. How different could his brother be?

And when the queen was executed in the middle of her beloved village, Leah would present her worthiness for the crown. It would shock everyone, but that was part of the excitement, really. She would be doing them a favor and she would get the respect she deserved.

This time she would be the one in control, and she needed no one to do that.

Well. . . *almost* no one.

. 21 .

CAROLINE'S TONGUE WAS HEAVY in her mouth, her heart pounding furiously as she shut her bedroom door with a final click. There was a fire burning across from the bed, and Amelia stood between both, lips wet from where she'd just licked them.

For being newlyweds less than an hour, they were standing quite far apart at the moment, something that must be rectified immediately.

"I am sorry there was no big celebration after the ceremony," Amelia said softly.

Caroline shrugged, strolling forward, and took her wife's hands in hers. Her wife's.

"I much prefer a more *private* celebration anyway."

With the heat from the fireplace licking at her ankles, Caroline reached up, turning Amelia back to face her with two fingers beneath her chin.

"Part of me does feel cheated we didn't get to dance in front of everyone we love, but we could dance here, now. If you'd like."

Caroline only smiled, stepping to the left where a music box rested on the mantel. She twisted it three times and returned it between a vase of dried lilacs and a stack of books. The tune she often hummed drifted toward them, mixing with the sounds of the crackling fire.

"You were never fond of dancing," said Amelia.

"No, but you are. And it turns out I am quite fond of you."

Caroline took Amelia's waist gingerly, doing her best not to trip over her own feet. Slowly they rotated, drifting closer to the bed, foreheads pressed together, eyes closed. It felt so natural to be with her like this. So right.

As the final click of the winding arm came around and the tune melted away into the air, Caroline spun Amelia out and back in. Then their mouths were pressed together and the queen's trepidation seemed to have evaporated as Caroline felt her body pressed against the small expanse of wall between the window overlooking the gardens and the fireplace.

She was trapped between soft curves and hard stone, and there was no place she'd rather be.

Amelia's fingertips floated from Caroline's hair to her neck before trailing over her breasts and down to her ribs with feather-light touches. Her other hand rested on Caroline's hip, soft and steadying at first, but growing warmer with every moment. Caroline trembled, recalling how Amelia had taken the lead their first night together.

Tonight, she wanted to prove herself as a lover. A partner. She could do this; she could love Amelia the way she deserved. The way a queen deserved to be loved.

She curled her fingers in the fabric of Amelia's blouse and tugged it loose, but before she could unfasten her trousers, Amelia slipped her hands away and took a small, unexpected step back.

"I almost forgot," she breathed, cheeks flushed and chest heaving.

Then she was dragging Caroline to the gold-framed mirror above the fireplace and turning her to face it. She stepped close; her left hand deep in her pocket, her right gripping Caroline's waist.

"Forgot what?"

Amelia grinned at her as she pulled out a necklace. "Your wedding gift. Well, technically, I meant to give it to you at Christmas, but..."

"Will you put it on me?"

Beaming, the queen obliged, swinging the necklace around to the front and draping it around Caroline's neck. She gulped, taking in her reflected appearance.

The delicate gold chain cascaded across her collarbone in a series of swooping loops, each web set with small pink crystals. A larger teardrop crystal hung from the center just before the dip of her cleavage.

It was breathtaking.

"Do you like it?" Amelia asked, her hands falling to Caroline's waist, tugging her back.

"I do, thank you."

The queen's lips curled as she moved Caroline's hair aside to press slow kisses along her shoulder. Her left hand slid up Caroline's spine, undoing the ties of her dress. The gown fell into a heap around Caroline's feet, leaving her with nothing more than jewels at her throat and flowers in her hair.

Amelia's eyes darkened and she made the most delicious sound in Caroline's ear. The kind of sound that started low in the gut and traveled up from the back of one's throat. It had Caroline's skin prickling. She was suddenly burning, as though her body had been plunged into the fire.

"You are not relaxed," Amelia observed, covering Caroline's fisted hands with her own.

"How can I be?"

Amelia chuckled. "Perhaps we should fix that before moving to the bed."

The way the word *bed* sounded on Amelia's lips was downright sinful. Caroline could only nod her head slowly, amazed she'd kept her eyes open this entire time. The queen's knee pressed against the backs of hers, spreading her thighs and sliding between them. Caroline obliged, though her legs were trembling.

"How?"

Amelia's eyes found hers in the mirror. "I wish to watch you touch yourself. Would that be alright?"

Caroline nearly choked on the air she'd quickly inhaled.

"What?"

"Show me how you touch yourself when you think of me... please."

Caroline felt Amelia's fingers slip between hers, opening her right fist, then holding it flat against her stomach. As though she'd left her own body, or like she was watching two other people in the mirror, she saw—rather than felt Amelia's hand guiding hers to the blonde curls between her thighs. Then lower.

Caroline gulped. "I... I—you..."

"You are the most beautiful thing I have ever seen. You are my wife and I am yours, and you are safe with me. Do you feel safe?"

"I... I do."

Amelia beamed. "Then please, show me. If you must, close your eyes to start."

Caroline's eyes fluttered closed gratefully as Amelia's middle finger applied pressure to her own, guiding her toward her own clit. When they found it, Caroline hissed. She was unbelievably sensitive.

"Ohhh."

Though her eyes were still closed, Caroline could hear the smile in Amelia's tone. The pride. "I'm going to pull my hand away, but do not stop, alright?"

"Alright."

Caroline's hand slipped out of place momentarily when Amelia released her, but she corrected immediately. She kept her eyes closed, her bottom lip already sore from where her teeth were gnawing away at it.

"You are so beautiful," Amelia repeated, her touch gliding up Caroline's abdomen, over her ribs and her breasts, to her shoulders and neck, then back to rest on her hips.

Caroline gasped. "Thank you."

Her own touch was familiar, practiced. She knew precisely what she liked. The right amount of pressure and how fast or slow to do at each moment, and her core responded accordingly. Though the pleasure never lasted long enough to do more than torture her.

First the heat within bloomed slowly, but with each passing second and every encouraging sound from the queen, it seemed to grow until it was almost boiling. Breathing had become a chore and coherent thoughts were fleeting. Amelia seemed content watching at first, but soon her fingers began kneading into Caroline's hips, drawing her back tighter and tighter against her body.

How she hadn't collapsed to the floor, Caroline didn't know.

"Alright," the queen whispered. "Now, open your eyes."

Caroline shook her head. "I, I can't."

"Do not be ashamed." Amelia's tone was soothing. "If you cannot look at yourself, look at me. See how I see you."

Somehow that sounded far, far worse.

Caroline forced her lids open, unable to avoid her own reflection. She looked positively wanton, legs somehow wider than when she'd first spread them. Her chest rising and falling rapidly, pupils blown wide.

"Can we go to the bed now?"

Amelia nodded, stepping back and taking Caroline with her. Then Caroline was on the edge of the bed, watching the queen of Dathoviel bending to her knees on the floor in front of her, still fully clothed.

Her hands slid up Caroline's thighs, coaxing them open once more. She pressed a series of hot, open-mouthed kisses from the inside of her knee up to her damp curls until she was nibbling at Caroline's hipbones.

"Lie back, please," Amelia coaxed. "It is *my* turn to worship you."

Caroline wanted to protest and say Amelia deserved the pleasure in this moment, but the need in the queen's eyes stopped her. She wanted this, perhaps more than Caroline did. And who was she to dismiss such a loving request?

Caroline slid back on the bed until her head was against the pillows, watching as Amelia stood and shed her wedding clothes. Then she was on the mattress next to her, pressing over her and slipping back between her legs. Caroline could only watch as the queen's head dipped and her face disappeared.

When her tongue swiped up and around, circling her aching, swollen core, Caroline cried out. Her hands flew to the ornate iron bars of her headboard, needing something to hold on to and wanting to avoid tugging at Amelia's dark locks.

For having never done this before, the queen certainly knew what she was doing. Almost as if she'd studied it.

Caroline had overheard from maids and female cousins how their partners had tried and failed at this very thing. Their complaints had lived in the back of Caroline's mind for many years, and she'd used them her first night with Amelia, but this was something else.

Oral pleasure wasn't just something Amelia happened to do. It was her own personal art form.

Her tongue alternated between slow but pressured, almost lazy circling licks to snake-like flicks. And then there was the sucking. And the vibrations from the blissful sounds coming from Amelia's mouth.

Caroline was trembling within moments.

"Oh. Please. Please." Caroline's capability to speak had been reduced to one-word sentences. "Don't. Don't. Stop. Please. Don't. Stop."

She was helpless and boneless, her body betraying any desire to prolong this pleasure.

She cried out, realizing her fingers had somehow released the headboard and found the queen's hair despite her best intentions. If her tugging hurt, Amelia said nothing. She didn't pull away to complain or slow down. She only went faster, applying more pressure with her tongue. Her hands had moved to the inside of Caroline's thighs, holding them open and pressing her hips down. Amelia looked up as Caroline glanced down. Their eyes locked as a hiss escaped Caroline's lips. Her hips began to buck, but the queen held on.

And when Caroline finally stopped writhing and collapsed back on the mattress, Amelia finally pulled back, grinning with wild, dark eyes.

"Are you alright?" she whispered, crawling up Caroline's body, pressing her hands on either side of her face.

"Not even a little," Caroline puffed. clutching at the necklace haphazardly tangled around her throat. "I've surely died. You've certainly killed me."

Amelia only chuckled and pressed their lips together, kissing her deeply. Caroline inhaled sharply, realizing just why this kiss tasted different from the rest. Her eyes flew open, then rolled back.

"Perhaps you can repay my sin with one of your own and kill me in return," Amelia teased when she finally pulled back.

Caroline was only too happy to oblige, pressing onto her elbows as Amelia slid away and lay down on the mattress. "You only have to tell me what you want."

She let her eyes rake over the queen's bare body unashamed. The sun had set entirely now, the windows dark around her bedroom. The only light came from the fire, the flickering flames dancing over Amelia's curves. Her smooth skin called out to Caroline's mouth, begging to be kissed and bitten.

"I want. . ." Amelia stuttered, her earlier confidence gone with the attention placed back on her.

Her eyes flickered back and forth nervously as Caroline settled between her legs, the mattress dipping low beneath her knees.

"You wanted to see me touch myself," Caroline teased. "Perhaps I should ask the same of you?"

Amelia pursed her lips, head shaking. "No, I want you. *Your* touch. I want. . . I want to feel—"

Caroline leaned forward, pressing her mouth to Amelia's, gently putting her out of her misery. Boldly, she slid her leg forward, pressing her thigh against Amelia's center. She could smell the queen's arousal, feel her heat. Pressing tighter, Caroline almost sighed in relief when Amelia began to rock her hips upward. A slight gasp escaped her mouth as she found her own ideal rhythm and Caroline took advantage of it, gliding her tongue between Amelia's teeth until it found hers.

The queen's gasp quickly turned to a moan and her rolling hips sped up. Caroline could have giggled at the sudden desperation that seemed to have taken over Amelia's fingertips. She was threading her fingers through Caroline's hair, pulling and tugging, her kisses turning wilder with each slant and tilt of her head.

Could she make Amelia orgasm like this? It seemed entirely possible from the sounds she was making. Sounds Caroline had no idea she could even make.

At the Inn they'd had to be quiet. Hardly breathing. But here, locked away in her tower with no one around, the queen seemed to have released all inhibitions.

She was damn near screaming.

"You're incredible," Caroline murmured in her ear. "I wish you could see how stunning you look like this."

Amelia's mouth opened, but no words came out. Only more delicious sounds, and perhaps a mumble for more. But Caroline couldn't be entirely sure. She pressed her thigh in tighter, higher, causing Amelia's wetness to spread across her skin.

"T—touch me," Amelia gasped. Begged. "Please."

She didn't need to beg. Caroline would give her anything and everything she wanted. Now and forever. And she told her as much, letting her left hand slide down Amelia's waist. She grasped her hip, then the back of her knee, and pulled it up. Amelia writhed beneath her, the increased pressure seemingly just what she needed.

Then Caroline's fingers seemed to take on a life of their own—with their own ideas and cravings. She hardly noticed her hand had slid down to grasp Amelia's behind, kneading the thick flesh there.

That sent the queen over the edge and she clapped a hand over her mouth.

"No," Caroline demanded, a little more forcefully than she meant to. "I want to hear everything."

Amelia's spine arched, her body quaking, her hips wild against Caroline's thigh, but she let her hand fall away as a chorus of prayers and curses tumbled from her lips. And Caroline captured them all greedily with her mouth, committing the image of her wife's blissful face to memory.

Her wife's.

April 16th, 1457

The following morning, Amelia awoke to the sound of someone knocking gently on the bedroom door. Groggy from lack of sleep, she gingerly shimmied out from under the tangle her lower half was in with the sheet and Caroline's legs.

By the time she had slipped back into her blouse, tiptoeing across the room toward the door, she had missed whoever had knocked. Luckily, they had left behind the breakfast spread they were trying to deliver. Amelia's stomach growled as she bent down to pick up the wooden tray. There was a vase of fresh roses, juice, fruit, eggs, and toast.

Amelia turned back to face the room, truly examining it for the first time. The white stone fireplace was opulent, though the flames within had died down to fading embers. She did not bother stoking it just yet. Beneath the window overlooking the gardens was a set of plush chairs in a pale green velvet and a small table between them. She approached, sliding the tray onto it before gazing around the rest of the room. On the opposite wall stood not one, but two wardrobes. Caroline had mentioned once how much she loved gowns. A different one for every day of the month, or something like that.

As if sensing she was being thought of, Caroline let out a soft sound, rolled over and reached across the mattress. When she found it empty, her eyes opened and she looked around, startled.

"Amelia?"

"Just here," the queen answered softly, gesturing to the tray. "Would you like to eat in bed or by the window?"

Caroline slid from the mattress, dragging the sheet with her as she stood. Amelia watched with heated eyes as her wife wrapped the sheet around her body.

"Window sounds lovely."

Amelia met her halfway, hooking her fingers around the necklace she had finally gifted Caroline last night. Even with her hair a mess and her eyes sleepy, the blonde still managed to steal her breath.

"You look lovely."

Caroline shook her head, smirking and playfully wagging a finger.

"I know that look in your eyes now. And sadly, you'll have to wait 'till we get home. Or at least 'till the inn. No doubt the Order is already gearing up to leave."

How lovely it was that she called Dathoviel home.

"I suppose you are right," Amelia sighed, holding her hands up in surrender. "Let us enjoy our first breakfast as wife and... well, wife."

They both giggled.

"I quite like the sound of that," Caroline said and stole a kiss before reaching toward the tray for a glass of juice.

Amelia had half a mind to drag her back to bed, but thought better of it. They had the rest of their lives for that, and her stomach was growling again.

An hour later, the newlyweds had made their way downstairs. Amelia was dressed in her riding clothes, and Caroline wore a fern-colored gown.

The Great Hall was bustling.

It appeared everyone had corralled here for final orders. The sea of faces was familiar now, and yet Amelia felt the absence of the others like a heavy, icy hand on her shoulder. A fresh wave of grief seemed to suck all the warmth from her bones that last night and this morning had created. She tried her best to focus on the fact they had won, and that tomorrow she would be back in her bed.

Caroline squeezed her hand. "I'm going to check on Spencer, alright?"

Amelia nodded, spotting him across the room speaking with Jacob the same time Caroline did. Then her eyes settled on the back of Eloise's head to the right.

"Of course."

"I'll find you in a few minutes," Caroline promised.

She pressed her lips to the queen's knuckles, their fingers unlacing as they parted.

Occasionally nodding at Order members who bowed or spoke her name, Amelia moved through the crowd towards the dark-skinned woman. It was comforting seeing her in armor once more. Other than Fredrick's memorial, Eloise had only worn plain trousers and the same tunic around the castle. She almost looked like her old self in profile, but when their eyes met, it was clear the dull ache of grief and anger remained. Even her braids looked sad in a way.

One did not overcome the pain of losing their father in a few short days.

"Are you looking forward to returning home?" Amelia asked.

Eloise's eyes flickered to the open doors. The horses were already saddled and hooked up to trailers stacked with pine coffins. Amelia recognized Eloise's stallion off to the side with a trailer with a single casket being attached by two Petrovian men.

Fredrick.

It made sense his body was not with the others. Eloise never let it out of her sight.

"I'm eager to put his body to rest."

Amelia could only nod. There was no right thing to say in these moments. She knew from experience one could only hear so many apologies over someone's loss before the bereaved went mad.

"We are leaving soon, yes?"

Eloise nodded, turning fully to face Amelia.

"May I ask you a personal question?"

"Certainly."

"How did you do it? Cope with losing your brother?"

Amelia almost laughed. Her behavior since Brantley's death hardly felt like coping. But that wasn't what Eloise needed to hear.

Eventually she had left her bed and started slowly living life again, so she must have done something right one day.

She thought of the hours Olive had spent holding her hand in comforting silence. The sound of Caroline's voice humming in the background or reading quietly to her when she pretended to be asleep. Of the way Regina prepared her plates with extra love and care, always with her favorite foods. She thought of Greta and riding and that day on the hill where she kissed Caroline.

"After a while, I let people in, let them help me. And I took as much time as I needed to process. Then I started doing the things I loved again. Some mornings the grief still sits heavy on my heart, but I know I can carry it, because I am not alone."

At first, Eloise grimaced as if she did not appreciate that answer. Then her face softened.

"My father would say the same thing, I'm sure."

Amelia reached out and caressed her elbow just as Spencer called for her over the crowd. "When we get back to the castle, ask Caroline to show you how to scream."

Eloise's eyes widened in alarm. "To what?"

Amelia only smiled and waved before making her way over to Caroline and the king.

April 17th, 1457

Julian tugged the satchel strap higher on his shoulder, slinking around the perimeter of the library. They'd been foolish to believe Alaric's death alone would ensure their freedom. Holding his breath, he craned his neck toward the door, ignoring the raindrops splattering against the window. Instead, he listened for any pause in the footsteps stalking the corridors. Whatever *this* was, it wasn't freedom.

Because of the king and queen's absence, Dathoviel was on the brink of collapse. The kingdom desperately awaited news, hoping for the best, while still bracing themselves for the worst. And despite Marcel *attempting* to watch over the kingdom, he'd done a terrible job. So terrible, that he'd been trapped in his own dungeon, by a servant no less.

Not that Leah was *any* servant.

She had released the guards Seb locked away before the Order departed, gaining their allegiance. Julian had no idea what she'd told them, but for the last two days they roamed the corridors like they owned the castle. They'd been rounding up anyone who fought back or showed loyalty to Amelia. Whatever leverage Leah had, it was powerful enough to turn brother against brother.

He doubted they held any true allegiance to Leah, but when you were locked in a cell and someone was dangling the keys outside of it, prepared to release you, agreeing to whatever they said was easy.

A few were stationed in the village; intimidating, creating fear. And if the smoke Julian had seen meant anything, they'd also burnt down the progress made this past year. Others were posted along the road to Petrovia, tasked with providing Leah advanced notice of the queen's arrival. At the first glimpse of the Order, the sentries to arrest Amelia on sight.

Or so Julian had heard.

Leah had all but threatened to have him killed if she saw him sneaking around again. Not taking her words lightly, he had quickly thrown together the few belongings he kept at the castle and had been attempting to escape ever since. He'd already been away from his daughters too long.

Maria could take care of herself, but expecting her to do that and protect her sisters under these circumstances was too much. He should be there with them. He *needed* to be.

Finally, the hall fell silent and he peeked out to look. The coast was clear, at least for the moment, so he made his way out of the library, looking left around a suit of armor missing its helmet, then right past the flickering torches. Heart pounding in his ears, he dashed toward the kitchens. It may be farther than the front door, but it was the safest way out undetected.

The aroma of fresh bread and the ominous slice of a blade urged him onward. Regina glanced up from the thick wooden butcher block and the fresh loaf she was carving when he appeared in the dimly lit entrance. Herbs dangled above the lopsided bun she'd tugged her hair into and a fire roared behind her. Her aged skin was smeared with flour, soot and sweat, and her sleeves were pushed to her elbows. She hadn't looked this stressed since Queen Diana had fallen ill.

He followed her flickering glance toward the sleeping guard seated in the corner. She slid him an uncut loaf and patted his cheek as he passed her. Her kind, maternal gaze followed him out the open back door and into the rain, her free hand lifting in a sorrowful wave. He returned it with what he hoped was a reassuring smile, then disappeared around the corner.

Leather boots slipping through the slick grass, he stuffed the bread inside his satchel and positioned the strap across his chest. Despite the refreshing comfort of cool air filling his lungs and the raindrops soaking his clothes, he forced himself to move fast. The more distance he put between himself and the castle, the better.

Once his feet hit gravel, he stopped and listened. A bell rang furiously in the distance, but it was too quiet to be the church bell. He crouched behind a tree as it grew closer; his tunic now plastered against his skin. Water was dripping from his fringe into his eyes, so he combed his dark hair back and prayed whoever was sprinting up the road was too busy to notice him.

Julian's gaze traveled to the northeast tower where he glimpsed Leah before she whipped around and disappeared. The ringing must be a signal.

Had someone spotted the queen?

His chest tightened as he looked longingly down the road. It would take less than an hour on foot to reach the village. Yet, even as his heart tugged toward his daughters, his feet turned back to the castle. He could warn Regina and perhaps help her gather some makeshift weapons from utensils and knives. Her meat tenderizing mallet alone could cause some serious damage.

"I'm sorry, Maria," he whispered, blinking against the wind.

~

The steady clopping of Greta's hooves against the gravel, the rhythmic swinging of Eloise's braids ahead and Caroline's humming on her right had nearly lulled Amelia to sleep despite the cool rain. But as the faint outline of her castle became visible through the grey skies, the tension in her neck and shoulders began slipping away.

It was far from the homecoming she had envisioned, but it felt good to be back. Everyone's hair and clothing were drenched, but a slower return trip was a small price to pay if it meant all the bodies returned home.

Just a few more minutes.

She could already imagine peeling off Caroline's wet gown and curling up with her in front of a fire.

Realistically that would have to wait, but the thought warmed her so she welcomed it. First, she must speak with her father. Hopefully things had been easy on him in her absence, and therefore he would go easy on her when she shared her plan.

Both she and Spencer agreed the quicker they explained to the court about Alaric, the quicker Dathoviel could move forward.

The court *would* hear and see reason. Especially if she came forward first and confessed. She refused to let the battle and all the lives lost to mean nothing at the end of this.

Her heart sang as she glanced in the village's direction. Even from a distance she could make out the thatched roofs and smoke billowing across the darkening sky. She could picture everyone in their homes away from the rain, cuddled around a fire and waiting to hear positive news.

Amelia threw Caroline a confident smile as they crested over the final ridge before the castle. Her heart fluttered as they turned onto the main path, approaching the entrance.

"Wait!" Eloise lifted her fist and everyone behind her came to an instant stop. "Something doesn't feel right."

"What do you mean?" Amelia reached out for Caroline's hand, eyes focused on her protector's rigid spine.

The castle's large double doors swung open with a sickening, ominous creak. At the very least, Amelia had hoped her father would greet her. Perhaps Regina and Julian. But only a sneering Leah wrapped in Alaric's fur, and a team of guards, appeared, and they looked the farthest thing from welcoming.

All confidence was sucked from Amelia as her eyes met Leah's. One guard stepped forward, presenting wrist chains as if they were a bouquet of roses. He looked her up and down slowly and Amelia flinched, quite aware of how exposed she must appear in her wet riding clothes.

"Leah!" In a flash, Seb guided Harlow forward, blocking the queen as best he could. "Why would you let them out?"

She wrapped the fur tighter around her middle, clutching herself almost protectively.

"Move that beast, traitor! *Your queen* is under arrest for treason and conspiracy against the king."

Both Spencer and Eloise drew their swords as Caroline nudged Gus forward to help cover Amelia.

Spencer addressed Leah next. "We've never met, miss. But you must recognize the kind of man my brother was. Think carefully before you go through with this."

There was a vicious chill in Leah's voice as she ignored Spencer, instead speaking to Amelia around Seb's torso.

"You can choose to come quietly into custody now and no one will be harmed. *Or* you can be taken by force, and the price of resistance will be your father's life. I have a guard with him now awaiting my order, and many more stationed throughout the village, ready to burn whatever remains to the ground. Surely you can imagine how far this could go should you choose wrong."

Amelia looked back to the smoke and her gut sank. She'd been foolish to think it had come from the chimneys. There was far too much of it.

Swallowing bile, she locked eyes with her wife.

Caroline shook her head, eyes pleading. "Don't listen to her."

She had no choice. She could not risk one more life for her cause.

"I am sorry," she whispered and slid from the saddle. "I love you."

Her feet nearly disappeared into the mud and she had to grip the billet strap to pull herself out. Just in case, she embraced Greta tightly at the last moment, burying her face in the horse's wet mane.

"Your Highness—" Seb began, but she silenced him with a wave of her hand.

"Please ensure the bodies are returned to their families and provide them whatever they may need to bury their loved ones respectfully."

"Yes, My Queen." Seb tipped his hat downward in acknowledgment, his beloved feather utterly destroyed by the storm.

"Eloise, you'll take care of the Order?"

Their eyes met, and Amelia was struck by their similarity to Fredrick's. He would tell her if she was making the right choice. Judging by the proud expression on Eloise's face, she was.

"Of course, Your Majesty."

"Olive. Caroline. As soon as you can, go to the village and ensure everyone is safe. Seb, go with them."

They nodded silently in response. Olive, who'd been riding close behind, struggled not to cry. She could barely make eye contact. Caroline however looked as if she could strangle Leah with her bare hands.

Spencer lowered his sword. "We'll get you out as swiftly as possible," he promised.

Amelia nodded half-heartedly. "Just take care of Caroline."

"I will."

Finally, Amelia faced Leah. "I shall go without a fight, on your word that no one else be harmed."

Leah placed her hand on her chest, lips thin, eyes narrowed. "Not a soul. It's *you* I wish to see suffer."

"Very well." Amelia surrendered and offered her wrists.

The guard moved forward, appearing thrilled to shackle her like a common thief. The cuffs bit into her skin. His height and broad shoulders menacing enough without the snapping flash of crooked teeth. He grabbed her by the shoulders, escorting her into the castle with a rough shove. The force and the weight of the iron threw her off balance and she fell, her knees cracking on the stone.

"Amelia!" Caroline jumped down from Gus's back and raced toward the door.

Leah quickly put an arm out to stop her.

"If you interfere, you may as well slit Marcel's throat yourself."

Before Amelia could see what happened next, the guard yanked her up, and toward the dungeons. His hand on the back of her head made it impossible to look back.

Judging by the way Olive's slippers kept sliding out of the stirrups, she'd clearly worn the wrong footwear for anything more strenuous than a simple trot. But despite all that, she rode hard and fast, closing in on the village before the others. She heard Caroline and Seb calling after her, but she refused to stop.

The moment her horse halted abruptly next to the fountain she tumbled from the saddle, barely managing to land on her feet. She spun around, her stomach lurching and the aroma of burning and destruction assaulting her nostrils.

The banners and flags she and Hannah had helped hang last month were singed black and hung in tattered shreds. The market carts were destroyed. They lay in a heap of wood and signage, as if mallets had been taken to them. Nearly every window of the surrounding homes and shops were smashed, and there wasn't a soul in sight.

Kwan.

The school.

Clutching her skirts, she dodged glass and debris, racing past rows of houses, the church and the clinic William had just begun framing. At the end of the road, she stopped dead in her tracks before a mountain of cinder, ash, and what vaguely resembled wood planks. Pressing the back of her hand to her mouth, she swallowed the sourness threatening to rise from her gut.

This had been her project. Her idea. Far too furious to cry, she stood watching the charred wood smoke as the rain extinguished the few hints of flame. If they'd been a few hours earlier, maybe she could have saved it.

"Olive?"

She turned toward the voice, relief flooding her as she saw Kwan's head poking out from around the corner. He looked wearily down the street, afraid of something. Someone?

She ran into his arms, and he held her hard against his body for a moment before tugging her down the road and into the tavern. He shut the door behind her and immediately latched it.

Then he was running his hands through her hair and his thumbs were caressing her cheek bones. Like he needed proof she was real. His eyes bore into hers, their familiar intensity dimmed. *Tarnished.* He was exhausted. Still, his lips pressed against hers roughly as he clutched her to his chest. He tasted like more booze than normal and smelled like smoke, but she didn't care.

His forehead pressed against hers and she kept her eyes closed, drinking him in, settling into the comfort of his embrace. Finally she pulled back slightly and looked up at him.

"I'm so glad you're safe. Where is everyone?"

"Hiding. These last few days have been hell."

With one hand on her lower back, he guided her over to a table, where a bottle of whiskey sat beside a half-full glass. His other hand clasped hers, perhaps afraid to release her. As she slid into the creaky chair, he grabbed another glass from behind the bar and filled it for her. Then re-filled his own, shooting it back with ease. She took the amber alcohol gratefully, ignoring the sting sliding down her throat.

"What happened?"

He swallowed hard, both hands tugging his hair. Even though it was black, she could see the grease and grime in it. She itched to draw him a bath, comb his hair back, massage the tension out of his shoulders. For the first time she noticed the blood on his shirt, but it didn't appear to be his.

Not that it being someone else's was better.

"Late last night, guards from the castle appeared in the village square. They were relentless—breaking everything they could and setting fire to what they couldn't. We all assumed the queen's plan had failed and Alaric was coming for us."

When his hands shook she covered them with her own. He smiled gratefully.

"No, we won. Alaric is dead."

"Yes, I overheard one of the guards last night saying Leah had sent them to destroy the village as punishment for our loyalty to the queen. I gathered as many people as I could. We hid in the church, but they soon chased us out. Then we made it to the schoolhouse."

He looked at her, apologies swimming in his eyes. He said none of them, and she was grateful. It would have broken her.

"I can guess the rest." Her grip tightened on him. "And now? Where are William and Hannah? The kids?"

His eyes flicked to the left where her gaze followed to a painting that hung on the farthest wall. It was crooked, showing it had been moved to the side in a rush.

He must have hidden whoever he could in the secret room she'd showed him his first day in Dathoviel.

"When I saw you, I thought my heart was going to explode," he said, drawing her attention back. "If you're here, Amelia must be too? She and Fredrick will know what to do."

Olive's eyes fell to the table as she clutched her empty glass. When she looked up, his curious eyes searched hers.

"Fredrick is dead," she said, watching the color drain from his cheeks. "And the queen's been arrested. Leah was waitin' for us when we arrived at the castle. One of her guards took Amelia into custody before we even made it through the door."

"And she let them take her?"

"They threatened her father's life. Believe me, she didn't want to go."

He steepled his fingers and leaned back in his chair, the two back legs bowing slightly under his weight. Sensing the impending snap, he tilted forward, elbows on the table, then he pressed his palms flat on either side of the bottle. She watched his nails begin to drum a slow rhythm on the cracked wood.

"So, what shall we do?"

"I saw no guards outside. They must have returned to the castle to help with whatever the bitch has planned."

"Then we best start moving. Amelia needs us."

Kwan tugged her chair close, pressing another kiss to her lips, gentler than before. Who knew when the next time they could be alone would be?

She caressed his cheek before he stood, watching as he pressed back from the table. He moved toward the framed painting and tilted it aside, revealing a small silver handle which he tugged on with both hands, and a portion of the wall pulled back. Like there had been a door all along.

Nervous villagers filed out one by one, and after quickly wrapping Hannah in a tight hug and receiving a relieved kiss on the cheek from William, Olive slipped outside. Seb and Caroline needed to be updated.

~

The flame from a single candle perched on a three-legged stool was the only light Amelia had once the sun set outside the small dungeon window. The rain may have stopped, but she had yet to wake from this nightmare.

Her cell was bare. So bare, she had been forced to sit huddled on the damp stone floor. Shuddering in the corner, she tucked her head between her knees and wrapped her arms around herself. What she would give for one of the gowns she had always loathed. The heavy skirts would have surely provided some escape from the chill settling in her bones.

The smell living in the shadows around her wasn't much better. She'd long since stopped trying to decipher the overwhelming stench, but that didn't make it disappear. If she ever got out, she swore future captives would be provided more humane conditions. No one deserved this.

The dungeon door swung open and light streaked across the floor before her. Eyes burning from the abrupt glow, Amelia clambered to her feet. Had they come to rescue her already? She blinked, attempting to make out the feminine silhouette in the doorway.

Caroline?

Her optimism plummeted when the lantern lifted revealing Leah's normally stunning features tainted by a sneer. She had shed Alaric's fur cloak but even in her simple serving dress she looked as threatening as a wild bear. Entering the room, she slipped the lantern's handle onto a hook above the cell. As it swung, the glow danced shadows across her hardened eyes.

"Enjoying your temporary new room?"

"Why are you doing this?" Amelia croaked, embarrassed that the other woman had heard the fear in her voice.

Leah laughed. "You left your kingdom in the care of a useless drunk. You took every loyal guard with you, leaving behind only servants and peasants. What *did* you think would happen?"

It stung how right she was. There was no one to blame but herself.

"I had no reason to believe you were a threat. You have lived in this castle your whole life. Our mothers were friends."

"Friends," Leah spat, laughing menacingly. "My mother *served* yours. Fetching this. Preparing that. She was forever in her shadow. Do you truly believe Olive respects you?"

"Yes, I do."

Leah's tone wavered between taunting and malicious. "No one has attempted to break you out, Amelia. Not even Caroline. Your people have lost too much because of you. They're tired of sacrificing."

Amelia shook her head, terrified of just that.

"No. I know them. They'll come. You cannot scare me."

"I don't want you to be scared, Amelia."

"Then what *do* you want?"

"To take back what is rightfully mine! To topple this hierarchy of nobles and those who serve them."

"You truly wish to be queen this badly?"

Leah slammed her hands on the bars, glaring into the cell. "I deserve this land!"

Amelia jumped back, heart racing. There was something she was missing. Something Leah was not telling her.

"I understand feeling powerless and trapped. I have struggled with that my whole life. I can help you."

Leah shook her head. "You understand nothing about me, and frankly, the best way you could help me is to die. It should have been *you* laid out on that battlefield, not Alaric!"

Leah's voice caught on his name, her lip trembling.

"Did you truly love him?"

Leah set her jaw and narrowed her eyes.

"The throne was always my main objective. I loved the opportunity he offered."

Amelia approached again, reaching through the bars for Leah's hand. She was clearly lying, at least about the last part.

"I am sorry he is gone. I did not want to kill him, but he left me no choice."

"No," Leah hissed, stepping back as if protecting something precious. "You can't trick or seduce me the way you have everyone else. I *will* take your kingdom and love the child Alaric gave me."

Amelia watched with wide eyes as Leah's hands caressed her stomach.

"His child?"

Her smile softened for a moment before she looked up, eyes flashing wickedly.

"I accomplished the one thing you couldn't. The primary necessity of a queen. No matter what, Amelia, you lose. One day, my son will rule Dathoviel, and he will finish what his father started."

Amelia gripped the bars to remain standing. If there was a baby, and if that baby were male, he *could* claim her throne for himself. And nothing she did or said could stop it.

"The court will require proof Alaric fathered the child. They may not believe a word you say."

"And you're praying my class will be enough to discredit my voice?"

Somehow, Amelia managed a sneer of her own.

"As a woman of God, I am called to pray."

"Best get on your knees then." Leah turned for the door, once more a silhouette against the shadows. "Though, I wonder. . ." she looked back from the top of the stairs. "Can *He* even hear you down here?"

22

"ARE YOU SURE YOU won't join us, Eloise?" Seb asked.

Again.

His feather had yet to recover even now the rain had stopped.

"Yes. Hannah needs my help organizing the coffins and ensuring everyone is reunited with their families."

Truthfully, the caravans were nearly empty, and there was nothing William and Hannah couldn't complete on their own now that the kids were in bed and Beatrice was watching over them.

Still, Eloise had made it clear she wouldn't leave her father's body. Seb's mouth opened, ready to object but Olive patted his shoulder and shook her head. The loose strands of her golden hair glowed in the light from the various torches held by the mourning villagers and the bonfire burning a few feet away.

With a shrug he headed to the fountain where Spencer waited next to the row of thirsty horses and pulled himself into Harlow's saddle. They slipped into hushed discussion with Caroline, no doubt finalizing their tactics for rescuing the queen.

She could have gone. *Should* have gone, but the last thing Eloise needed to see right now was more violence. Even she was tired of it. As her fingertips caressed the carved edge of her father's casket, she bit her bottom lip. None of this was supposed to be happening. He should be here. Standing at her side. She wasn't ready to be alone.

Olive's timid voice snuck into her thoughts.

"Do you need anythin'? Can I help in some way?"

Their eyes met over the coffin. They weren't exactly friends, but they weren't *not* friends either.

On her left, Hannah stepped away, giving them privacy and assisted a couple who'd arrived to identify their son's remains. Come sunrise, the bodies would be buried in the graveyard behind the church, and a collective ceremony would be held. At least that was the plan. How tonight played out would determine that.

"Thank you, but I'll be alright. I still need to check on my grandmother and ensure she's recovering. Doc said she inhaled a lot of smoke during the fire and requires rest, which is not an easy thing to enforce with her. Besides, I have orders of my own to follow."

The handmaiden came around the side of the coffin to face her. "I admire your strength, Eloise, but no one is asking you to put on a brave face for their sakes."

"The brave face is for myself," Eloise admitted. "I spent the days after the battle locked in sadness. I didn't eat. I could hardly move. I couldn't even do my job and protect Amelia. I can't afford to fall back into that darkness right now. We all lost people we care about, but we must keep going and finish this." Eloise eyed

Olive's arms as they extended toward her. "And if you hug me I'll break—so please don't."

Olive nodded, her hands falling to her sides. "I understand. I'll be waitin' whenever you wish to talk."

"It's time," Kwan called from the group now gathered around Seb and Spencer.

He was excited to utilize his useful skills for good. Or so he said during the meeting a few hours ago while Spencer and Seb had planned their attack. Not that Eloise had any idea what skills he had.

Olive threw him a quick nod before turning back to Eloise. "Wish us luck?"

Eloise couldn't bring herself to return the handmaiden's smile. "Good luck."

"Oh!" Olive stopped and turned back. "Is there anythin' you want me to tell Julian when I see him?"

"Julian? Why would—"

"Everyone knows, Eloise. Keepin' secrets at court is near impossible."

Eloise fumbled, her cheeks feeling warm.

"I'm not part of court."

"You're stuck with us whether you like it or not." Olive grinned, backing herself towards Kwan. "I'll just tell him you said hi, yeah?"

Eloise watched her struggle onto the back of the horse. Winking, her arms slid around Kwan's waist and she pressed her cheek to his back.

"Ready?" Spencer shouted from the front of the group.

A chorus of affirmative answers flooded in, and they charged off, dozens of hooves spraying rocks and dirt as they galloped into the darkness.

It was strange, Eloise decided, having so many people care for you for no reason other than they wanted to. Weeks ago she'd hardly known them, but an undeniable bond was forming, shifting the group dynamic. They were making room for her. Not because they had to, but because they wanted to. Now she had to decide if she wanted to accept.

Inviting people into your heart also welcomed pain. And she was uncertain how much more her soul could tolerate right now.

Turning back to her father's coffin, she focused on giving him the burial he'd wished for as a man, not a soldier. If he hadn't been so skilled with a sword and diplomacy, he would have surely been a sailor or a fisherman.

Her heart ached as she realized they would never again sit at the edge of the mountain and fish together. She would never again hear his voice or see his smile. His hand would never reach up and caress her face.

She had never thanked him for teaching her how to sit in nature and breathe. How to listen to the animals and the wind dance through the leaves.

Eloise struggled to remember the last time they'd been together like that. Had she been as intentional in the moment as he'd always hoped she would be? If she'd known it would be the last time, would she have done anything differently?

Out of nowhere, a young woman raced into the square, cursing at the retreating backs of the Order. She collapsed on the side of the fountain, chest heaving. Any villagers nearby backed away, throwing her odd looks.

"Are you alright?"

Eloise regretted the words the moment they slipped out.

The girl looked over; her resemblance to a certain jester impossible to ignore. The warm copper skin and piercing gaze were unmistakable. This had to be one of Julian's daughters. The eldest perhaps? Maria?

"I told him to wait for me." She gestured wildly. "But of course, he didn't."

"Who?"

"My fool fiancé. I must get to the castle and find my father. He was meant to return days ago, and he's never late."

"You know what's going on in the castle right now, don't you?" Eloise asked, her left brow raised. "Is that really the best place for you?"

The girl's eyes narrowed, flickering over Eloise's armor and the sword hanging from her hip.

"*You* are the last person to lecture me about wanting to fight. My father is in there. Don't you understand? I can't just sit around and wait anymore. I must try to save him."

The shattered pieces of Eloise's heart plummeted to her ribs.

She understood perfectly.

"You can take my horse," she whispered, working open the latches of her vest. She could feel Maria's eyes on her.

"What are you doing?"

"This is a metal breastplate wrapped in leather. It's molded to my body, but it will do you better than nothing. If you're going in there, you'll need some kind of protection."

She gestured for the young woman to join her next to the stallion tied to a nearby post.

"Alright..."

Eloise eyed the girl's skirt.

"You'll ride easier and fight better if this is shorter. Do you object?"

Maria studied the dagger as Eloise pulled it from her boot.

"Do it."

Eloise tore into the fabric until the rough hem rested just below the young woman's knees. Then she slipped out of her vest and helped Maria into it.

Her fingers trembled, remembering the first time her father had dressed her in armor. It had weighed more than her, and the helmet always slipped over her eyes.

She'd tripped right over the wooden sword and gone sprawling across the cottage floor. He somehow convinced her to try again. And again.

"You'll grow into it," he promised, lifting her back onto her feet and dusting her off.

The girl grunted, steadying herself as she adapted to the literal weight on her shoulders.

"I know it's heavy," Eloise said. "but it should help keep arrows or blades from piercing your torso."

She undid her belt next and wrapped it around the girl's waist, adjusting the sword.

"Why are you helping me?"

"Because...maybe it's not too late."

The girl eyed the sword dangling against her thigh. "I don't actually know how to use this."

Eloise coughed away the thickness building in her throat, helping the girl into the saddle.

"If you keep both eyes open and swing like hell, you'll at least scare them all away."

The armor didn't fit correctly and she was clearly uncomfortable, but she still focused in with the same knowing look as Julian.

"He told us about you, you know? Says he'll marry you one day. If we let him."

Eloise swallowed. "Don't worry. I'm not the marrying kind."

At the corner of the girl's lips Julian's cheeky grin taunted her, and hope to see him again sprouted through the grief that had weighed Eloise down since the battle.

"Will you come with me?"

This time it was harder to say no.

"I can't."

"Well, wish me luck at least?"

Somehow, Eloise managed a small smile this time. "Good luck."

Crouched behind a tree, Seb's exhausted eyes strained through the darkness covering the clearing between the forest and the castle, where he and the Order were hiding.

On his left, Olive knelt behind a tree of her own, frozen, holding her breath. Or so he assumed, since he was holding his. Her gaze remained locked on Kwan, who was currently climbing the northeast tower toward one of Leah's guards. Easily.

It was a sight, watching him leap and slink up the stone. The young soldier above paced back and forth, looking around periodically but overall appearing uninterested in his task. Seb couldn't blame him, he'd spent many a night on watch and it was utterly boring, especially alone.

"He'll be alright," Seb whispered.

Olive nodded, but the moonlight cascading through the trees illuminated her worried expression. No one spoke as Kwan skillfully utilized choice vines and cracks in the wall on his final ascent toward the battlement. Seb however, had to consciously keep his mouth from hanging open. Who was this guy? And where had he learned to move like *that*?

A relieved sigh slipped from Olive's lips as Kwan landed gracefully between the merlon and crenel nearest him. In the flickering light of the torches perched around the tower, he squatted, preparing to disarm the guard. From this distance they heard nothing, but Seb doubted the bartender's swift moves made any noise. The guard marching at the front door a few feet below certainly seemed unaware anything was happening over his head.

After a moment, Kwan released his tight hold around the man's neck and lowered him to the floor.

As Spencer instructed, he then lifted one of the torches, waving it back and forth twice as a signal of his success.

Step one of reclaiming the castle was complete, but many more steps lay before them. They must move quickly. There was no telling when Leah had set the guards shift change at. They could have hours, or moments before more knights emerged.

Seb looked over his shoulder to where Spencer hid in the tall, damp grass. Eyes on the stoic marching guard at the door, the king maneuvered forward through the brush until he was crouching at Seb's side.

"You remember your side of things?"

They'd only gone over it ten times back at the tavern.

"Olive and I enter through the front with our men. You, Caroline, and your team will breach through the kitchen. We'll both remove any obstacles in our way. My team frees Amelia and her father. Yours captures Leah."

Spencer nodded affirmatively. "See you inside."

He motioned for Caroline and his five chosen soldiers to follow. Seb watched them go, still surprised Caroline had chosen to go after Leah rather than stick with the team tasked with rescuing Amelia.

The two cousins and their companions headed east, silently disappearing into the darkness.

"Shall we go?" Olive asked, her hands wringing impatiently.

"Yes."

Seb led his own group of six out into the field, motioning silent orders to each of them. He followed the same shadowed path Kwan had, careful to keep his back to the cold stone and his feet quiet. As he reached the edge of the castle wall, he drew an arrow from the quiver resting between his shoulder blades and set it into his bow. An exhale shuddered from between his lips.

Keep it together.

Ignoring the rush of blood in his ears, he listened for the guard's footsteps to fade, signalling his back was turned. Without hesitating, Seb stepped into the light, aimed, and fired. The soldier fell with a sickening thud, face down into the gravel.

"Go," Seb ordered.

Olive and a male member of the Order rushed forward, pulling the fallen guard from sight. They returned with his armor a minute or so later, though it felt like hours.

"Will it fit?" Olive hissed, her eyes furiously shifting left to right, and then up to where Kwan was peering down at them.

"No idea."

Seb removed his vest and cap, irritated at having to wear another man's armor. Olive supported the metal chest plate, securing it around his shoulders.

"Hurry!"

"Yes, thank you," he bit back through gritted teeth and she flinched at his tone. "Sorry, I'm just nervous."

It was definitely too small.

"So am I." He forced the helmet on and tucked his cap behind a large boulder at the base of the tower. "If I die tonight, make sure that's buried with me."

"Don't say that."

He dropped the visor over his eyes and gestured for her to duck behind him into the shadows. The thick wooden doors blocked any noise from inside. There could be ten men waiting, or one, or none. As much as he hated the uncertainty, he couldn't wait around for someone to discover them.

Anxiety coursed from his pounding heart to his fingers as he reached for the iron handle and pulled. Olive mumbled something behind him but he couldn't hear her through the helmet compressing his skull. The piercing creak of the door however sliced through his aching head, but he pressed on. Another couple inches and they could slip inside.

He hedged through the thin opening; breath held tight in his lungs. The familiar sleek stone floors and glowing torch lined corridors was almost comforting.

Empty. Not a soul in sight.

As the rest of the team entered the hall behind him, Olive bumped into him and he stumbled forward slightly. There was barely time to curse before approaching footsteps echoed from a corridor on their left. Olive scurried everyone back outside, leaving the door ajar.

A knight in full armor stepped forcefully into the hall. His visor lowered, obscuring his identity.

"Aren't you supposed to be patrolling outside?" he demanded.

Seb panicked. "I was given orders to find you."

The knight advanced, suspicion lacing every word. "Who gave you these orders?"

"The king."

"King Alaric? He's alive?" He sounded so hopeful it was near nauseating. "Answer me!"

When he was close enough, Seb tugged the ridiculous helmet off his head and tossed it aside, exposing himself.

"No, he's long gone."

They both drew their swords, assessing one another. The knight sneered.

"Sebastian, the traitor. Bold of you to return here alone. Leah will be pleased to kill you."

Seb rolled his shoulders back. "Bold of you to assume I'll give her the chance."

If their blades clashed, the sound would echo through the halls and announce their presence too early. He must think carefully. Seb lunged forward, faking a frontal attack, before darting to the side at the last moment. The knight stumbled forward, and Seb was grateful he couldn't see the man's face. Killing him would be easier if he remained a faceless barricade between them and the queen who needed removing.

As the knight regained his balance Olive appeared, sword in hand, distracting him.

"What the hell is going on?" the knight demanded.

"We're takin' back the castle," Olive said. "And you have ten seconds to decide if you're prepared to surrender, or die."

~

Across the castle, Julian glanced up with wide eyes when the kitchen's back door flew open. It slammed against the guard he'd tied up in the corner, assumedly breaking his nose—given how the man cried out through his now blood-soaked gag.

"Shut it." Regina pointed at him with her knife. "I've had just about enough from you."

Julian watched as Spencer stepped into the room, sword drawn. Caroline stood at his side, eyeing the bloody, howling knight with caution. A few other Order members trickled into the room as well, all seeming on guard.

"Julian, right?" the king asked.

"Yes, Your Highness."

"We've come to help. Can you tell me where Leah is?"

"Unfortunately, no. We interrogated this one, but all he could tell us was that Leah has twelve men working with her. She could be anywhere, but you'll no doubt find her if you go that way."

Julian pointed at the door leading into the main corridor on his right.

"Thank you." Spencer turned to Caroline. "Ready?"

"Yes." She took his sword, eyeing it with uncertainty.

Julian watched as the king selected two knives from the butcher block where Regina had arranged them. He turned to her.

"Do you mind if I borrow these, madam?"

"Not at all."

"Seb's likely already inside," Caroline said to the room as a whole. "Olive is with him and a few others. They should be headed toward the dungeons to free Amelia if nothing's gone wrong on their end."

"Is Eloise with them?" Julian asked.

Caroline's lips twisted momentarily into a smirk. "She stayed in the village."

The guard at Regina's feet started grumbling again, and she kicked him with her heel "Fredrick's with the other group?" she asked, hopefully.

Spencer and Caroline exchanged a long look. Finally, Caroline stepped forward, shoulders fallen. She took the cook's hands gingerly. Regina's lip was already trembling.

"I'm so sorry, Regina..."

"He didn't make it, did he?"

Caroline slowly shook her head.

Silent tears poured from Regina's eyes. Julian stepped close, wrapping his arm around her quaking shoulders.

"He died a hero," Spencer offered, unaware Fredrick and Regina had been lovers.

"He didn't want to be a hero," she shouted, blowing her nose into a kitchen rag. "He just wanted to be a man."

She turned to Julian and he held her tightly. Eventually, she sniffed loudly and wiped her eyes with her apron. "Eloise has his body," Caroline said. "You can take my horse and meet her in the village?"

"No, no. It's alright," Regina coughed, arming herself with a cleaver and a paring knife. "Saving the queen should be our priority. Besides, I've never felt more inclined to fight than I do right now."

Spencer headed for the exit first, gesturing for a blonde man to join him. As his mouth opened to administer orders, the back door slammed open for the second time. The injured knight rolled out of the way just in time, but Julian couldn't see past the vision of Maria entering the kitchen. He shook his head, blinking. Was that Eloise's armor?

"Maria?"

"I found you." Her steps were unsteady from the weight of the breastplate and sword, but she made it to him, gripping his arms tightly. "I had to make sure you were safe."

The blonde next to Spencer spoke. "Maria, what are you doing here?"

Julian's eyes narrowed, turning to the man currently glaring at his daughter. He'd seen him around the village a few times, but judging by the way he eyed Maria, they knew each other well. Too well.

"Following through on my word," she spat, eyes flashing in his direction. "Something you wouldn't know anything about."

"This is no place for you," he said, crossing his arms over his chest. "Do you think I want you here distracting me? I have a job to do."

She threw her hands in the air. "And I have a duty to my father. You don't even support the queen!"

"Go home, Maria. Let the men handle this."

His words were met with hisses from both Caroline and Regina. Was he blind to their weapons?

"Alright, enough."

Julian stepped in front of his daughter, facing her. . . *her what*?

"Quite right." The young man gestured to Julian as if they were on the same side. "If she won't listen to me, maybe she'll listen to you."

Julian felt Maria lunge forward, but he stepped between them, shaking his head at her.

"I don't know you, but you shall never speak to my daughter like that again."

"I'm going to be her husband, so I will speak to her however I please."

"The hell you will!" Maria pushed past forward. "I will never marry you!"

Julian crossed his arms, both proud and infuriated. Now was not the time to learn all the details involved, but he *would* get answers soon. Including why Maria had been secretly engaged.

Spencer, who'd been watching the entire scene with his mouth open cleared his throat. "May we carry on with the mission, please?"

"Certainly, sir." The guard snapped to attention, awaiting the orders he'd been about to receive before Maria's arrival.

"I think you'll be best suited staying here actually. Guard this man and ensure he doesn't escape." Spencer gestured to the bloody, whimpering knight on the ground.

The young man's face fell. "But, sir—"

"Are you rejecting a direct order?"

"N-no, sir."

Spencer turned to Julian. "Would you be willing to lead us through the castle? I'm unfamiliar with the layout."

"Certainly."

Julian armed himself with three kitchen knives; the last tucked into his belt, and advanced through the door, glancing back at Maria. She looked so mature in Eloise's leather with a sword swinging from her hip. It scared the hell out of him.

She was seventeen now, and her mother had warned him their relationship would change. But what about the other girls? Hattie was only two years behind her. Would she be next? Would holding her closer help? Or would it push her farther away? Perhaps he had forced her to age quicker than necessary by splitting his time between castle life and the village.

Well, after this he'd make sure his girls knew he was there for them. Even if that meant moving back to the village full time. Yes, much needed to be discussed when this was all over. With both Maria and Eloise.

If they were going to continue their relationship, she deserved to know where his priorities lay.

~

Blessing the brightness of the full moon, Eloise followed its trail from the beach into the glittering water, her top and trousers clinging tight as she pulled on the rope.

Thankfully, the boat carrying her father grew easier to maneuver with each step forward. She knew the practices his soul required to pass successfully into the next life. It was the same ceremony they'd performed years ago for her mother, and a decade prior for her grandfather.

Though this time she was doing it with only the memory of his voice instructing her.

When the water reached her ribs, she stopped, drew the boat close, folding her arms on the trim. Trim she'd helped carve as a young girl when he'd grown tired of borrowing the local fisherman's boats and decided he needed his own. Trim full of divots and scratches from her attempts to copy his work, that he never sanded away to perfection. To him, that would have erased her hard work, and the memory of them building it together.

Slowly, she let her eyes travel to him.

He lay peacefully inside, hands resting on his bare stomach, just above simple linen trousers. His sword and shield were tucked beside him to his left. His spear to his right.

At his feet lay a box with preserves and bread his spirit could enjoy or offer any deities who might discover him. A pillow of frankincense-soaked moss and greenery surrounded his head.

"To provide grounding dreams into the afterlife," his voice whispered in her mind.

Just the memory of his instruction was comfort enough to encourage her on. Humming a familiar chant, she unhooked a string of flora she had tied herself from her neck and draped it over his scarred chest.

"Rosemary for remembrance and irises to honor."

This was it. The last time she would ever look upon his face. That chill of realization ran deeper than the cool midnight air ever could. Gently, she caressed his cheek, imprinting every faint wrinkled inch of dark skin into her memory. Each one a booming laugh from an inside joke or a hearty, proud grin.

She closed her eyes, remembering the way he'd beamed at her the morning of the battle, his reflection amused as she told him about Julian.

Quiet tears fell, becoming one with the water, flowing out in faint ripples. Digging her toes into the soft sand, she guided the boat in three circles.

"East to west, summoning protection for the next stage of this journey."

Her humming continued as her fingers lifted one by one, releasing the boat. It bobbed, slowly floating away on faint waves.

She was burying him as a warrior, but also as a man of the earth. The side of him only the rare people got to see. It was shameful really, for it was a beautiful side. One he should have been allowed to explore more. One he could have, if she hadn't failed to keep him safe.

Eyes trained on his face, she backed onto the beach and reached for her bow. With the water lapping at her toes, she selected an arrow from her quiver. After securing a scrap of linen behind the arrowhead, she dipped it into a glass of whiskey resting in the sand with a trembling hand.

"Water for a smooth journey. Earth to cushion and ground. Air to cleanse. And fire to—"

She froze. Fuck! How had she forgotten the candle?

Shivering and cursing herself, she looked frantically down the beach, hoping that somehow a candle would appear.

And like she'd been summoned by magic, an old woman stood on the edge of the trees, her long nightdress rippling in the wind against legs nearly too thin to support her. Yet, she always managed it. The contrast of white linen against her dark complexion was familiar and comforting. A sight Eloise had seen every night of her life.

"Ye didn't think ye would have to do this alone, did ya?"

At her grandmother's side, William had his arm around her waist, guiding her frail body onto the beach. He smiled sheepishly, silently apologizing for failing to stop her. He needn't feel guilty. No one could keep her grandmother from doing anything she set her mind to.

"Certainly not, Grandmama. Thank you for bringing the flame."

The older woman contemplated the solitary candle in her left hand as if having forgotten it was there. Her kinked grey hair stuck up wildly as her confusion faded into a grin.

"I suppose I did."

Eloise could picture her sneaking out of bed against doctors' orders, taking the candle from her bedside table and waddling barefoot out into the street, peering toward the trees. William had probably found her wandering and knew it was better to help her reach the beach than argue with the eldest witch in the village.

"Seems to be the one thing I've forgotten." Eloise gestured between them at the altar and tools she'd set out before uncovering her father's boat and dragging it to the water.

"Good thing there's two o' us."

Allowing herself a matching smile to her grandmother's, Eloise met them halfway and took her arm. William dismissed himself without being asked.

"It's just the two of us now..." Eloise faltered, eyes returning to the boat.

It floated close enough she could complete the ceremony, but further than she'd originally planned. The shot would be tricky now and she wouldn't forgive herself if she missed. Never had a more important arrow flown from her bow.

"For now," Grandmama said, patting Eloise's braids, then her cheeks with wrinkled but soft hands. They smelled of lavender, as usual. "The sooner ye' release him soul, the sooner we can feel him wit' us again."

Those same hands brought the candle to the edge of the arrow and they both watched the flame licking at the alcohol.

Nodding and inhaling deeply, Eloise aimed at the boat with a final blessing of love and protection. When her eyes opened, she released the arrow, following its arch across the water. It landed somewhere in the moss, just as she intended it to.

The tightness in her jaw and shoulders melted away, leaving her feeling exhausted and drained. But she couldn't drag her gaze from the boat.

She had done it. He was free.

The flames grew as calm spread slowly through her muscles. First in her fingertips and toes, then through her arms, and up her legs. It uncoiled the knots in her gut and trickled through her chest, massaging her lungs. She gasped, as if she'd been holding her breath for days. Finally, it settled in her heart. And ever so slowly, the tightness of her throat melted away.

Since the battle she'd been hurting, wishing she had died, unable to fathom life without him. But as his soul escaped the binds of his earthly body, the comfort of his spirit wrapped around her. Embracing her. She didn't look up hoping to see him. He was there; along with a sense of peace she never imagined finding again.

Slowly, Eloise sunk down into the sand with her grandmother. Their arms wrapped around one another, humming the same chant as the burning boat drifted further and further away.

"Him here wit' us now," whispered her grandmother, eyes closed, wrinkled lips smiling. "Him free."

23

OLIVE WATCHED THE SHADOWED hall as Seb shed the last of his inappropriately sized armor. Relieved at the freedom, he chucked the greaves and gauntlets into a closet next to the bodies of the two unconscious knights they'd just captured and disarmed.

"Alright," he said, shutting the door. "Aside from a guard watching over Amelia, that should be the last of our worries on this side of the castle."

Olive moved next to him. The sword in her hand shook, and he reached out to steady her.

"Are you sure we won't run into anyone else?" one of the two remaining Order members asked.

"I'm sure of nothing. However, I locked up thirteen men before we left for Petrovia. If Leah has any sense she'll have spread them throughout the castle."

Olive shook her head. "It's terrifyin', basin' every move we make on hopes that Leah knows what she is doin', but not so much we can't beat her."

"It certainly is." Seb rolled his shoulders and drew his sword. "Shall we?"

Olive followed his gaze toward the dungeon entrance.

"Yes."

~

Numbness had overtaken Amelia's limbs as she huddled in the corner of her cell. She no longer felt the chill of the stone beneath her trousers or repulsion from the surrounding smell. Though she'd mentally surrendered to the filth, she had yet to follow through with her desire to collapse on the floor.

Her hands still bled from trying to break open the lock, but the sting had dulled and her heart was beating slowly. Almost too slowly. She'd had far too much time alone with her thoughts, and fears, and doubts.

Hopes of rescue continued fading as a tear slid down her cheek.

She had no way of knowing her wife's fate and there was nothing she could do about it. Bile tried to rise from her gut, but there was nothing in her stomach to expel as the image of Caroline dead somewhere tormented her.

The once faint buzzing in her ears had grown so loud she barely heard the door as it flung open. She blinked her searing eyes against the light flooding in. Before her head fell back onto her knees, she caught the fuzzy glimpse of a silhouette.

Leah had returned.

This was it, after all.

Everything she'd done, everyone who'd sacrificed themselves on that battlefield. It was all for nothing. She'd had mere days with her bride when she should have had decades. And now she wouldn't even get to say goodbye. To kiss her one last time or gaze into her glittering eyes. No, the last eyes she would see would be Leah's.

And maybe that was exactly what she deserved.

Her stomach rolled as two hands gripped her shoulders, dragging her to her feet. When her legs failed to support her, she crumbled back to the icy stone, boneless and hopeless. Let it be trouble for them. If they wanted her, they could drag her out.

The hands gripped her once more, shaking her this time. They were speaking, but she couldn't hear anything. The buzzing was too loud, as if a beehive had erupted in her brain.

Then she was soaking wet. Had they dumped a bucket of water on her head? Oh, please let it have been water.

She threw herself back against the wall, sputtering and dragging her hair from her eyes.

"Oh, thank god. She's movin'. Seb, I need help!"

Was that... It couldn't be. Could it? Had she finally started hallucinating? Was one night in a cell all it took for her to lose her mind?

"Your Highness." The knight's tone was gentle, but hurried.

Now she was imagining him too? Why not Caroline? Or her mother? Even Brantley.

Olive's voice quivered. "What's wrong with her?"

"Shock."

A flask met the queen's lips and she drank greedily, eyes still shut. They refused to open.

"She's in no condition to get on a horse right now."

"We'll have to improvise." Seb tucked the flask away and wrapped his arms around her. "Amelia, I'm going to pick you up and carry you out of here, alright?"

Silently, she allowed her body to slump against the hard planes of his chest as he lifted her.

"You're safe now, Amelia," Olive whispered. "We're takin' you to Caroline."

~

Caroline seriously regretted not taking more time to refresh her swordplay skills before tonight. She was barely holding her own, but thankfully Spencer's skills were unmatched.

He threw a single blade, taking out the knight attacking her. The man fell to his knees, clutching his arm and bellowing.

"Get out of here!" Spencer ordered.

"Are you sure?"

"Yes!" He took back his sword, eyes locked on Leah as she cowered in the far corner of the throne room behind one of her guards. "Help the others find Amelia."

She briefly squeezed his arm. "Don't die."

He managed a wink before turning back to the fight. "Not planning on it."

Caroline raced through the open doors, only to immediately skid to a halt at the sight of her wife cradled in Seb's arms. She looked near death and smelled it too. Still, Caroline rushed to her side, brushing back the wet hair matted to her face.

"Is she alright?"

The look in Olive's eyes said no.

"She needs time to recover," Seb assured them both. "and water and food."

"Bring a chaise from that room," Olive ordered the men behind her, pointing to a closed door a few feet away.

Her authority was not questioned and they returned moments later carrying a blue velvet lounge. Gently, Seb lay the queen down on it, unsheathing his sword. Caroline was already on her knees clutching Amelia's clammy hand between hers.

Lip trembling, she took in the sight of her wife's unsteady breaths, willing her eyes to open.

"Where's Leah?" Seb demanded.

Caroline pointed to the doors she'd just exited. "We managed to back her and the remaining four guards into that room. But they are putting up one hell of a fight to protect her."

Olive's hands shook. "I'll run to the kitchens."

"Thank you."

Caroline beamed gratefully at the handmaiden before she raced off, clearly having reached her fill of battle.

Seb however angled toward the grunting, curses, and clanging weapons. "This will be over soon," he promised.

As he disappeared through the doors, Caroline tucked closer to the chaise, caressing Amelia's grimy, bloody hand with her thumb.

"I hope so."

On guard and out of breath, Seb observed the action as he entered the throne room. He wiped the dripping sweat from his forehead, gaze travelling left to right.

Regina was crouched behind the door, her normally flour smeared skirts splattered with blood. She was restraining a yelping guard who had a dagger jutting from his arm. A pair of Order members were seated against the wall, their wounds already attended to. One deceased guard lay on the ground. Seb looked away, recognizing the face.

The cook removed the blade from the yelping knight before her, sliding it across the floor toward Spencer before slicing a strip of cloth from the basket next to her and tying it around the injured arm.

"You're a fool for choosing their side, son," she whispered. "If you're lucky, I can convince them to spare your life."

Seb's eyes flicked to where Julian and a young woman faced off with a guard. Spencer was battling two more to his left who were shielding a cowering Leah. She had one hand clutching the arm of Alaric's throne, the other wrapped around her stomach. As Seb stepped toward Spencer to offer his assistance, the unknown young woman let out a shriek.

"Father!"

Julian was on the floor, clutching his leg as blood soaked through his linen trousers.

"Maria, get out of here now," he yelled.

Seb lunged forward, blocking the guard's sword as it came down over the young woman's head. Their blades clashed beside her ear and she shrieked, crawling hastily toward Julian.

Seb dealt with the knight. A slice to his arm, leg, and finally, a kick to the chest sent the man onto his back. He slid a few inches, sword clattering to the floor as Regina rushed forward, a rope in her hands—ready to capture him.

Seb chanced a glance at Spencer. The king needed help.

"Are you alright?" Seb knelt next to an increasingly pale Julian.

His hands quickly coated in blood as he applied pressure to the wound, buying Regina time as she tied up the knight.

The jester gulped, looking like he may faint. "I've been better."

"He struggles with blood." The young woman pressed her hands on either side of his, doing her best to help her father. "Thank you for saving me."

A lump formed in Seb's throat and his already pounding heart slammed against his ribcage.

God, she was beautiful.

"Ah. . ." He couldn't speak for a moment. "You're welcome."

"Eyes off my daughter," Julian warned, voice uncharacteristically weak.

That was not a great sign.

"Regina!" Seb threw her a look.

"Coming." She threw him one right back.

The girl shook her head. "I was only thanking him."

"Yes, well, I think he has a king to save now."

"I do."

Seb pushed back to his feet, tearing his eyes from the young woman as Regina took his place on the floor.

Of course, he would meet a woman like her in a situation like this. He darted across the room, wiping his bloody hands on his trousers with a promise to find her—*Maria*—when this was all over.

Tasting the rusty tang of his own blood on his lips, Spencer spat. He was so close to ending this.

"That's enough, Leah," he said to the sliver of her he could glimpse between the two guards poised between them. "Enough people have died. Don't let these two men sacrifice themselves for you as well. Don't let this lead to your death."

"You won't kill me," she sneered.

"I will do what I must. Whatever you force me to."

Spencer spotted Seb slipping behind the thrones, eyes trained on Leah. This could work. He just needed to let the knight get close enough to capture her.

"You won't kill me," she repeated. "because your flesh and blood grows inside me."

His sword quaked in his hand. "You're with child?"

"Not just any child." She took one step closer, though the guards remained protectively in front of her. "A son. An *heir*."

His eyes searched her body. The only sign of pregnancy were her hands clasped around her abdomen. "It could just as easily be a daughter."

It could also be a lie.

"Regardless of gender, King Spencer, the soul growing here is your blood. Can you kill me knowing the child would die as well?"

He took an involuntary step forward, throat tight. No, he couldn't.

"How do I know you're not lying to save your own skin?"

"You don't." She smirked. "But the chance I could be telling the truth is enough to secure my life."

Seb was one, maybe two feet from Leah. They *could* end this without another drop of blood spilled.

Hidden in the shadow of the throne chairs, Seb's questioning gaze locked on Spencer's. Slowly, the king nodded, so indiscreetly it was almost impossible to see.

Seb grabbed Leah, his right arm around her, his sword held at her throat. A stream of curses flung from her lips as she struggled and failed to get loose.

Unprepared for an attack from behind, the two guards swung around on clumsy feet. Spencer took advantage of their confusion, springing forward. He captured the smaller one, his arm tight around the man's quivering chin and kicked the legs out from underneath the second.

Regina was already at his side, chest heaving, her cleaver pointed at the fallen guard's nose.

~

Amelia felt water dripping over her stomach from the cloth, caressing the length of her arm as the heat from the bathwater coaxed her aching muscles to relax. There was no telling how long she had been here, but she hardly had the energy to care. She would take any improvement over the dungeon.

One by one, her other senses awakened. Flexing her feet against the porcelain tub, she deduced the scent of lilacs, melting wax, and soap. Then Caroline's familiar humming broke through the buzz at the center of her brain until it faded away completely.

If this was heaven, it was more than acceptable.

Allowing her face to turn toward the sound, her eyes fluttered open in the gently lit room. A few candles were spaced around them, providing enough glow to identify her wife without overwhelming her tired eyes. She blinked a few times, finding it easier now to move her body than the last time she'd been conscious.

Her hand lifted from the water, and Caroline gasped.

"Oh, thank goodness."

A curtain of blonde hair surrounded Amelia as Caroline knelt over the tub to kiss her, the tips of her curls meeting the water and caressing the queen's naked skin.

"Am I dreaming?"

It felt real, but Amelia was unsure what to trust anymore. Had being captured by Leah been a dream? Were they still in Petrovia?

"You're awake," Caroline answered, the edge of her nose brushing over Amelia's.

She leaned in, nearly slipping into the tub as Amelia pulled her close, desperate to feel grounded to this reality. The bathwater soaked Caroline's gown, causing it to cling to her skin. Heated inside, as well as outside now, Amelia's hands turned greedy. She ignored the pulses of pain in her limbs as Caroline sighed, breath hot and sweet against her face.

The sound drifted from Amelia's ears to her now clenching gut. Then Caroline's hand pressed against her face, and Amelia was mirroring the movement, turning into her touch, pressing soft kisses to damp skin.

"Are we safe? Is it all over?"

"Yes. Spencer has Leah in custody. He'll be dealing with her shortly. Your father has been released as well and wishes to see you, but Seb convinced him it could wait till morning. Olive drew you this bath, and I've been here since, praying you would wake up."

"You? Praying?"

Caroline smiled softly, still half in, half out of the tub.

"In desperate times."

"I was so terrified I might never see you again," Amelia admitted, caressing both of Caroline's cheeks.

"Part of me was too. I'm sorry I wasn't there to release you from that horrid cell."

"We are together now."

"And don't expect me to let you out of my sight again. For at least... twenty years."

Caroline submitted to the bath, dragging the rest of her skirts in behind her and settling her knees on either side of Amelia's thighs. Water sloshed from both sides of the tub to the floor, but neither cared. They clung desperately to one another, pounding hearts meeting beat for beat as their chests pressed close and their lips met.

Caroline's eyes were glazed with lust, and Amelia welcomed it, wishing the pale green fabric was already gone. Impatient fingers gripped Caroline's hips, needy kisses were pressed to the base of her throat, drifting back to her already swollen lips.

Twenty years sounded quite reasonable if it meant this moment would last just as long.

April 18th, 1457

Leah had no choice but to move forward as the tip of Kwan's dagger pressed threateningly against the bottom of her spine. She moved stiffly, leaving behind the same cell Amelia had been locked in, up the dark dungeon stairs, through the corridors, and into the Great Hall.

One foot in front of the other, eyes seeing only the toes of her slippers and the disheveled edges of the fur cloak that hung crookedly off her shoulders.

She had been so close, but now she had nothing. Except the life growing inside her, and she would do *anything* to protect it. Whatever they did to her, she would survive. Her son would live, even if she had to beg, or stay in that cell until he drew his first breaths.

One step at a time.

Kwan *encouraged* her forward again and she stumbled into the early morning sunbeams streaming across the floor of the throne room. The rope around her wrists bit as she struggled to regain balance. Her gaze shifted forward, finding blood splattered boots a few feet ahead. One was tapping impatiently, wrinkling the cuff of black leather pants.

She didn't bother hoping it was Alaric. The permanent crack in her heart would forever remind her she would have to go on without him.

Slowly she looked up, finding Spencer towering over her with his arms crossed.

Their eyes met—hers cautious and his stoic. With his handsome features twisted by contempt and disgust, it was startling how closely he resembled Alaric in this moment.

Seb stood to her left, his sword unsheathed and Olive sneered at her right. Ignoring them, she eyed the thrones for the briefest of moments, thinking of all that could have been.

Slipping a dagger from his thigh sheath, Spencer approached and her heart stuttered, but she didn't step back. He eyed her with a hard gaze, as she hooked the tip of the blade into the ropes at her wrists and tugged. Her binds fell to the floor between them. She rubbed at the sore skin, prepared to thank him when the point of his blade slid beneath her chin, forcing her gaze to meet his. She held her breath, not daring to move.

"I await whatever punishment you deem fit," she said, voice still and even.

They wouldn't see her quiver.

"Banishment," he said. "A carriage with adequate provisions awaits you outside. You may go with your life and the life of your child, but you may never return to Dathoviel. If either of you set foot on this soil after today, the consequences shall be grave," he promised

"Yes, Your Majesty."

The words tasted like poison, but she was prepared to do whatever she had to, to get her son as far away from them as possible. Seb stepped forward, gripping her elbow tightly, directing her from the room.

"Good riddance," Olive hissed as they passed.

Leah's fists clenched, but she didn't pause.

One day her child *would* return to seek justice for his father's death.

And then, Dathoviel would burn.

. 24 .

AMELIA TOOK A DEEP, calming breath as she knocked on the door of her father's study.

"You can do this," Caroline whispered as it swung open.

Shockingly, Marcel tugged Amelia against his chest, embracing her for a long moment. Her arms hung limp at her sides, unsure what to do.

"Hello, Father," she croaked, finally patting his back awkwardly before he held her at arm's length, grinning.

"I'm so thankful you're safe."

He even beamed at Caroline as he ushered them both inside.

Amelia hardly recognized the bright, tidy space. The fireplace was clean, the drapes pulled back, and only a single book lay on the table next to his favorite sofa. In fact, he looked like a brand-new man himself.

Despite having been locked in a cell just hours ago, his boots were oiled, his clothes wrinkle free, and every grey hair was in place. Most surprisingly, there wasn't the faintest scent or sight of brandy anywhere. Instead, it had been replaced by lemon and peppermint; a familiar combination from her childhood.

"You wished to speak with me?" Amelia stuttered.

Nodding, he gestured to the love seat, taking his usual spot. Amelia and Caroline accepted, fingers still laced. If he noticed, he said nothing.

"I wished to apologize for failing to stop Leah."

Amelia shook her head, far more disappointed in herself than him. "Leah took advantage because she knew the opportunity was there. I should not have given her the chance."

"Where is that dreadful woman now?" Marcel asked.

Caroline grinned. "Spencer banished her just this morning."

"Oh, good."

Amelia opened her mouth once, then shut it. She might as well get all this over with, but it would not be pretty.

"Father, the court must be called to order."

Hands on his knees, he inhaled a shaky breath.

"So, it's true? You are responsible for Alaric's death?"

"Technically Spencer took his life, but yes."

"His father and I had an arrangement. He cannot take our land."

"I assure you, he does not want it. Dathoviel will be officially returned to me at my coronation."

The light in Marcel's eyes turned hopeful. "Has Spencer chosen *you* as his bride? It will be a bit of a scandal, marrying one brother, and then the other, but it certainly wouldn't be the first time..."

Amelia glanced nervously at Caroline. She nodded and squeezed her hand.

"No, *however*, I will not be ruling Dathoviel alone."

The confusion etched across his aging face was swiftly replaced by objection. His eyes turned hard, settling on her and Caroline's clasped hands. He understood, but of course would force her to say it.

"Explain."

A mere spark of confidence appeared behind Amelia's ribs, and she snatched it up, letting it drive the words tumbling from her mouth. She would not act like anything was wrong, or that she had done anything bad. She would simply tell him the same way she would if she had chosen a man to spend her life with.

"Caroline and I have married."

His skin paled and eyes bulged.

"Be serious!" he exclaimed.

"We *are*, Your Grace," Caroline bravely said.

He bristled, ignoring her. Luckily, his temper and disappointment were no strangers to Amelia. She knew how to shield herself from this pain. At least part of it.

"Y—you cannot be—e married! Women can't... they can't..." He slammed his fist on the side table, rattling her mother's music box "Have you gone mad? What will people think?"

Amelia drew in a deep breath, her resolve threatening to fail, but she dug deep for another dash of confidence. It was hiding, but Caroline was still clutching her hand, so she focused on the warm pressure and narrowed her eyes.

"Take whatever time you need to process this, but Caroline and I have chosen one another and there is no changing it."

"Is this," he gestured flippantly between them. "because of Alaric? The way he treated you? Certainly, we can find you a suitable man to properly marry."

"*No*. Caroline is where my heart truly lies."

His head shook. Disappointed. Disgusted.

"Do you honestly believe the court will name two queens? You'd do better keeping this a secret," he advised, though it sounded more like a threat than concern. "No one needs to know about this, unfortunate *predicament.*"

"Father, you must—"

He cut her off desperately.

"There is a doctor I heard of in the eastern kingdoms. He's quite renowned for a type of treatment helpful for your. . . confusion." His eyebrows lifted in hope. "We could send you both. Today."

Amelia straightened her spine. "You are mistaken if you believe I require your blessing or understanding to move forward with my life."

He glared. "Amelia—"

"I wish I had it," she interrupted, a lump of sadness forming in the back of her throat. "but your lack of support is far from shocking. I will never please you, and so, I am done trying."

He, however, had more to say. "How can you be so selfish as to end our bloodline? Without a husband, you cannot provide Dathoviel with an heir. What legacy will your rule leave behind if our kingdom dies with you?"

"I will find a way."

Marcel stood, his jaw tight. Unable to look her in the eye, he pointed at the door.

"I'd like you both to leave."

Caroline opened her mouth to speak, but Amelia shook her head. Her lack of surprise at his behavior did not dull the ache in her chest as they rounded the corner. She collapsed into Caroline's warm embrace, a sob tearing through her.

April 20th, 1457

The village bustled with rumors, murmured speculation, and indignant huffs the next two days.

Kwan had expected the tavern to be full following the Order's return. But he'd been prepared for a celebration, and it seemed nervous, frustrated villagers drank far more than happy ones. Barrels continued to run low as tensions rose.

He groaned when Olive brought him another towering tray of soiled mugs, tossing aside his rag and setting down the goblet he'd just cleaned with a clink.

"Tell me that's the last of it."

"Unfortunately, that lot wants another."

Her chin jutted towards the table in the far corner where five men sat. They'd grown progressively louder with each round and showed no signs of stopping, but at least the things they said were supportive of Amelia.

Kwan took the tray and rolled his sleeves further up while Olive licked her lips. What was it about *those* muscles in particular she couldn't resist?

Grumbling about inventory in his eastern dialect, he handed her an empty tray and walked over to the remaining barrels behind the bar. She followed, eyes drifting to the way his tan trousers pulled across his backside.

"Explain to me again why all this is happening?" he asked, beginning to fill the mugs one by one. "I thought Amelia and King Spencer had an agreement."

"They did. Historically in Dathoviel when crimes are committed, or someone is suspected of treason, the king presides over the case and decides if the defendant before him is guilty or innocent and chooses the punishment at his own discretion."

"What if the king is dead, or the one on trial himself? Or, the queen, in our case."

"Then a Justice is appointed to take his place. He is tasked with hearin' all statements and deliverin' a verdict."

"But, Spencer became king when he killed Alaric, right?"

Olive slid her hands flat beneath the tray as the weight increased with every new mug. "When the initial ministers were called to reinstate Amelia as queen on Spencer's order, they refused. They also denied him authority altogether, makin' Dathoviel a kingdom without a ruler and inevitably throwin' yet another dagger into our plans."

"They can do that?"

"They also have the power to remove a leader if they believe he or she is unfit."

Kwan's eyes narrowed as he set the last mug down. "Yet they didn't with Alaric."

"Amazin' what gold can buy, ain't it?"

He nodded. "So, they're involvement isn't good news?"

"They've never been particularly fond of Amelia."

"They certainly took no time at all charging her with conspiracy."

"We have Leah's summons to thank for their quick response callin' in Justice Carlyle."

She spat the man's name and had no intention of apologizing for it.

Once she'd successfully delivered the drinks, she stepped behind the bar to help Kwan with the remaining dirty glasses.

"You know the man they're bringing in?" he asked, watching her from of the corner of his eye.

She froze. "What makes you think that?"

"His name sounded like a curse on your sweet lips."

He kissed them for good measure.

She grinned, at first.

"His mother and mine were siblings, but it was he and I who grew up like brother and sister after my aunt died, leavin' him in my mother's care. That's how he came to live in the castle. But somethin' changed in him when he was chosen to apprentice with the ministers. He suddenly thought himself better than everyone on staff. Includin' me. So I grew up, and moved on."

"Sounds like he got lucky, and it went to his head."

"Precisely. From the number of women I've heard he's shared his bed with, it's clear he regards us with little value."

"That doesn't bode particularly well for Amelia."

"No shit."

Kwan turned back to the tray and reached for a glass, dipping it into the bucket of soapy water between them.

"The hearing still expected to happen tomorrow?"

"Yes. I'll need to head back to the castle soon and ensure Amelia has everythin' she needs."

Kwan eyed the men at the table. "I'll close up here after they've finished their round and give you a ride. I could use a break."

Her bottom lip found its way between her teeth as she watched the bubbles drip down his arms.

"Maybe we could run upstairs first? I forgot to make your bed this mornin'."

His slick, soapy hands captured her hips, tugging her chest against his. Hot breath ghosted over her throat as he nibbled on her earlobe. He smelled like spice and whiskey.

"Only if we can muss it up immediately after."

Her only reply was a moan as his hands slid down, cupping her arse. She was definitely going to be late returning home.

April 21st, 1457

Straightening his cap, Seb scanned the sea of faces swarming the throne room. All eyes remained trained on the doors as the villagers awaited Amelia's arrival. He and his recently steamed feather had been shooed from her tower just under an hour ago, and if Caroline's estimations were correct, they'd be arriving any minute.

If the ruling today went poorly, the kingdom would undoubtedly erupt in chaos, making finding Maria quite difficult. And he must find her, for he'd been unable to stop thinking about her since.

He moved through the crowd, spotting Julian first. A lump formed in his throat. It was hard enough requesting a date, never mind doing so in front of the father. Seb approached, his heart pounding so loud, certainly everyone around could hear it.

"Why, hello, Seb." The jester grinned, clapping him on the shoulder. "How's Amelia doing? Have you seen her yet this morning? Maria, you remember Sir Seb?"

Maria stood next to him, peering around her father's chest with a small smile and dark, curious eyes.

Seb's lungs nearly forgot how to work for a moment.

Julian gestured to the bench next to them. "Would you care to sit with us?"

The knight couldn't bring himself to tear his eyes away from her. "If you don't mind."

"Not at all." The jester waved him closer.

"It's lovely to see you again," Maria said, eyes sparkling.

"You as well." Seb bowed.

Julian cleared his throat, a hint of joviality in his tone, but not much. "I vaguely recall telling you to keep your eyes off my daughter."

"Don't start, Papa," she warned. "I'm well beyond courting age." Then her eyes were on Seb and his cheeks were burning. "He is free to look all he likes."

He swallowed. Twice.

"There is meant to be a celebration this evening, should things go in our favor. I was hoping you'd accompany me."

Maria eyed a man a few feet from them who glared possessively through bruised lids, his arm wrapped in a tight sling. She merely rolled her eyes and shifted so her back was to him.

"I'd be honored to arrive on the arm of a hero."

Julian coughed, clearly uncomfortable at being caught in the middle.

"The honor will be all mine, I assure you. From what I hear you're a hero in your own right, charging the castle all on your own to save your father."

Maria beamed proudly, but before she could speak, trumpets sounded from outside the doors and a guard began shouting.

"Announcing! Queen Amelia of Dathoviel!"

The group parted, separating Seb from Maria as the villagers backed themselves to opposite walls, forming an aisle down the center of the room. They turned to look as Amelia entered in a simple, pale blue gown, her sapphire and pearl crown perched proudly atop her head. Determined, even in the face of her judge and every member of Dathoviel, she proceeded toward the long table where Justice Carlyle sat, his desk, a few feet before the thrones. Her eyes raked over the crowd, most likely searching for familiar faces.

When she found Seb he nodded encouragingly, hoping she could see his smile. Across from him, William and Hannah waved, Brianna's arms wound tightly around her father's neck. She looked frightened, but Amelia gave the child a wave and that seemed to help.

Squaring her shoulders, the queen stood firm as Justice Carlyle's emerald eyes scanned the length of her body. It was painful to watch, but surely more agonizing to be subjected to. The pale, ginger haired judge signaled for everyone to be seated, his gaze remaining locked on Amelia. His voice booming around the room, silencing any remaining whispers.

"We are now in session!"

As everyone shuffled to sit, Amelia visibly quivered.

25

A LUCKY MAN WAS one who loved his job, and Carlyle happened to be one of those men. He relished in the power of holding another's life in his hands. And there was nothing sweeter than having the royal family at his mercy. *Especially,* Amelia.

Though he had hoped she would look far more devastated by her circumstances. The mere fact she wasn't already weeping and begging at his feet disappointed him. He did so like it when they begged.

There was still time, of course. The trial had just begun.

"Queen Amelia of Dathoviel. You have been brought before the court on charges of treason and conspiracy to assassinate the king. What say you to these charges?"

Amelia inhaled deeply.

"Guilty."

The crowd gasped, whispers erupting like a wave from front to back. Every soul knew the truth, but her outright admittance would surely move the trial along quickly. And hardly in her favor. They also knew *his* reputation and the rarity with which he permitted pardons. Looking around the room, then back to Amelia he attempted to hide his surprise. Where was the fun if she was going to submit immediately? Where was the sport?

"You understand what a guilty admission means?" he warned.

"I plead guilty to treason by the court's definition. Though in my heart, I committed no crime."

Ah, yes. She would fight after all.

"Explain."

"Alaric should have never been king. I did not commit a crime by travelling to Petrovia for assistance. I was doing my people a service."

His quill scratched across the parchment in front of him, but his eyes remained on her. "Do you truly believe that?"

"Yes."

Carlyle leaned back in his chair, dropping his quill to the tabletop and crossing his arms.

"Convince me," he dared with a wave of his hand.

Amelia only glared.

"Alaric was cruel, unjust, and thirsty for power at any cost. We learned he planned to sell our men into slavery for King Bartholomew of Winvoltor's gold mines in exchange for a cut of their findings. Our court jester intercepted a letter to his mistress explaining his success."

"And is this mistress available for questioning?"

The queen's resolve faltered for a moment. "No. She was recently banished from our land."

"Do you have this letter to enter as evidence?"

She looked helplessly into the crowd. "I believe so?"

After a moment, a man with deeply tanned skin stepped forward, handing an envelope to one of the court's staff members.

Scanning the letter briefly, Carlyle absorbed the familiar, neat scrawl of the now deceased king. It was disappointing to learn Amelia had been telling the truth—about this at least. Hard to argue with evidence like that.

Or was it?

"It appears your words are truthful. However, this letter is without the late king's official seal. Without his confirmation—something the dead cannot provide—the court is unable to authenticate the document." Carlyle folded the letter and flicked it aside as if it were worthless trash to be tossed out later. Then he refocused his attention on Amelia. "Do you have further justification of your actions to present before I deliberate your sentence?"

"It *is* fact that the king murdered Prince Brantley."

The room was impossibly silent.

Carlyle's eyes narrowed. "Don't forget it is *you* on trial today. Not the late king."

Amelia quivered with frustration, but she spoke calmly.

Disappointing. How sweet it would be to have her break. Then he could deem her unfit to rule and have his officers drag her out of here.

"With all due respect, *sir*, my duty is to prove Alaric's low moral character and his transgressions. Only this way will you understand my actions were far from criminal."

"And this proof you speak of?"

"I have witnesses willing to provide testimony from both accounts."

"Very well." Carlyle spread his hands in vague acceptance. "Let's hear their testimony, assuming they have not also been banished."

Two men, one from either side of the room, stepped forward.

"Sir Seb, Your Honor. I am a knight in the Queen's Order. Once I was considered Alaric's closest confidant. I was also present the day he took Prince Brantley's life."

Carlyle's fingers drummed on the desktop.

Fuck.

"And you wish to testify *in* support of Queen Amelia?"

"I do."

Carlyle gestured impatiently, briefly noting the knight's presence on his scroll. "Begin."

"When I first met the former king, I was just a homeless orphan in Petrovia. He welcomed me into the castle, offered me clothing, food, and friendship. I realize now his charity was simply the start of his manipulation. He needed someone to do his bidding. To worship him and follow him everywhere. He prepared me from a young age to support every decision he made, promising rewards for my loyalty with the one thing I craved most."

"Which was?"

"Leave behind a legacy as something more than a poor man covered in mud. He delivered on his promise when we arrived in Dathoviel, and was crowned king. I was given my knighthood, but his manipulations did not end there. He asked me to spy on the queen and report back any wrongdoings so *he* may overthrow *her*. When there was none, he became infuriated. I was not privy to this information at the time, but we know now he soon began to work out a plot with King Bartholomew. A few weeks before his death, he confided in me his plans to trade Dathoviel's subjects to Winvoltor for gold."

Carlyle nodded slowly, quill scratching. "And the queen's accusations regarding Prince Brantley's death? Have you any information about this?"

Regret laced the man's voice.

"Prince Brantley's death was not a hunting accident as Alaric wished the kingdom to believe. I discovered them in the woods, where Alaric stood over the prince's body. There he admitted that he needed the prince eliminated."

"And did he share why?"

"He'd begun to view him as a threat."

Carlyle's eyes narrowed, quill freezing over the ink pot. He threw a sneer at Amelia, watching as more colour drained from her face.

Yes, Your Highness. Now is the time to panic.

"But, you did not see the physical act of murder. You cannot describe to me how he did it?"

Seb slowly shook his head. "No. I arrived afterward and demanded to know what was going on. I wanted to save the boy, but there was no hope."

"Hmmm." Carlyle pressed his palms to the table. "It seems this tale is simply your word against the king's. And since he can neither confess—nor defend himself, your story becomes impossible to corroborate."

The knight sputtered. "I may not have anything substantial to present to you other than words, but I swear on my life that Alaric admitted he was responsible. He even threatened to blame the prince's death on me if I told the truth."

Carlyle tapped his quill free of excess ink, free hand waving dismissively. Covertly, he glanced the knight open his mouth to speak, but Amelia shook her head. A second man stepped forward, hands clasped behind his back, face set like stone. He looked impossibly regal.

"King Spencer of Petrovia," he stated for court record.

Carlyle sat up at attention, quite ready to listen.

Now *this* was stimulating.

"Your Highness, please, tell the court just how Queen Amelia convinced you to take your own brother's life?"

King Spencer didn't shift a muscle below the neck, but his lips pursed and his left eyebrow rose.

"Queen Amelia presented concerns regarding Alaric's behaviors. He had threatened her life numerous times and was a great menace to her kingdom. She felt she had no other choice than to reach out for assistance. She never asked me to end his life. Alaric's death was a result of battle."

"This battle was a surprise attack, was it not? An ambush?"

"We've no way of knowing what word reached Alaric prior to meeting us on the battlefield. Surely he must have known to find our location."

Carlyle wasn't sure which part of Spencer's story was false, and that was perhaps more irritating than being lied to.

"Can you explain to the court how you found the strength to take his life? As I understand, he was your last remaining family member."

"On the contrary. I have an aunt and a cousin." Spencer gestured to Lady Caroline standing a few feet behind the queen. "One of the reasons only they remain is *because* of Alaric. He is responsible for the death of my younger brother as well."

The crowd gasped.

"A bold accusation," Carlyle admitted. "But one I believe you cannot prove?"

"Alaric was a menace to this land and its people," Seb proclaimed from the right side of the room. "The state of the village during his reign is proof enough!"

"King Alaric is not the one on trial!" Carlyle bellowed, fist banging, demanding order. "We are here to discuss the charges placed upon Queen Amelia. Besides, I dare say the current state of Dathoviel is far better than it has ever been."

He'd seen the destruction of Leah's men with his own eyes as he rode through the village last night, but he'd also seen the people working together to try and salvage whatever they could. It *almost* warmed his cold heart.

"Thanks to the queen." Lady Caroline stepped forward. "Amelia, tell him everything you've done for the people."

Everyone could see her wrestling internally, but somehow, she found the words. It was displeasing to see the faint glimmer in her eyes and the color returning to her cheeks.

"The truth is, many changes *were* made in our kingdom, but I cannot take credit for them alone. We worked together. The improvements in Dathoviel are much more a testament to my people's strength, than mine."

The crowd parted to the left, and a blonde man stepped forward. A young girl wriggled from his arms, heading for the queen, who crouched down to meet the child. They whispered to each other, but Carlyle was focused on the man.

"My name is William Carpenter, sir, and I'd be grateful for the opportunity to address the court today."

Purely unable to resist, he allowed the unusual request. "Very well."

"The food in our bellies, the warmth on our cheeks, and the progress made in the village is due to the hard work of Queen Amelia and her companions. Even while mourning the beloved Prince Brantley, she ensured we remained cared for. She easily could have left us behind. Instead, she sent hope in the form of aid and doctors. As she healed, so did we. Now we are in the process of re-building a school and a pharmacy—two things we've desperately needed for decades."

Carlyle peered at the man over his steepled fingers. "You are stating, for the record, King Alaric was not responsible for any progress?"

"None. His increased taxes consumed our resources at a rate we couldn't endure. Prior to Queen Amelia implementing changes, we were starving. Dying. Without Amelia, my family and many others would not be well enough to stand in this room."

A quick scan around the space proved the villagers did look healthier than the last time he had visited Dathoviel. Perhaps even better than when he'd lived here.

"Do you agree with this man's words? Does he speak for you all?"

"He does," someone shouted.

"Yes," exclaimed others.

Feet began stomping in unison throughout the hall, and heads nodded.

Amidst the villagers rallying call, Carlyle caught his first glimpse of Olive.

As usual, her glaring golden eyes cut right through him. She clearly still hated him, and that was for the best. It was doubtful there were enough words to repair the damage he'd caused by abandoning her.

He slipped from the throne room as everyone surrounded the queen protectively.

Pushing thoughts of his cousin aside, he moved to the chaise someone had placed for him beneath the window in this poor excuse for a makeshift office. He let his head drop into his hands and reflected on everything he'd learned. Though he could take as many hours, days, or weeks to make his final decision, Amelia clearly had the support of her people. And their support would no doubt turn to uproar if provoked. He had power, title, and a fancy robe, but they had the numbers. And they clearly had no issues rebelling.

LET IT REIGN

Behind closed lids, he envisioned a riot following the queen's sentencing. He *might* escape the castle, but they'd find his carriage, topple it, tear the wheels off and drag him from the splintered wooden remains. They'd beat him to death in the same village square he'd once played.

Indeed, lies were told this morning. But even though he'd never met Alaric, it was clear the king had been wicked. To say the least.

All Carlyle knew for sure was the people all desired the same thing. For Amelia to be their queen, and he would be a suicidal fool not to deliver it—even if it were an act to save his own skin. As much as he valued power, he valued his life more.

She would undoubtedly fail them sooner or later. Then it would be her hanging in the village square. Either way, it would not be his concern after today.

~

Amelia's heart pounded in her ears as she gripped Caroline's wrist tightly. Every set of eyes in the throne room, including hers snapped up when the door opened and Carlyle reappeared. Those who had taken to sitting during his absence rose, gathering behind the queen. The room was painfully silent, save for the click-clack of his footsteps approaching his table. He pulled his chair out; the legs scraping offensively across the floor, then thought better of it and remained standing. His hands clenched atop the chair back.

The scroll he held was either execution orders or a full pardon. There was no middle ground for Carlyle hated paperwork and complicated rulings.

She felt a small hand patting her hip. Looking down, she glanced at Brianna and did her best to return the girl's hopeful smile. The justice cleared his throat, and her head turned, meeting his gaze once more, his eyes icy as a frozen forest.

"We've heard testimony today on behalf of Queen Amelia, the accused. She pled guilty to both charges of treason and conspiracy, and yet the court has listened to justifications for her actions. Despite causing the loss of a man's life, you've painted her as a savior. If anyone wishes to testify on behalf of the late king, now is the time."

The displeased crowd murmured as the hair at the back of Amelia's neck prickled. Any of the guards once loyal to Alaric could step forward and tell the truth regarding the ambush. Or even spin a lie and prolong the hearing. She held her breath, teeth grinding.

"It'll be alright," Caroline whispered, though her own jaw was clenched.

Eloise nodded from her left. "He's stalling."

When no one volunteered, the mild hope in Carlyle's voice faded.

"As judge and jury, I have the power to decide the future of this woman and your kingdom. But I can only do so with the evidence and testimony before me. Given that, I clear the queen of all charges."

Amelia blinked.

Was he toying with her? Surely, he would burst into laughter at any moment, send his agents to pull her from the protective cocoon formed around her.

Expression blank, he set the scroll on the desk and simply turned away, robes billowing behind him as he exited the room. His job complete. Part of her wished to thank him, but she was immediately enveloped in hugs from Caroline and Olive. The crowd around her chanted, joyful and loud.

"Long live the queen! Long live the queen!"

Her mind spun, trying to understand how this happened. Then Spencer was pushing himself through the crowd and placing his hand on her shoulder, his grin making her smile. So much like Caroline.

"Congratulations, Your Highness."

She accepted his embrace, returning it tightly. "Thank you for sharing your story. I was certain my head was minutes away from being removed."

Spencer smirked. "I'm sure he would have loved nothing more. Though I can see the man's a bastard, he's no fool. He was most likely frightened we would revolt and tear him limb from limb. That it would be *his* head lost if he ruled against you."

Eloise chuckled. "He was right."

"Whatever his reason, I am grateful."

"Quite." Spencer nodded. "There is the matter of returning your kingdom to you that we must handle before I return to Petrovia."

She beamed, her scattered pulse hammering unevenly inside her chest.

"When?"

He looked around, arms spread out.

"Now?"

Her eyes widened.

"Now?"

"Everyone is already here. Besides you've waited long enough, I think." He leaped atop Carlyle's table, clapping his hands together. "Silence, please! I have an announcement to make."

Gradually the voices faded as all eyes fixated on the king. He extended his hand to Amelia, nodding encouragingly for her to take it. After a short hesitation, she joined him on the table, blushing at the peculiar situation.

She'd nearly convinced herself this day would never come.

"Before King Spencer makes his announcement, I just wanted to thank you all." Amelia's hand pressed over her heart. She would *not* cry. "Your support today certainly impacted the justice's verdict, and I will not forget that. Thank you for saving my life. Especially *you*, William."

William nodded with a warm smile, his arm around Hannah's waist as she cuddled baby Winslow close.

"As you've saved ours. It was my pleasure."

At their feet, Brianna and some of the other children continued to dance. Spencer commanded their attention as well with a final clap.

"Are you ready?" he whispered.

With pursed lips and sweaty palms, Amelia nodded and accepted his hand.

"I am."

"Queen Amelia, on this day, I willingly release your throne, your crown, and your people back into your care. Where it's always belonged."

"Thank you, King Spencer," she choked out, tears pooling in the corner of her eyes.

She decided to let them fall.

He stepped down, fingers slipping from her grip. "You are now the sole, reigning monarch. Long live Queen Amelia of Dathoviel!"

The room erupted into celebration.

. 26 .

AMIDST THE CLINKING GLASSES and soft music, Eloise circled the edge of the packed ballroom once more, sweeping past sharply dressed servants holding dessert trays. One eye stayed on Amelia while the other searched.

She had yet to see Julian since returning to Dathoviel save for a brief, shared glimpse at the queen's hearing yesterday, but he must be here somewhere. Nearly everyone in the kingdom was in attendance, either twirling around the dance floor in celebration or indulging in drink and sweets from the train of buffet tables Regina had somehow managed to prepare in time.

Perhaps baking and decorating opulent treats was how the cook processed stress and grief? And perhaps she ought to talk with the woman soon about her father. Eloise hadn't the slightest idea what to say to her, but saying nothing felt wrong.

With her tight, gravity defying curls springing wildly around her head, Eloise changed course and sauntered through the center of the room. Her hair—an entity all its own—moved freely now that she'd released it from its usual braids. And she welcomed the newfound freedom its wildness instilled in her. She rarely allowed herself to indulge this way, but if her father's passing had taught her anything, it was that life was too damn short to spend it wrapped in armor every minute.

To solidify this new ideal, she'd ensured to dress for the occasion tonight, and she had no regrets. The apricot colored silk of her gown glowed against her dark, lemongrass scented skin. It was draped over one shoulder, tied at her hip and shockingly low in the back, where it cascaded to the floor. As the gold band on her bicep glinted in the candlelight, the bangles at her wrists jingled along with every step.

Olive had said she looked like an ancient goddess and she certainly felt like one.

A melodic laugh from the right froze her in her tracks, forcing her to turn toward it. She recognized more faces than not, but one in particular stood out. Julian's daughter was nearly doubled over in laughter, holding tightly to Seb's arm. If anyone could lead her to Julian, surely Maria was a wise place to inquire?

"Hello again," she said, putting on her best smile as she approached them.

The pair faced her, their smiles warm in return. "You look stunning, Eloise," Seb said, tipping his hat toward her.

"Thank you. I see you also took the time to clean up."

He smoothed his ivory jacket. "A gift from Olive. She made one for Kwan and Julian as well. Have you seen your father tonight, Maria?"

Wonderful. She didn't even have to ask and make things obvious.

"We arrived together." The young woman pressed onto her tiptoes, peering around the room. "But I haven't seen him since."

Maria stumbled forward into Seb's arms, tripping on her lavender skirt, and he caught her hands stayed gentle.

"Perhaps we should sit for a few moments?" he asked. "I doubt you've ever drank wine this quickly before."

Maria blushed. "Might not be the worst idea."

"Excuse us," Seb said with a nod, guiding Maria over to a table and swiping a breadbasket along the way.

Eloise set her sights on the head table where the queen indulged in yet another glass of champagne. Perhaps she should return to Amelia's side and be content with observing what remained of the festivities. Surely the party wouldn't continue past midnight. She could try to find Julian tomorrow.

Then she stopped.

Had he been there the whole time? Surely not, she hadn't taken her eyes off Amelia long. So how had he gotten there without her seeing? Maybe he was avoiding her.

Though how any man could avoid this dress, was unthinkable. Dozens gawked at her in this moment, but she didn't care. There was only one person's attention she wanted, but his eyes were currently squeezed shut, head thrown back in laughter.

Who gave that man the right to look so exquisite? The corners of his mouth crinkled, and he slapped Spencer's shoulder, the buttons of his own ivory coat undone, revealing a blue tunic. The king was also beside himself, chuckling into his wine, shoulders quaking as Julian managed to gasp out a response to whatever joke she'd missed.

Eloise marched toward the table, the slits in her gown flicking out, showing far more toned leg than she typically preferred, but this moment had one focus. One target.

Julian stood straight when he noticed her approaching the round table, Adam's apple bobbing as he swallowed.

He cleared his throat twice, struggling to meet her eyes. She took it as a compliment.

"Evening, Eloise."

She opened her mouth to respond but Spencer interrupted them.

"Good lord, Eloise!" the king spluttered from across the table.

She let herself chuckle. "Eyes up here, Your Highness."

He shook his head, reaching for a napkin to sop up the wine he'd spewed everywhere. "Your request is practically impossible. A woman like you in armor is one thing. I became accustomed to the sight eventually. But this dress..."

Eloise risked a glance at Julian and found him tapping his fingers against his champagne flute, eyes narrowed at the king over the glass. With one eyebrow quirked like that, he almost looked dangerous and she was torn between how handsome he looked and how childish she believed jealousy to be. Thankfully there wasn't long to battle because whatever wild possessiveness he'd felt, he quickly got a handle on, his face relaxing once more.

Amelia, clearly drunk, pushed back from the table, a smirk on her painted lips. "I almost died when I first saw her! Truly stunning, Eloise."

"Truly stunning," Julian echoed, voice low so no one but the two of them would hear.

The queen fixed the cuffs of her flowing sleeves and re-tucked her pale-yellow blouse into the loose black trousers she wore. Her crown was crooked, but she righted that next.

"Julian, you make sure this woman has a wonderful time. Queen's orders!"

"Of course." He nodded, tongue darting out to wet his lips.

Eloise's core tightened, recalling just how soft they'd felt slanting against hers in the garden. That night felt like years ago now. So much had changed since then.

"My wife and I are going to dance, in fact," Amelia announced. "Join us?"

Caroline looked up sadly from the chocolate cake she was delighting in. "Dance?"

"Yes, dance. Come on."

Sighing, the blonde relinquished her fork, throwing a glare Spencer's direction.

"Olive, guard this with your life."

The handmaiden seated across from them giggled. "I'll do my best."

As Caroline and the queen found a spot on the dance floor, Olive slid the plate towards her and away from Spencer, eyeing him and the piece of cake he'd just cleared.

"Don't worry about me," he said defensively. "I prefer my limbs attached to my body."

He held up his hand, showing a scar resembling the prong marks of a fork.

As they all laughed, Kwan sidled over to the table, his ivory jacket tossed over his arm. He leaned down to Olive, gripped her shoulder, and pressed his lips to her ear. Whatever he whispered made her blush and swallow thickly. She stood, cleared her throat, and patted her mouth with a napkin.

"Excuse us," she said politely.

Then she and Kwan raced out the door.

The moment she disappeared, Spencer reached around the candelabra, his fork piercing the abandoned dessert.

"Mm-mm. So good," he murmured, mouth full. When he opened his eyes he blinked, staring at Eloise and Julian widely. "You're still here?"

Julian chuckled, arms crossed. "And just what do you have to say for yourself?"

The king hopped to his feet, hands clasped in prayer.

"Please don't tell Caroline. I'll grab her a new slice right now. She won't even notice."

He tackled a servant who appeared to have the last slice on his tray, before apologizing and tripping his way back to the table. He ducked at the last minute as a dark green slipper flew in his direction from the dance floor.

When Eloise turned back to Julian the laughter in her throat bubbled away. His eyes were trained on her and suddenly *she* felt like the target.

"Follow me?" he requested, offering his arm.

"That would be a first," she teased, taking it.

They maneuvered toward the glass doors Kwan and Olive had escaped through as the music picked up tempo and the bodies turned wild. Once outside the rushing energy of the ballroom, Eloise drank in the warm night air while Julian borrowed a lantern from one of the guards. A light breeze tickled her exposed spine, but the anticipation made her shiver, made her ache for his mouth. Not just his lips against hers, but for his mouth to be on her *everywhere*. She might even allow him to push her up against the castle wall if he asked.

He didn't, and she attempted to hide her disappointment.

Instead, they walked away together, the noise of the ballroom fading as his fingers slipped beneath her hair, painting fire across her shoulder blades and caressing the back of her neck. The limp she noticed he was walking with helped detour her from acting on her many impulses.

Trees often looked the same to an average person, but Eloise easily recognized where they stopped as the spot he'd nearly gotten himself killed by stepping in front of her bow.

"I wish to ask you an important question," he said, hanging the lantern on a nearby branch.

She shivered again, this time from the loss of his touch. "I may have an answer."

The light from the flame flickered in the wind, shadows dancing across his jaw. It quivered momentarily before he moved closer again and took her hands.

"I know it's sudden, and you are free to say no, or to even change your mind if you do say yes."

Eloise smirked when he paused, awaiting her response. "You've yet to actually ask me anything."

"Of course." He cleared his throat, and her heart leapt as he slid down to one knee. "Eloise, you are an incredible woman. I have not felt so ignited by another person as I am in your presence, in years. I would be honored if you'd consider taking me as your husband."

Her mouth fell open.

"You—you wish to... marry me?"

"Your father said it wouldn't be easy for you to say yes, but I would like to spend my life with you. So, I had to ask."

"You spoke to him about this?"

"Just once."

Eloise blinked—a million questions swarming in her mind. She longed to love and be loved in return; there was no denying that. Or the inexplicable pull she felt to this man. But seeing the pain her parents had gone through had always deterred her from the idea of marriage.

"We hardly know each other well enough to commit so intensely. And there is your daughters..." she trailed off, overwhelmed. I'm officially the new constable after tomorrow."

He stood, the patience in his eyes unwavering. "I will wait for you to feel comfortable with the idea. In the meantime, we can have more time together, and you'll have the chance to meet my girls. They will love you. My youngest cannot stop talking about the first female knight. And earlier Maria mentioned your kindness to her."

He took an impossible step closer, holding her gaze. Her chest brushed with every inhale.

"She did?"

He nodded. "As for your duty, I will never ask you to stop doing what you love. You have my support, now and always."

Her head spun.

"I don't think I can be the wife you need, or a mother of sorts to your daughters."

"I wish for nothing more than to see your face in the morning, watch you lead and inspire, and tell you about my day in the evenings. The world is changing, Eloise. Our kingdom is changing. I know who you are, and I will always expect a sword in your hand over a broom."

She inhaled deeply, wanting to believe.

"I need someone who believes in me. Who won't hold me back, and wants a life full of excitement. Adventure. Do you think you're capable of handling all that?" she prodded.

His hands captured her face, thumbs stroking her cheeks.

"I can and will handle anything you throw my way, Eloise."

"Even if we spend the rest of our days together without vows and rings?"

"Of course. Marriage *can* be wonderful, but if you're offering love and loyalty, that commitment is enough." His voice trembled and she could feel the shudder in his fingertips. Though he kept her gaze locked on his and his breath was ghosting over her lips, they still felt too far apart. She let out a long breath, longing to tear the jacket from his body and feel her skin against his.

"You almost sound afraid."

Perhaps reading her mind, he brought her lower body flush against his. "I never thought I feared strong women, but I fear you."

"What do you fear?"

"How easily you could hurt me. But I would be lying if I said I didn't want you to make my life wild. If you agree, I promise to create a haven for you in return. Our home would be a place you can be gentle. Where you don't need to prove anything about yourself, to anyone. Where you could let go."

He laced their fingers, her bangles rattling as he brought her wrist to his lips and she gulped. Could he feel how her pulse raced?

"You would do that for me?"

"I *will* do anything for you, Eloise."

She pressed her lips to his fiercely, fingers gripping his hair, tilting his head left and right. He met her beat for beat, his moans pouring into her mouth. He walked her back, pressing her spine against a thick trunk; his own wildness unleashed. Not out of control—just simply open. Asking her to open for him in return. In fact, he was utterly in control. Every move he made was intentional. Even when he pulled back, gazing into her eyes, his fingertips grazing across her collarbone to the knot of fabric on her shoulder. He didn't untie it like she thought he might. He simply slid it over, his teeth and tongue attaching to the newly revealed flesh.

"Julian," she gasped, her head tilting back against the bark.

"Do you want to stop? Slow down?"

She shook her head, knowing she was safe with him. He *could* handle her, and finally, for the first time in perhaps her entire life she softened, and fully and completely surrendered.

"Never."

April 22, 1457

Amelia woke the next morning with the blissful memories of chocolate-flavored kisses and tangled sheets.

Too soon the sweetness faded into a heavy pressure as realization struck her. It was coronation day. She wiggled deeper into her pillow and into Caroline's arms. They had all worked so hard for today. Sacrificed greatly for it.

A sharp rap on the bedroom door stirred Caroline awake.

"It is far too early, Olive," she called gruffly and Amelia could have kissed her.

"It's quite late actually." The doorknob turned. "Come on, ladies. The day is waitin' for you two to make history, and I await to tame your hair."

The handmaiden entered with a tray displaying fresh flowers, three kinds of savory meat, orange juice, and steaming eggs. She set it on the bed as Amelia and Caroline sat up and snatched a slice of toast for herself.

Amelia greedily munched on her bacon. "All the pinning and curling is exhausting. Perhaps we should just cut my hair off," she suggested, gauging Olive's reaction.

Olive quickly transformed from a life-giving goddess who brought breakfast, back to a hairdressing, dream-crushing general. She tapped the brush against Amelia's vanity and her foot against the floor. Her lips were silent but her eyes spoke volumes.

Amelia groaned and slipped from the mattress, taking the platter of bacon with her.

~

When Caroline reached for her pale sage gown a few hours later her hair was twirled elegantly at the base of her neck and her lips were pink. She shed her night clothes, rejoicing in the lack of corsets present. Amelia had converted her away from wearing them, and she intended to never go back.

"There!" Olive clapped her hands together as she stepped back from lacing Amelia's gown and turned toward Caroline. "You both look lovely, but I demand we find a second handmaiden soon. Gettin' you both ready myself is too much work."

Amelia swayed in front of the mirror, admiring the simple lines of her powder blue gown. She looked stunning and regal.

"Actually, we hoped to speak with you about that."

"Oh?"

Olive's eyes widened as the queen took her hands, leading her toward the still unmade bed where they sat.

The excitement bubbling inside Caroline made keeping a straight face impossible. She knew exactly what this was about.

"After a bit of consideration," Amelia began. "I think it's time you left the castle."

Blood drained from Olive's already porcelain skin. "I—I don't understand."

"You have been nothing but loyal, supportive, and a true friend whenever I have needed you most. But it is time for you to have your own life now." Amelia patted her hand. "Kwan makes you happy, yes?"

"Yes."

"But you two can never be properly together while you live in the castle and he's in the village."

Olive gnawed her bottom lip. "True."

Hazel eyes glistening with tears, Amelia placed a copper key into her palm. Olive looked down at it, and then back up curiously.

"If it pleases you, we think you should move to the village with him. And open a shop where you sell clothes. Anyone can see you have a talent for it. I don't think Seb shall ever remove the jacket you made him."

Olive tilted her head to the side, gazing off into the distance as if trying to picture a life in the village. Then she smirked, clearly imagining Kwan.

"I *have* been sewing a lot lately, but it's been to keep my hands busy. Everythin' has been so stressful."

"And you've held us together, perhaps most of all," Amelia said.

Caroline sat on the bed, Olive between her and the queen. "This way, you'll be nearby to supervise the school rebuild as well."

Olive wrapped her arms around them both, happy tears pouring down her now flushed cheeks. "Thank you."

"Thank *you*," Amelia said, tears forming in her own eyes. "For being the greatest friend I could ask for. For supporting our love and keeping me sane."

"We couldn't have done it without you," Caroline said.

Olive gave a watery wink. "You certainly couldn't have."

After the three women had repaired their makeup, they left the tower arm in arm.

At the bottom of the stairs awaiting to escort them stood Seb, Kwan, and Spencer. Caroline also spotted Julian and Eloise off to the side, both smiling with their foreheads pressed together.

She thought of how Fredrick's trust in Amelia helped make today possible. Of Kwan's skill, Seb's bravery, Julian's loyalty, and of course, Spencer's support.

It wasn't just Olive they wouldn't be here without. For without them and all the men who'd willingly volunteered for the Order, Amelia would not be standing here today.

Lost in thought, Caroline took Seb's arm, watching Spencer escort Amelia to the throne room with Eloise shadowing close behind. Kwan and Olive rushed ahead to ready the guards.

Undoubtedly, her father's controlling and harsh nature during her youth had tainted her view of men. Not to mention the countless examples she'd seen growing up and heard from other ladies in the castle. She'd had this image in her mind from an early age that men were the dominant force she *must* submit to. So, she'd done everything in her power to keep them further than arm's length. Even Seb, who she'd been close with as children, she'd pushed away. But her father's behaviors, and the other dastardly men she encountered reflected *their* character. *Not* the entire male gender.

After all, Leah had been the farthest thing from an ally. A person's value could not be blindly measured by their gender, military rank, or royal title alone. There was only character, kindness, integrity, and reliability. Things anyone could have or lack. Just as her strength did not erase the might of the men supporting them, neither did their existence discolor her triumphs.

She'd always considered Spencer the exception to the rule, and perhaps he was. Perhaps these good men she found herself surrounded with *were* rare, but that could change. In many ways, her mother's outdated views had been right. All genders served a purpose.

What would it mean for young boys if they learned a true man's traits? Instead of subconsciously learning a twisted sense of masculinity. It wasn't enough to see these issues. Soon she would officially have the power to do something—and perhaps she could enlist the help of a few trustworthy friends to assist.

But first, she would need to make amends.

Just outside the doors, she tugged on Seb's sleeve, bringing him to a stop as everyone else filed in. His shoulders tensed, suddenly on guard.

"Is everything alright?"

"Yes, I. . . I just wanted to say thank you."

He didn't, or maybe *couldn't* hide his surprise.

"Thank me?"

"I may never understand how hard you fought to be free of Alaric's influence, but I do know it was crucial to our success."

Seb smiled, clearly startled. Their relationship had dissolved to nothing but glares since she'd thrown mud in his face when they were twelve years old and cursed him until he'd run away. She couldn't even remember why she'd been so angry that day, but she had a feeling it had little to do with him.

"Thank you. Your words mean more than you know."

"Amelia is grateful as well," she continued, words rushing out. "I believe she plans to award you a higher rank after the ceremony."

The guards at the door coughed, a warning to finish their conversation as the drumming began—the signal for everyone to take their seats. The coronation was moments away.

Seb inhaled deeply. "That's kind of you, but I believe my time in armor has ended. I wish to create a life for myself outside of nobility. Have a family perhaps. Leave behind a legacy through honest work and love, not titles and ranks. Coveting those things turned me down a terrible path, and it's one I don't intend to travel again."

"Does this have anything to do with Maria?"

Seb looked down quickly, his left boot scuffing twice against the stone floor. "I decided a while ago I needed change, but we'll see where it goes, with her."

She squeezed his arm, smiling. "If loving Amelia has taught me anything, it's that whatever is meant for you, will find you. You deserve a happy ending too, Seb."

Spencer's head poked into the hall, eyes wide.

"*What* are you two doing? Come on!"

Seb grinned and guided her through the open doors. "One happy ending at a time."

~

The throne room was once again warm, bright and full of life. Servants, villagers, and friends rejoiced as Spencer placed a new crown atop Amelia's head. It was gold, set with a rainbow of colored gems and fit perfectly.

Rising from her knees, she worked to grow accustomed to the new weight as her eyes met Spencer's. She had wished her father would have proceeded over the ceremonies, but the bigoted coward had fled from the castle without a word following her trial, probably too ashamed or afraid to face her. His lacking acceptance and support stung. It even broke her heart a little, but it came as no surprise.

She'd never had his approval to lose in the first place, so expecting it today was a foolish way to spoil her own moment. Later, she could mourn, but today she was going to enjoy this. Plus, the excited roar from the crowd proved she was far from alone.

"You fought bravely for our kingdom," Spencer proclaimed so everyone could hear. "You avoided submission when others made it clear they did not believe in you. You fought for your beliefs and those who needed you, saving many lives. And you honored those who willingly gave themselves so the people they love may live peacefully. You are the true definition of a queen, Amelia. May you reign long and true."

They bowed to one another before turning to face her people. Everyone cheered loudly, but they must have been anxious to hear her speak because a collective hush came over them after a moment or two.

Caroline beamed on Amelia's left, tears streaming down her cheeks.

"Dathoviel embarks on a fresh chapter today. With a clean slate for us all. I vow to hear every voice in our land. No matter race, religion, or gender. Laws will be made based on the greatest outcome possible for all. I do not promise perfection; however, I do guarantee progress! Hard work will still be needed by everyone, but I vow no one will work harder for our kingdom than I. We allied with Petrovian strength without the need for arranged marriage, and should we need their support in the future, King Spencer assures me he *will* provide for us in exchange for our continued allegiance. To further expand our riches and resources, I plan to open trade routes responsibly with far kingdoms, while keeping your families whole."

The crowd cheered, hollering, feet stomping so hard she could feel the vibration even through the platform. Joyful trumpets sounded off, and drums beat in customary celebration from each corner.

Amelia beamed, relishing in the love and support. She prayed it would continue beyond her final announcement. Her eyes roamed to Caroline, who took a deep breath and released Seb's arm, joining her on the platform.

"We're sure about this?" she whispered.

"I am, are you?"

Caroline's blue eyes glistened. "I know I love you."

"Then I'm sure." Amelia took her left hand, gripping it tightly, then called for silence again.

Soon all eyes transfixed on them.

"This *is* a special day! For there is more than one reason to rejoice." Amelia straightened, resolved to withstand any negativity. "Caroline and I are married. As your duchess, she will serve our land by my side."

The crowd murmured with spreading opinionated looks of surprise mixed with nods of acceptance or smugness.

"Keep smiling," Spencer whispered through gritted teeth as he stepped forward to present a second crown set with morganite and peridot atop Caroline's curls. "Don't let those who disapprove smell your fear. You have far more support than hate, I assure you."

Amelia nodded.

"We understand this is new to you," she called. "If you feel unsure, we pray you come around in time. We do not ask for you to understand today. We simply hope for the opportunity to prove our love is just as true as yours. Our kingdom has been a fair one for many years, unlike those who forbid the love between two men or two women. They call it a sin, and their behavior is punished. No longer will Dathoviel blindly support diverse love simply by default. We shall *intentionally* support and protect it! We must fight this hate with love! *All* love will be accepted and celebrated within our kingdom, and it will be safeguarded. I decree this ruling not for myself alone, but for you, your children, and theirs. May love never again cost those blessed by it, their lives or freedom."

Though she could not ignore the displeased looks staring back at her, the majority of faces were smiling, or at least curious. This was never going to be easy, but it would be worth it.

For a moment, she even caught a glimpse of two men in the back sharing a kiss. Her eyes fell to William, Hannah, and the children. Their support radiated toward her, along with many others.

Bravely, Caroline stepped forward, pulling the attention toward her.

"I do not yet understand everything there is to know about Dathoviel, your land, and customs or your personal desires. But I do vow to learn and love this kingdom like I'd been born here. Please, support a new dawn for Dathoviel together with us. Please take this opportunity to rise up, and build a world for future generations we can all be proud of. One free of hate, prejudice, and broken hearts. Queen Amelia and I vow to serve, with you as our focus for all our days."

A momentary silence hung where everyone, including Amelia, held their breath. Then cheers and applause slowly erupted from the crowd, and though it was not unanimous, it seemed louder than before. Amelia couldn't help herself. She tugged Caroline into her arms, kissing her deeply. The new duchess raised her arm in triumph, fingers still linked with Amelia's.

There was no turning back now.

As trailblazers, they would face judgment and bigotry the rest of their lives, but the greatest power they had was the effort they put into the kingdom and their reactions to those who rejected their love. They should not have to prove themselves worthy, but they would. They would do so gladly if it meant the lives that came after were easier and their love was free.

History had been made, and a new age reigned.

Epilogue

May 10th, 1458

THE MAYPOLE STOOD PROUDLY in the village square, colorful ribbons twirling as the children danced and sang around it. Amused, Queen Amelia and Duchess Caroline strolled by, inhaling the sweet floral air and whispering to one another.

In addition to celebrating spring's arrival, villagers lined up to tour the newly completed schoolhouse before indulging in various eats from the decorated caravans and carts surrounding the fountain.

Now six years old—and quite proud of it, Brianna leapt from the circle and ran toward Amelia. Laughter poured from her bright, broad smile, the daisy crown around her soft blonde locks slipping forward over her eyes as she skidded to a halt. She hastily pushed it back into place. Her brothers followed, their long legs easily keeping up with her. Each child had gained nearly a foot in height since the last festival.

"Let the queen be," William called, stepping from the front stoop of the schoolhouse where he'd been showing off his hard work to interested villagers.

Hannah sauntered out through the open double doors a moment later, looking relaxed and comfortable in her new teaching skirt and blouse from Olive's shop. She smiled, hands in the deep pockets, her cheeks pink and eyes full of life. The whole image was a far cry from the first time Amelia had met the family.

"Yes. Come along, children."

"No need to worry," Amelia promised, waving the parents off.

With a surrendering smile, William wrangled the boys back to the pole while Brianna took the queen's hands, guiding her to sit on the edge of the bubbling fountain.

"I've a secret to tell you," the child whispered.

Amelia grinned. "What is it?"

With a low voice, Brianna leaned in.

"When I grow up, I wish to be a queen just like you."

A spark ignited in Amelia's heart, and her mind.

"I believe anything is possible." She tapped the floral crown atop the girl's head. "Including you wearing a real one of these someday—if your heart truly desires it. The only person capable of stopping you from becoming whoever you want *is* you. You are a brave, strong girl, and you shall do amazing things."

Brianna's hips wiggled with excitement on the stone wall, exactly where Amelia had once stood, addressing the Order's first members.

Her gaze darted to Caroline, then back to Amelia.

"I think I'd like to have a king, though."

"You are free to love whomever you choose. Just ensure they are kind and respectful."

"You cannot tell Papa or Mama about my kingdom!" the young girl urged in a loud whisper. "I want them to be surprised."

Amelia nodded conspiratorially, pressing a finger to her lips. Pleased, Brianna jumped down and sprinted across the square toward her brothers.

Caroline took her place, fingers fitting perfectly within Amelia's. The queen rested her head on her wife's shoulder.

"Everything alright?"

"We may have found our heir."

Caroline nodded thoughtfully, observing Brianna take charge of the other children, despite being the youngest and shortest.

"Seb says her eldest brother has been doing well since he started mentoring him. Perhaps it's time we match more of the willing knights with the boys in town."

Amelia smiled up at her wife. "I wondered when you would admit you were working on a project."

"Just doing my duty as your duchess."

A few feet away, Constable Eloise stood guard, despite having direct orders from the queen to relax and enjoy the festival. And for the most part it appeared she was. But a little help wouldn't hurt.

She'd been on edge since the letter from King Bart had appeared a few weeks ago, demanding his slaves. That would have to be dealt with soon...

Across the way, Julian danced with his youngest daughter on the impromptu dance floor of leftover wooden planks from the schoolhouse. He made silly faces, earning screeching giggles for his efforts. Maria and Seb were embracing close by; swaying slowly despite the lively tune sweeping through the square. It was newly wedded Olive and Kwan who seemed built for this particular beat. They spun circles around everyone else, laughing and kissing.

It was glorious. All this love. All this joy. Amelia craved to be part of it. Dragging Caroline toward the dance floor, the queen also grabbed Eloise's hand as she passed by.

"Time to dance!" she ordered. "Even you, Constable."

Eloise opened her mouth to protest, but Caroline shook her head. "You know it's easier to do as she asks."

Amelia watched gleefully as Julian took Eloise into his arms, holding both her and his daughter close. Eloise wrapped herself around them both, surrendering to the music with a bright grin.

Behind them two men danced together next to their market cart of handmade jewelry.

As complete and happy as she felt spinning her wife around their friends, Amelia could not ignore the permanent void in her heart left open by Brantley's absence. Though she'd been successful at saving her kingdom and avenging his murder, nothing could bring him back. A fact that still stung, especially in moments like these when she craved to know if he would be proud of her.

"I'm always proud of you."

His words from the last night they had ridden together slipped to the forefront of her mind, and she didn't realize she was crying until Caroline reached up to brush away the single tear that had escaped down her cheek.

Her kingdom would stay like this. Full of laughter and music and love. She would ensure it.

Enjoy this special preview of the
companion novel
to Let It Reign

BORN TO REIGN

COMING SOON

MILES AND MILES AWAY, in a small cottage beside the sea in a kingdom called Salvown, Leah cradled her nursing son close. Still so overwhelmed by her love for him, she stared into his striking blue eyes between the sleepy flutters of his lids. All babies had them at first, but perhaps his would remain.

His little mouth finally unlatched, lips puckering, still sucking on air as deep sleep took him. Cradling him close, she tugged the corner of his father's fur wrap under his chin.

Like Alaric, the infant had soft dark curls, and stroking it often caused Leah's thoughts to drift back to Alaric. To what her life should have been.

Her gut clenched violently but she ignored it, pressing a gentle kiss to the infant's smooth forehead. Eyes closing, she shut out the small, plain room surrounding them and rocked.

"We are far from the castle you deserve," she whispered. "but I promise you, baby Henric. We *will* return home one day."

Would *you* like to join

The Queen's Order?

Interact with author Cathrine Swift and other fans in the official Facebook Fan Club.

- ➢ Get first looks at all things *Born to Reign*
- ➢ Author Talks
- ➢ Book Club Details
- ➢ Deleted Scenes
- ➢ And MORE

www.facebook.com/groups/thequeensorder

gratitude

How does one even begin to comprehend the outpouring of love and support this story received before it became this physical thing you're now holding in your hands?

I did this, and my ability to have overcome self-doubt, anxiety and depression to write this novel and finish it, is not something I take lightly. However, there are a few people—quite a few actually—who deserve praise and thanks. Because this book would not exist without them. I'm going to start at the top and work my way down, because I work best with lists.

First off, I must say a huge, ridiculously loud, rooftop screaming THANK YOU to Chelynne & Kaitlyn.

You were the ones who read the very first, very messy, very imperfect draft of this book. You fell in love with these characters and supported me when they were hardly more than fuzzy figments of my imagination. You kept me going and reminded me not to give up. And you pushed me to keep going. I am forever in your debt, my beautiful alpha readers.

Secondly, my beta readers. You goddesses, you. Audrey F., Natacha, & Kathleen. If my book was a cake and my characters were the icing, you would be the sprinkles.

Thirdly, to Ashley Weiss. My critique partner and friend. Whether we're talking about puppies, Draco Malfoy, distracting one another with TikTok's or ACTUALLY focused on our stories, sharing advice and boosting one another's confidence, you're always there for me night and day.

Thank you for having the guts to tell me I wasn't writing historical fiction after all and giving me the gentle kick I needed to take my passion for steamy romance seriously. To own it.

And of course, thank you to my husband, Sid Isaac.
For your military advice, your passion for all things Fredrick and for your support as I brought this book to life, which I'm sure in many ways often felt like a third person in our marriage or a second child I had to care for.

There are quite a few special people in particular that checked in with me often, reinforcing and supporting in their own special ways, offering encouragement and advice and care. Without you – Keri, Dalton, Audrey W., Candase, Tarn, and my badass grandmother Cheryl, this book straight up wouldn't exist. Thank you so much.

Certainly, I can't forget about my talented professional team. My INSANELY talented and patient cover designer; Fran at *Cover Dungeon Rabbit*. And Madii at *Bound by Words*, my passionate and understanding editor. Your guidance as I learned and grew was such a blessing. Thank you for working with me, and I can't wait to see what magic we make together next time!

And last, but never, ever least, the online community I found through BookTok and Bookstagram. The readers, writers and fans who liked and commented and shared their excitement for this book every day. Who sent me inspiration and reassurance and boosted me on tough days. (Stephen McClellan & Gabriela Lavarello & Sabrina Ulicki, just to name a few!)

Let it Reign was a labour of love, and you all loved me through it, so thank you.
From the bottom of my heart.

LET IT REIGN
OFFICIAL SOUNDTRACK

Castle- Halsey
Rise Up- TheFatRat
I Walk the Line- Halsey
Queen- Loren Gray
Everybody Wants to Rule the World- Lorde
Yellow Flicker Beat- Lorde
Titanium- Jasmine Thompson
Love Me Like You Do- Nanasheme
Take Me to Church- Neon Jungle
Skyfall- Madilyn Bailey
Hallelujah- Hannah Trigwell
She Keeps Me Warm- Mary Lambert
Look What You Made Me Do- Taylor Swift
The Story of Tonight- Hamilton
Unsteady- X Ambassadors
How Bad Do You Want It- Sevyn Streeter
Kings & Queens- Ava Max
Salute- Little Mix
Give 'me Hell- Robbie Nevill
Just Like Fire-Pink
That's My Girl-Fifth Harmony

Available on
Spotify

About the Author

Cathrine Swift is an indie author and Youtuber with a passion for intentional living and steamy fanfiction.

Recognizing how authors have changed her life, she hopes to utilize her growing talent to do the same. To change the world, for at least one person. She's dedicated her adult life to learning, practicing her craft and uncovering her true voice through heartbreak, hardship and human interaction.

Cathrine lives in Alberta, Canada with her husband and wild toddler.

www.authorcathrineswift.com
@authorcathrineswift on Instagram & TikTok

Did you enjoy Let it Reign?

PLEASE RATE & REVIEW

on GOODREADS and Amazon

ALSO BY THIS AUTHOR

Words & Music: A Jet Set Romance
August 2022

Unhappily Forever Ever After: A Short Vampire Love Story (Gone Before Morning anthology)
October 2022

Mistletoe Messes & Peppermint Kisses
December 2022

Born to Reign
Coming Soon

Printed in Poland
by Amazon Fulfillment
Poland Sp. z o.o., Wrocław